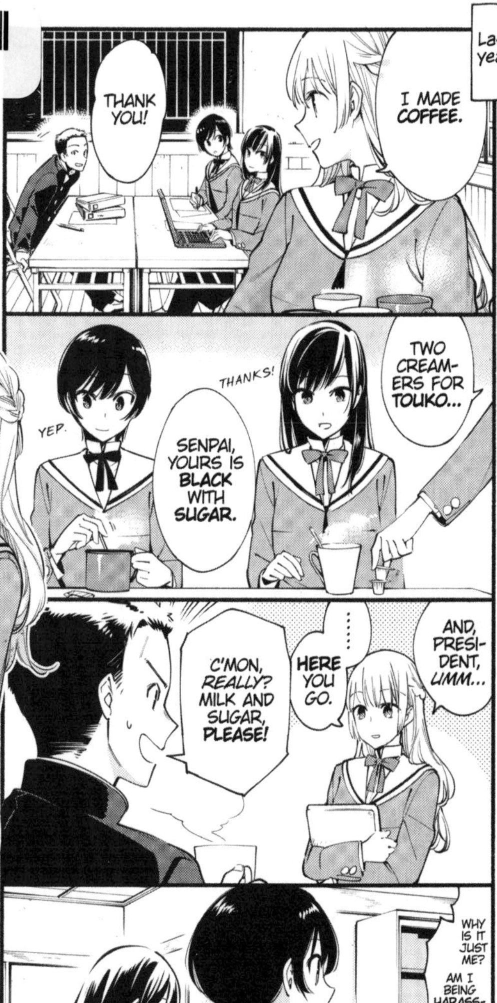
Last year.
I MADE COFFEE.
THANK YOU!
TWO CREAMERS FOR TOUKO...
THANKS!
SENPAI, YOURS IS BLACK WITH SUGAR.
YEP.
AND, PRESIDENT, UMM...
......
HERE YOU GO.
C'MON, REALLY? MILK AND SUGAR, PLEASE!
WHY IS IT JUST ME?
AM I BEING HARASSED?
SAYAKA-CHAN REALLY DOESN'T REMEMBER, HUH...? THAT'S AMAZING.
YEAH, WHEN SHE DOESN'T CARE, SHE REALLY DOESN'T CARE...

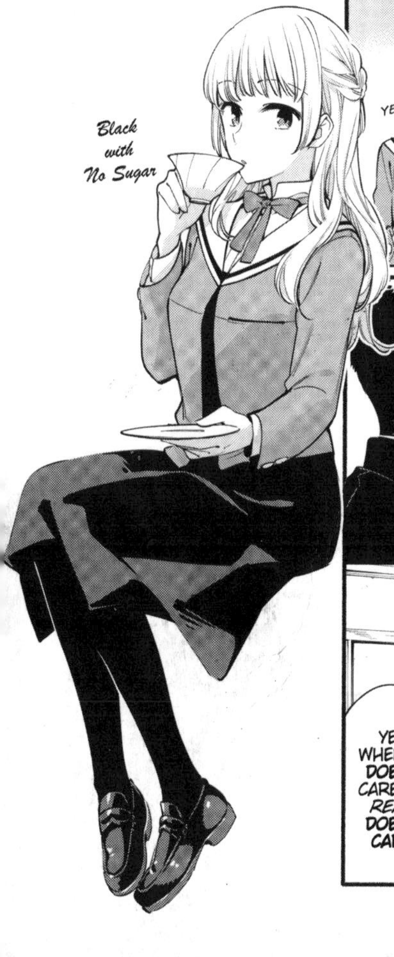
Black with No Sugar

## ONLY TIME CAN TELL...

Student council president Nanami Touko is in love with her friend, Koito Yuu! Even though Yuu doesn't love her back, she stuck by her side and joined the student council, too. She's accepted Touko's feelings—but what about her own? Yuu *still* doesn't have anyone she likes...but now, a new thought is growing in her heart: "I want to fall in love with Nanami-senpai!"

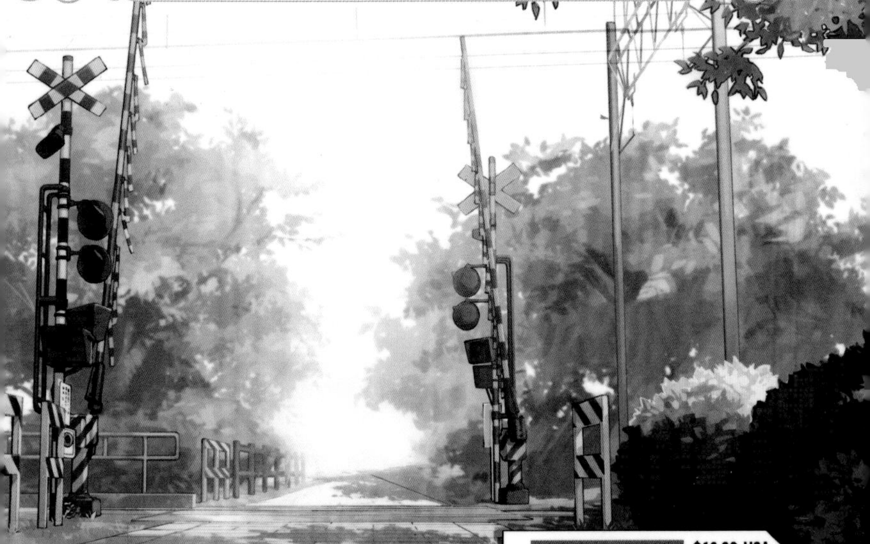

Rated: TEEN
$12.99 USA
($14.99 CAN)
ISBN 978-1-626924-79-6
51299>
9 781626 924796

Seven Seas Entertainment, LLC.
www.gomanga.com
Distributed by Macmillan

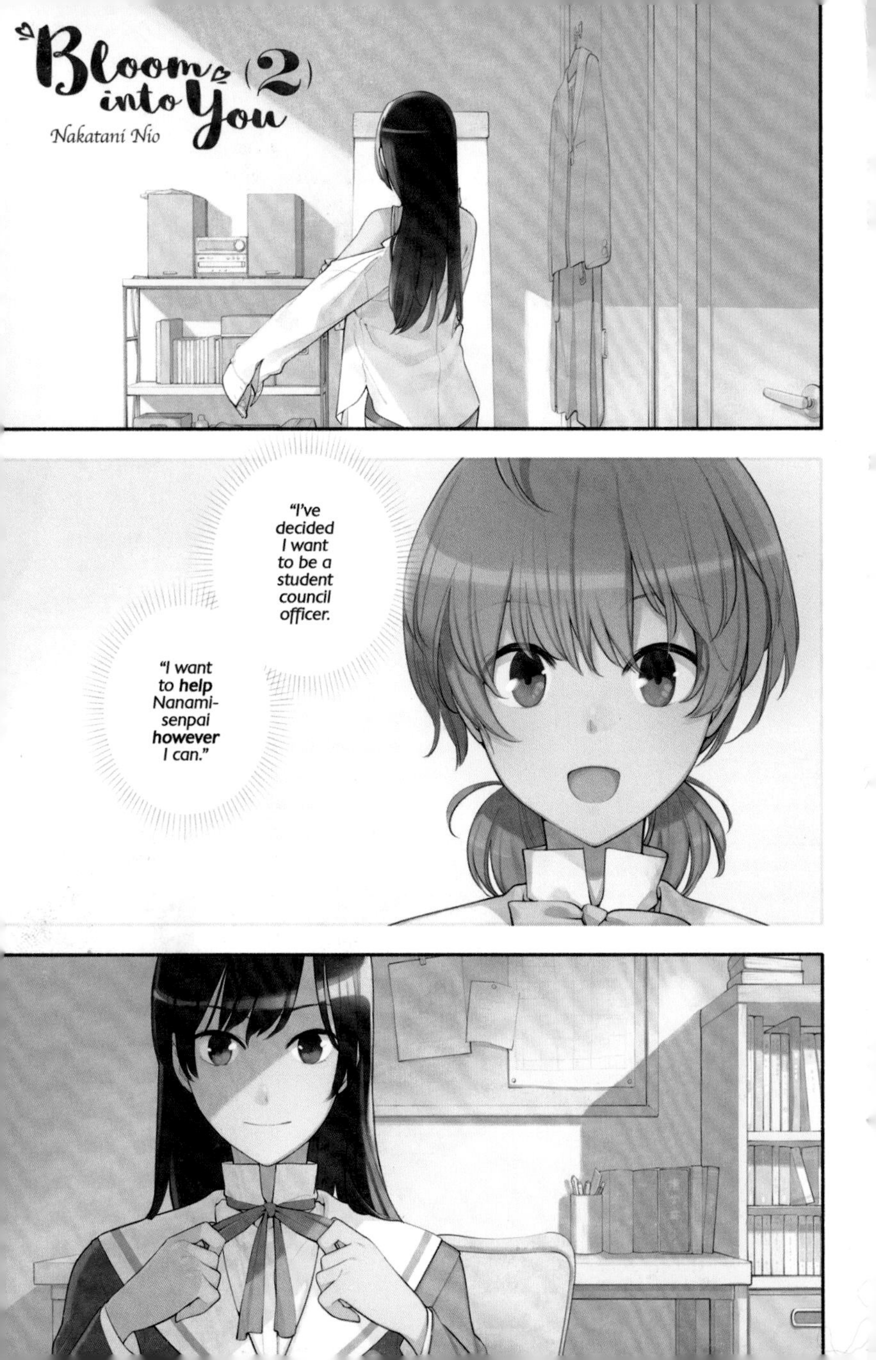
Bloom into You (2)
Nakatani Nio
"I've decided I want to be a student council officer.
"I want to help Nanami-senpai however I can."

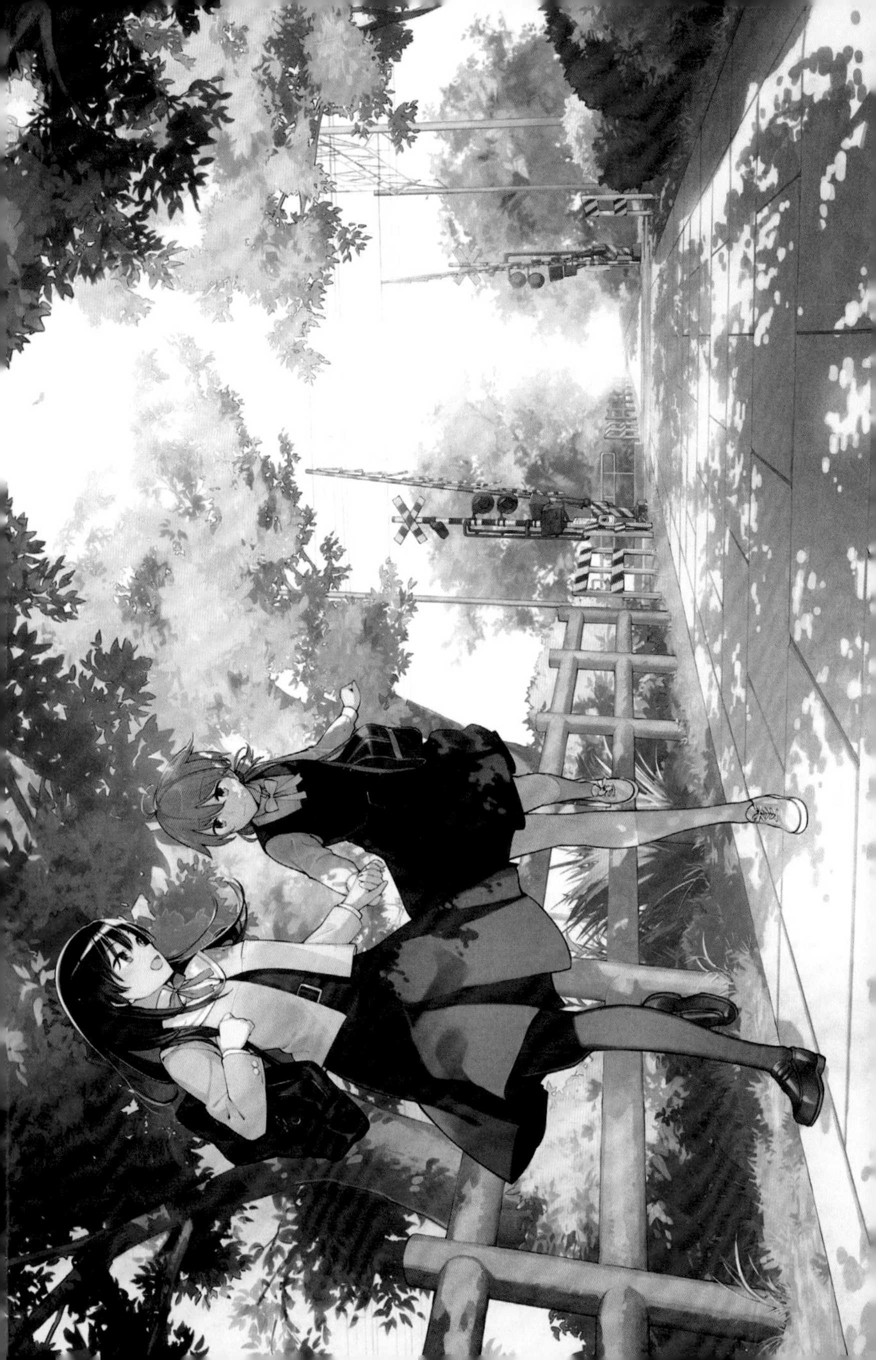

# 6 A Kiss is Just a Kiss EPISODE SIX

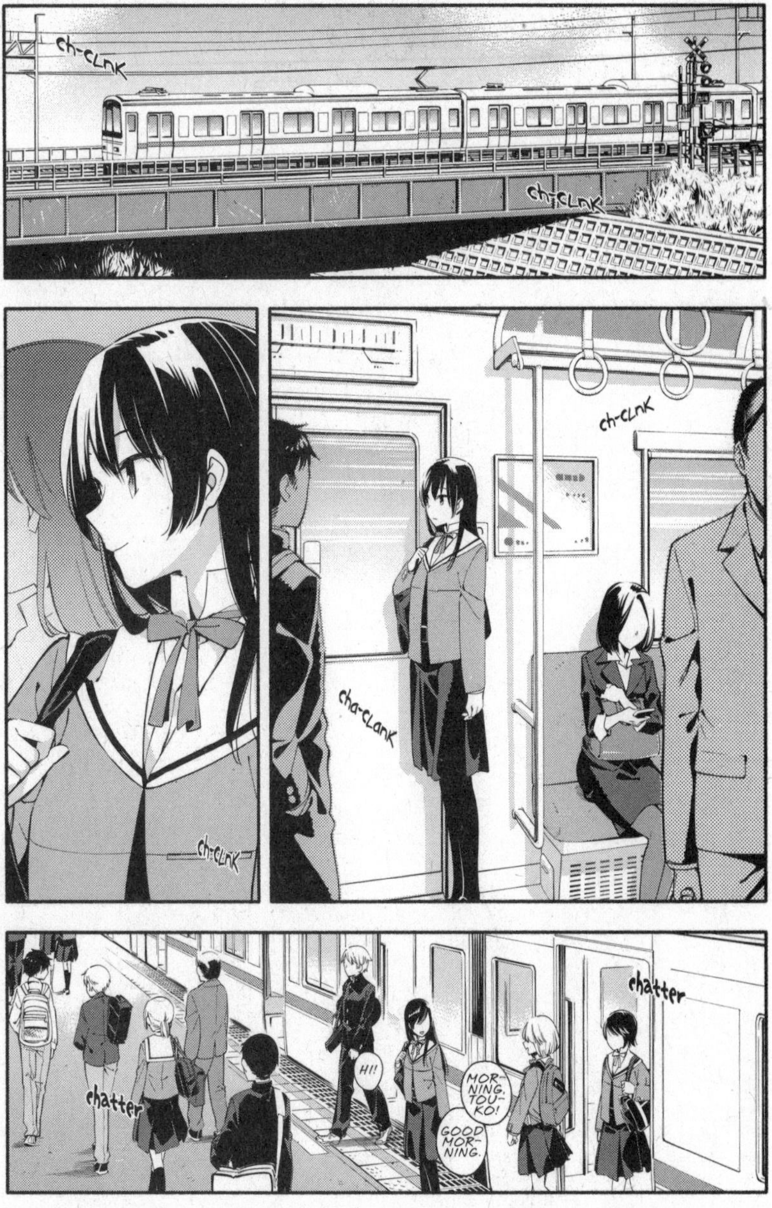
ch-clnk
ch-clnk
ch-clnk
cha-clank
ch-clnk
chatter
MORNING, TOUKO!
GOOD MORNING.
HI!
chatter

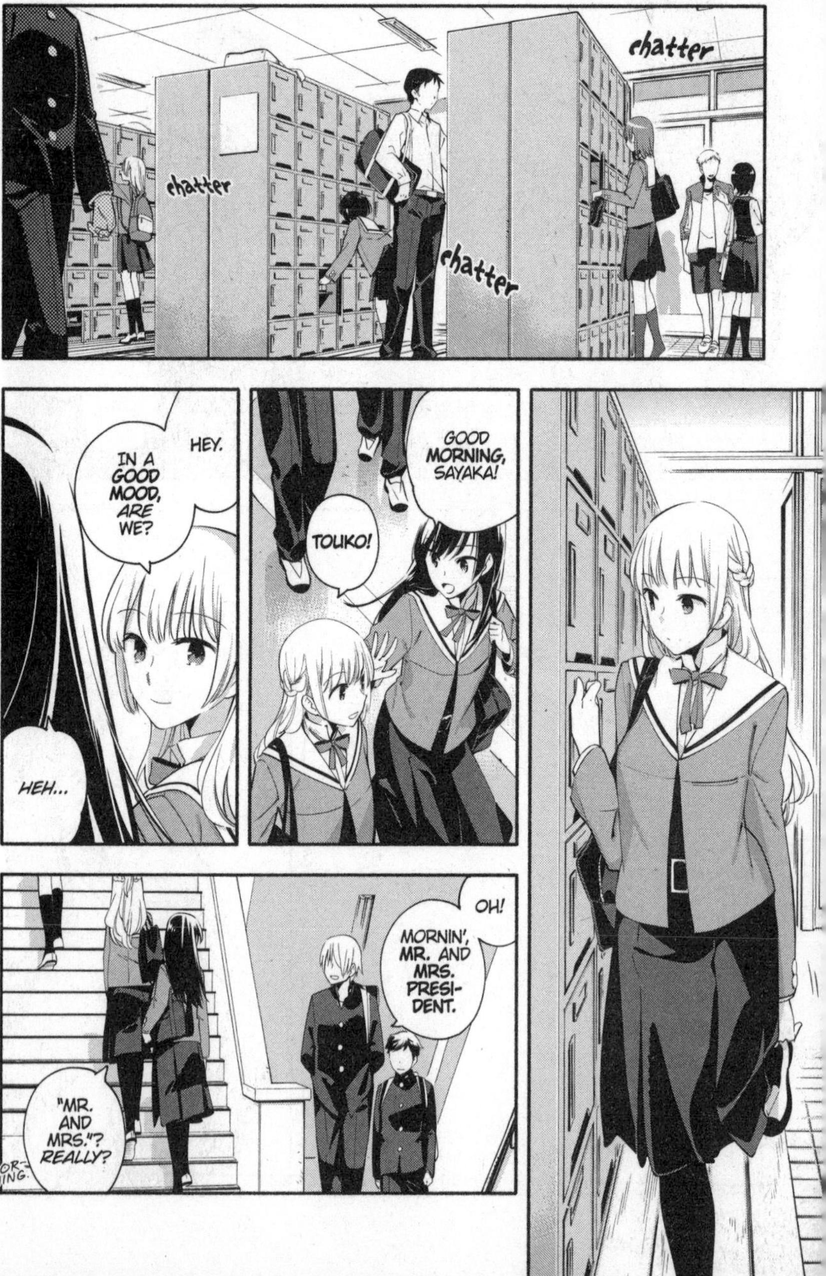
chatter
chatter
chatter
GOOD MORNING, SAYAKA!
TOUKO!
HEY.
IN A GOOD MOOD, ARE WE?
HEH...
OH!
MORNIN', MR. AND MRS. PRESI-DENT.
"MR. AND MRS."? REALLY?
MOR-NING.

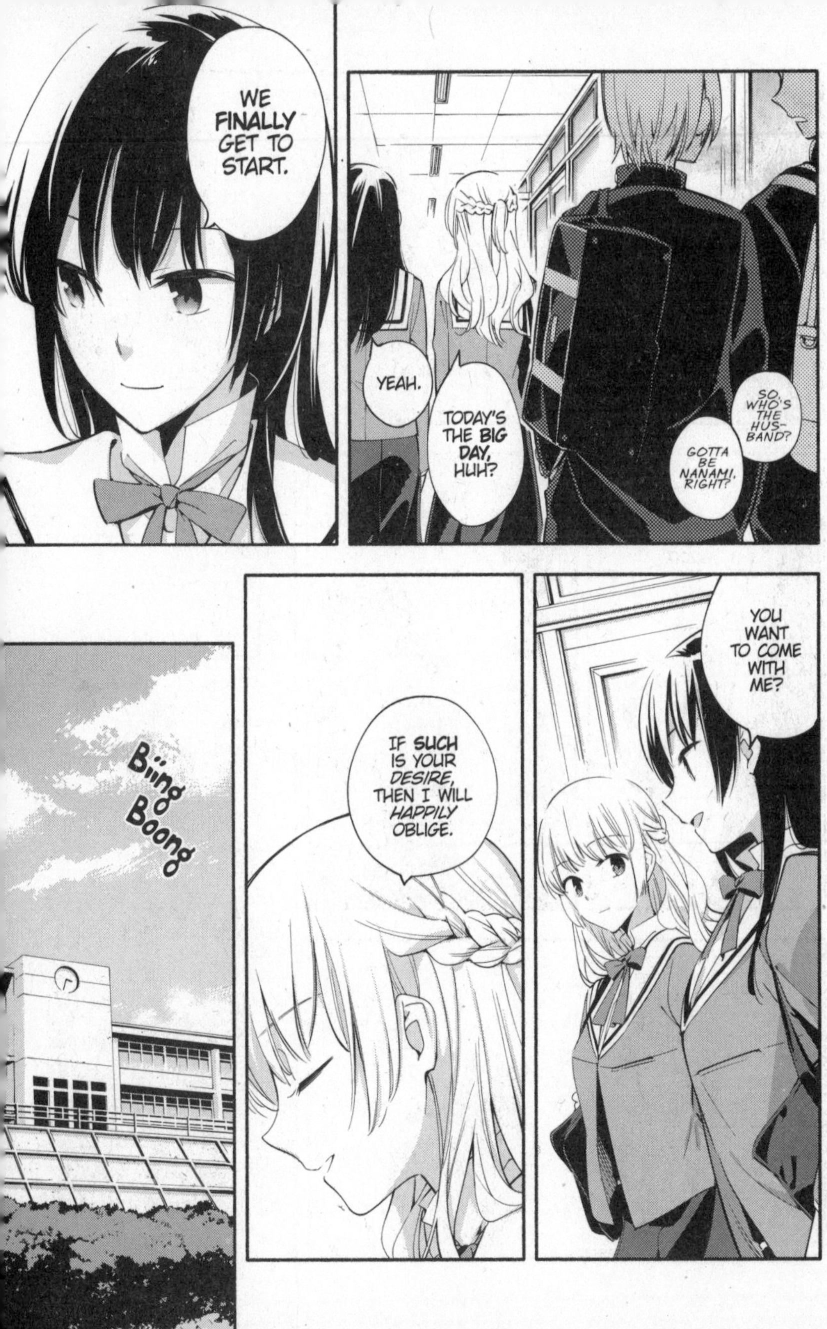
SO, WHO'S THE HUS-BAND?
GOTTA BE NANAMI, RIGHT?
TODAY'S THE BIG DAY, HUH?
YEAH.
WE FINALLY GET TO START.
YOU WANT TO COME WITH ME?
IF SUCH IS YOUR DESIRE, THEN I WILL HAPPILY OBLIGE.
Biing Boong

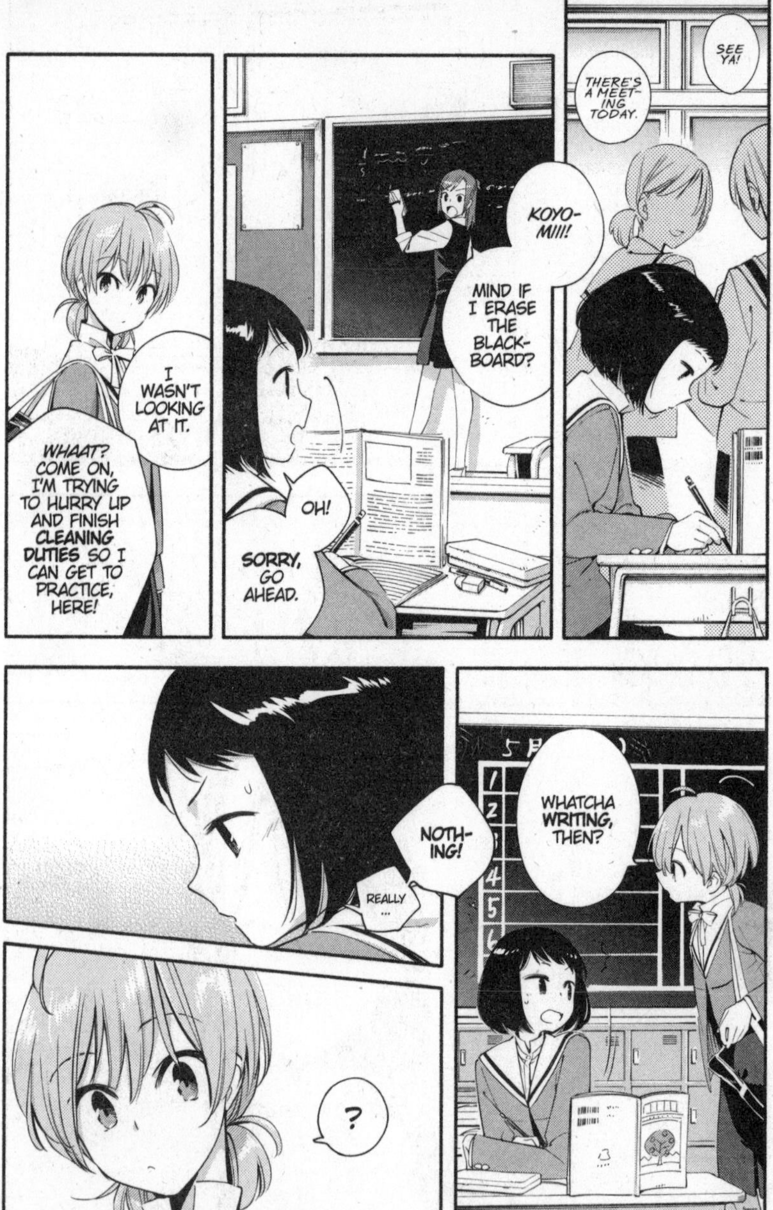
SEE YA!
THERE'S A MEETING TODAY.
KOYO-MIII!
MIND IF I ERASE THE BLACKBOARD?
OH!
SORRY, GO AHEAD.
I WASN'T LOOKING AT IT.
WHAAT? COME ON, I'M TRYING TO HURRY UP AND FINISH CLEANING DUTIES SO I CAN GET TO PRACTICE, HERE!
WHATCHA WRITING, THEN?
NOTHING!
REALLY...
?

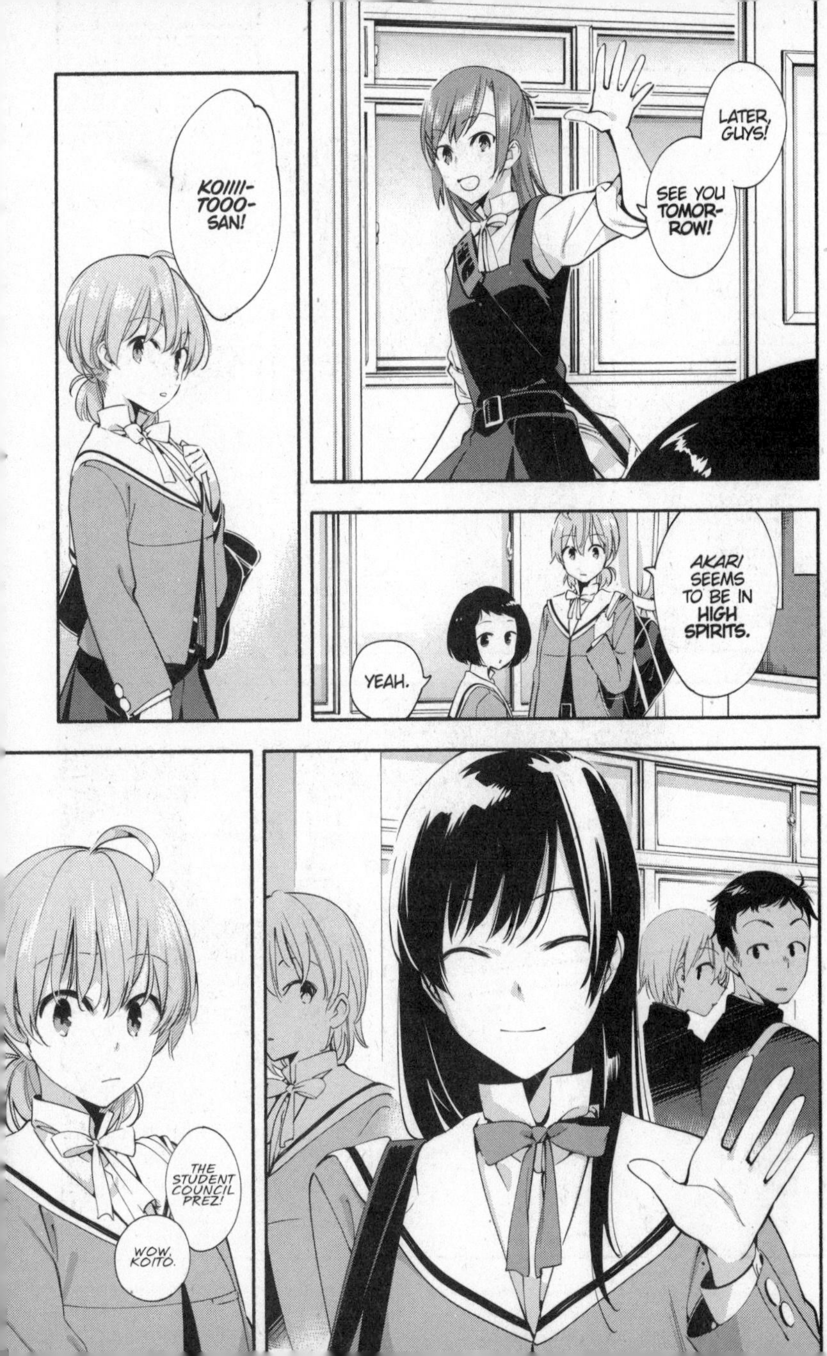
LATER, GUYS!
SEE YOU TOMORROW!
AKARI SEEMS TO BE IN HIGH SPIRITS.
YEAH.
KOIIII-TOOOO-SAN!
THE STUDENT COUNCIL PREZ!
WOW, KOITO.

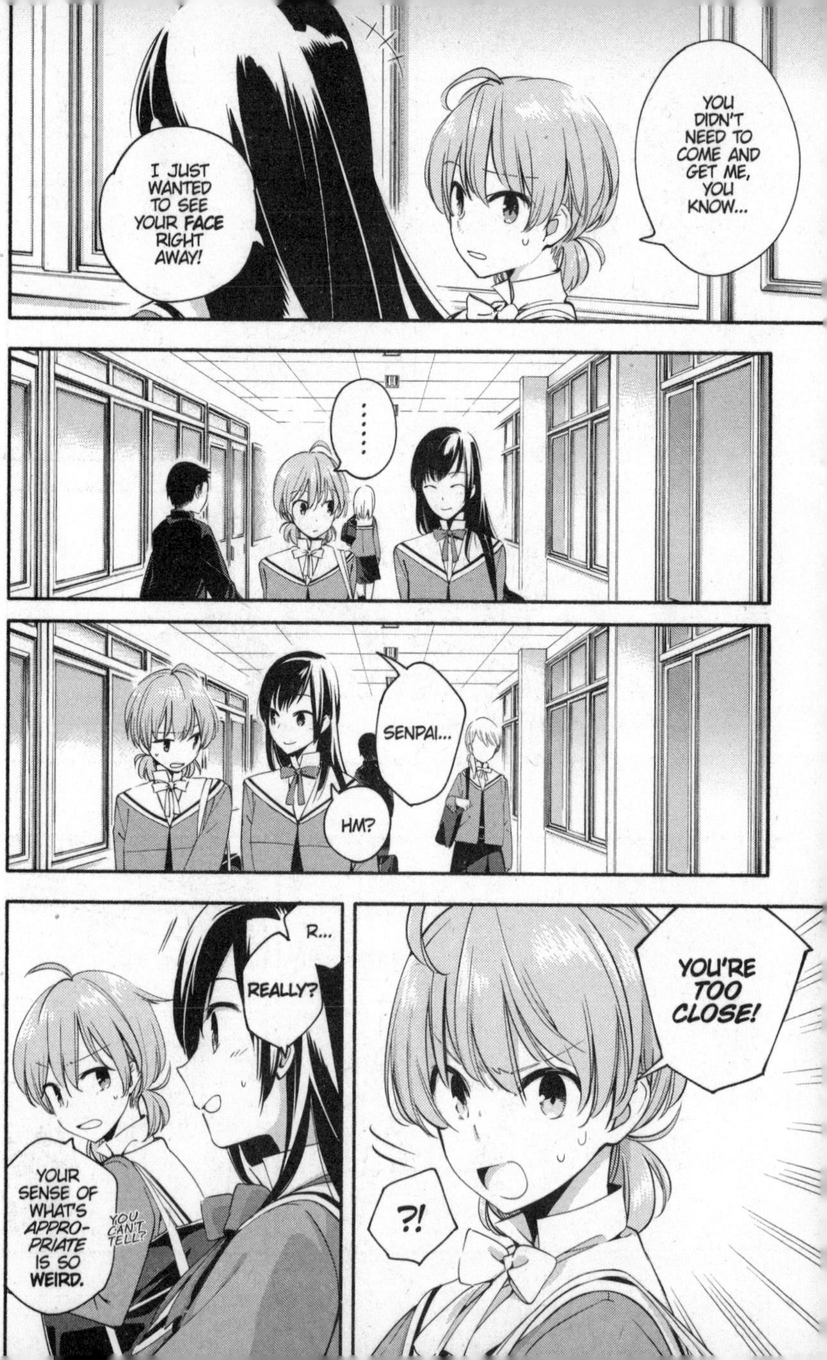
YOU DIDN'T NEED TO COME AND GET ME, YOU KNOW...
I JUST WANTED TO SEE YOUR FACE RIGHT AWAY!
......
SENPAI...
HM?
YOU'RE TOO CLOSE!
?!
R...
REALLY?
YOUR SENSE OF WHAT'S APPRO-PRIATE IS SO WEIRD.
YOU CAN'T TELL?

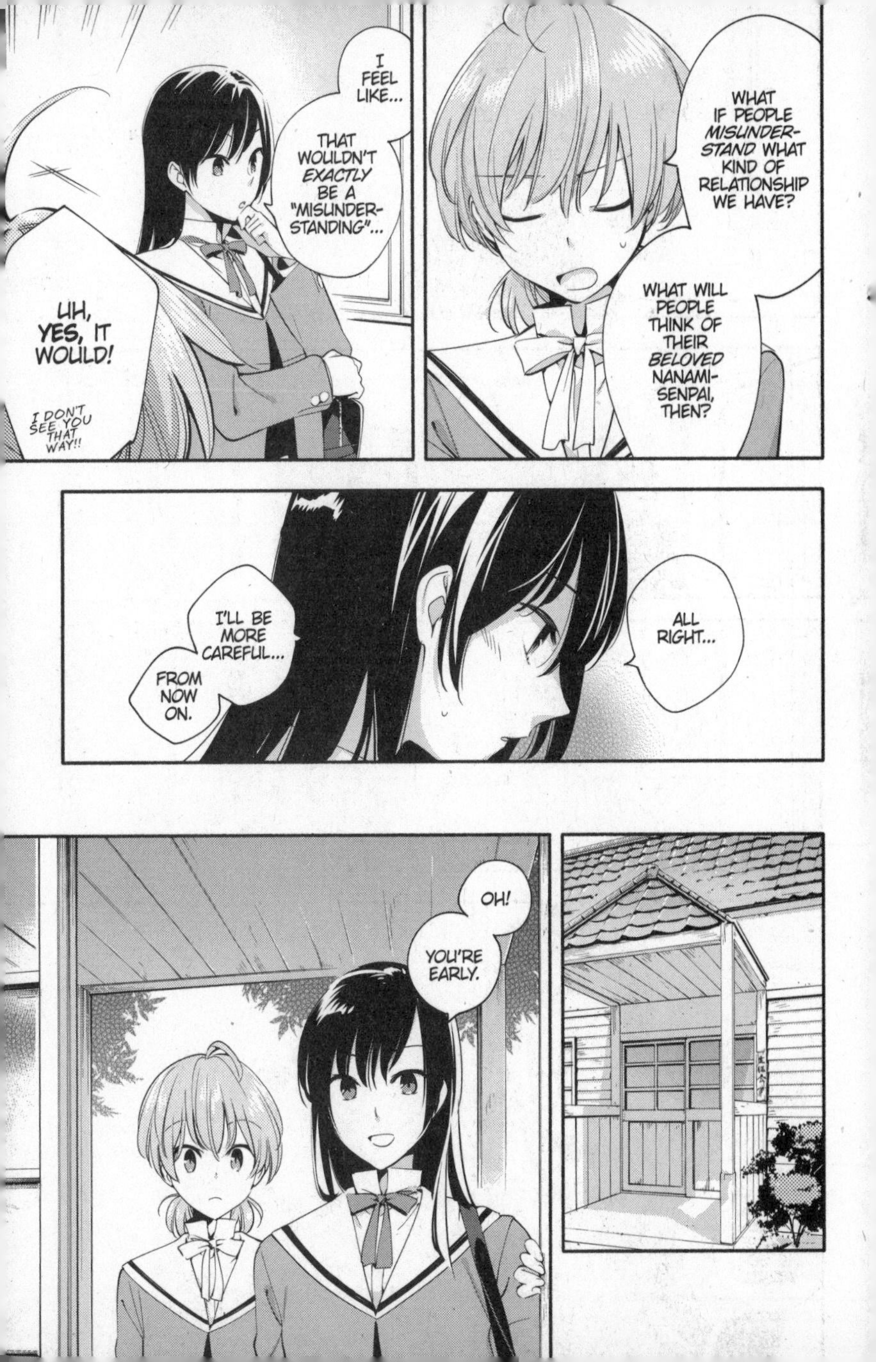
WHAT IF PEOPLE MISUNDERSTAND WHAT KIND OF RELATIONSHIP WE HAVE?
WHAT WILL PEOPLE THINK OF THEIR BELOVED NANAMI-SENPAI, THEN?
I FEEL LIKE...
THAT WOULDN'T EXACTLY BE A "MISUNDERSTANDING"...
UH, YES, IT WOULD!
I DON'T SEE YOU THAT WAY!!
ALL RIGHT...
I'LL BE MORE CAREFUL...
FROM NOW ON.
OH!
YOU'RE EARLY.

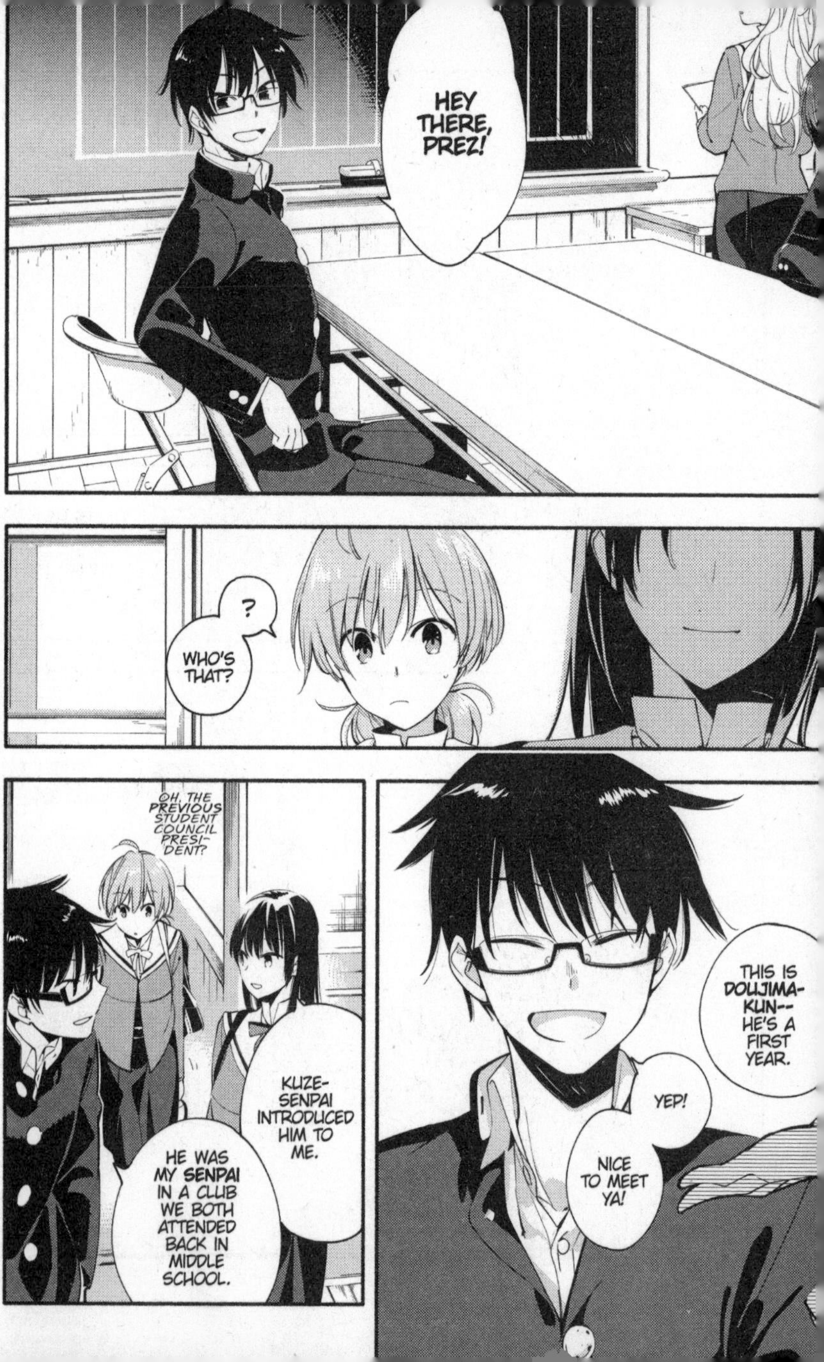
HEY THERE, PREZ!
?
WHO'S THAT?
THIS IS DOUJIMA-KUN-- HE'S A FIRST YEAR.
YEP!
NICE TO MEET YA!
OH, THE PREVIOUS STUDENT COUNCIL PRESI-DENT?
KUZE-SENPAI INTRODUCED HIM TO ME.
HE WAS MY SENPAI IN A CLUB WE BOTH ATTENDED BACK IN MIDDLE SCHOOL.

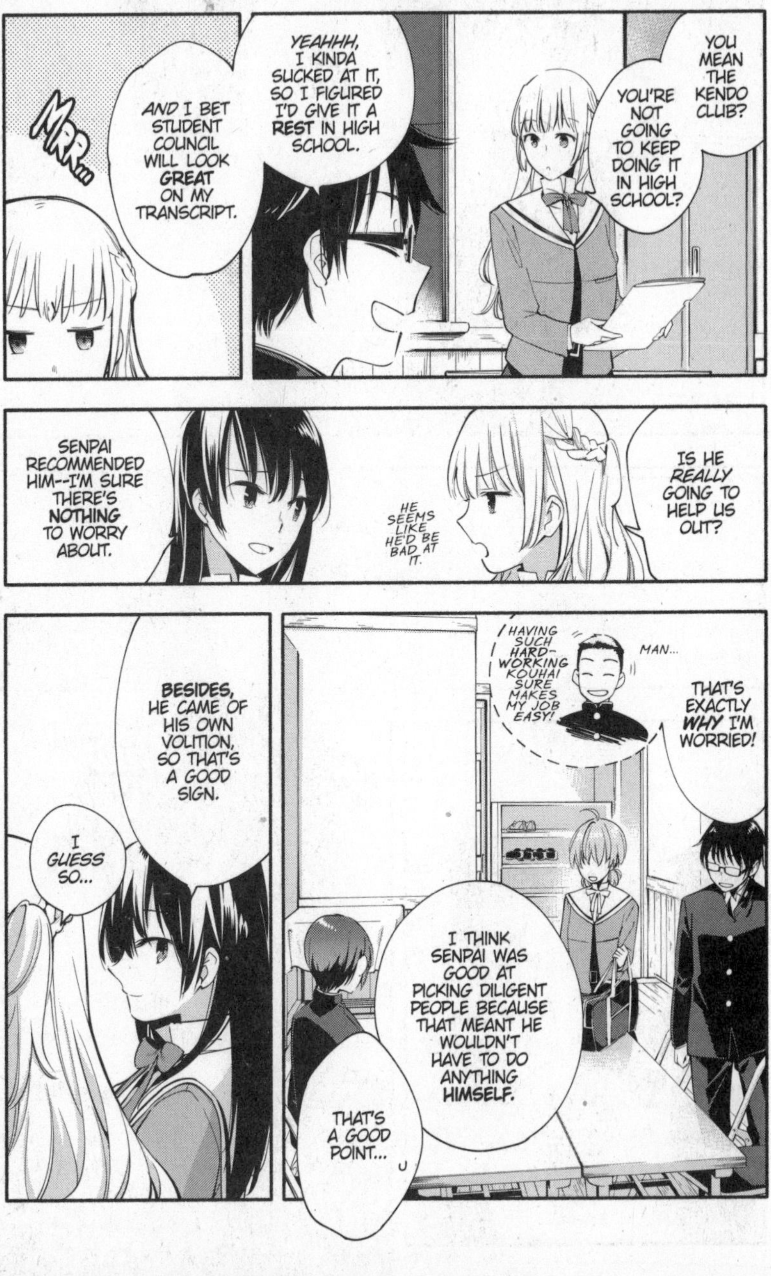
YOU MEAN THE KENDO CLUB?
YOU'RE NOT GOING TO KEEP DOING IT IN HIGH SCHOOL?
YEAHHH, I KINDA SUCKED AT IT, SO I FIGURED I'D GIVE IT A REST IN HIGH SCHOOL.
AND I BET STUDENT COUNCIL WILL LOOK GREAT ON MY TRANSCRIPT.
MRR...
IS HE REALLY GOING TO HELP US OUT?
HE SEEMS LIKE HE'D BE BAD AT IT.
SENPAI RECOMMENDED HIM--I'M SURE THERE'S NOTHING TO WORRY ABOUT.
HAVING SUCH HARD-WORKING KOUHAI SURE MAKES MY JOB EASY!
MAN...
THAT'S EXACTLY WHY I'M WORRIED!
I THINK SENPAI WAS GOOD AT PICKING DILIGENT PEOPLE BECAUSE THAT MEANT HE WOULDN'T HAVE TO DO ANYTHING HIMSELF.
THAT'S A GOOD POINT...
BESIDES, HE CAME OF HIS OWN VOLITION, SO THAT'S A GOOD SIGN.
I GUESS SO...

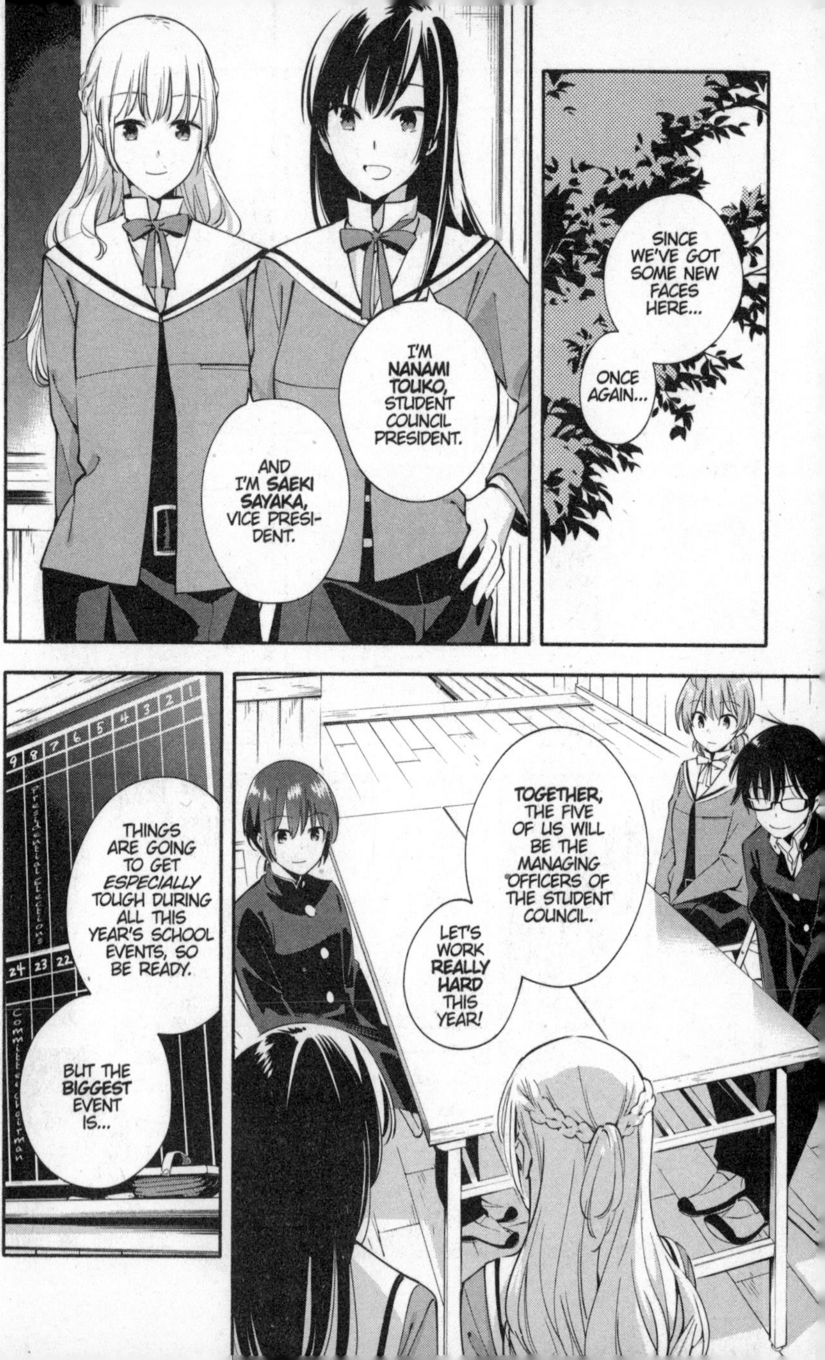
SINCE WE'VE GOT SOME NEW FACES HERE...
ONCE AGAIN...
I'M **NANAMI TOUKO**, STUDENT COUNCIL PRESIDENT.
AND I'M **SAEKI SAYAKA**, VICE PRESI-DENT.
**TOGETHER**, THE FIVE OF US WILL BE THE MANAGING OFFICERS OF THE STUDENT COUNCIL.
LET'S WORK **REALLY HARD** THIS YEAR!
THINGS ARE GOING TO GET *ESPECIALLY* TOUGH DURING ALL THIS YEAR'S SCHOOL EVENTS, SO BE READY.
BUT THE **BIGGEST** EVENT IS...

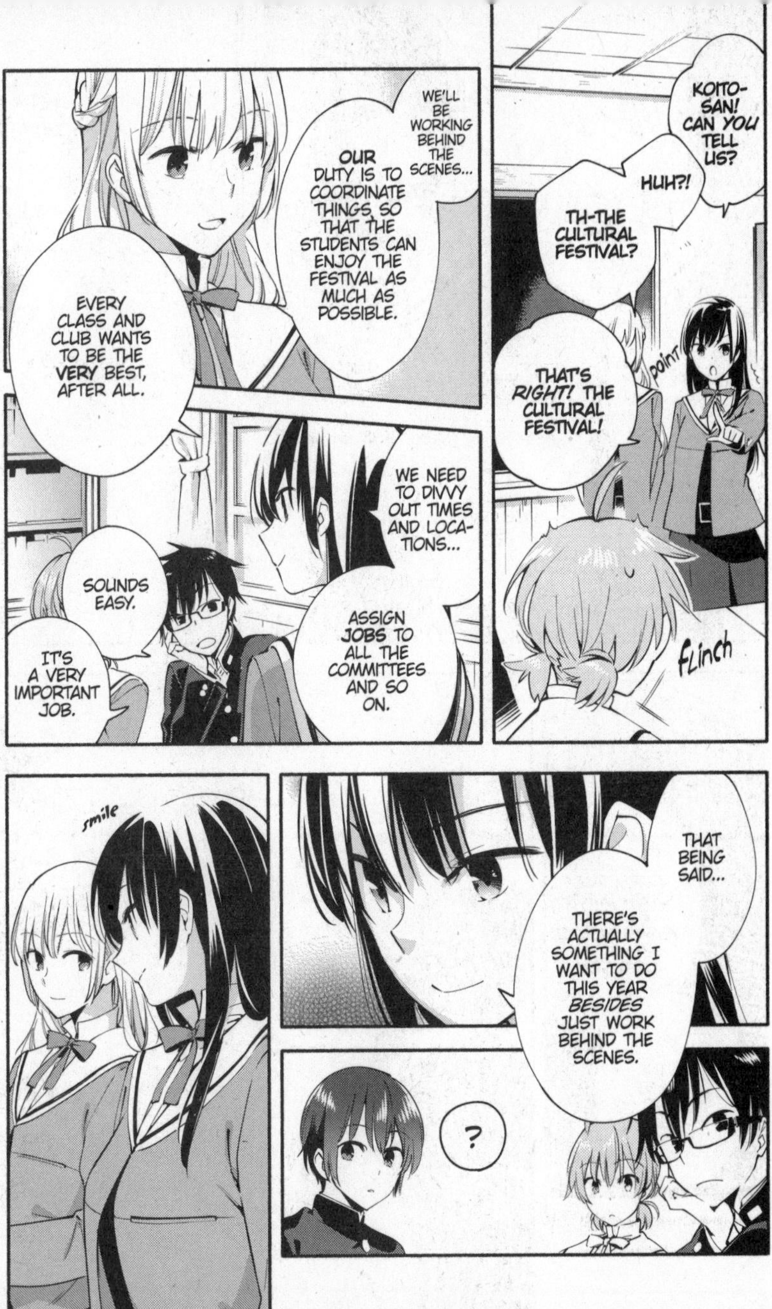
KOITO-SAN! CAN YOU TELL US?
HUH?!
TH-THE CULTURAL FESTIVAL?
point
THAT'S RIGHT! THE CULTURAL FESTIVAL!
FLINCH
WE'LL BE WORKING BEHIND THE SCENES...
OUR DUTY IS TO COORDINATE THINGS SO THAT THE STUDENTS CAN ENJOY THE FESTIVAL AS MUCH AS POSSIBLE.
EVERY CLASS AND CLUB WANTS TO BE THE VERY BEST, AFTER ALL.
WE NEED TO DIVVY OUT TIMES AND LOCATIONS...
ASSIGN JOBS TO ALL THE COMMITTEES AND SO ON.
SOUNDS EASY.
IT'S A VERY IMPORTANT JOB.
THAT BEING SAID...
THERE'S ACTUALLY SOMETHING I WANT TO DO THIS YEAR BESIDES JUST WORK BEHIND THE SCENES.
?
smile

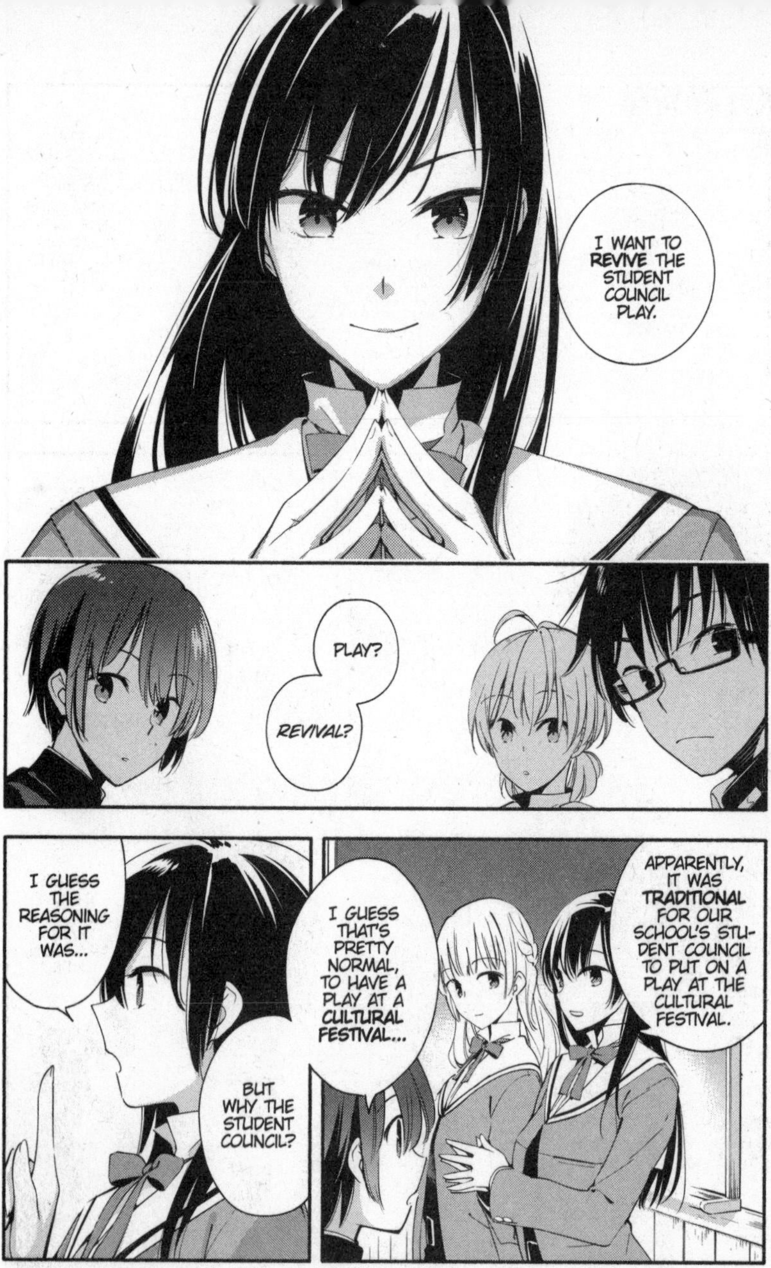
I WANT TO REVIVE THE STUDENT COUNCIL PLAY.
PLAY?
REVIVAL?
APPARENTLY, IT WAS TRADITIONAL FOR OUR SCHOOL'S STUDENT COUNCIL TO PUT ON A PLAY AT THE CULTURAL FESTIVAL.
I GUESS THAT'S PRETTY NORMAL, TO HAVE A PLAY AT A CULTURAL FESTIVAL...
BUT WHY THE STUDENT COUNCIL?
I GUESS THE REASONING FOR IT WAS...

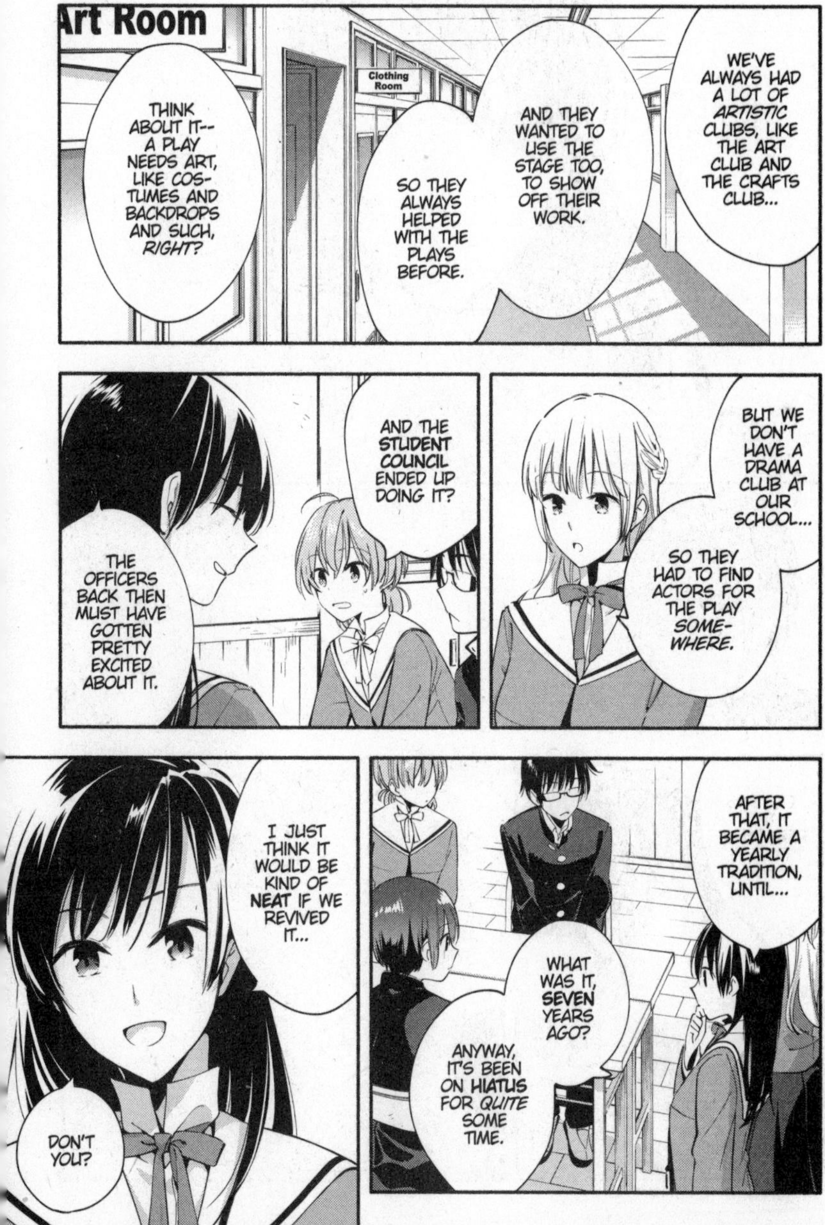
Art Room
Clothing Room
WE'VE ALWAYS HAD A LOT OF *ARTISTIC* CLUBS, LIKE THE ART CLUB AND THE CRAFTS CLUB...
AND THEY WANTED TO USE THE STAGE TOO, TO SHOW OFF THEIR WORK.
SO THEY ALWAYS HELPED WITH THE PLAYS BEFORE.
THINK ABOUT IT-- A PLAY NEEDS ART, LIKE COS-TUMES AND BACKDROPS AND SUCH, *RIGHT?*
BUT WE DON'T HAVE A DRAMA CLUB AT OUR SCHOOL...
SO THEY HAD TO FIND ACTORS FOR THE PLAY *SOME-WHERE.*
AND THE **STUDENT COUNCIL** ENDED UP DOING IT?
THE OFFICERS BACK THEN MUST HAVE GOTTEN PRETTY EXCITED ABOUT IT.
AFTER THAT, IT BECAME A YEARLY TRADITION, UNTIL...
WHAT WAS IT, **SEVEN** YEARS AGO?
ANYWAY, IT'S BEEN ON HIATUS FOR *QUITE* SOME TIME.
I JUST THINK IT WOULD BE KIND OF **NEAT** IF WE REVIVED IT...
DON'T YOU?

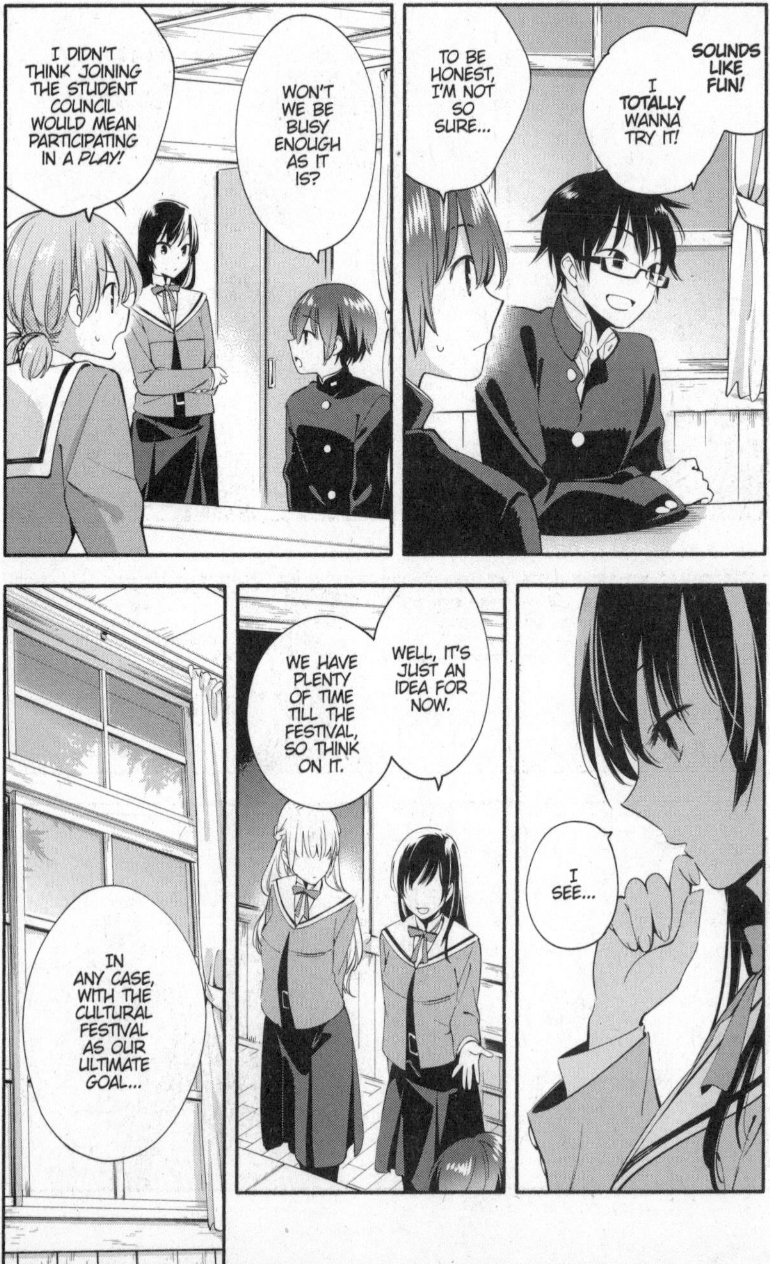
SOUNDS LIKE FUN!
I TOTALLY WANNA TRY IT!
TO BE HONEST, I'M NOT SO SURE...
WON'T WE BE BUSY ENOUGH AS IT IS?
I DIDN'T THINK JOINING THE STUDENT COUNCIL WOULD MEAN PARTICIPATING IN A *PLAY*!
I SEE...
WELL, IT'S JUST AN IDEA FOR NOW.
WE HAVE PLENTY OF TIME TILL THE FESTIVAL, SO THINK ON IT.
IN ANY CASE, WITH THE CULTURAL FESTIVAL AS OUR ULTIMATE GOAL...

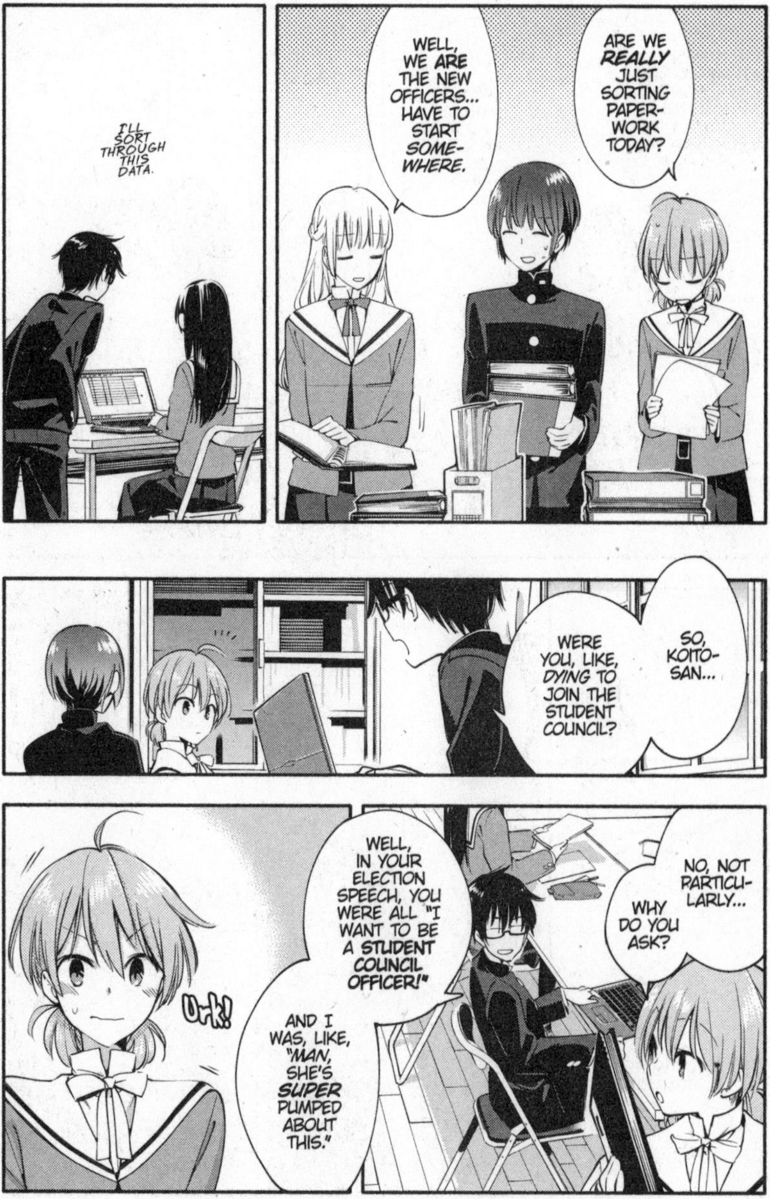
ARE WE REALLY JUST SORTING PAPER-WORK TODAY?
WELL, WE ARE THE NEW OFFICERS... HAVE TO START SOME-WHERE.
I'LL SORT THROUGH THIS DATA.
SO, KOITO-SAN...
WERE YOU, LIKE, DYING TO JOIN THE STUDENT COUNCIL?
NO, NOT PARTICU-LARLY...
WHY DO YOU ASK?
WELL, IN YOUR ELECTION SPEECH, YOU WERE ALL "I WANT TO BE A STUDENT COUNCIL OFFICER!"
AND I WAS, LIKE, "MAN, SHE'S SUPER PUMPED ABOUT THIS."
Ork!

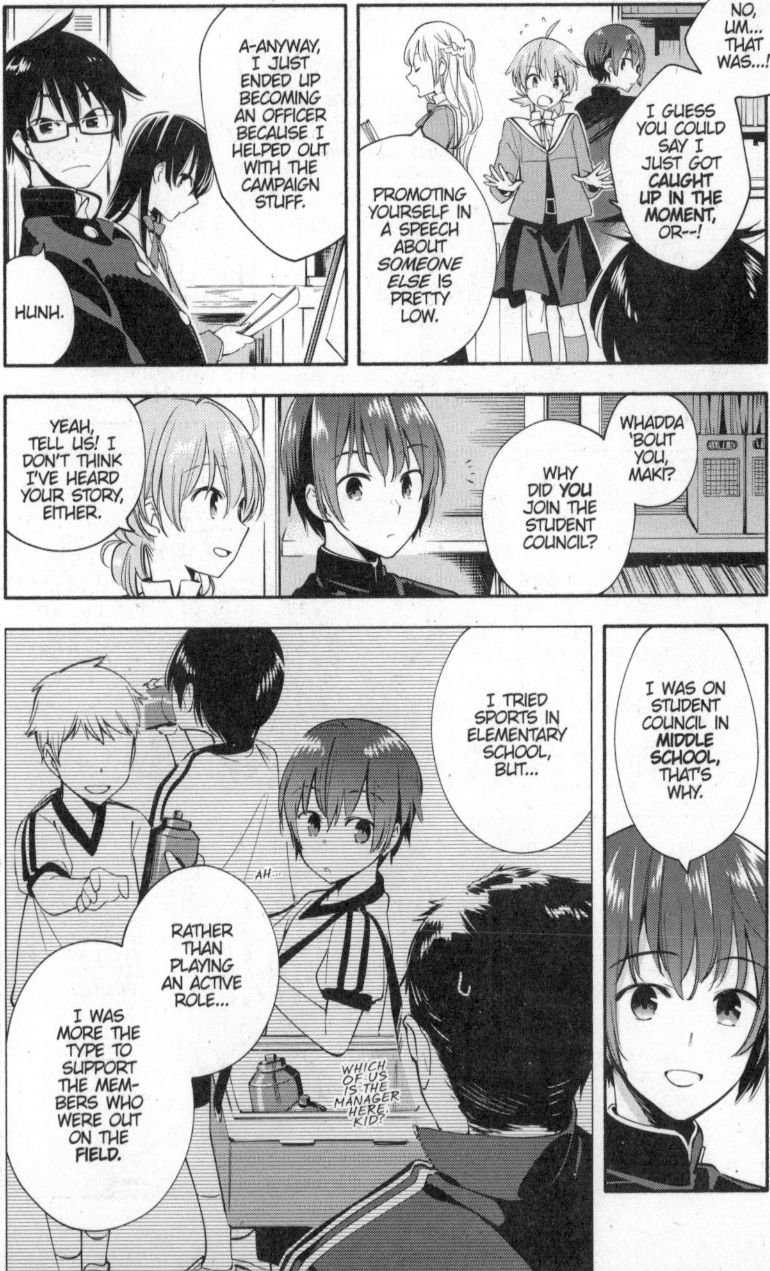
NO, UM... THAT WAS...!
I GUESS YOU COULD SAY I JUST GOT CAUGHT UP IN THE MOMENT, OR--!
PROMOTING YOURSELF IN A SPEECH ABOUT SOMEONE ELSE IS PRETTY LOW.
A-ANYWAY, I JUST ENDED UP BECOMING AN OFFICER BECAUSE I HELPED OUT WITH THE CAMPAIGN STUFF.
HUNH.
WHADDA 'BOUT YOU, MAKI?
WHY DID YOU JOIN THE STUDENT COUNCIL?
YEAH, TELL US! I DON'T THINK I'VE HEARD YOUR STORY, EITHER.
I WAS ON STUDENT COUNCIL IN MIDDLE SCHOOL, THAT'S WHY.
I TRIED SPORTS IN ELEMENTARY SCHOOL, BUT...
AH...
RATHER THAN PLAYING AN ACTIVE ROLE...
I WAS MORE THE TYPE TO SUPPORT THE MEMBERS WHO WERE OUT ON THE FIELD.
WHICH OF US IS THE MANAGER HERE, KID?

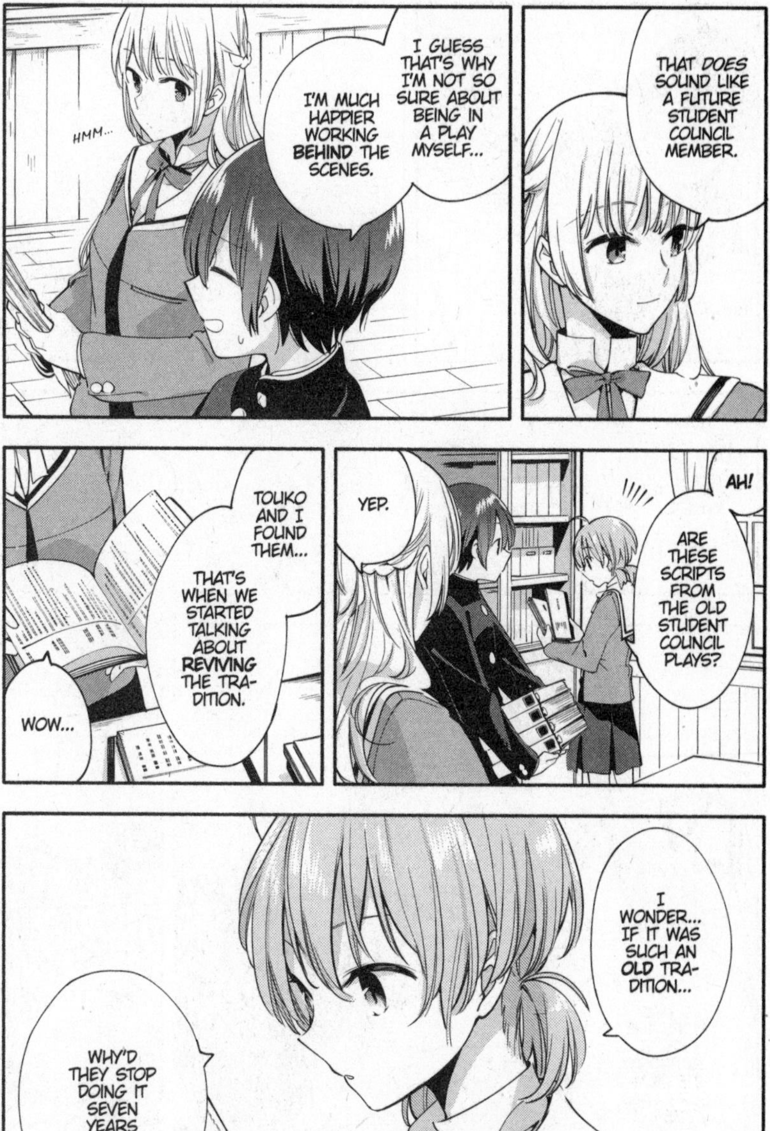
THAT *DOES* SOUND LIKE A FUTURE STUDENT COUNCIL MEMBER.
I GUESS THAT'S WHY I'M NOT SO SURE ABOUT BEING IN A PLAY MYSELF...
I'M MUCH HAPPIER WORKING **BEHIND** THE SCENES.
HMM...
AH!
ARE THESE SCRIPTS FROM THE OLD STUDENT COUNCIL PLAYS?
YEP.
TOUKO AND I FOUND THEM...
THAT'S WHEN WE STARTED TALKING ABOUT **REVIVING** THE TRA-DITION.
WOW...
I WONDER... IF IT WAS SUCH AN OLD TRA-DITION...
WHY'D THEY STOP DOING IT SEVEN YEARS AGO?

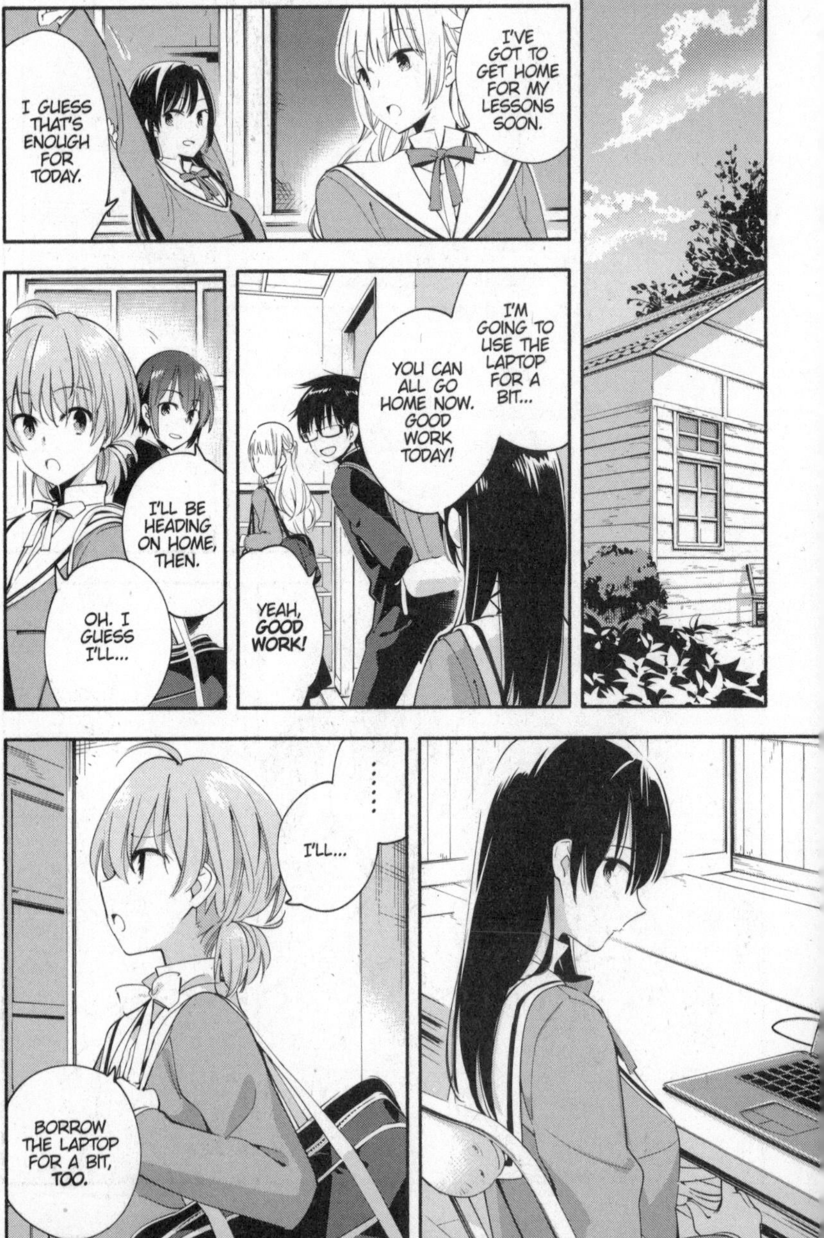
I'VE GOT TO GET HOME FOR MY LESSONS SOON.
I GUESS THAT'S ENOUGH FOR TODAY.
I'M GOING TO USE THE LAPTOP FOR A BIT...
YOU CAN ALL GO HOME NOW. GOOD WORK TODAY!
YEAH, GOOD WORK!
I'LL BE HEADING ON HOME, THEN.
OH. I GUESS I'LL...
......
I'LL...
BORROW THE LAPTOP FOR A BIT, TOO.

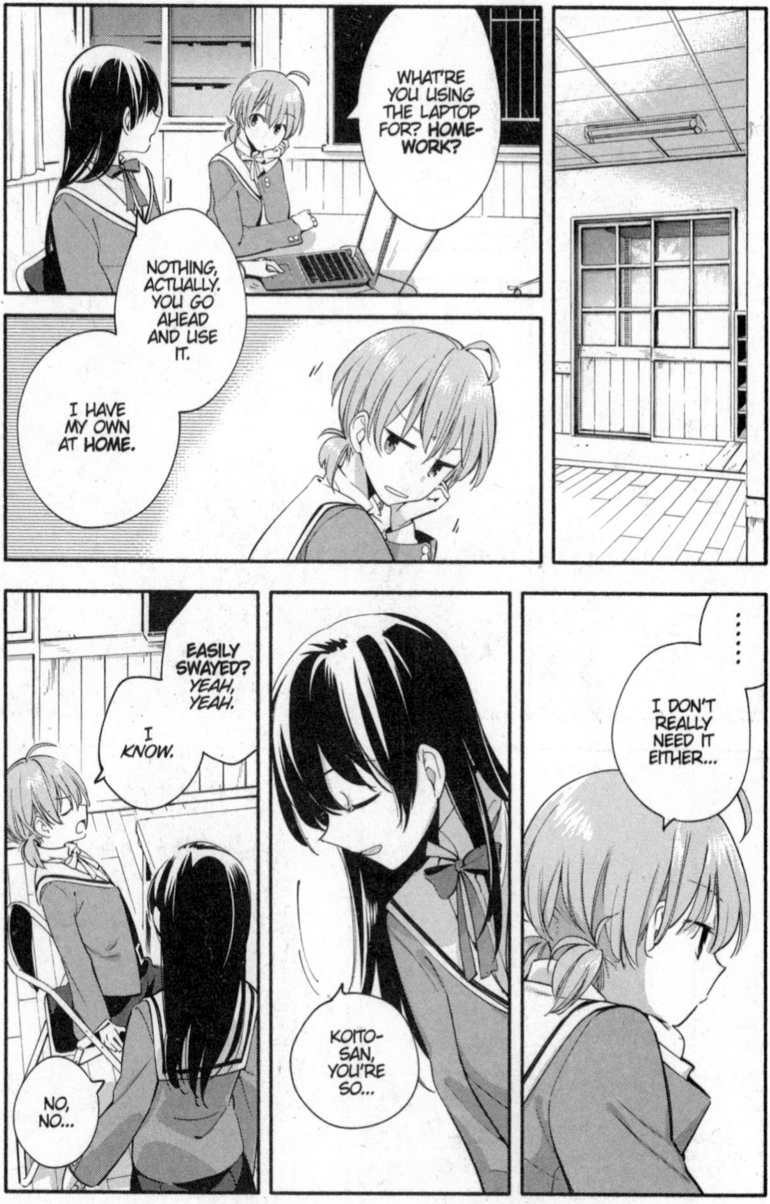
WHAT'RE YOU USING THE LAPTOP FOR? HOME-WORK?
NOTHING, ACTUALLY. YOU GO AHEAD AND USE IT.
I HAVE MY OWN AT HOME.
......
I DON'T REALLY NEED IT EITHER...
KOITO-SAN, YOU'RE SO...
EASILY SWAYED? YEAH, YEAH.
I KNOW.
NO, NO...

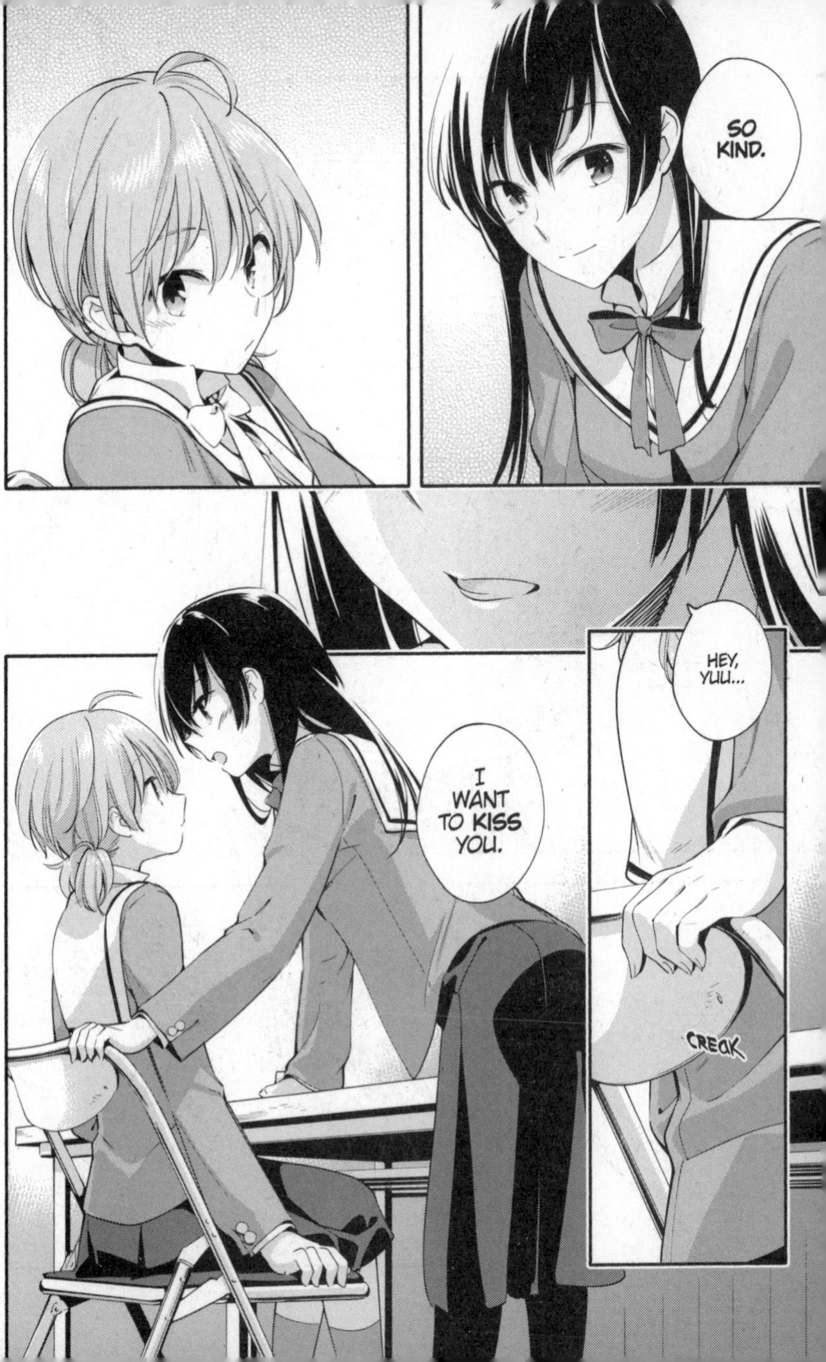
SO KIND.
HEY, YUU...
CREAK
I WANT TO KISS YOU.

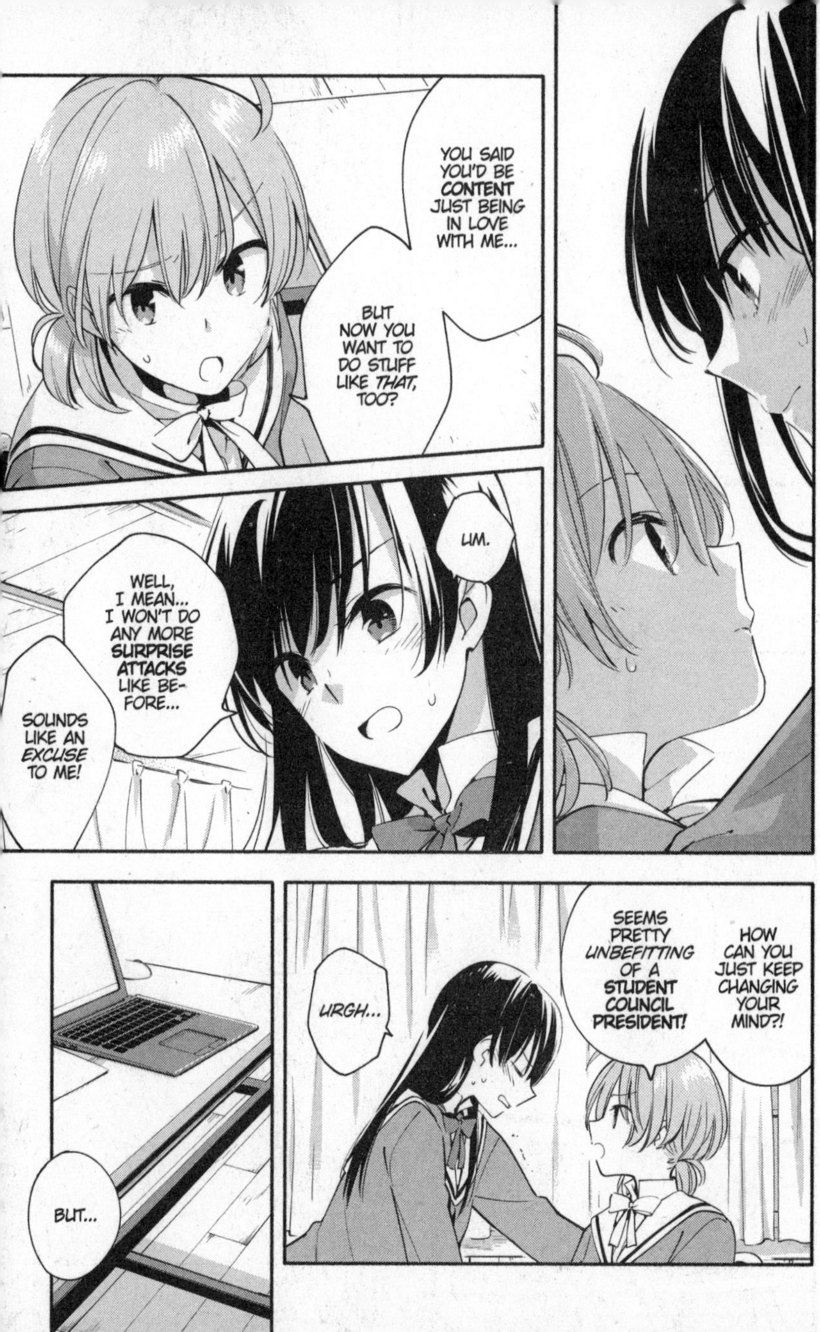
YOU SAID YOU'D BE CONTENT JUST BEING IN LOVE WITH ME...
BUT NOW YOU WANT TO DO STUFF LIKE *THAT*, TOO?
UM.
WELL, I MEAN... I WON'T DO ANY MORE SURPRISE ATTACKS LIKE BE-FORE...
SOUNDS LIKE AN *EXCUSE* TO ME!
HOW CAN YOU JUST KEEP CHANGING YOUR MIND?!
SEEMS PRETTY *UNBEFITTING* OF A STUDENT COUNCIL PRESIDENT!
*URGH...*
BUT...

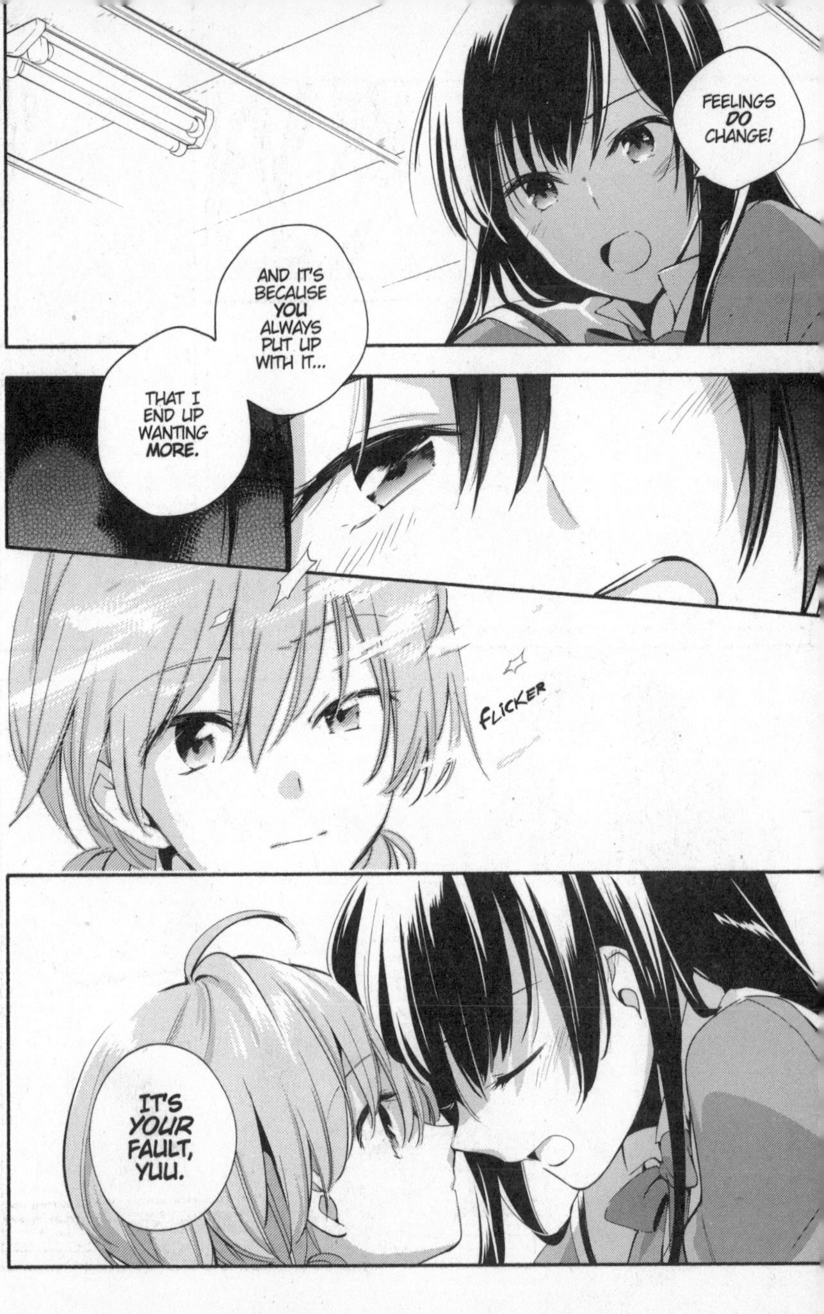
FEELINGS DO CHANGE!
AND IT'S BECAUSE YOU ALWAYS PUT UP WITH IT...
THAT I END UP WANTING MORE.
FLICKER
IT'S YOUR FAULT, YUU.

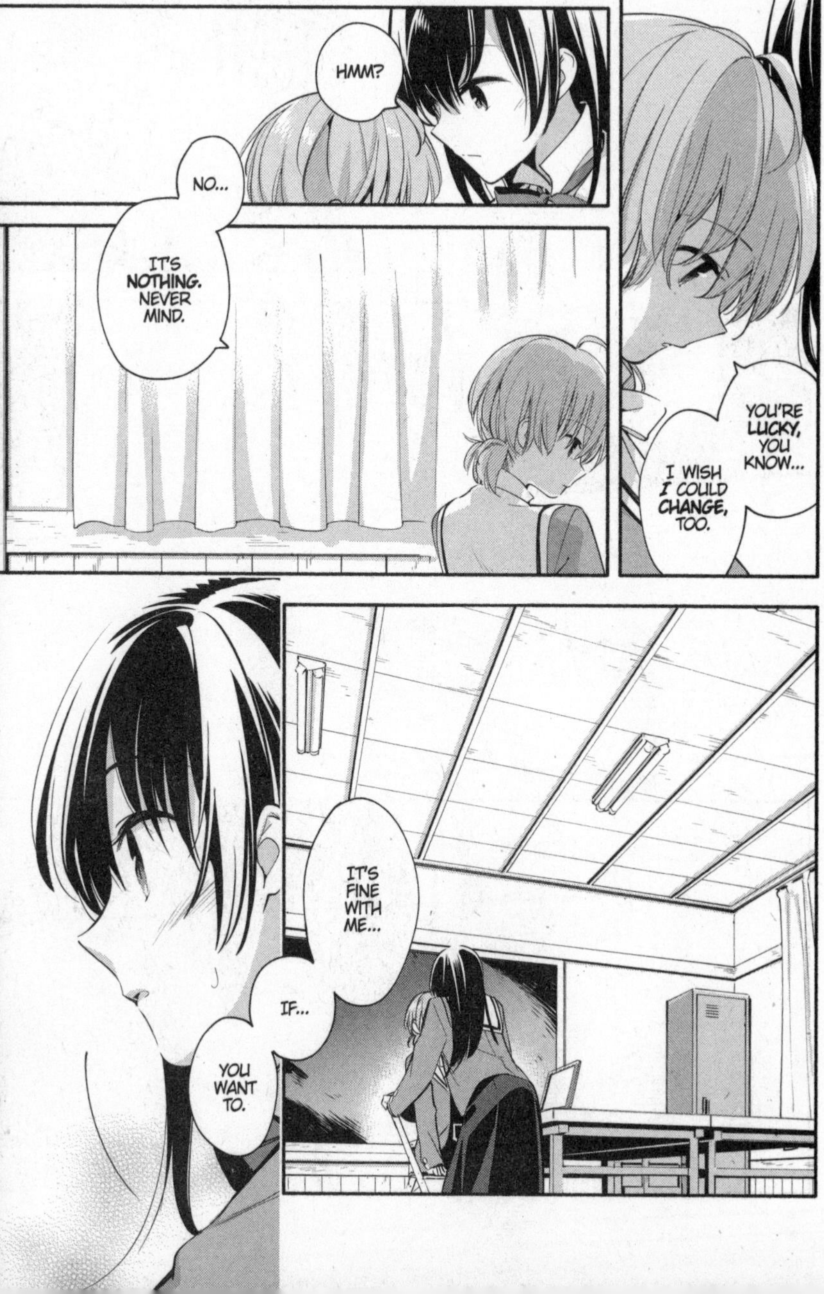
YOU'RE LUCKY, YOU KNOW...
I WISH *I* COULD CHANGE, TOO.
HMM?
NO...
IT'S NOTHING. NEVER MIND.
IT'S FINE WITH ME...
IF...
YOU WANT TO.

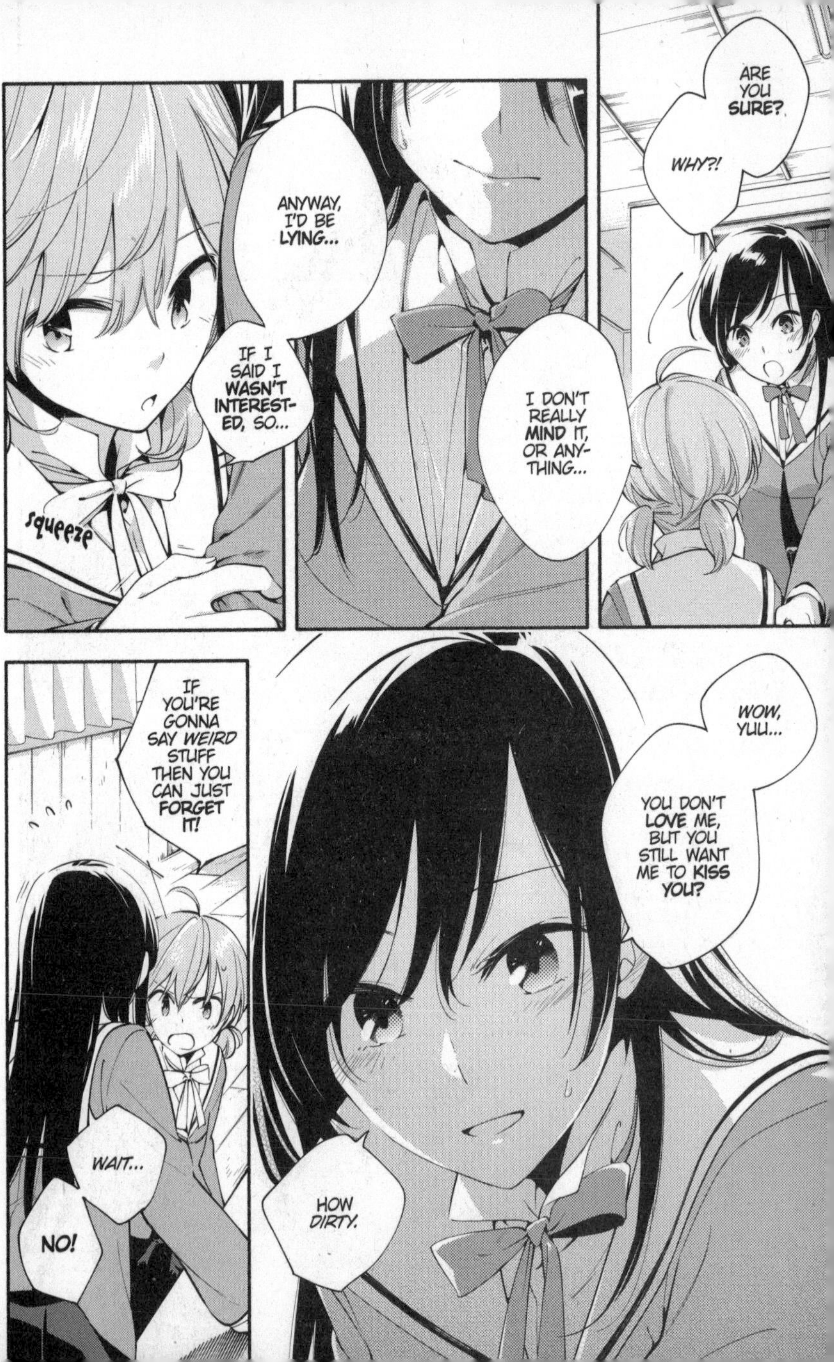
ARE YOU SURE?
WHY?!
I DON'T REALLY MIND IT, OR ANYTHING...
ANYWAY, I'D BE LYING...
IF I SAID I WASN'T INTEREST-ED, SO...
squeeze
WOW, YUU...
YOU DON'T LOVE ME, BUT YOU STILL WANT ME TO KISS YOU?
HOW DIRTY.
IF YOU'RE GONNA SAY WEIRD STUFF THEN YOU CAN JUST FORGET IT!
WAIT...
NO!

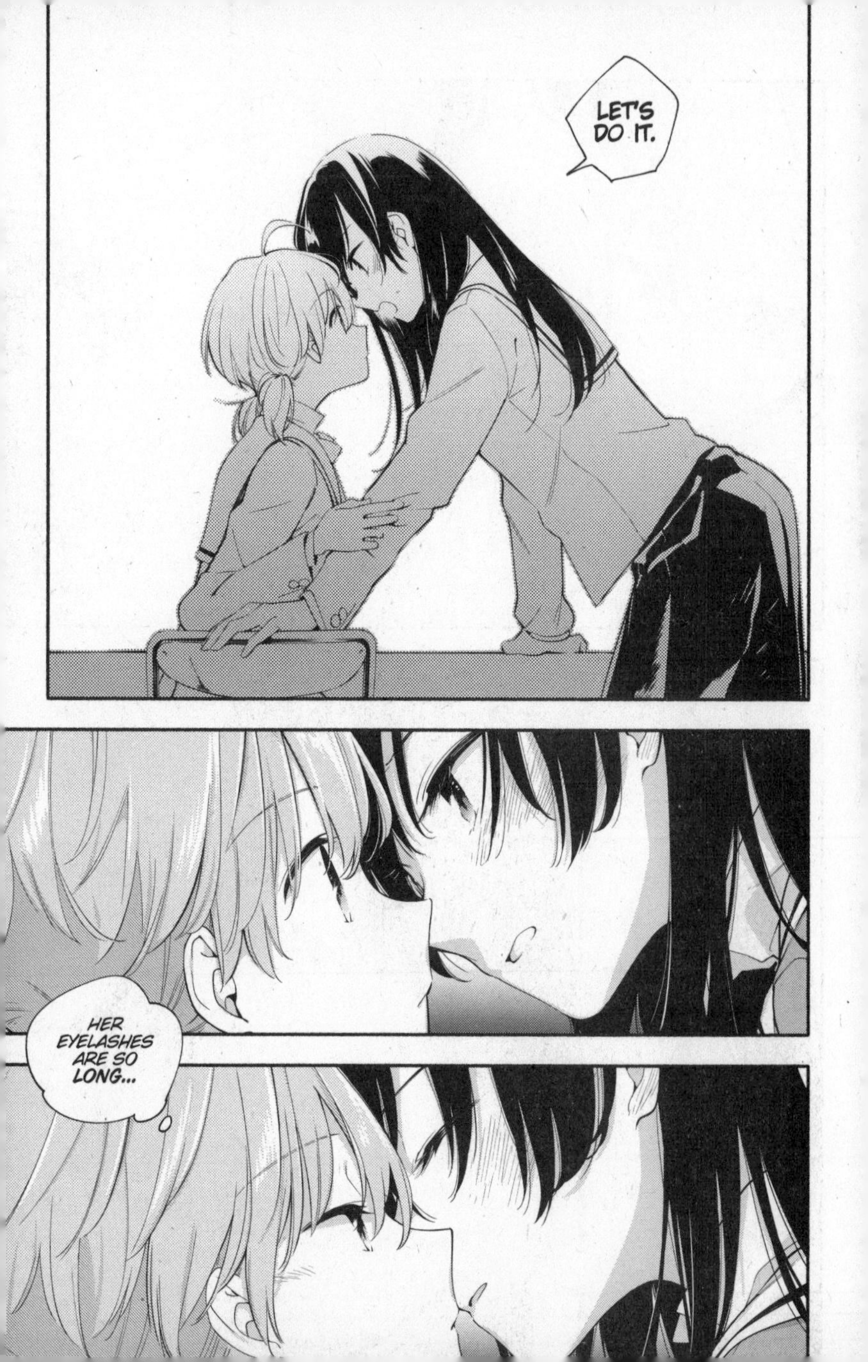
LET'S DO IT.
HER EYELASHES ARE SO LONG...

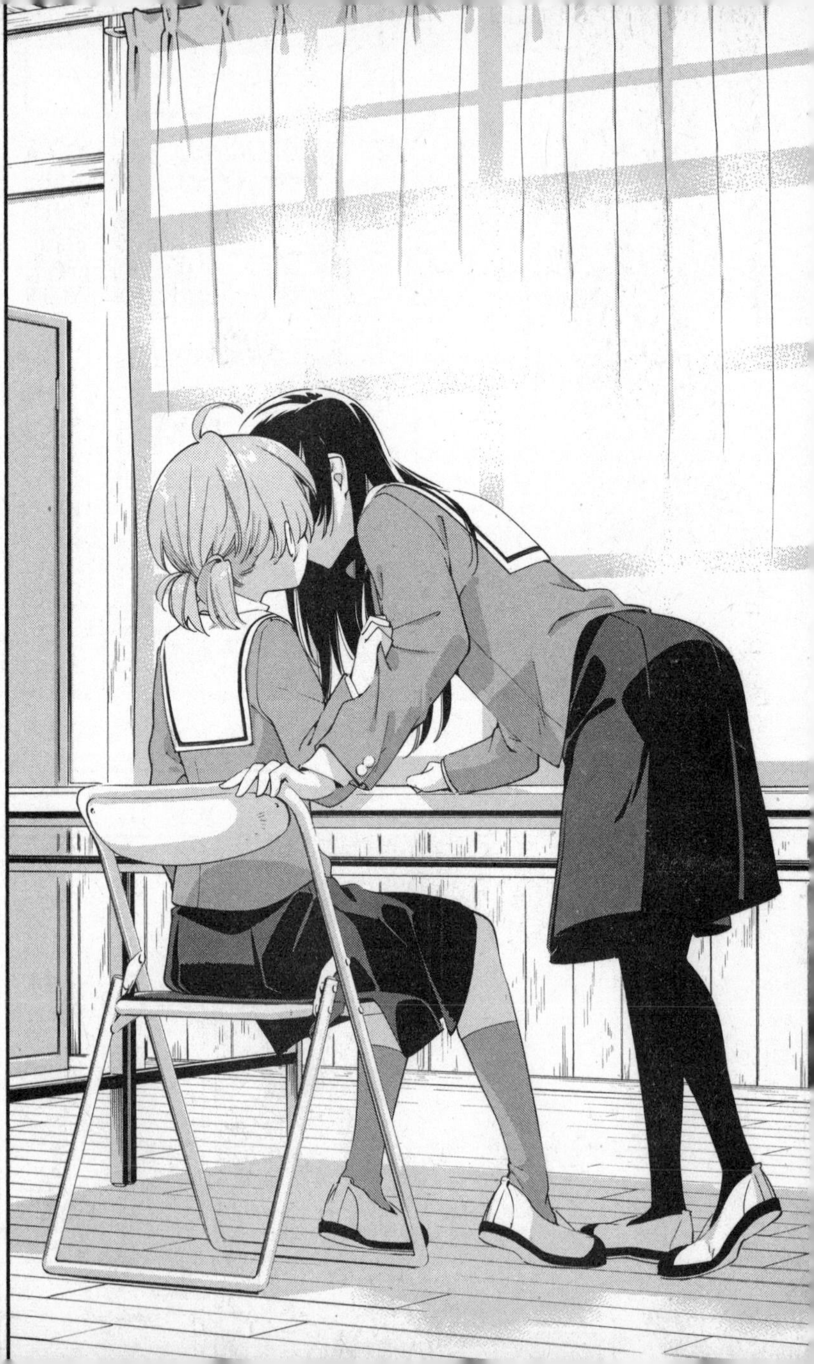

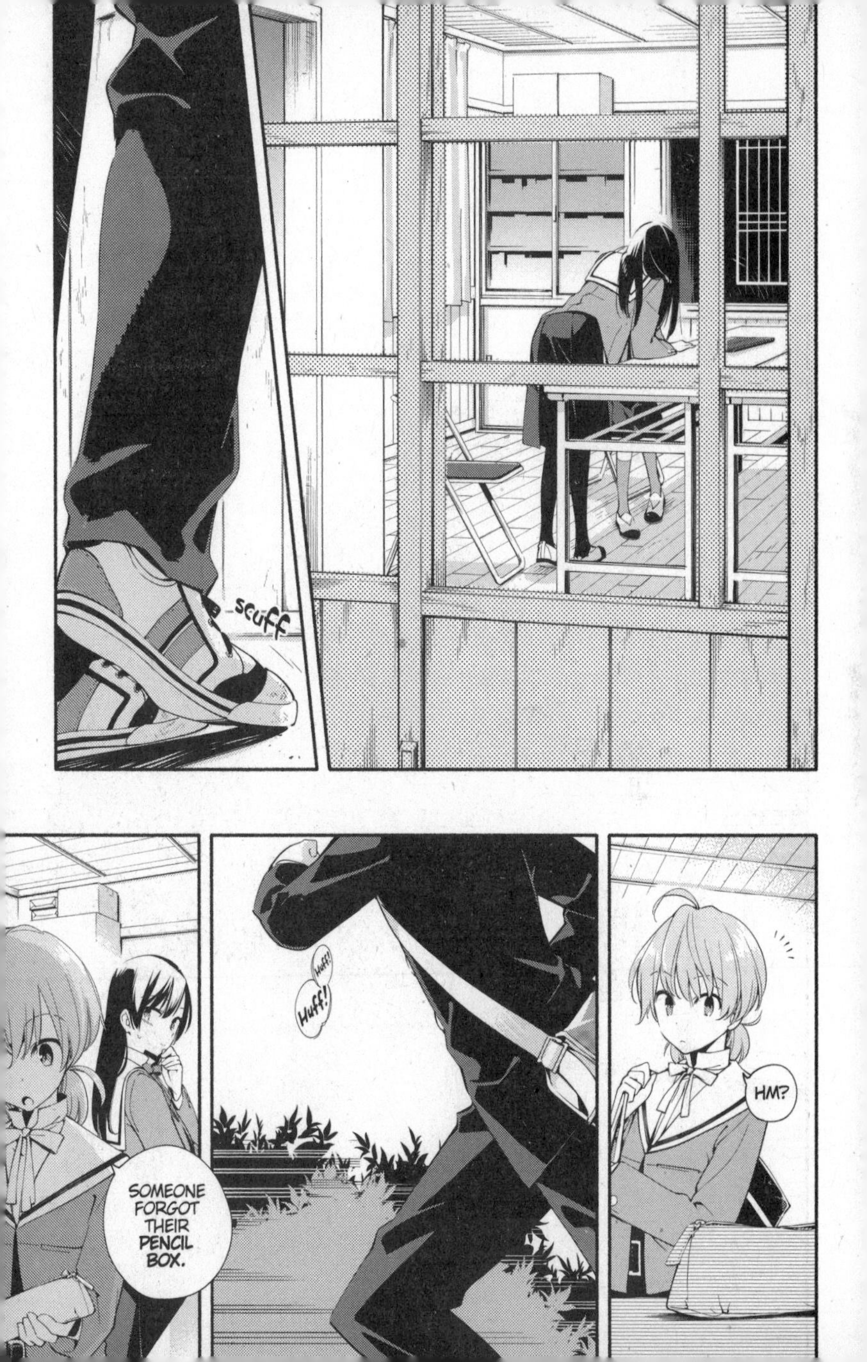
scuff
HM?
Huff!
Huff!
SOMEONE FORGOT THEIR PENCIL BOX.

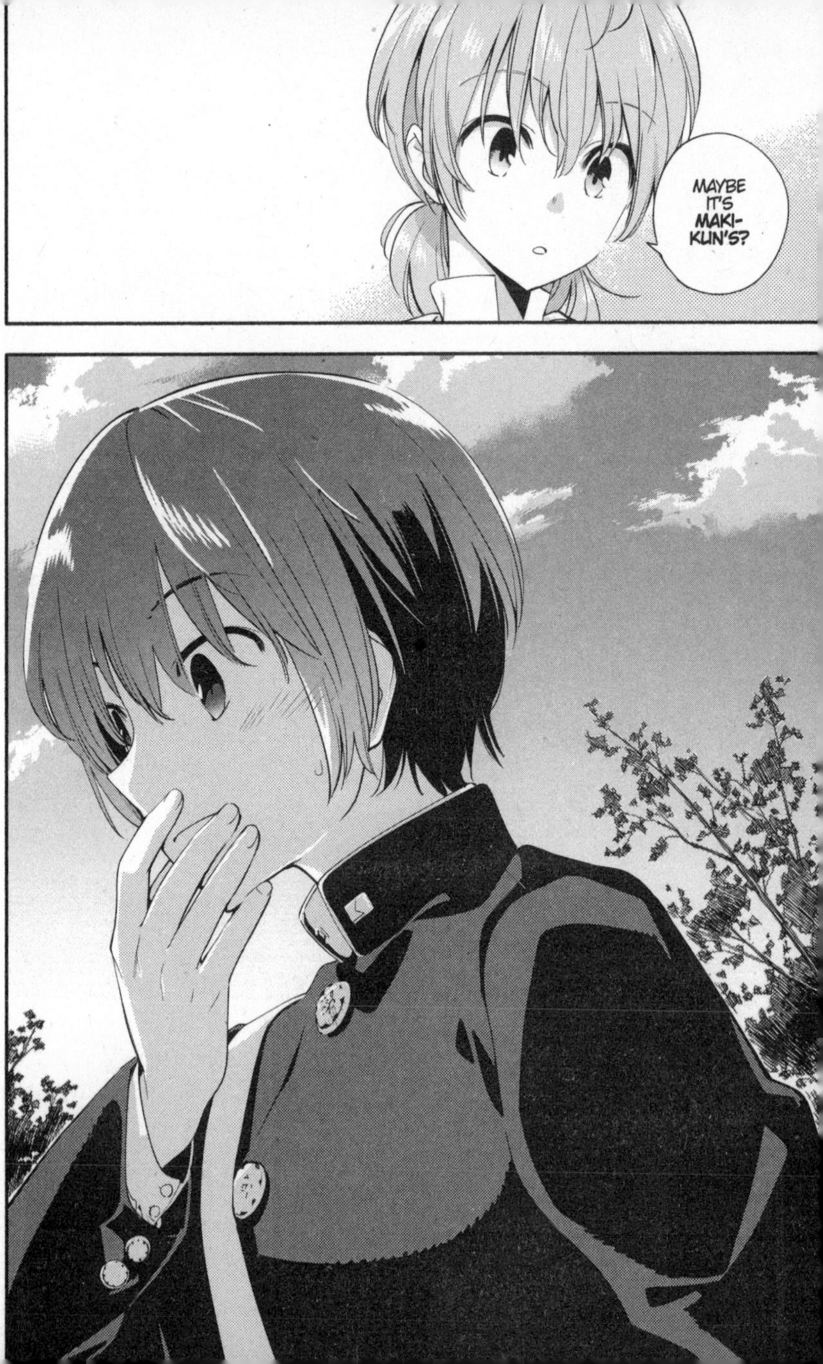
MAYBE IT'S MAKI-KUN'S?

HE
PLAYED
TABLE
TENNIS...

IN THE
BOY
SCOUTS
SPORTS
PROGRAM.

( Bloom Into You )

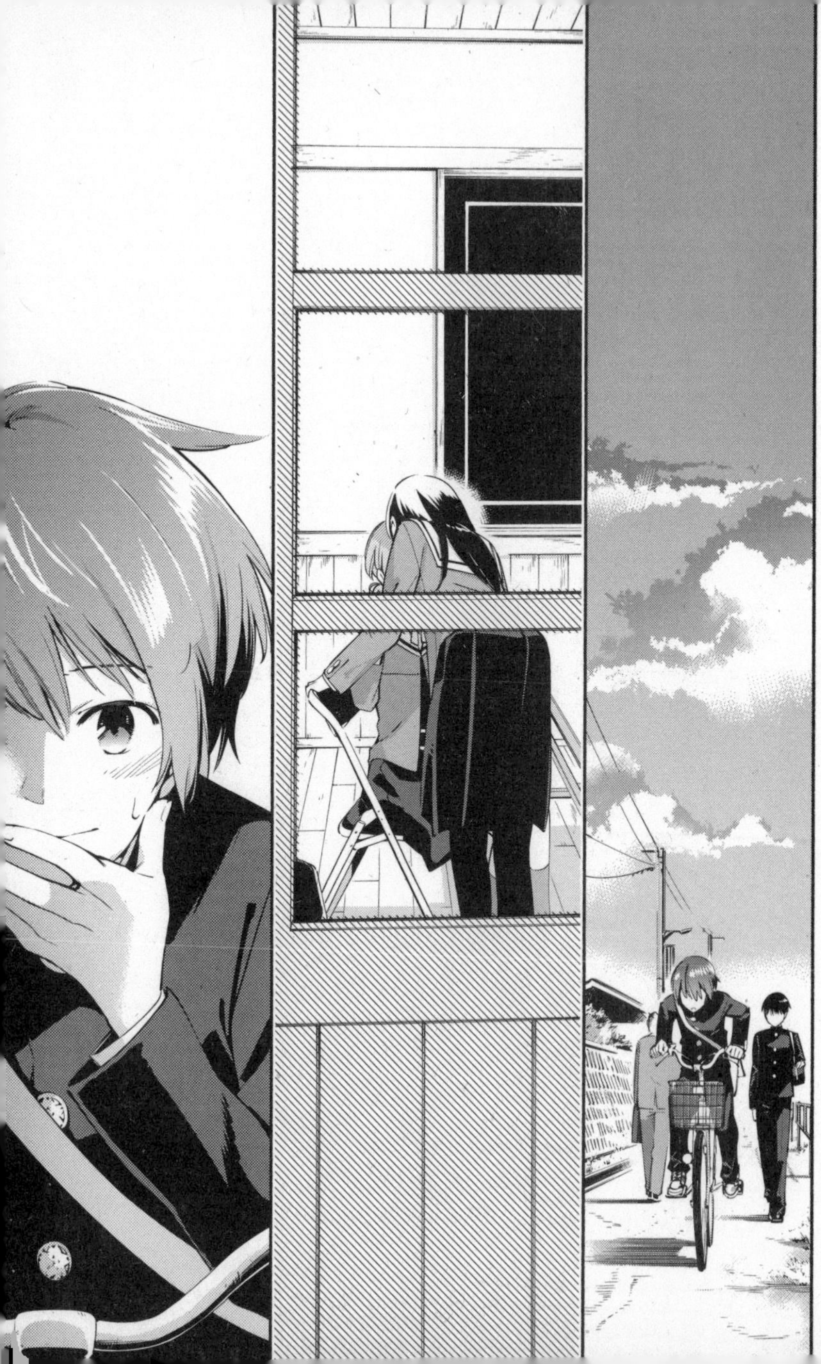

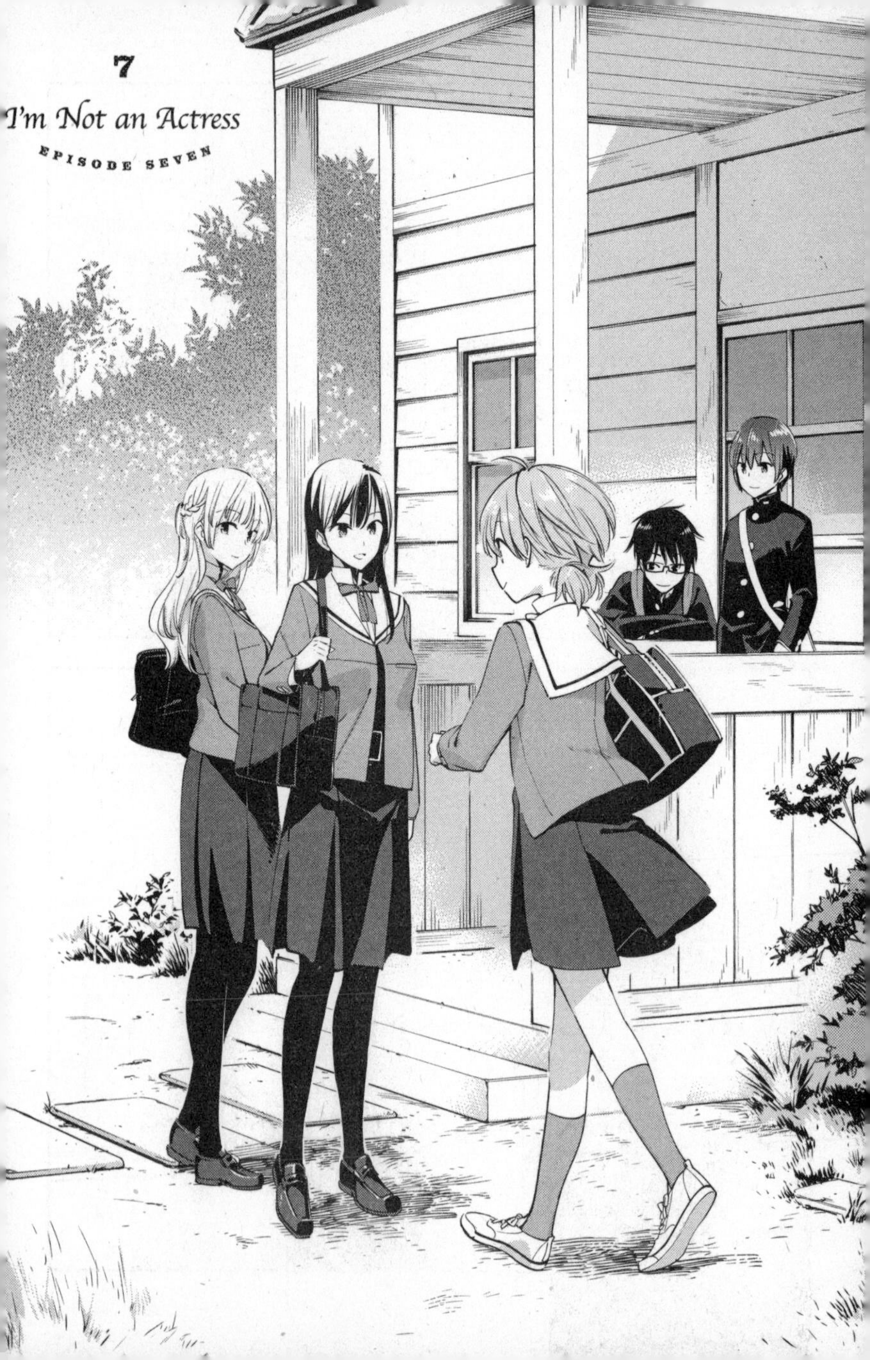
7
I'm Not an Actress
EPISODE SEVEN

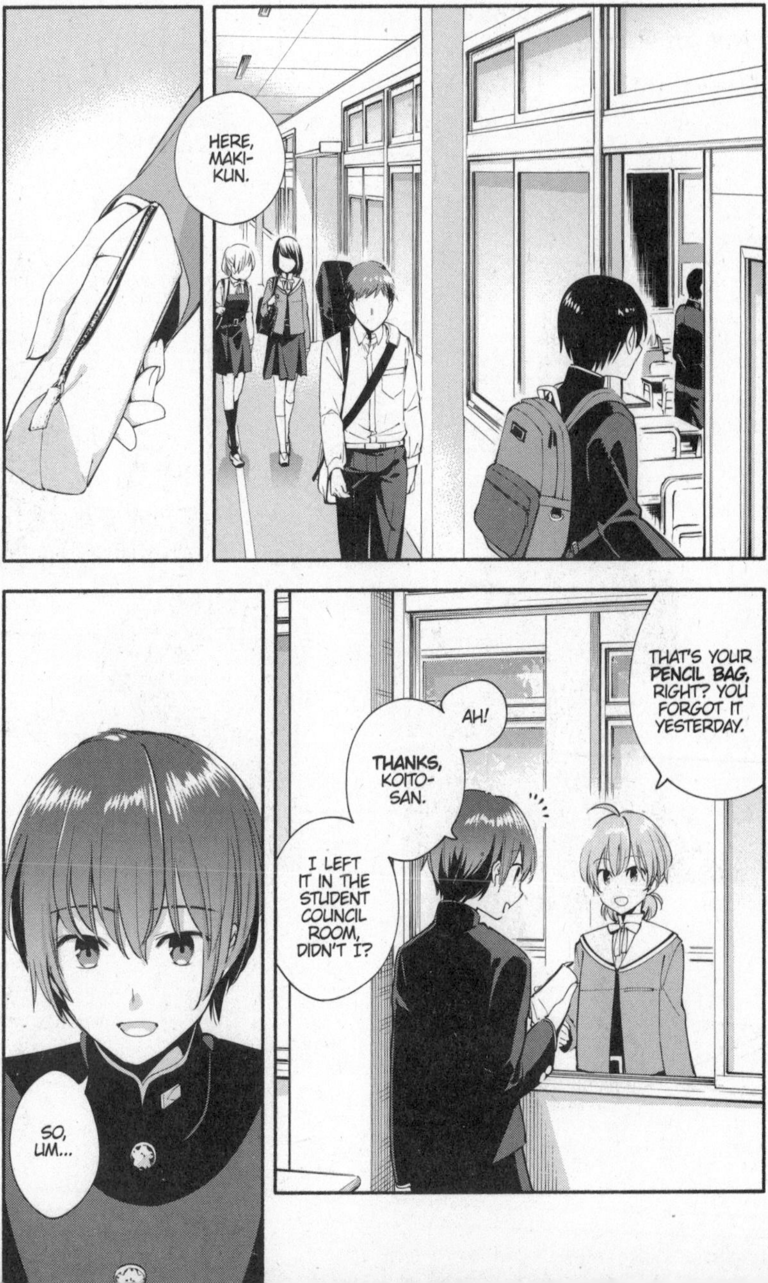
HERE, MAKI-KUN.
THAT'S YOUR PENCIL BAG, RIGHT? YOU FORGOT IT YESTERDAY.
AH!
THANKS, KOITO-SAN.
I LEFT IT IN THE STUDENT COUNCIL ROOM, DIDN'T I?
SO, UM...

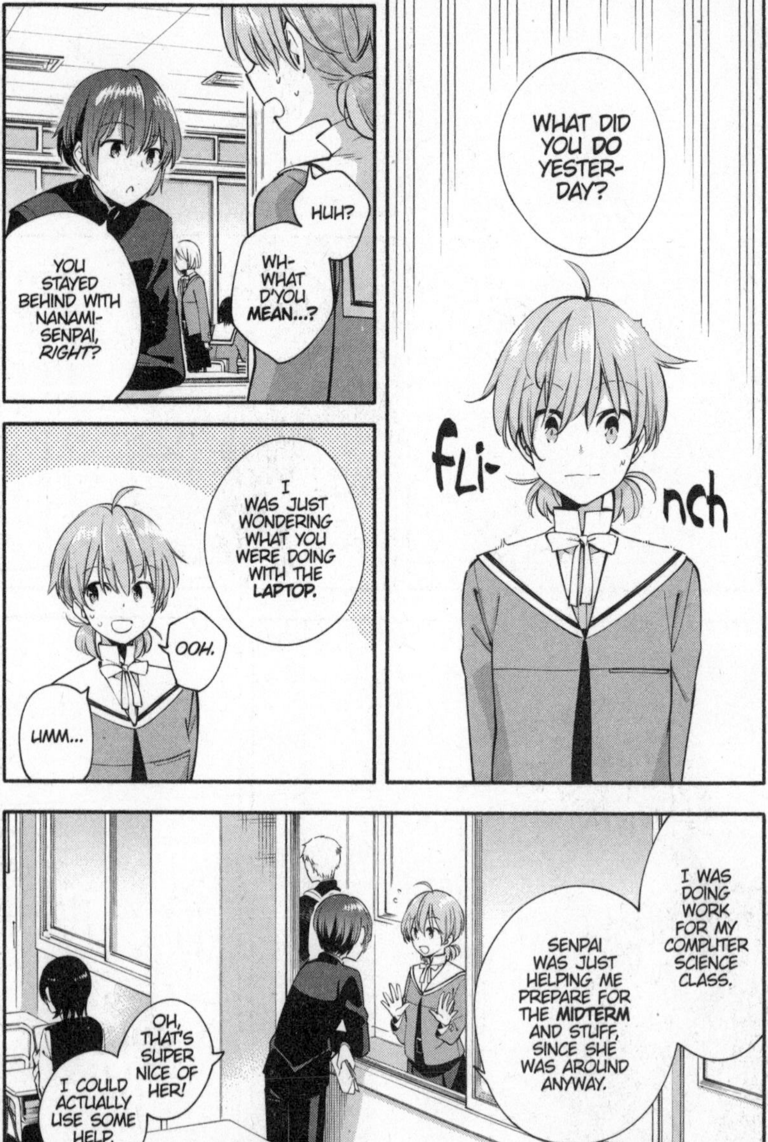
WHAT DID YOU DO YESTER-DAY?
FLI-NCH
HUH?
WH-WHAT D'YOU MEAN...?
YOU STAYED BEHIND WITH NANAMI-SENPAI, *RIGHT?*
I WAS JUST WONDERING WHAT YOU WERE DOING WITH THE **LAPTOP.**
*OOH.*
UMM...
I WAS DOING WORK FOR MY COMPUTER SCIENCE CLASS.
SENPAI WAS JUST HELPING ME PREPARE FOR THE **MIDTERM** AND STUFF, SINCE SHE WAS AROUND ANYWAY.
OH, THAT'S SUPER NICE OF HER!
I COULD ACTUALLY USE SOME HELP, TOO.

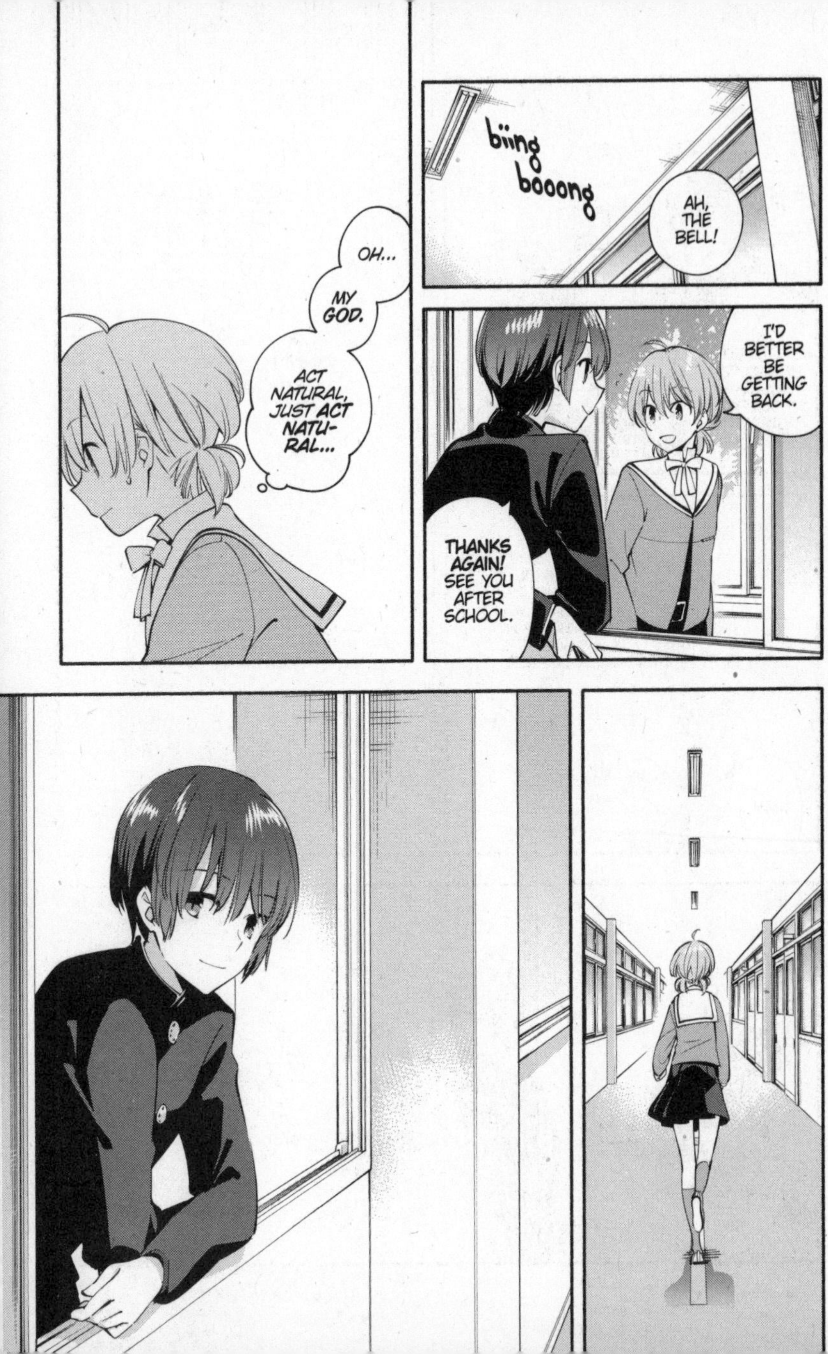
biing
booong
AH, THE BELL!
I'D BETTER BE GETTING BACK.
THANKS AGAIN! SEE YOU AFTER SCHOOL.
OH...
MY GOD.
ACT NATURAL, JUST ACT NATURAL...

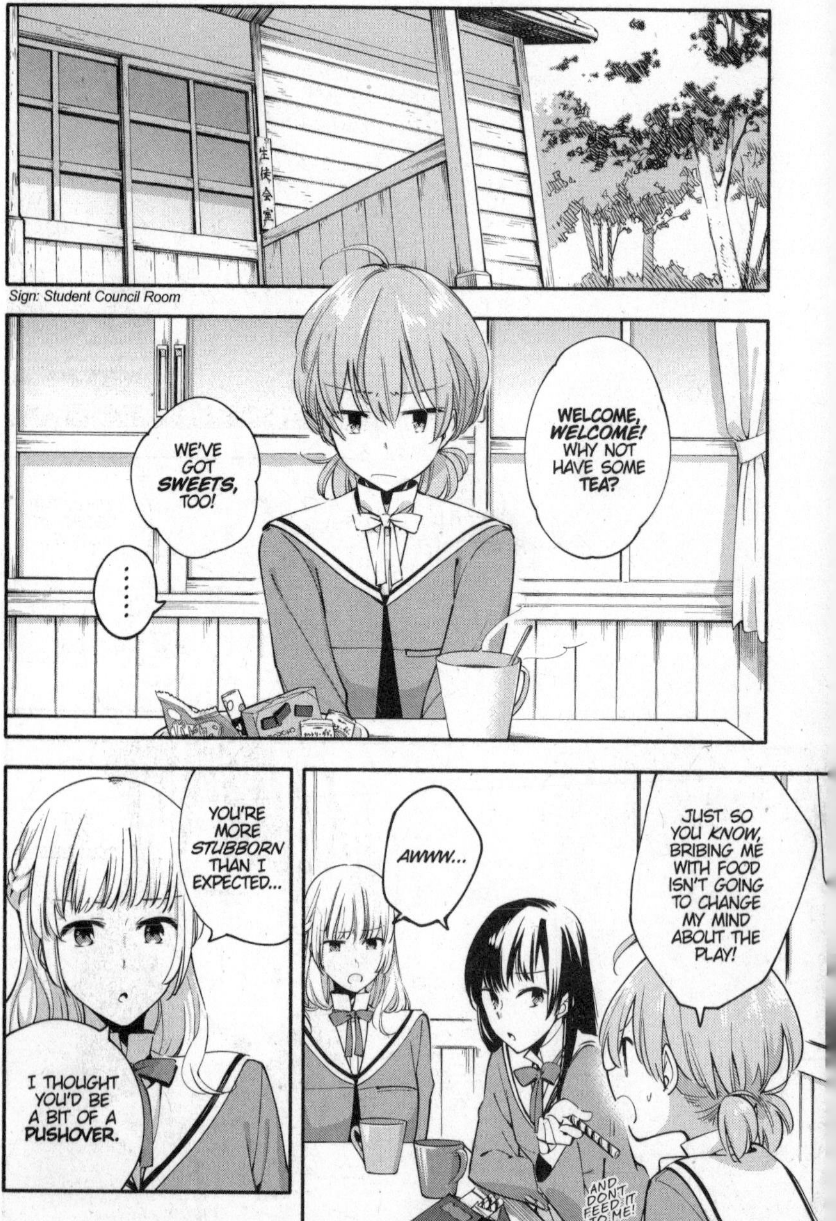
生徒会室
WELCOME, WELCOME! WHY NOT HAVE SOME TEA?
WE'VE GOT SWEETS, TOO!
......
JUST SO YOU KNOW, BRIBING ME WITH FOOD ISN'T GOING TO CHANGE MY MIND ABOUT THE PLAY!
AWWW...
AND DON'T FEED IT TO ME!
YOU'RE MORE STUBBORN THAN I EXPECTED...
I THOUGHT YOU'D BE A BIT OF A PUSHOVER.
Sign: Student Council Room

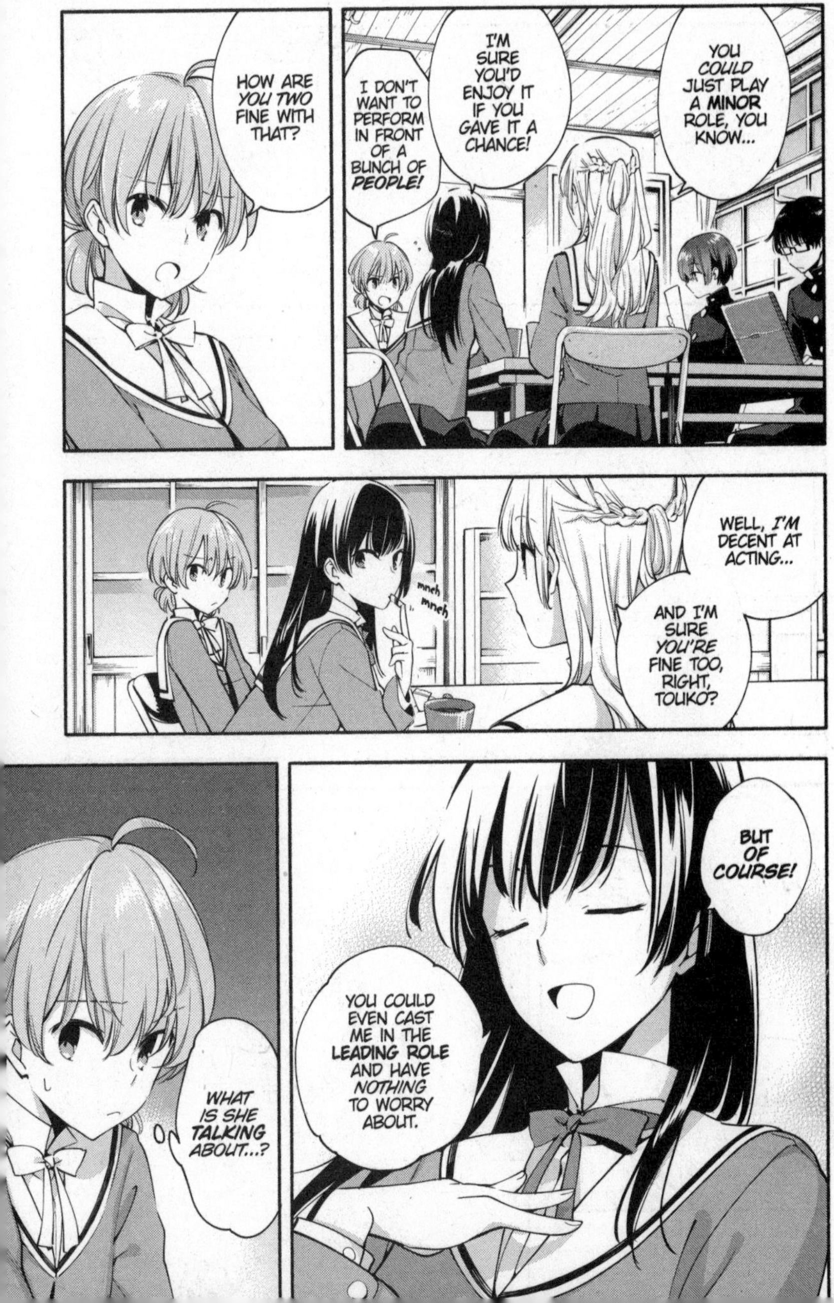
YOU COULD JUST PLAY A MINOR ROLE, YOU KNOW...
I'M SURE YOU'D ENJOY IT IF YOU GAVE IT A CHANCE!
I DON'T WANT TO PERFORM IN FRONT OF A BUNCH OF PEOPLE!
HOW ARE YOU TWO FINE WITH THAT?
WELL, I'M DECENT AT ACTING...
AND I'M SURE YOU'RE FINE TOO, RIGHT, TOUKO?
mneh mneh
BUT OF COURSE!
YOU COULD EVEN CAST ME IN THE LEADING ROLE AND HAVE NOTHING TO WORRY ABOUT.
WHAT IS SHE TALKING ABOUT...?

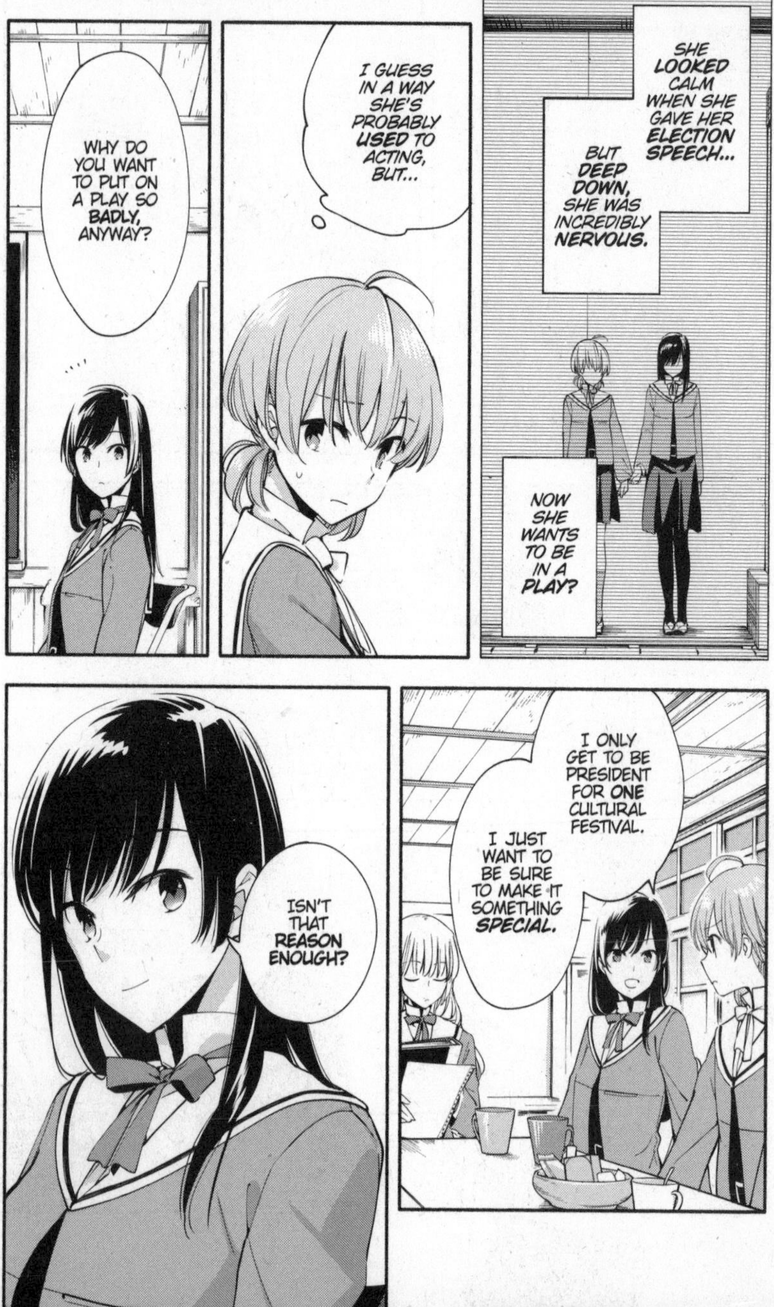
SHE LOOKED CALM WHEN SHE GAVE HER ELECTION SPEECH...
BUT DEEP DOWN, SHE WAS INCREDIBLY NERVOUS.
NOW SHE WANTS TO BE IN A PLAY?
I GUESS IN A WAY SHE'S PROBABLY USED TO ACTING, BUT...
WHY DO YOU WANT TO PUT ON A PLAY SO BADLY, ANYWAY?
...
I ONLY GET TO BE PRESIDENT FOR ONE CULTURAL FESTIVAL.
I JUST WANT TO BE SURE TO MAKE IT SOMETHING SPECIAL.
ISN'T THAT REASON ENOUGH?

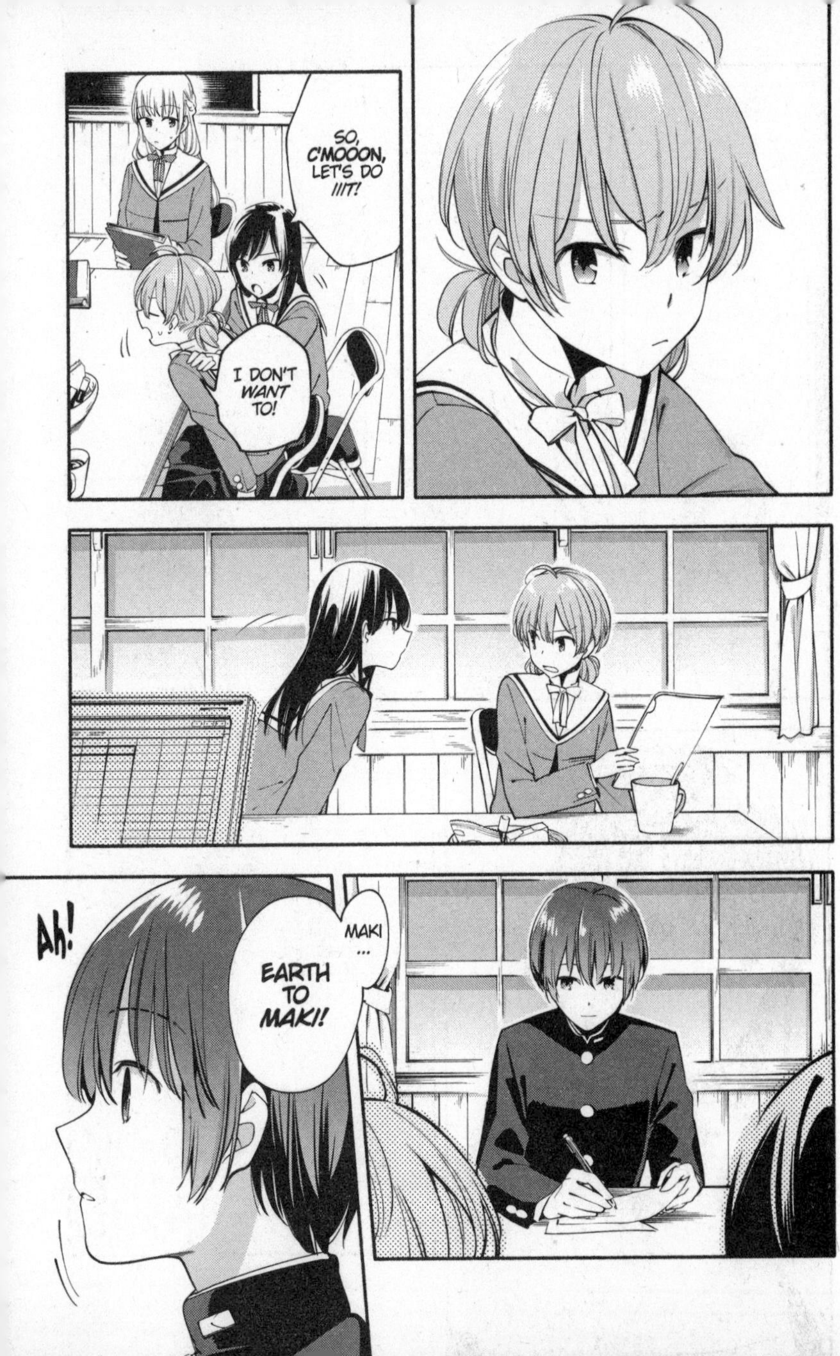
SO, C'MOOON, LET'S DO IIIT!
I DON'T WANT TO!
MAKI ... EARTH TO MAKI!
Ah!

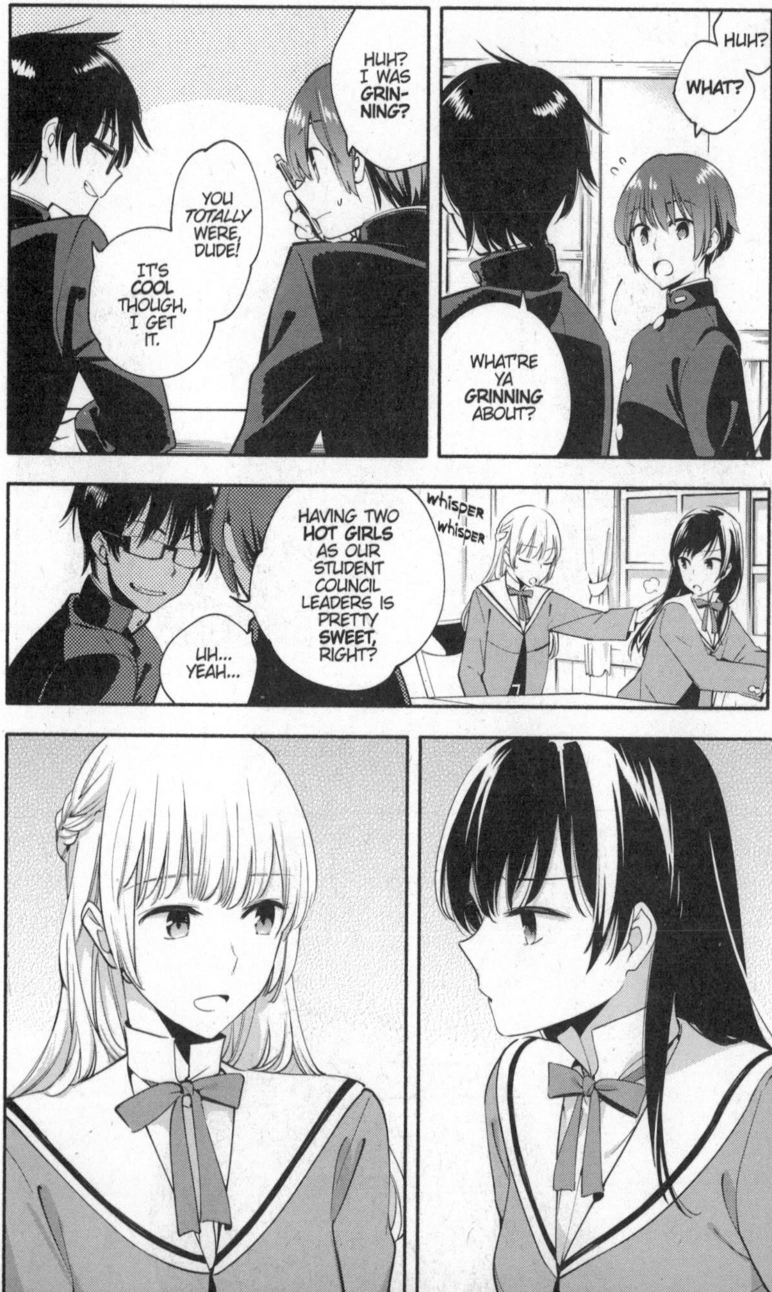
HUH?
WHAT?
WHAT'RE YA GRINNING ABOUT?
HUH? I WAS GRIN-NING?
YOU TOTALLY WERE, DUDE!
IT'S COOL THOUGH, I GET IT.
whisper whisper
HAVING TWO HOT GIRLS AS OUR STUDENT COUNCIL LEADERS IS PRETTY SWEET, RIGHT?
UH... YEAH...

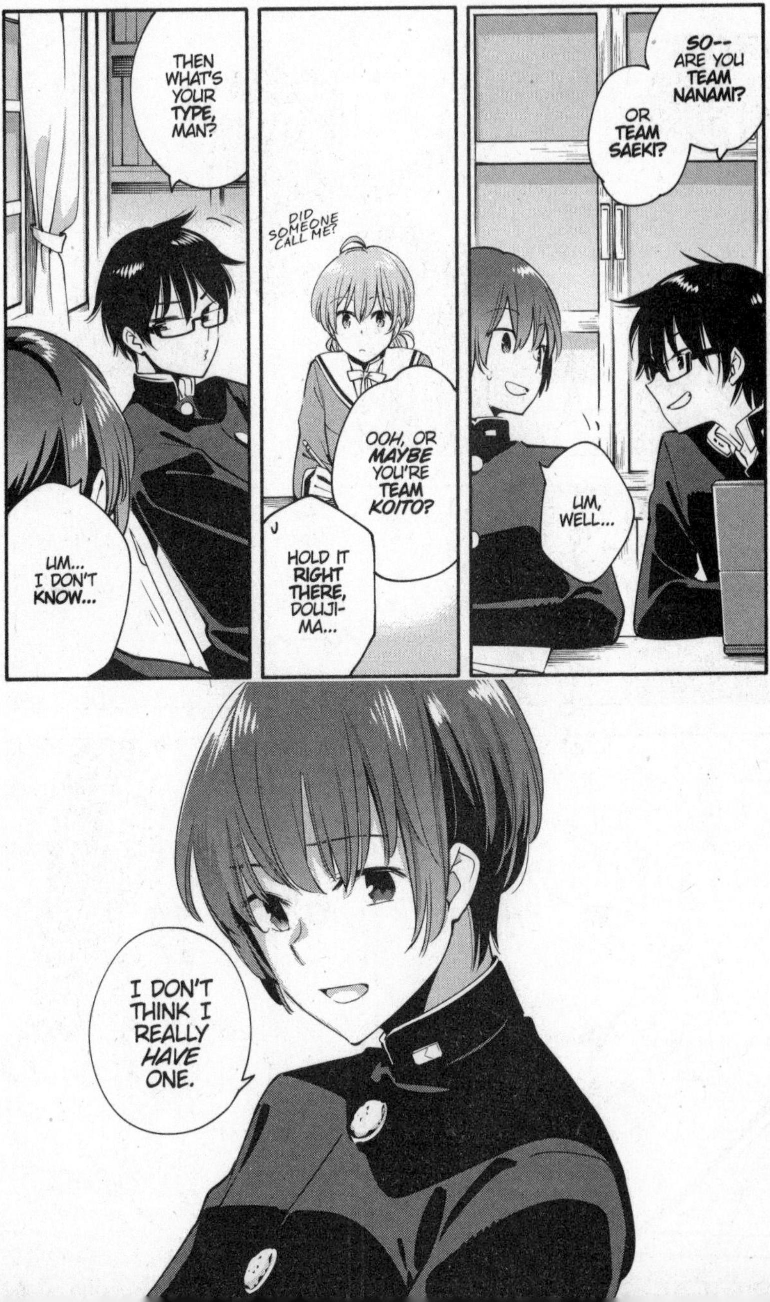

SO-- ARE YOU TEAM NANAMI?
OR TEAM SAEKI?
UM, WELL...
OOH, OR MAYBE YOU'RE TEAM KOITO?
DID SOMEONE CALL ME?
HOLD IT RIGHT THERE, DOUJI-MA...
THEN WHAT'S YOUR TYPE, MAN?
UM... I DON'T KNOW...
I DON'T THINK I REALLY HAVE ONE.

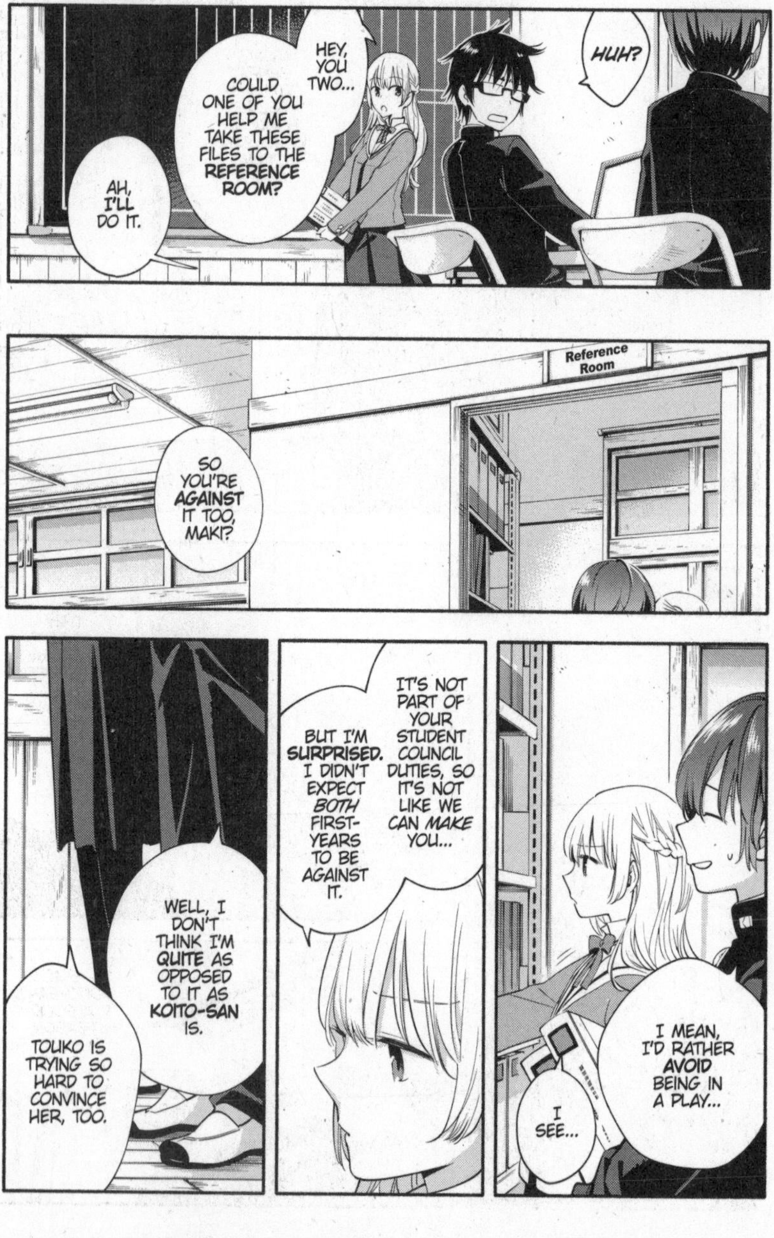
HEY, YOU TWO... COULD ONE OF YOU HELP ME TAKE THESE FILES TO THE REFERENCE ROOM?
HUH?
AH, I'LL DO IT.
Reference Room
SO YOU'RE AGAINST IT TOO, MAKI?
I MEAN, I'D RATHER AVOID BEING IN A PLAY...
I SEE...
IT'S NOT PART OF YOUR STUDENT COUNCIL DUTIES, SO IT'S NOT LIKE WE CAN MAKE YOU...
BUT I'M SURPRISED. I DIDN'T EXPECT BOTH FIRST-YEARS TO BE AGAINST IT.
WELL, I DON'T THINK I'M QUITE AS OPPOSED TO IT AS KOITO-SAN IS.
TOUKO IS TRYING SO HARD TO CONVINCE HER, TOO.

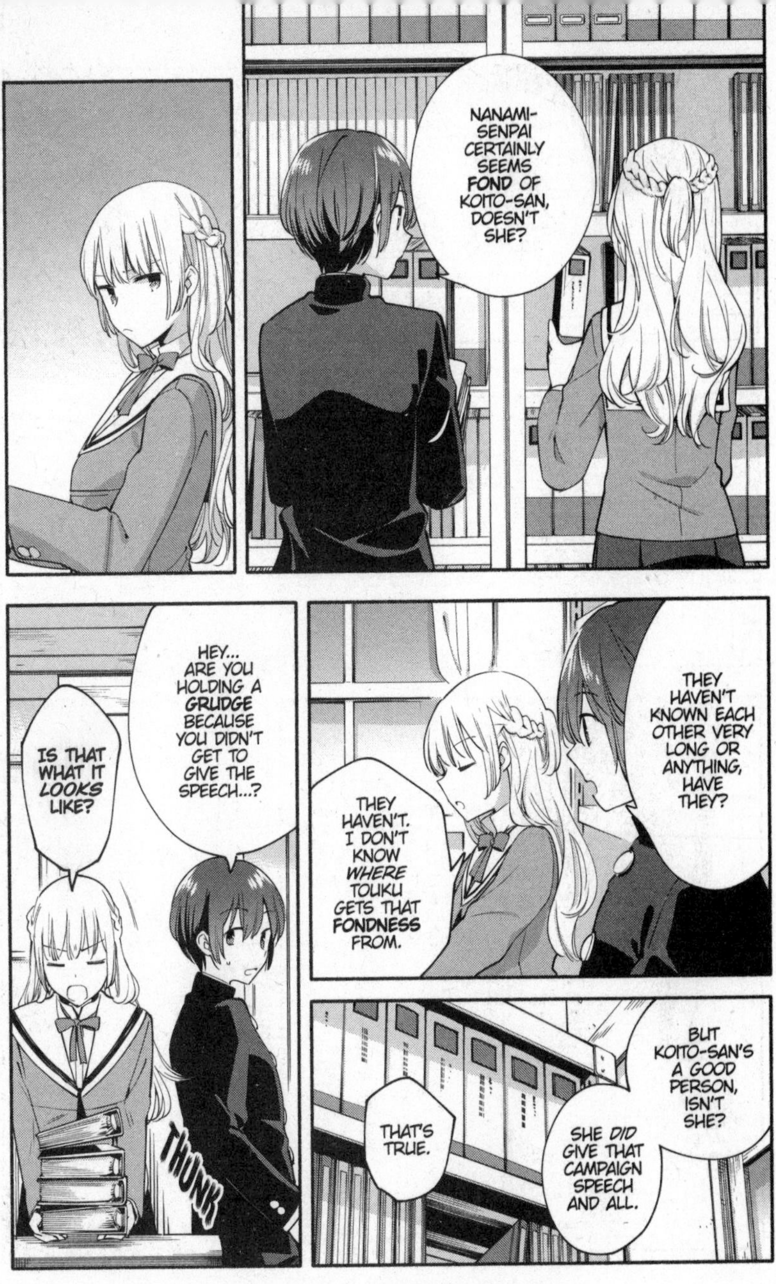
NANAMI-SENPAI CERTAINLY SEEMS **FOND** OF KOITO-SAN, DOESN'T SHE?
THEY HAVEN'T KNOWN EACH OTHER VERY LONG OR ANYTHING, HAVE THEY?
THEY HAVEN'T. I DON'T KNOW *WHERE* TOUKU GETS THAT **FONDNESS** FROM.
BUT KOITO-SAN'S A GOOD PERSON, ISN'T SHE?
SHE *DID* GIVE THAT CAMPAIGN SPEECH AND ALL.
THAT'S TRUE.
HEY... ARE YOU HOLDING A **GRUDGE** BECAUSE YOU DIDN'T GET TO GIVE THE SPEECH...?
IS THAT WHAT IT *LOOKS* LIKE?
THUNK

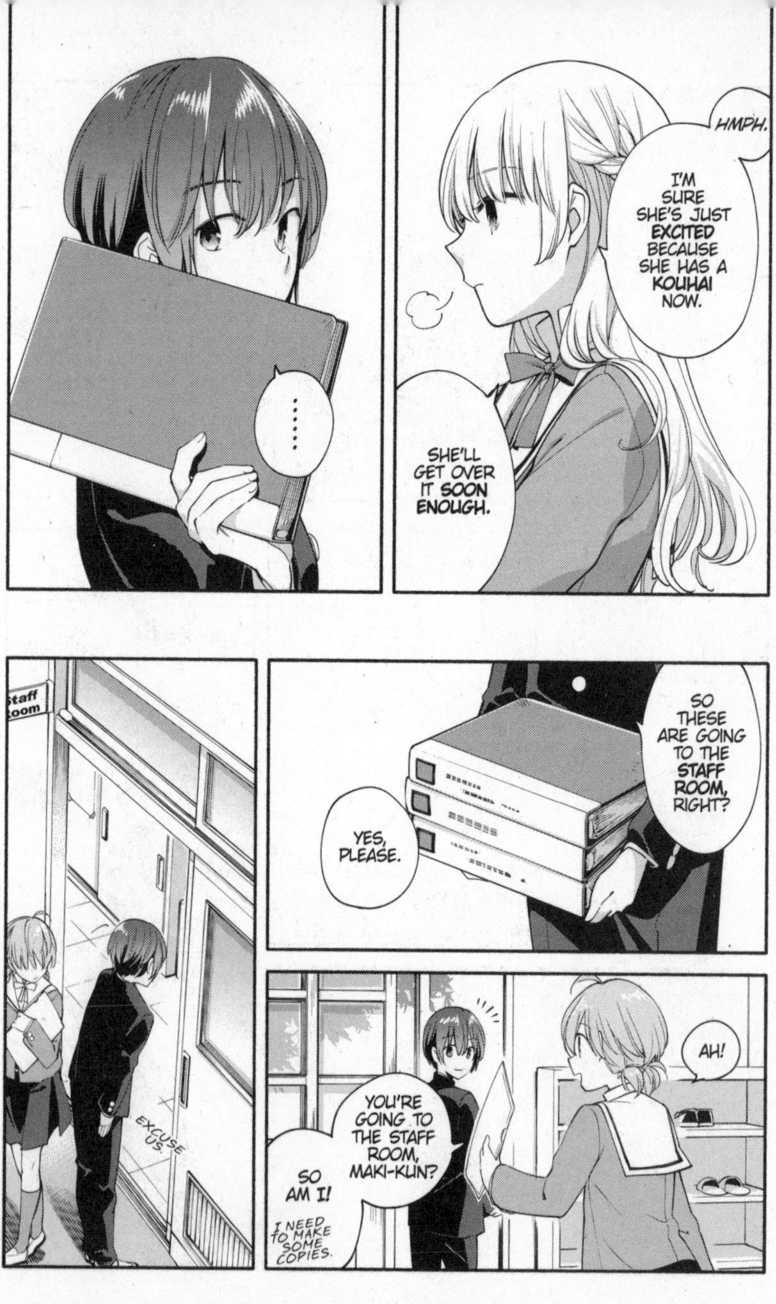
HMPH.
I'M SURE SHE'S JUST EXCITED BECAUSE SHE HAS A KOUHAI NOW.
SHE'LL GET OVER IT SOON ENOUGH.
......
SO THESE ARE GOING TO THE STAFF ROOM, RIGHT?
YES, PLEASE.
AH!
YOU'RE GOING TO THE STAFF ROOM, MAKI-KUN?
SO AM I!
I NEED TO MAKE SOME COPIES.
Staff Room
EXCUSE US.

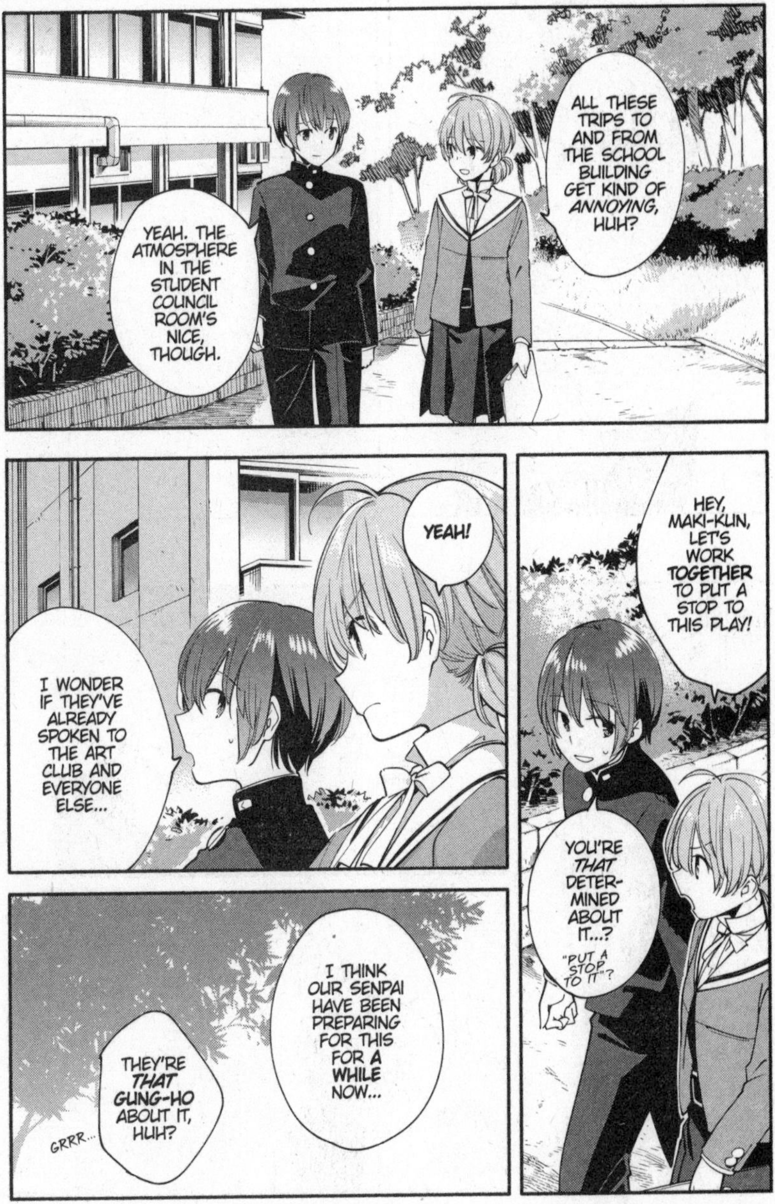
ALL THESE TRIPS TO AND FROM THE SCHOOL BUILDING GET KIND OF ANNOYING, HUH?
YEAH. THE ATMOSPHERE IN THE STUDENT COUNCIL ROOM'S NICE, THOUGH.
HEY, MAKI-KUN, LET'S WORK TOGETHER TO PUT A STOP TO THIS PLAY!
YOU'RE THAT DETERMINED ABOUT IT...?
"PUT A STOP TO IT"?
YEAH!
I WONDER IF THEY'VE ALREADY SPOKEN TO THE ART CLUB AND EVERYONE ELSE...
I THINK OUR SENPAI HAVE BEEN PREPARING FOR THIS FOR A WHILE NOW...
THEY'RE THAT GUNG-HO ABOUT IT, HUH?
GRRR...

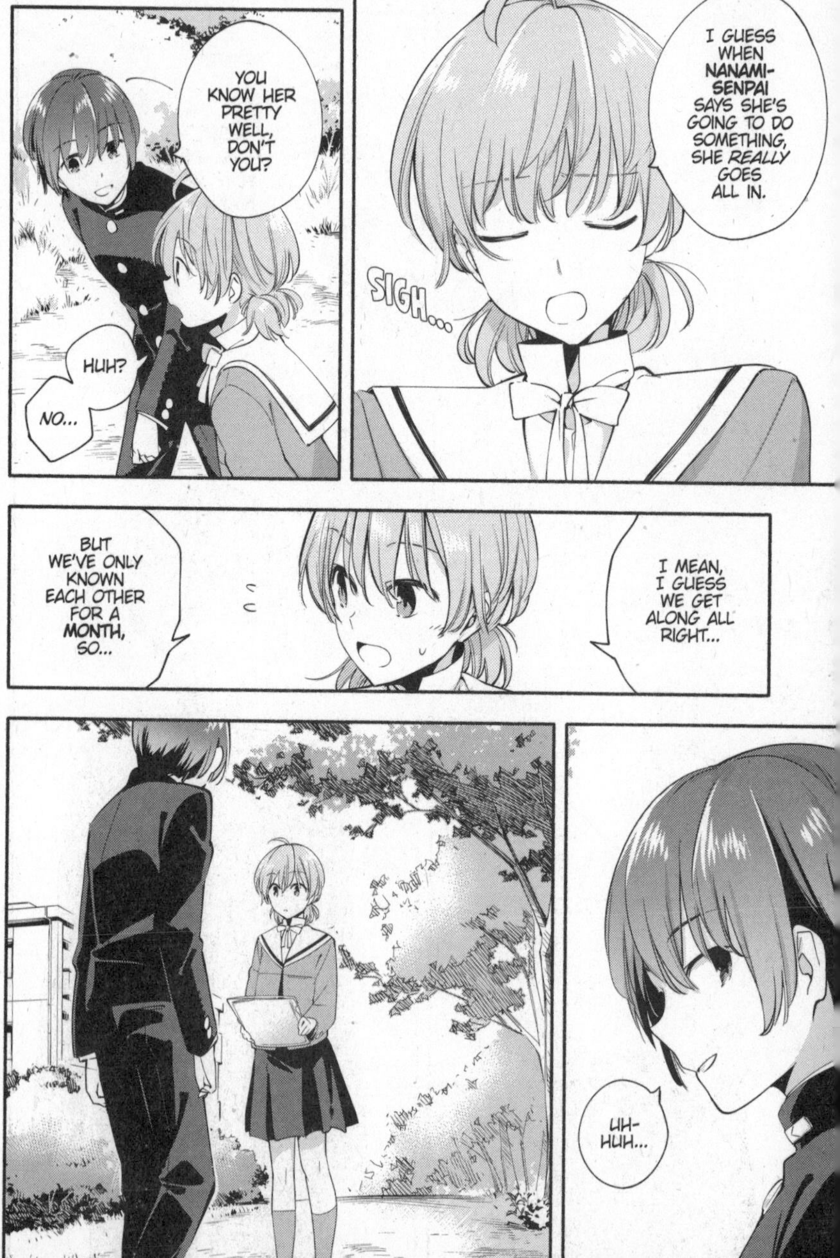
I GUESS WHEN NANAMI-SENPAI SAYS SHE'S GOING TO DO SOMETHING, SHE *REALLY* GOES ALL IN.
SIGH...
YOU KNOW HER PRETTY WELL, DON'T YOU?
HUH?
NO...
I MEAN, I GUESS WE GET ALONG ALL RIGHT...
BUT WE'VE ONLY KNOWN EACH OTHER FOR A MONTH, SO...
UH-HUH...

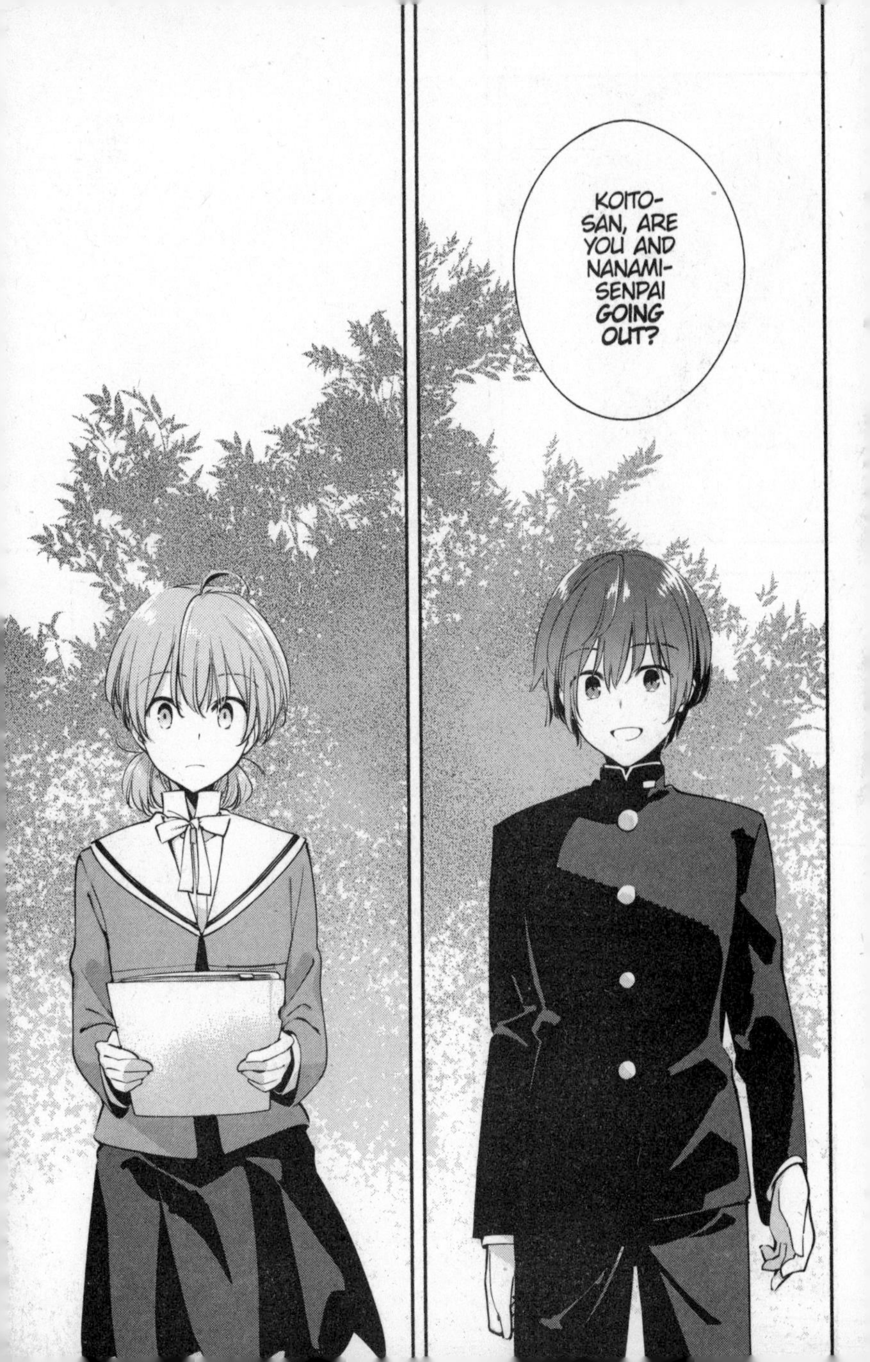
KOITO-SAN, ARE YOU AND NANAMI-SENPAI GOING OUT?

"........"

I SAW YOU TWO YESTERDAY.

SORRY.

"NANAMI-SAN DID **WHAT** WITH A FEMALE KOUHAI?"

"SHE HAD HER **GIRLFRIEND** GIVE THAT SPEECH?

"TALK ABOUT **BUSINESS** AND PLEA-SURE..."

"SHE ALWAYS SAID SHE **DIDN'T** WANT TO GO OUT WITH ANYONE!"

"SO THAT'S WHAT TOUKO'S INTO, HUH...?"

"I DIDN'T THINK SHE WAS THE TYPE TO DO THAT SORT OF THING."

HE **SAW** US...

HE KNOWS?

IF...

IF WORD GETS AROUND ...!

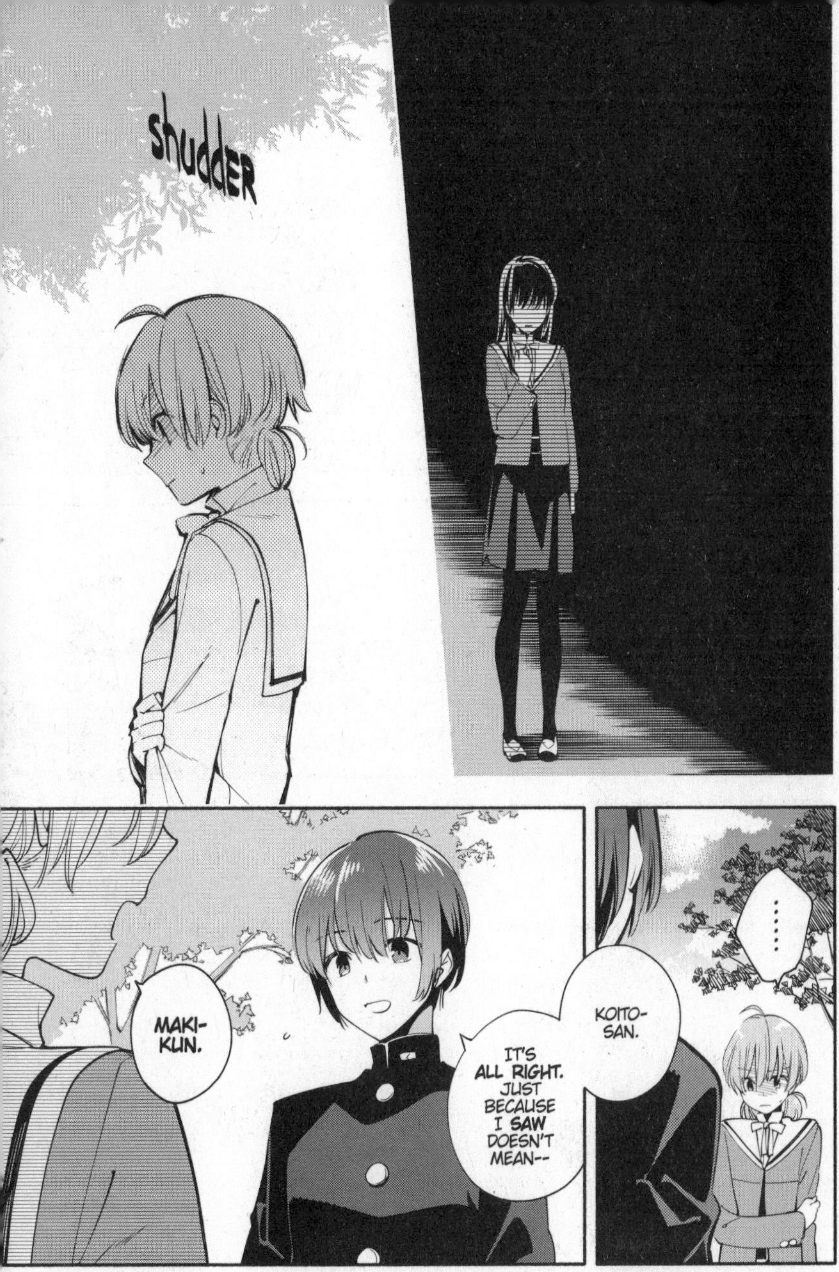
shudder
......
KOITO-SAN.
IT'S ALL RIGHT. JUST BECAUSE I SAW DOESN'T MEAN--
MAKI-KUN.

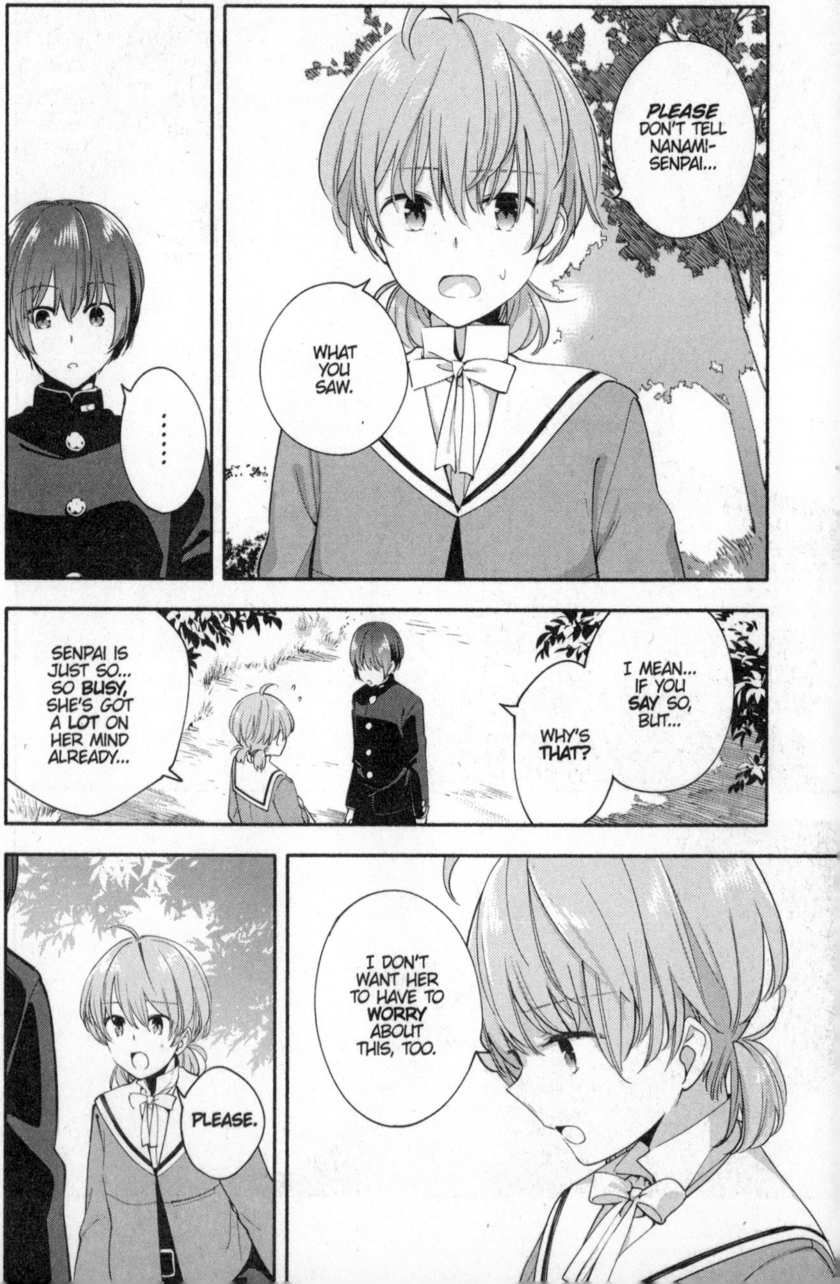
PLEASE DON'T TELL NANAMI-SENPAI...
WHAT YOU SAW.
......
I MEAN... IF YOU SAY SO, BUT... WHY'S THAT?
SENPAI IS JUST SO... SO BUSY, SHE'S GOT A LOT ON HER MIND ALREADY...
I DON'T WANT HER TO HAVE TO WORRY ABOUT THIS, TOO.
PLEASE.

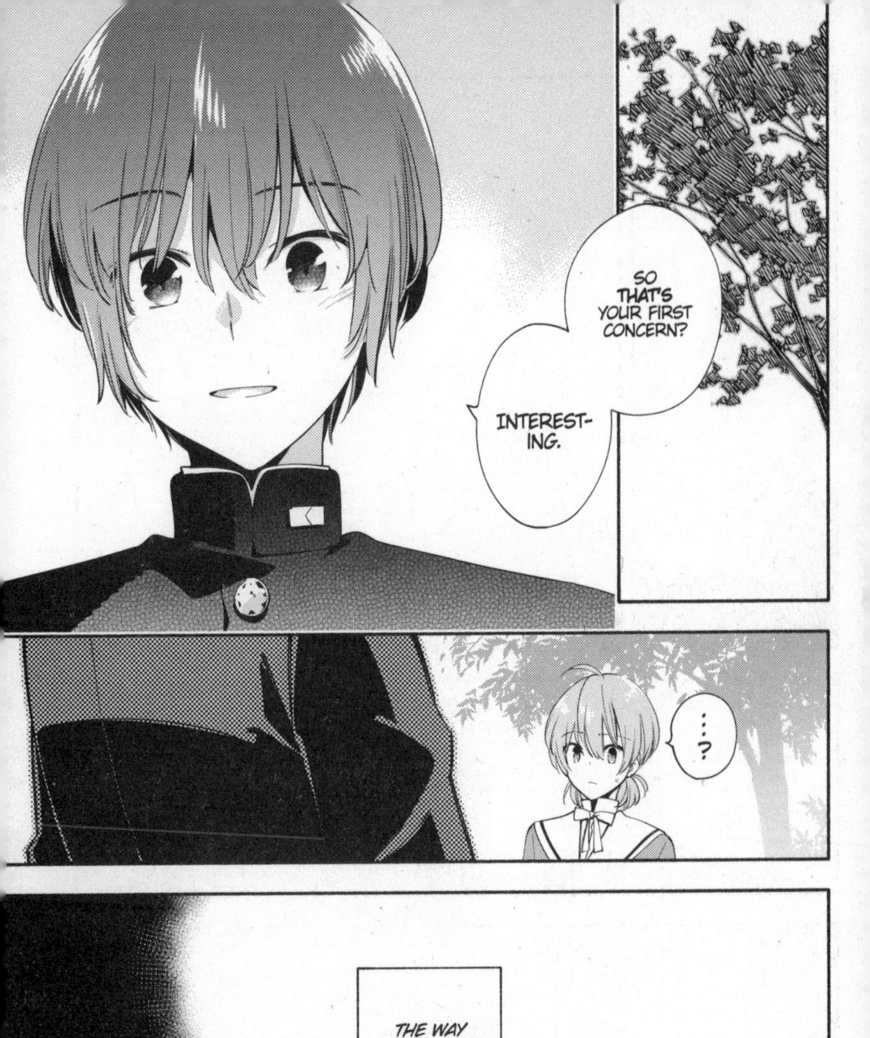
SO THAT'S YOUR FIRST CONCERN?
INTEREST-ING.
...?
THE WAY PEOPLE ACT WHEN THEY'RE IN LOVE IS REALLY REMARKABLE.

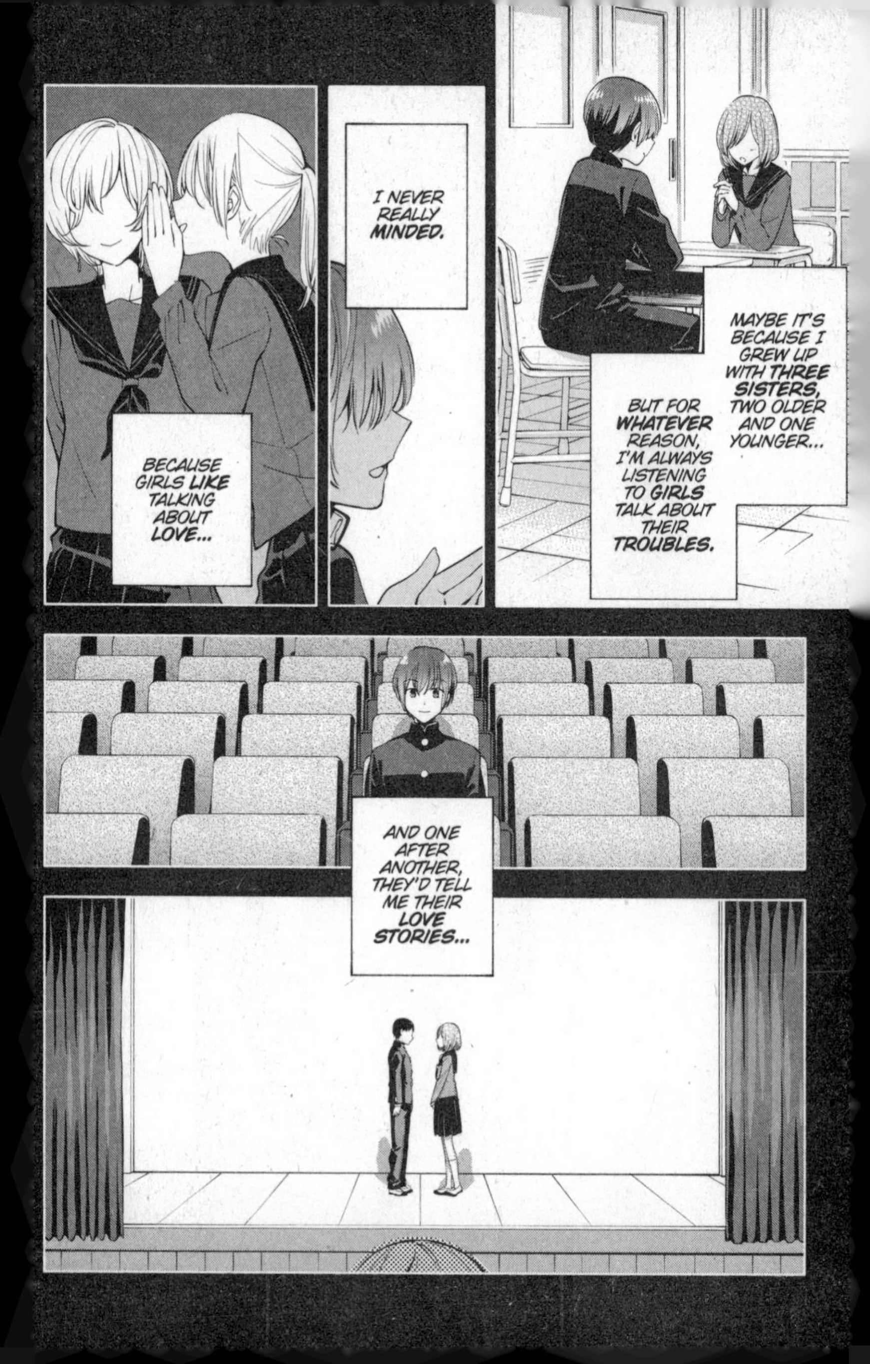
MAYBE IT'S BECAUSE I GREW UP WITH THREE SISTERS, TWO OLDER AND ONE YOUNGER...
BUT FOR WHATEVER REASON, I'M ALWAYS LISTENING TO GIRLS TALK ABOUT THEIR TROUBLES.
I NEVER REALLY MINDED.
BECAUSE GIRLS LIKE TALKING ABOUT LOVE...
AND ONE AFTER ANOTHER, THEY'D TELL ME THEIR LOVE STORIES...

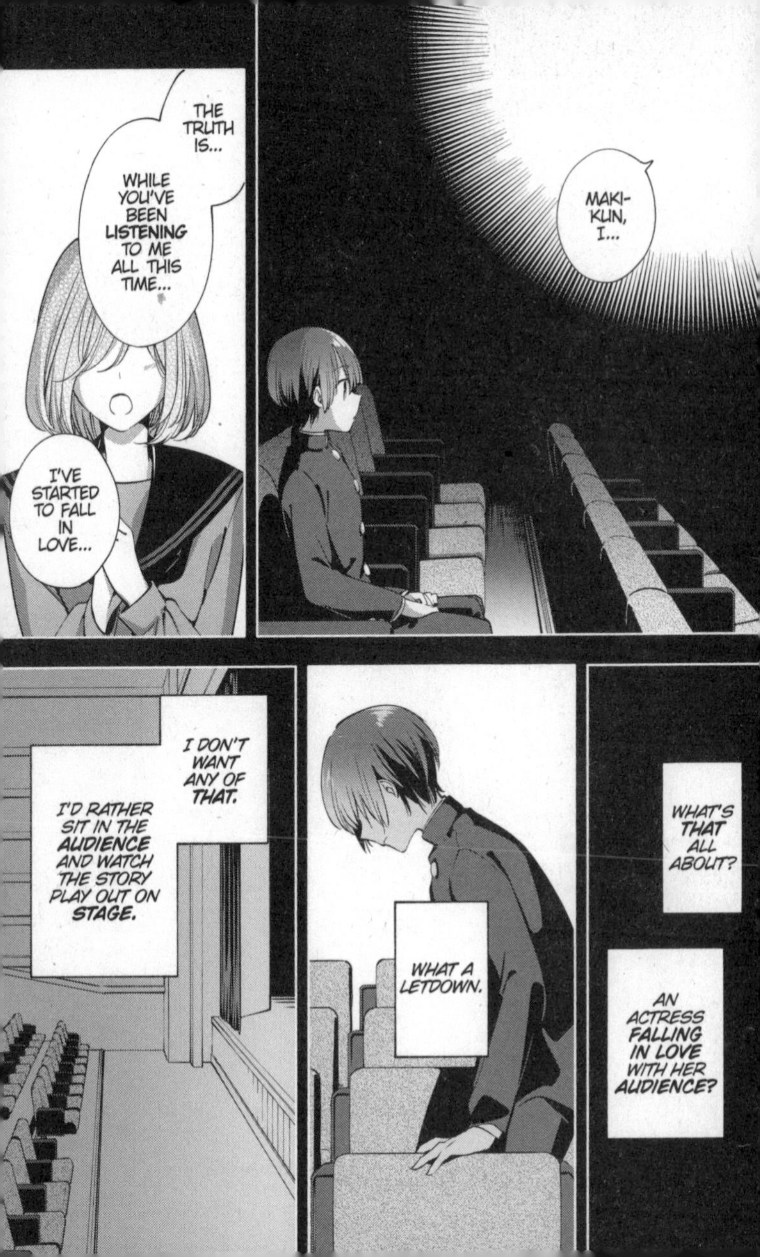
MAKI-KUN, I...
THE TRUTH IS...
WHILE YOU'VE BEEN LISTENING TO ME ALL THIS TIME...
I'VE STARTED TO FALL IN LOVE...
WHAT'S THAT ALL ABOUT?
AN ACTRESS FALLING IN LOVE WITH HER AUDIENCE?
WHAT A LETDOWN.
I DON'T WANT ANY OF THAT.
I'D RATHER SIT IN THE AUDIENCE AND WATCH THE STORY PLAY OUT ON STAGE.

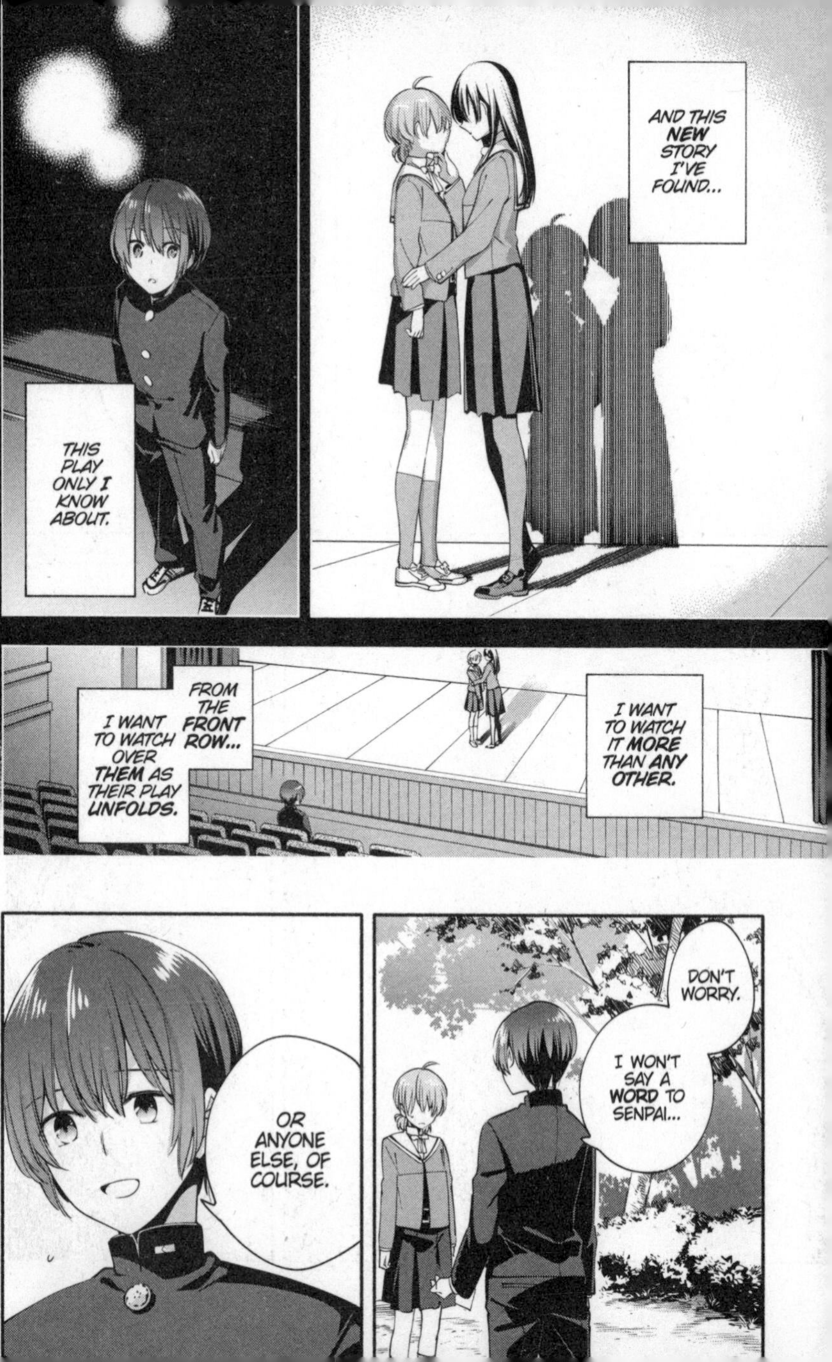
AND THIS NEW STORY I'VE FOUND...
THIS PLAY ONLY I KNOW ABOUT.
I WANT TO WATCH IT MORE THAN ANY OTHER.
FROM THE FRONT ROW...
I WANT TO WATCH OVER THEM AS THEIR PLAY UNFOLDS.
DON'T WORRY.
I WON'T SAY A WORD TO SENPAI...
OR ANYONE ELSE, OF COURSE.

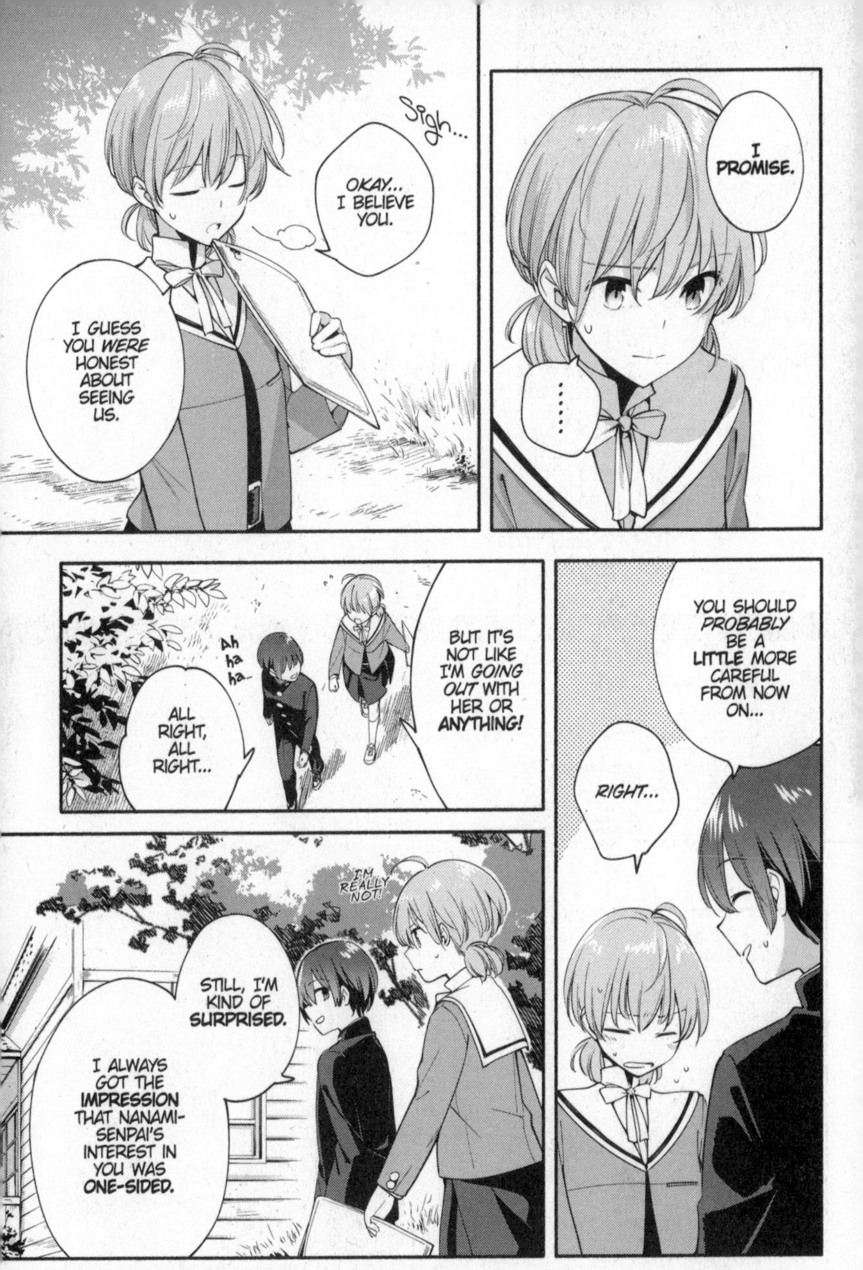
I PROMISE.
......
Sigh...
OKAY... I BELIEVE YOU.
I GUESS YOU *WERE* HONEST ABOUT SEEING US.
YOU SHOULD *PROBABLY* BE A LITTLE MORE CAREFUL FROM NOW ON...
*RIGHT...*
BUT IT'S NOT LIKE I'M *GOING OUT* WITH HER OR **ANYTHING!**
Ah ha ha...
ALL RIGHT, ALL RIGHT...
I'M REALLY NOT!
STILL, I'M KIND OF **SURPRISED.**
I ALWAYS GOT THE **IMPRESSION** THAT NANAMI-SENPAI'S INTEREST IN YOU WAS **ONE-SIDED.**

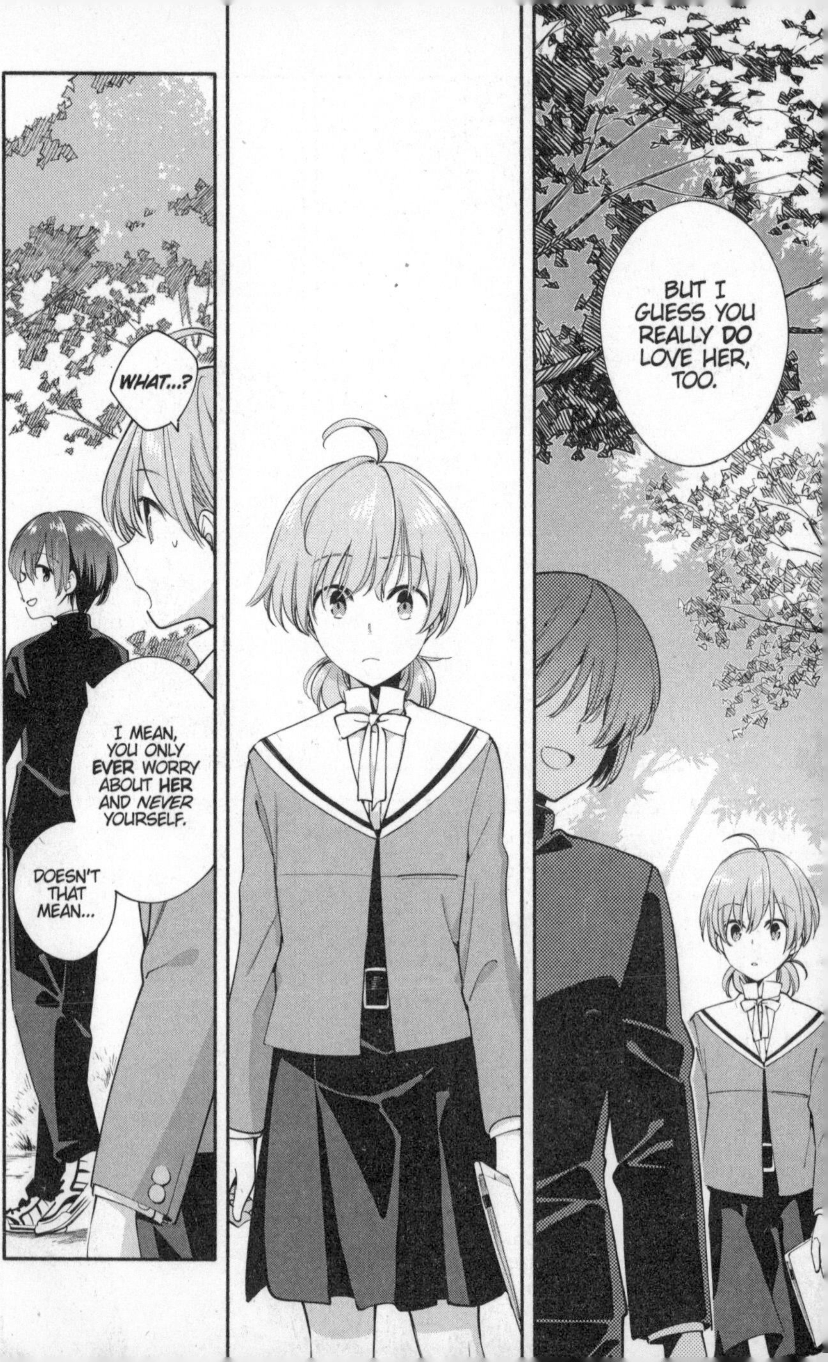
BUT I GUESS YOU REALLY DO LOVE HER, TOO.
WHAT...?
I MEAN, YOU ONLY EVER WORRY ABOUT HER AND NEVER YOURSELF.
DOESN'T THAT MEAN...

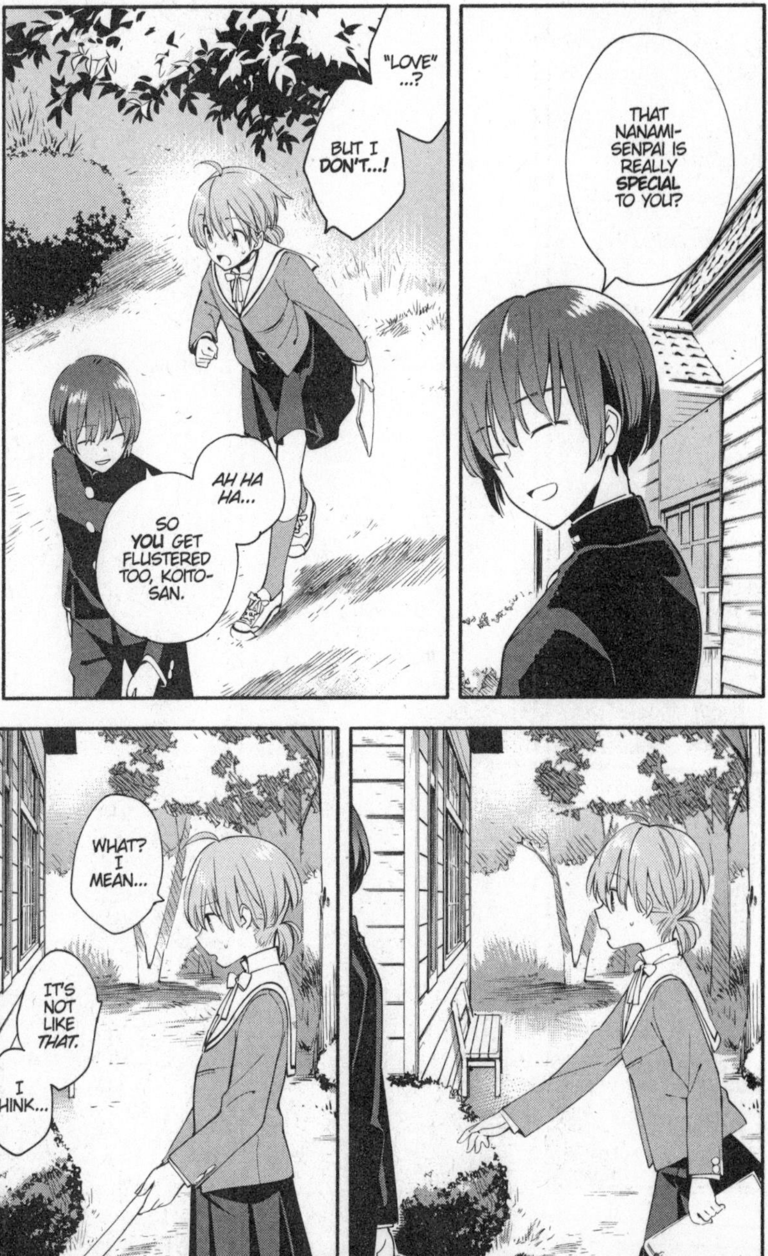
THAT NANAMI-SENPAI IS REALLY SPECIAL TO YOU?
"LOVE" ...?
BUT I DON'T...!
AH HA HA...
SO YOU GET FLUSTERED TOO, KOITO-SAN.
WHAT? I MEAN...
IT'S NOT LIKE THAT.
I THINK...

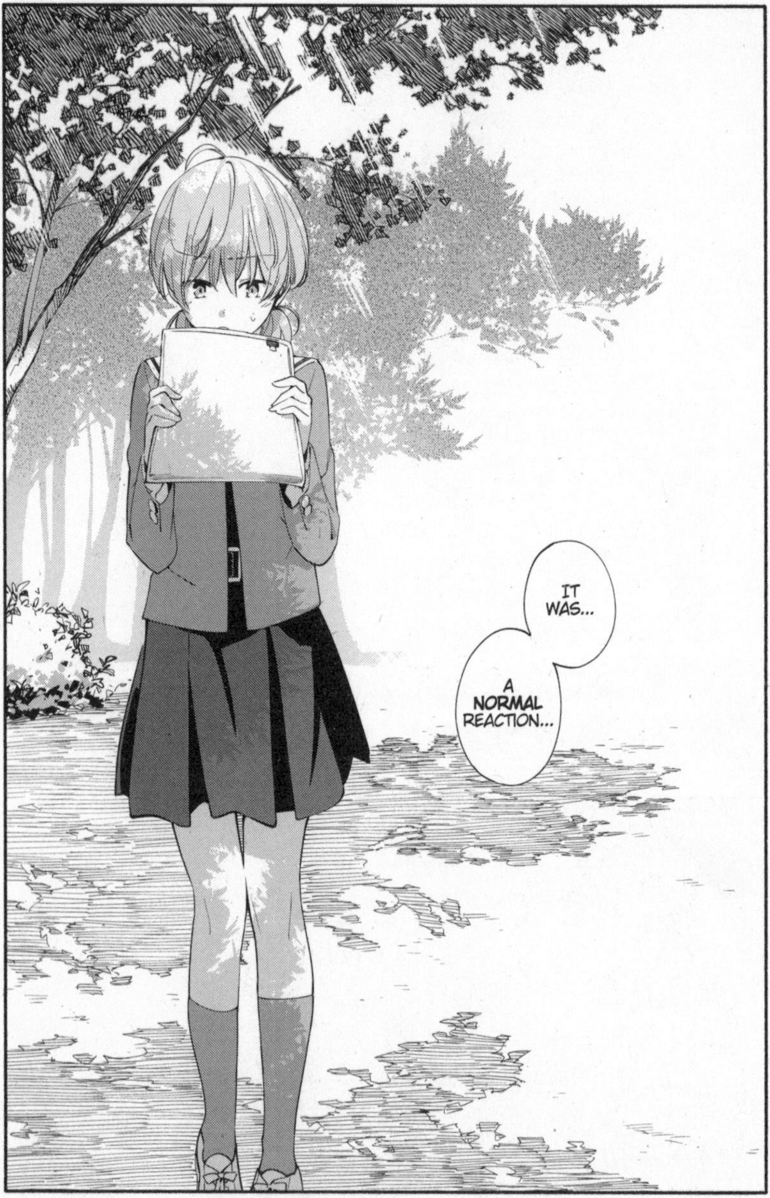
IT WAS...
A NORMAL REACTION...

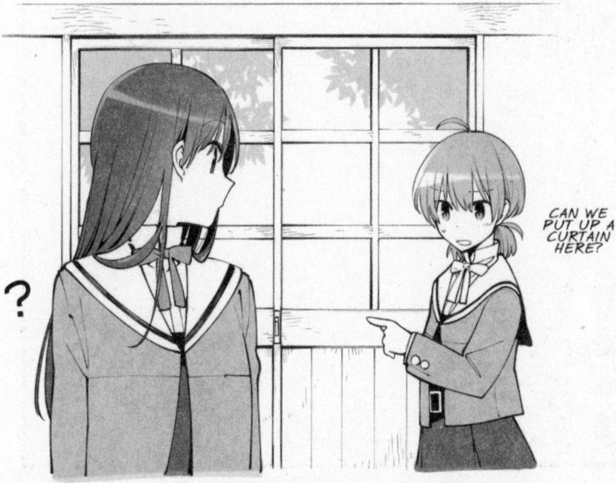
CAN WE PUT UP A CURTAIN HERE?
?

( **Bloom Into You** )

# Interlude: Reading Too Much Into Books

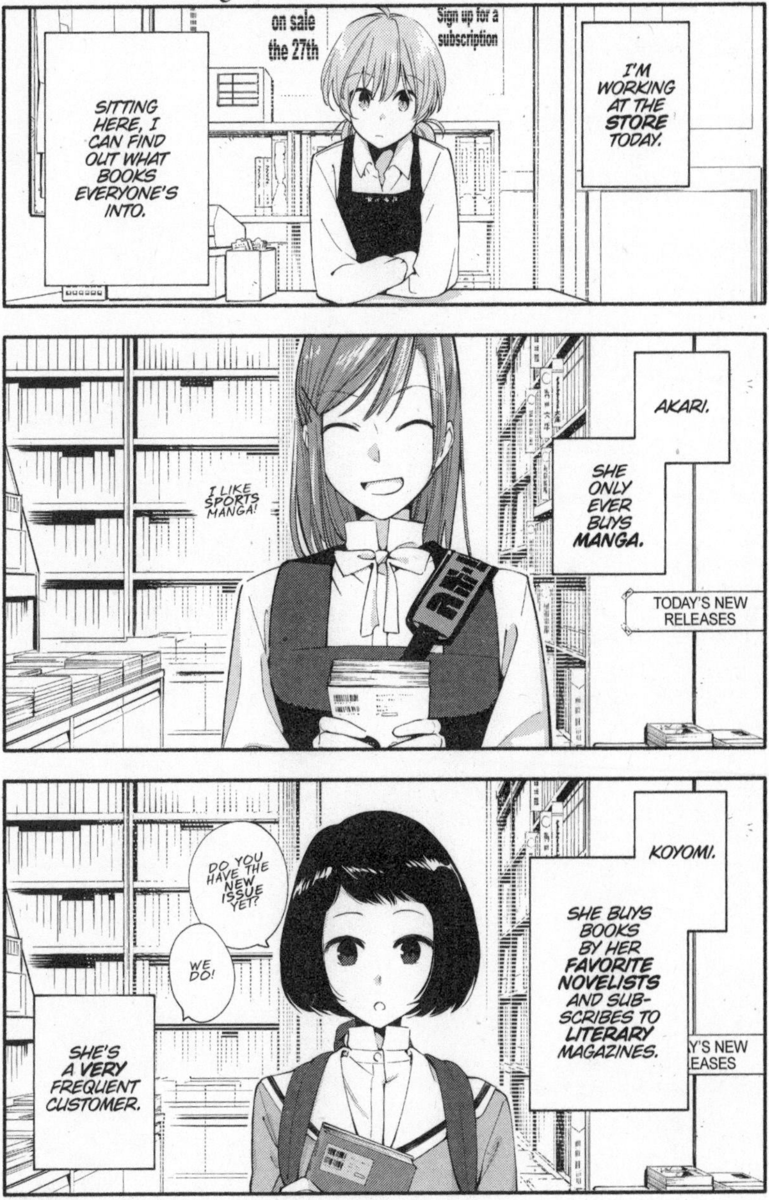
Sign up for a subscription
on sale the 27th
I'M WORKING AT THE STORE TODAY.
SITTING HERE, I CAN FIND OUT WHAT BOOKS EVERYONE'S INTO.
AKARI.
SHE ONLY EVER BUYS MANGA.
TODAY'S NEW RELEASES
I LIKE SPORTS MANGA!
KOYOMI.
SHE BUYS BOOKS BY HER FAVORITE NOVELISTS AND SUB-SCRIBES TO LITERARY MAGAZINES.
Y'S NEW LEASES
DO YOU HAVE THE NEW ISSUE YET?
WE DO!
SHE'S A VERY FREQUENT CUSTOMER.

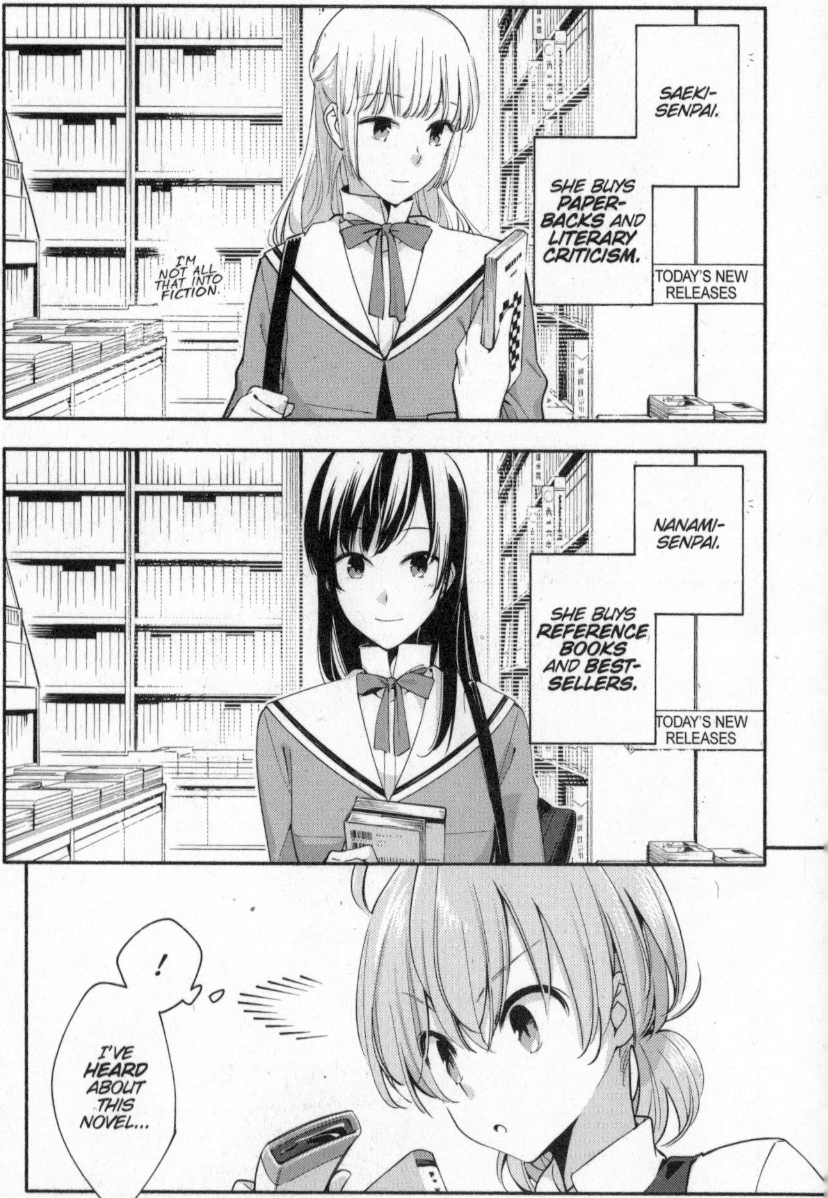
SAEKI-SENPAI.
SHE BUYS PAPER-BACKS AND LITERARY CRITICISM.
TODAY'S NEW RELEASES
I'M NOT ALL THAT INTO FICTION.
NANAMI-SENPAI.
SHE BUYS REFERENCE BOOKS AND BEST-SELLERS.
TODAY'S NEW RELEASES
!
I'VE HEARD ABOUT THIS NOVEL...

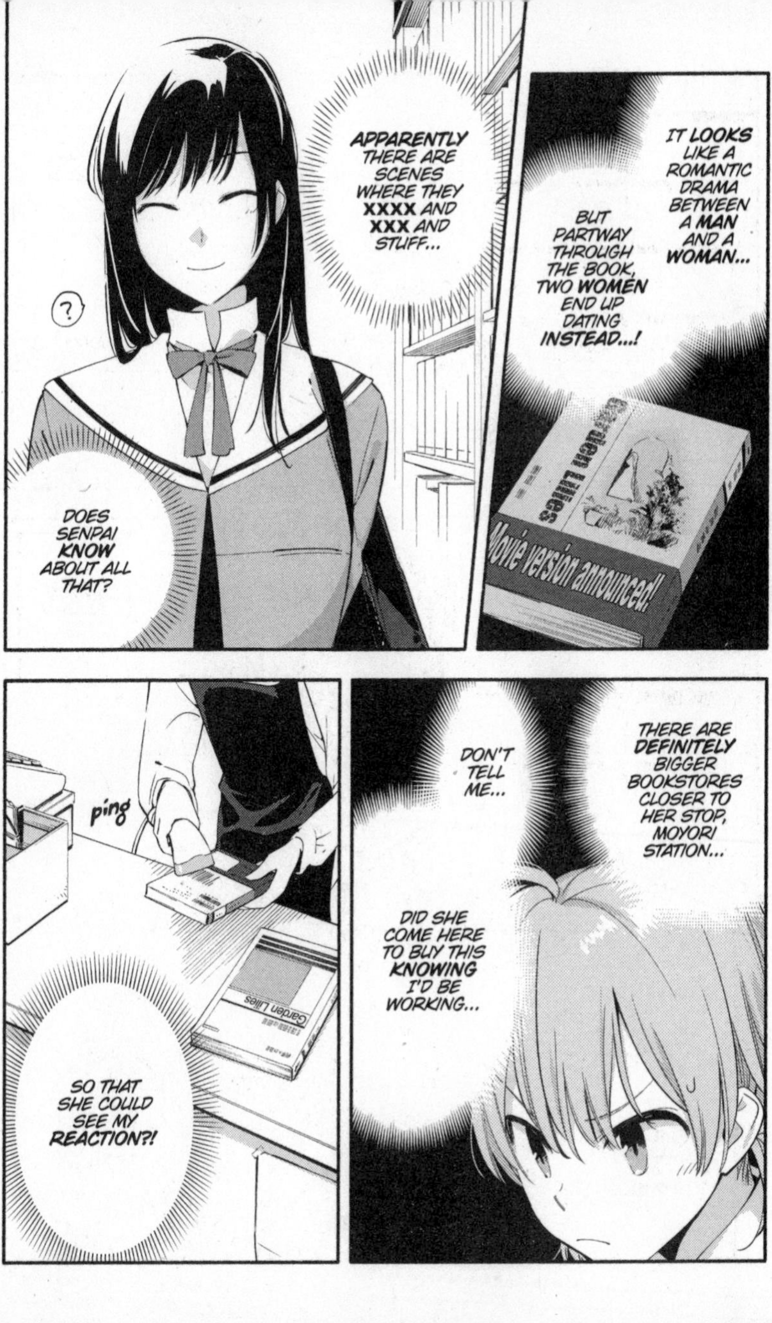
IT LOOKS LIKE A ROMANTIC DRAMA BETWEEN A MAN AND A WOMAN...
BUT PARTWAY THROUGH THE BOOK, TWO WOMEN END UP DATING INSTEAD...!
Garden Lilies
Movie version announced!
APPARENTLY THERE ARE SCENES WHERE THEY XXXX AND XXX AND STUFF...
?
DOES SENPAI KNOW ABOUT ALL THAT?
THERE ARE DEFINITELY BIGGER BOOKSTORES CLOSER TO HER STOP, MOYORI STATION...
DON'T TELL ME...
DID SHE COME HERE TO BUY THIS KNOWING I'D BE WORKING...
ping
Garden Lilies
SO THAT SHE COULD SEE MY REACTION?!

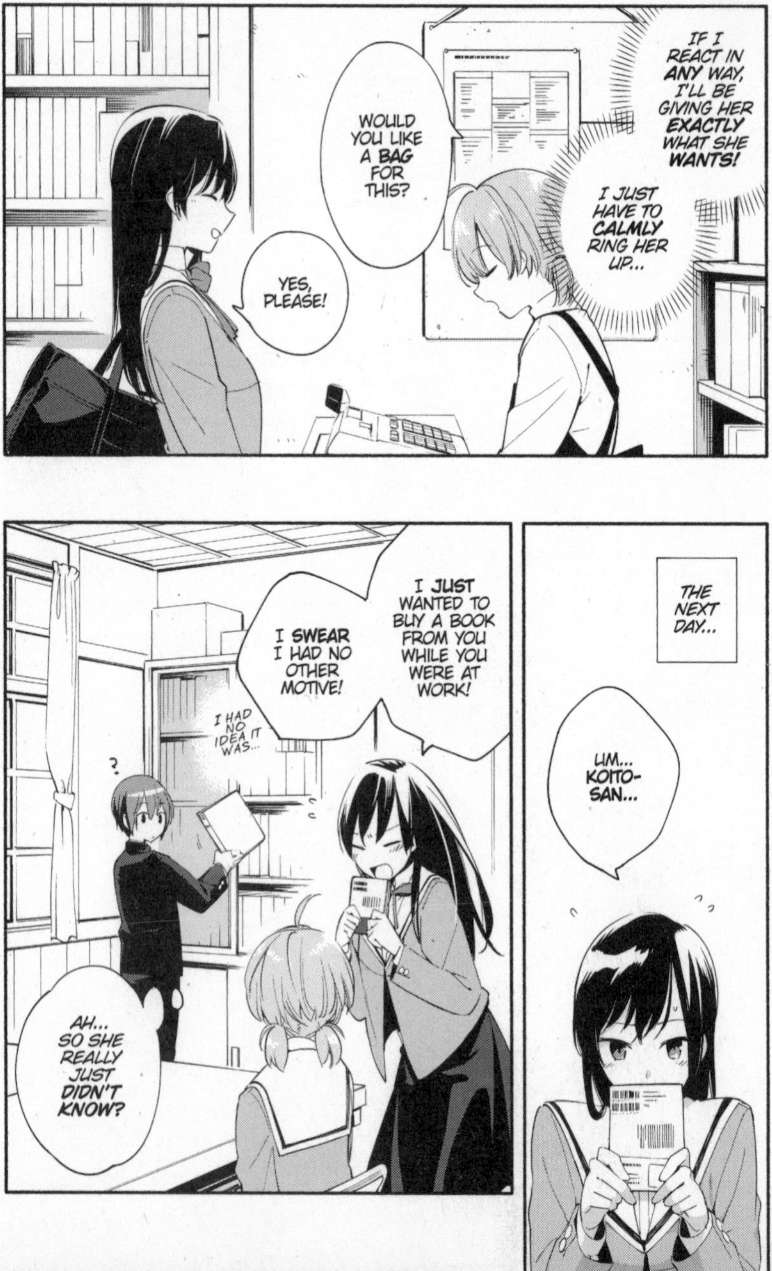
IF I REACT IN ANY WAY, I'LL BE GIVING HER EXACTLY WHAT SHE WANTS!
I JUST HAVE TO CALMLY RING HER UP...
WOULD YOU LIKE A BAG FOR THIS?
YES, PLEASE!
THE NEXT DAY...
UM... KOITO-SAN...
I JUST WANTED TO BUY A BOOK FROM YOU WHILE YOU WERE AT WORK!
I SWEAR I HAD NO OTHER MOTIVE!
I HAD NO IDEA IT WAS...
?
AH... SO SHE REALLY JUST DIDN'T KNOW?

AS FOR ME, I LIKE MYSTERIES AND SCI-FI AND STUFF.

FUJISHIRO BOOKSTORE

( **Bloom Into You** )

# 8

## Multiple Choice

EPISODE EIGHT

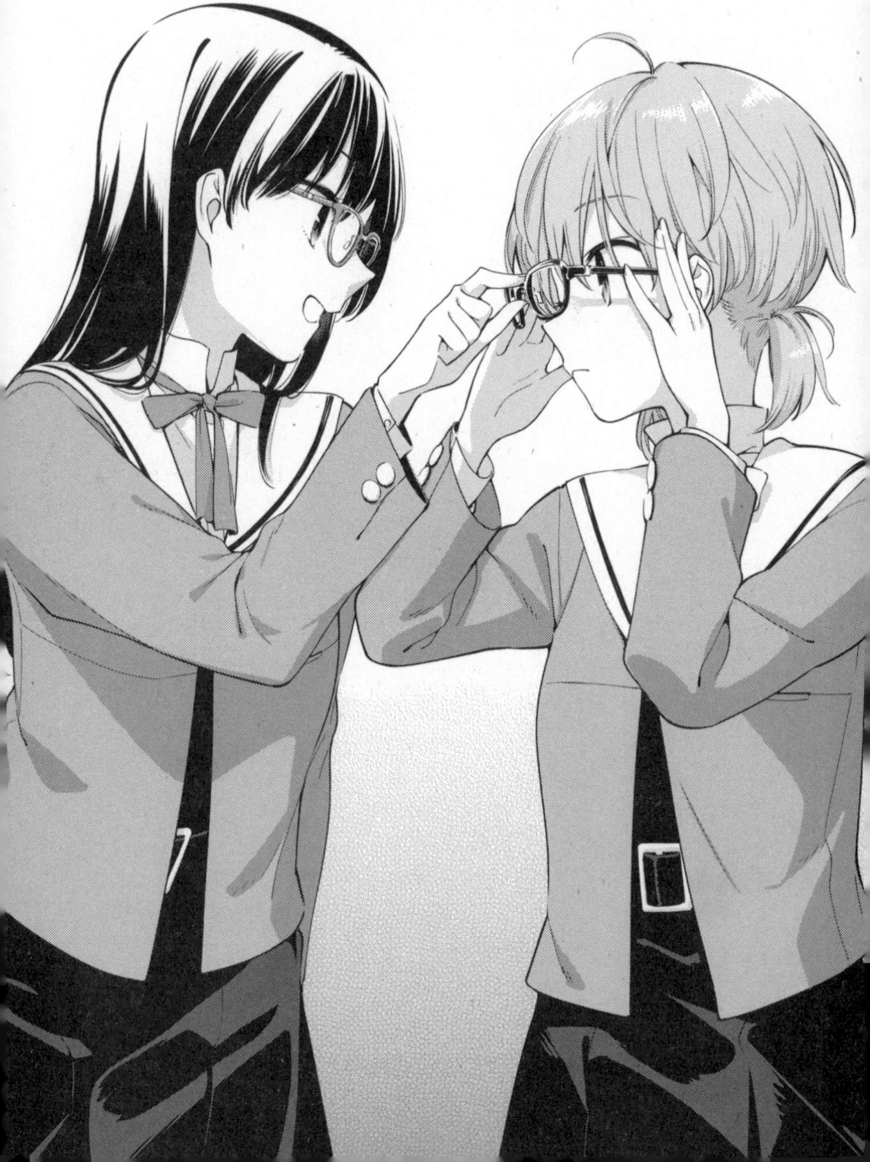

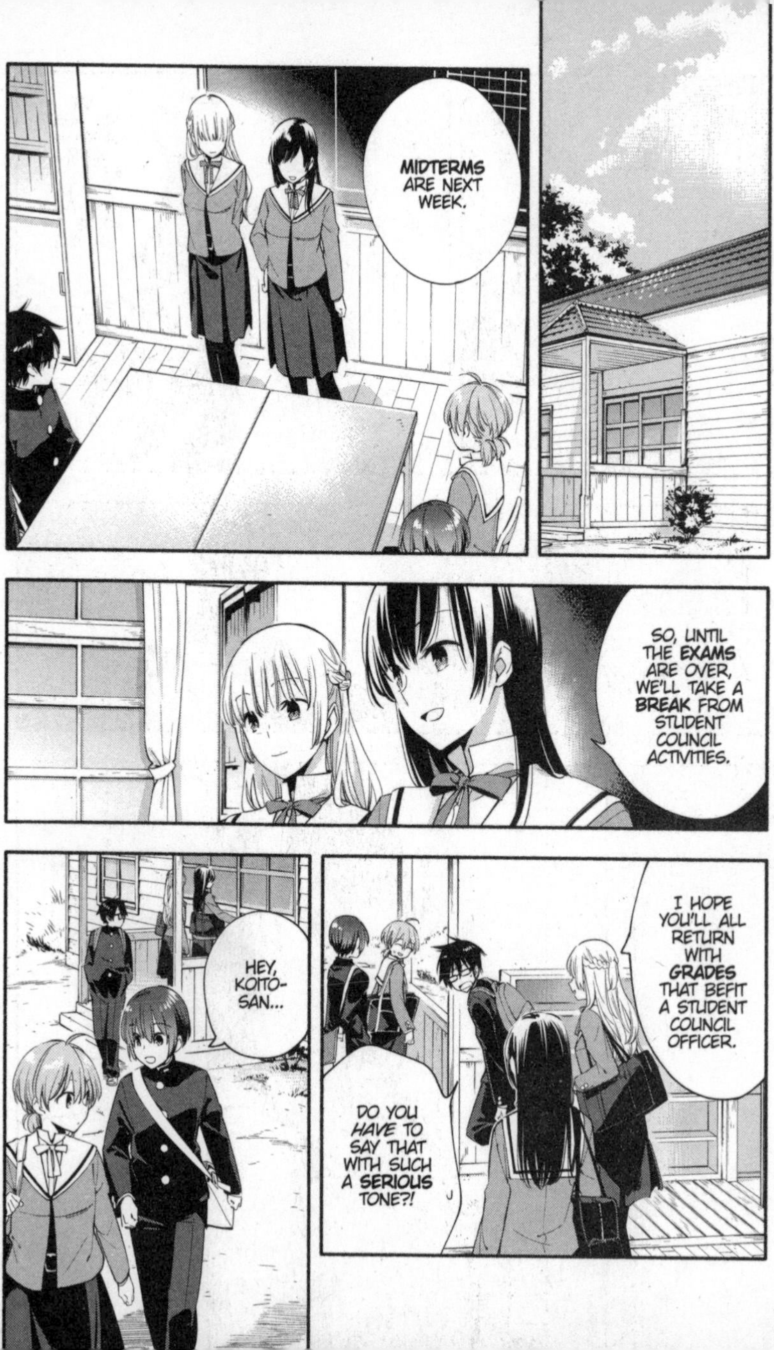
MIDTERMS ARE NEXT WEEK.
SO, UNTIL THE **EXAMS** ARE OVER, WE'LL TAKE A **BREAK** FROM STUDENT COUNCIL ACTIVITIES.
I HOPE YOU'LL ALL RETURN WITH **GRADES** THAT BEFIT A STUDENT COUNCIL OFFICER.
DO YOU *HAVE* TO SAY THAT WITH SUCH A **SERIOUS** TONE?!
HEY, KOITO-SAN...

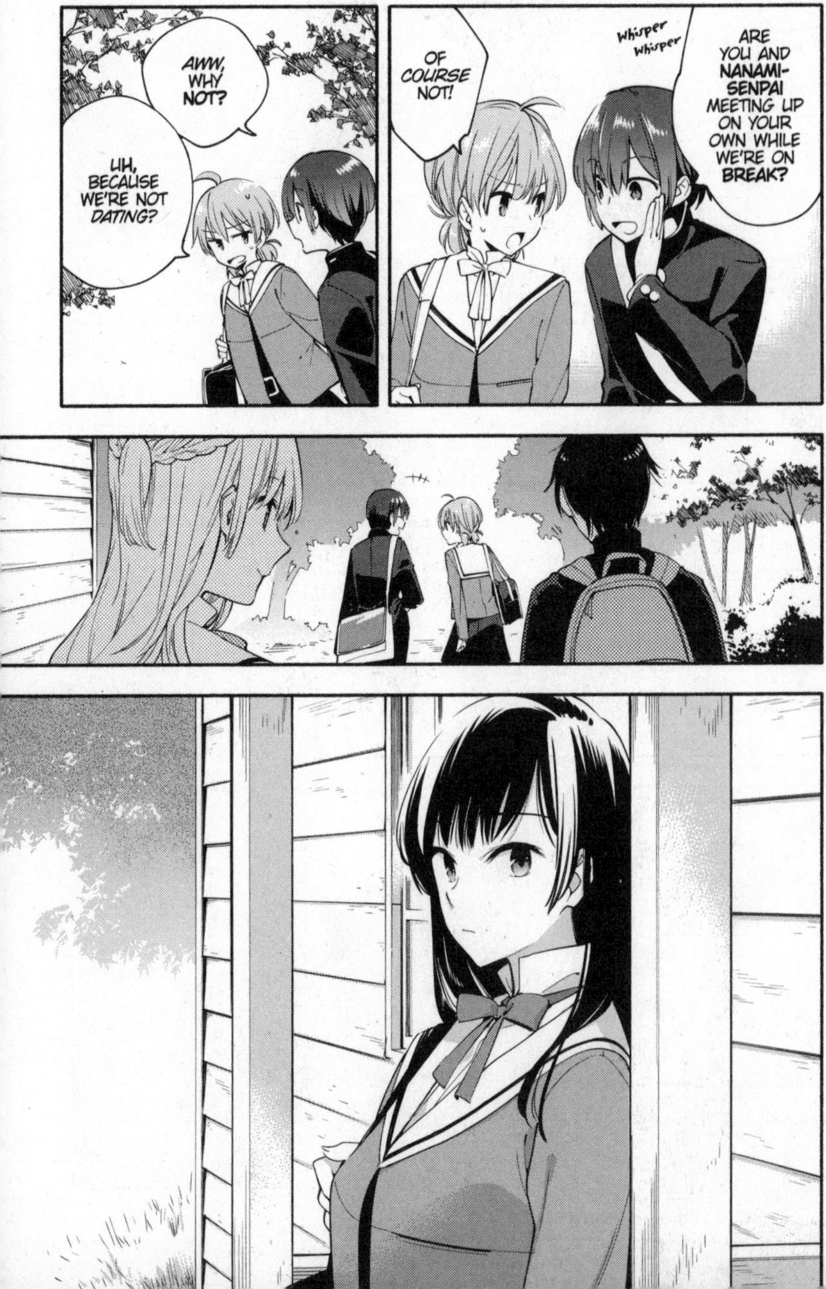
ARE YOU AND NANAMI-SENPAI MEETING UP ON YOUR OWN WHILE WE'RE ON BREAK?
Whisper Whisper
OF COURSE NOT!
AWW, WHY NOT?
UH, BECAUSE WE'RE NOT DATING?

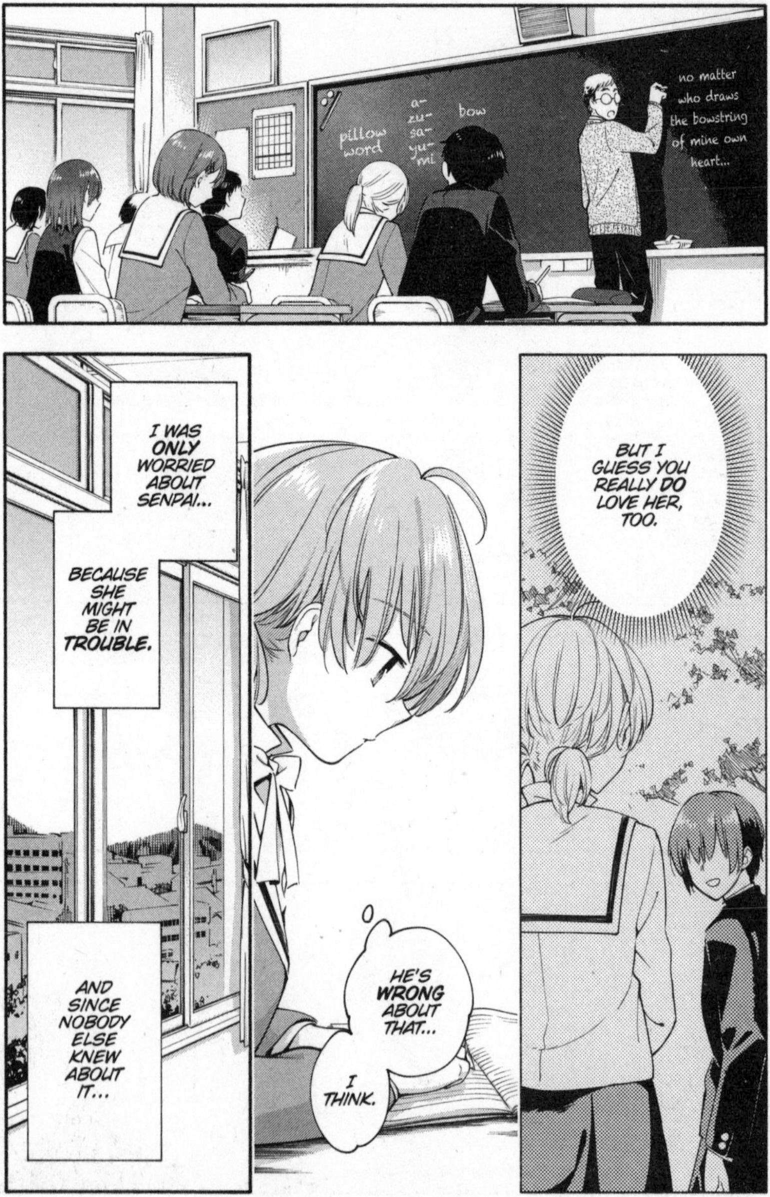
no matter who draws the bowstring of mine own heart...
bow
a-zu-sa-yu-mi
pillow word
BUT I GUESS YOU REALLY DO LOVE HER, TOO.
I WAS ONLY WORRIED ABOUT SENPAI...
BECAUSE SHE MIGHT BE IN TROUBLE.
AND SINCE NOBODY ELSE KNEW ABOUT IT...
HE'S WRONG ABOUT THAT...
I THINK.

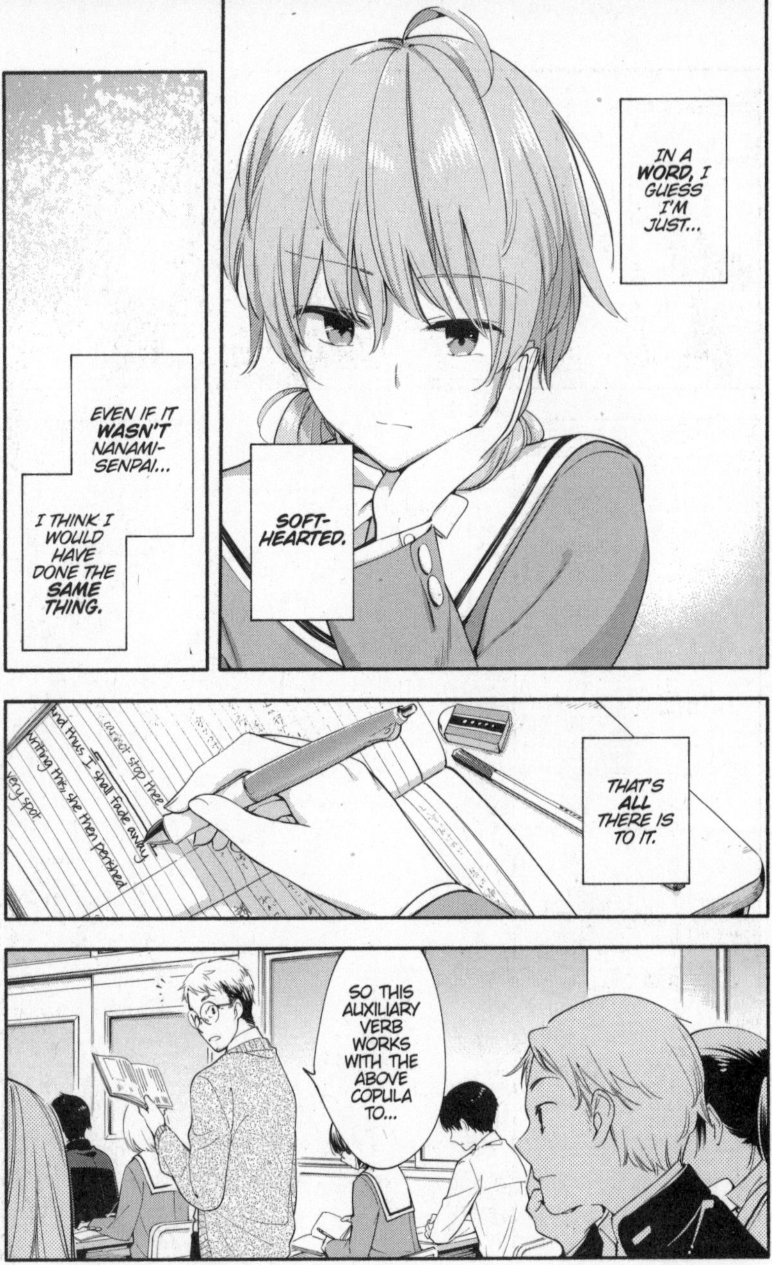
IN A WORD, I GUESS I'M JUST...
SOFT-HEARTED.
EVEN IF IT WASN'T NANAMI-SENPAI...
I THINK I WOULD HAVE DONE THE SAME THING.
THAT'S ALL THERE IS TO IT.
cannot stop thee
and thus I shall fade away
writing this, she then perished
very spot
SO THIS AUXILIARY VERB WORKS WITH THE ABOVE COPULA TO...

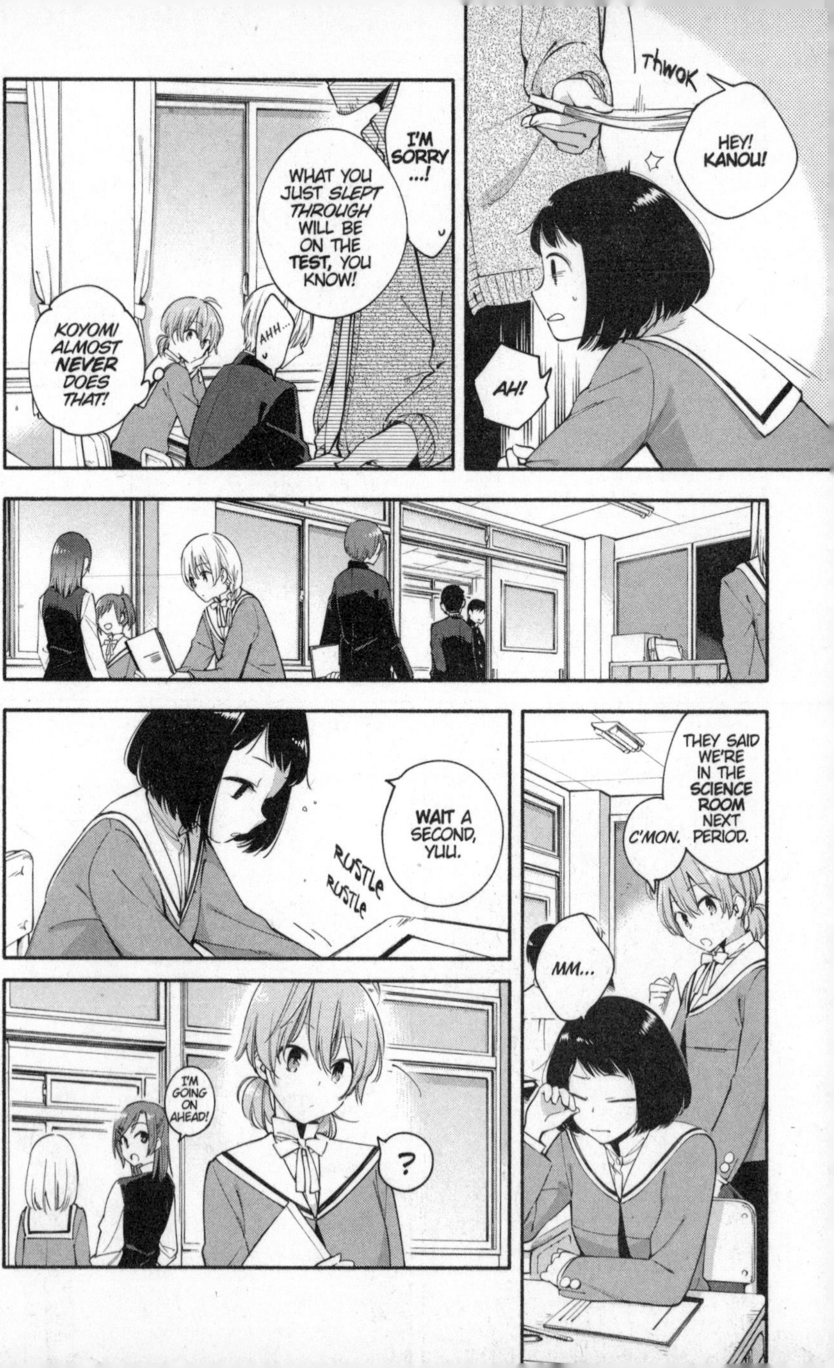
THWOK
HEY! KANOU!
AH!
WHAT YOU JUST SLEPT THROUGH WILL BE ON THE TEST, YOU KNOW!
I'M SORRY ...!
AHH...
KOYOMI ALMOST NEVER DOES THAT!
THEY SAID WE'RE IN THE SCIENCE ROOM NEXT PERIOD.
C'MON.
MM...
WAIT A SECOND, YUU.
RUSTLE RUSTLE
I'M GOING ON AHEAD!
?

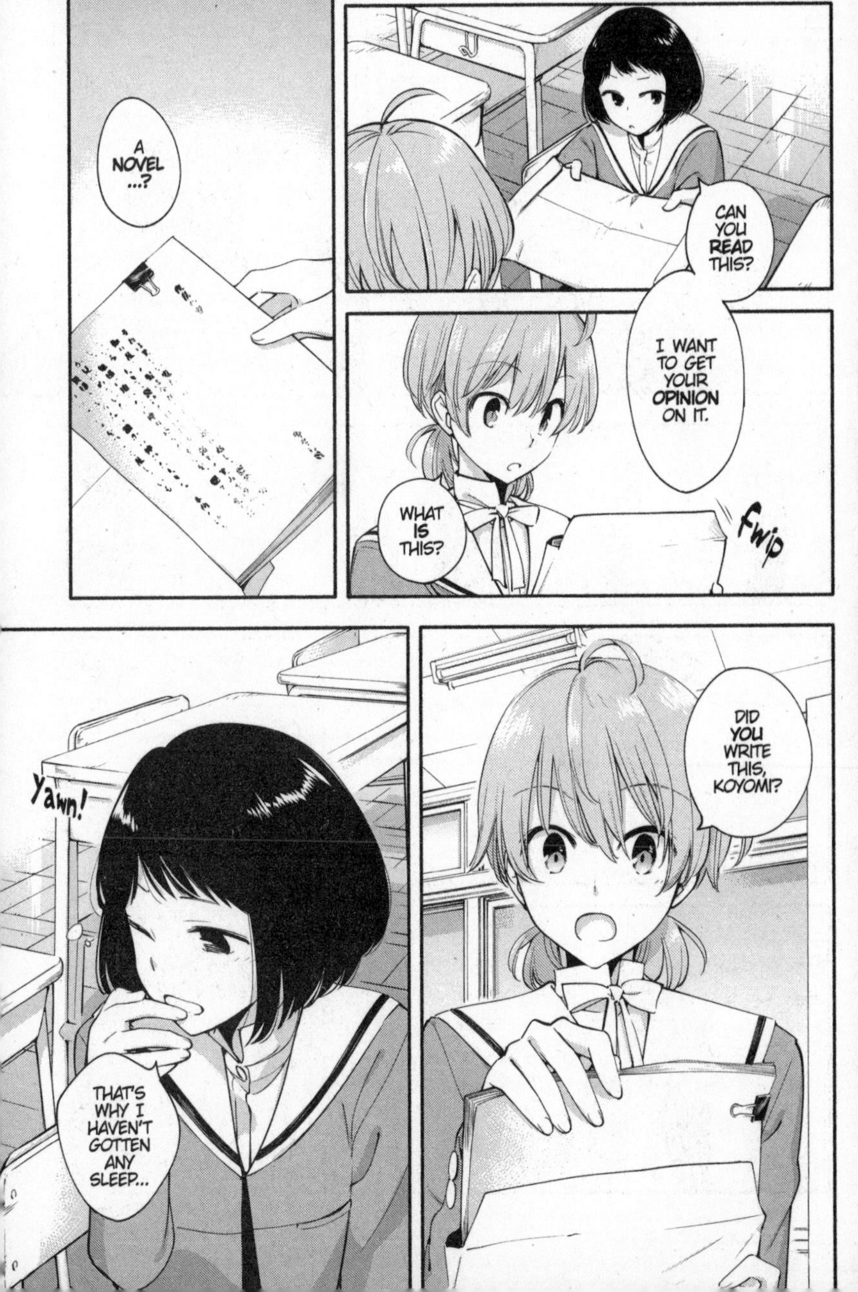
CAN YOU READ THIS?
I WANT TO GET YOUR OPINION ON IT.
fwip
WHAT IS THIS?
A NOVEL ...?
DID YOU WRITE THIS, KOYOMI?
Yawn!
THAT'S WHY I HAVEN'T GOTTEN ANY SLEEP...

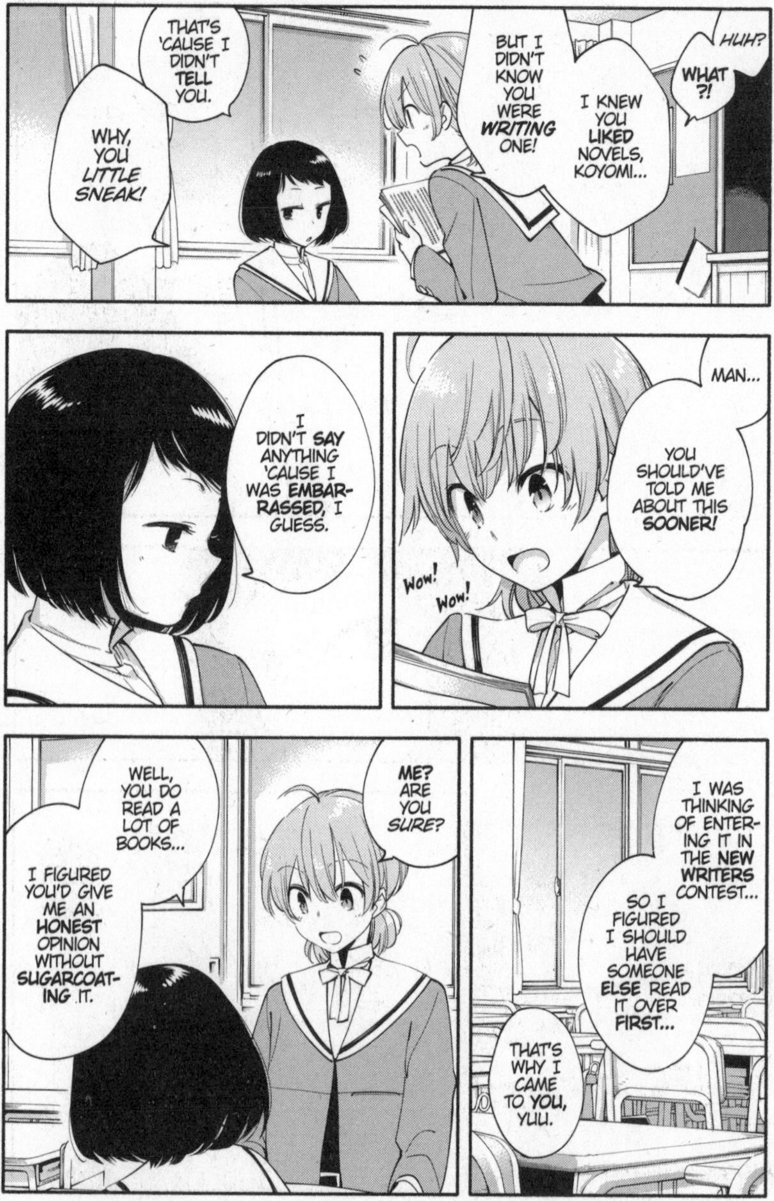
HUH?
WHAT?!
I KNEW YOU LIKED NOVELS, KOYOMI...
BUT I DIDN'T KNOW YOU WERE WRITING ONE!
WHY, YOU LITTLE SNEAK!
THAT'S 'CAUSE I DIDN'T TELL YOU.
MAN...
YOU SHOULD'VE TOLD ME ABOUT THIS SOONER!
Wow!
Wow!
I DIDN'T SAY ANYTHING 'CAUSE I WAS EMBARRASSED, I GUESS.
I WAS THINKING OF ENTERING IT IN THE NEW WRITERS CONTEST...
SO I FIGURED I SHOULD HAVE SOMEONE ELSE READ IT OVER FIRST...
THAT'S WHY I CAME TO YOU, YUU.
ME? ARE YOU SURE?
WELL, YOU DO READ A LOT OF BOOKS...
I FIGURED YOU'D GIVE ME AN HONEST OPINION WITHOUT SUGARCOATING IT.

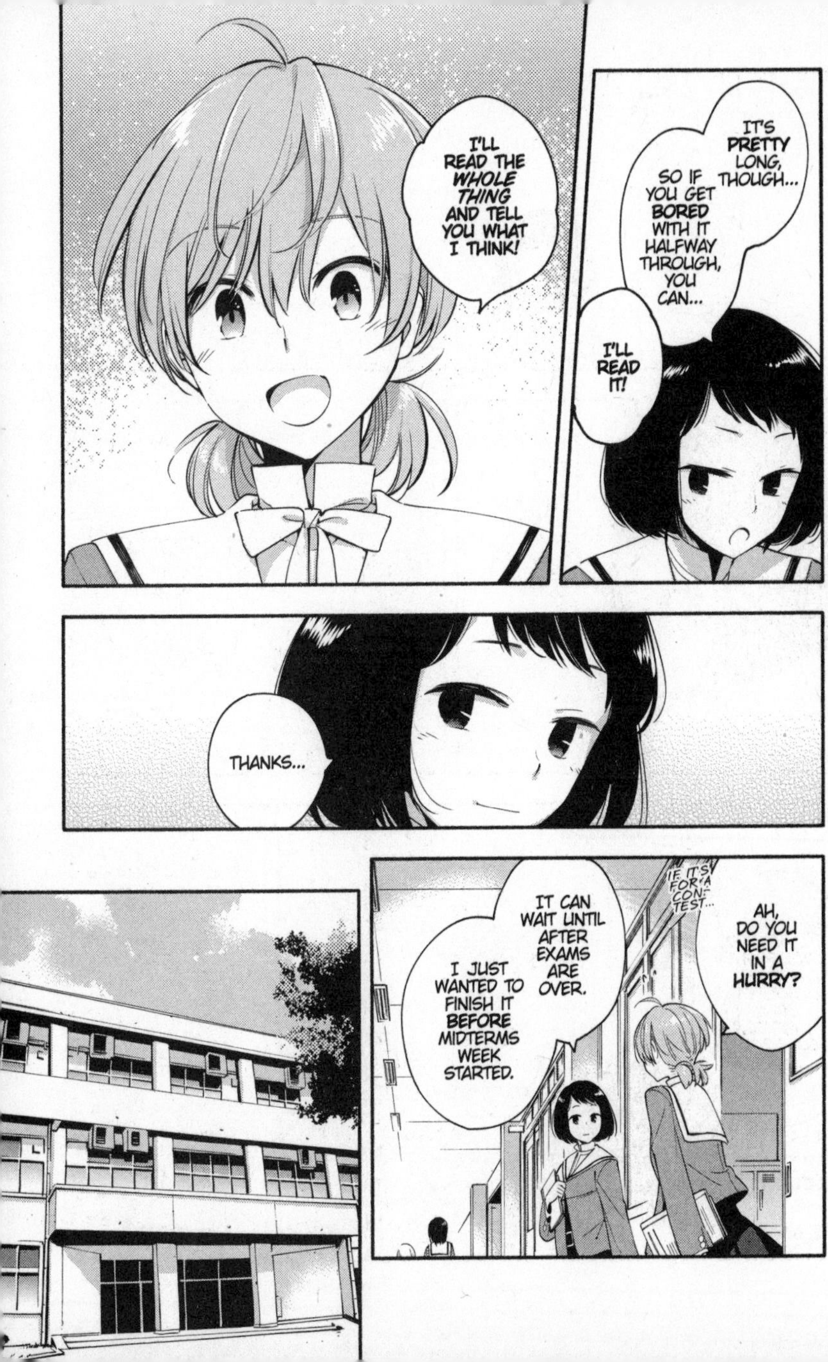
IT'S PRETTY LONG, THOUGH...
SO IF YOU GET BORED WITH IT HALFWAY THROUGH, YOU CAN...
I'LL READ IT!
I'LL READ THE WHOLE THING AND TELL YOU WHAT I THINK!
THANKS...
AH, DO YOU NEED IT IN A HURRY?
IF IT'S FOR A CONTEST...
IT CAN WAIT UNTIL AFTER EXAMS ARE OVER.
I JUST WANTED TO FINISH IT BEFORE MIDTERMS WEEK STARTED.

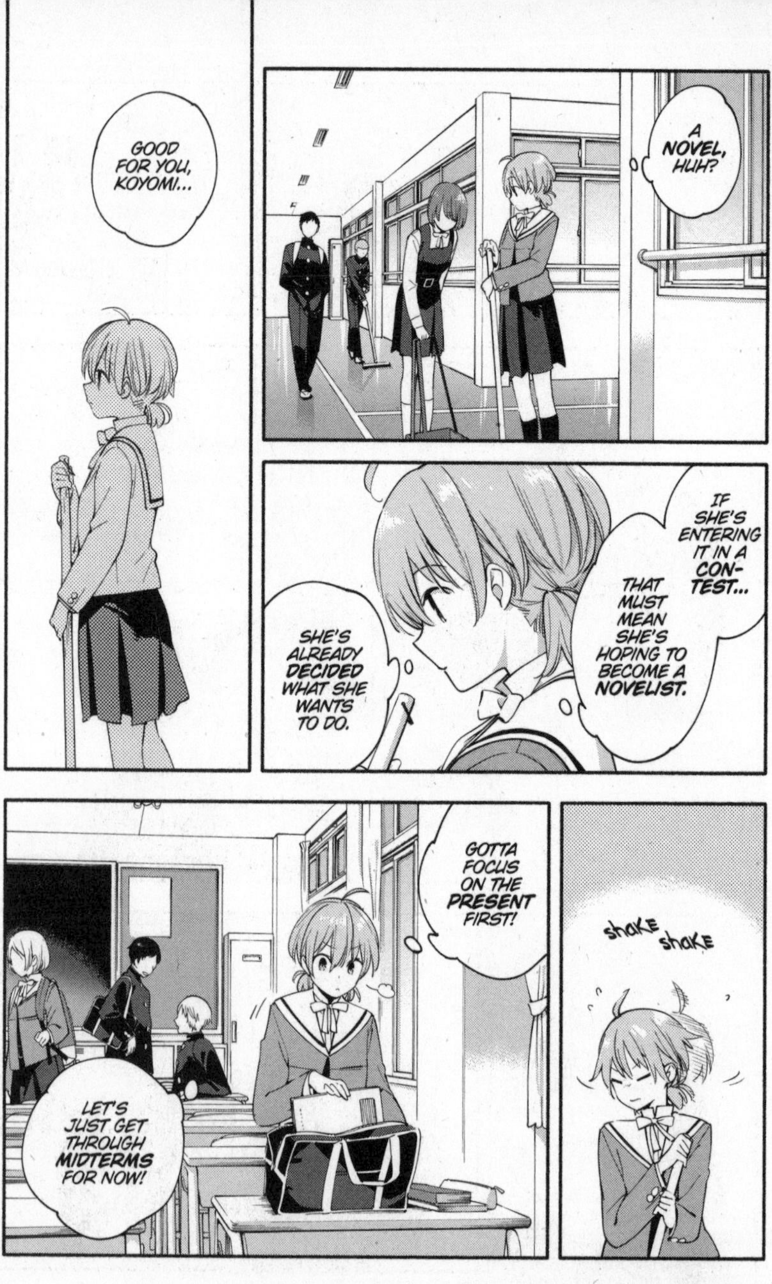
A NOVEL, HUH?
IF SHE'S ENTERING IT IN A CONTEST...
THAT MUST MEAN SHE'S HOPING TO BECOME A NOVELIST.
SHE'S ALREADY DECIDED WHAT SHE WANTS TO DO.
GOOD FOR YOU, KOYOMI...
shake shake
GOTTA FOCUS ON THE PRESENT FIRST!
LET'S JUST GET THROUGH MIDTERMS FOR NOW!

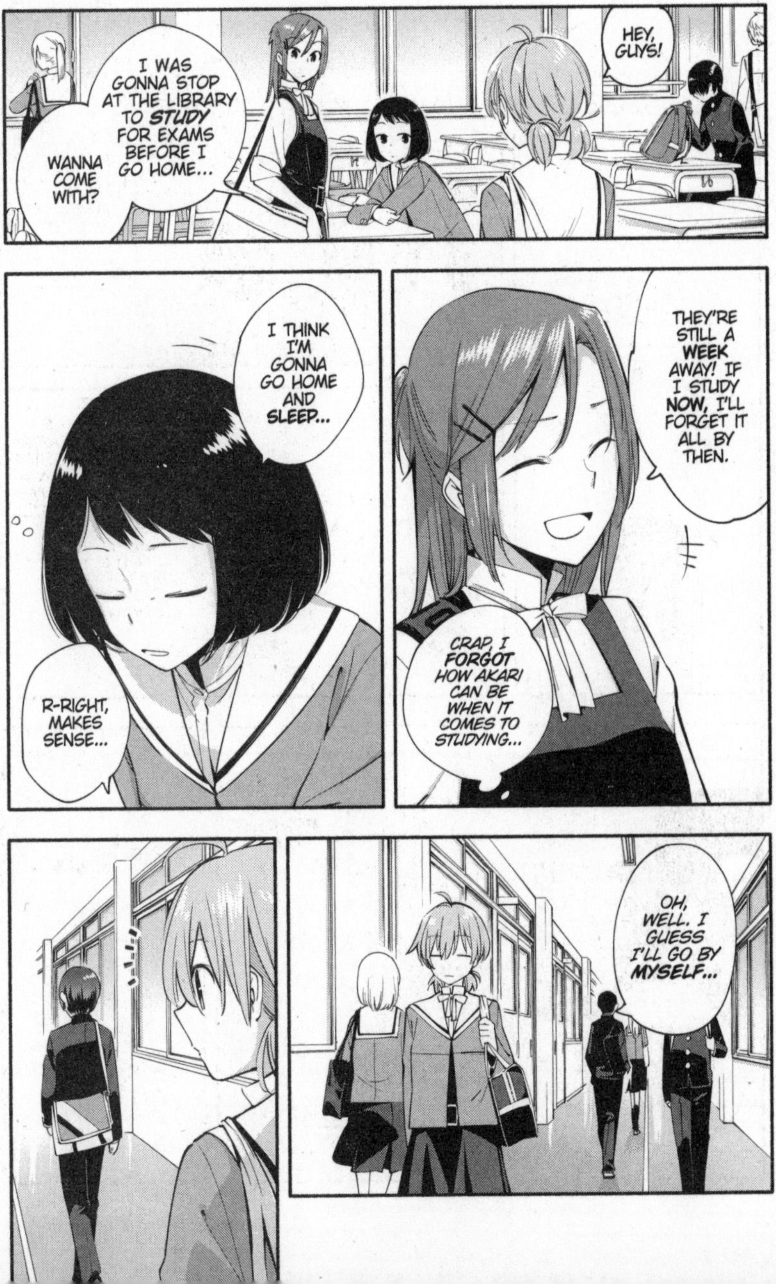
HEY, GUYS!
I WAS GONNA STOP AT THE LIBRARY TO STUDY FOR EXAMS BEFORE I GO HOME...
WANNA COME WITH?
THEY'RE STILL A WEEK AWAY! IF I STUDY NOW, I'LL FORGET IT ALL BY THEN.
CRAP, I FORGOT HOW AKARI CAN BE WHEN IT COMES TO STUDYING...
I THINK I'M GONNA GO HOME AND SLEEP...
R-RIGHT, MAKES SENSE...
OH, WELL. I GUESS I'LL GO BY MYSELF...

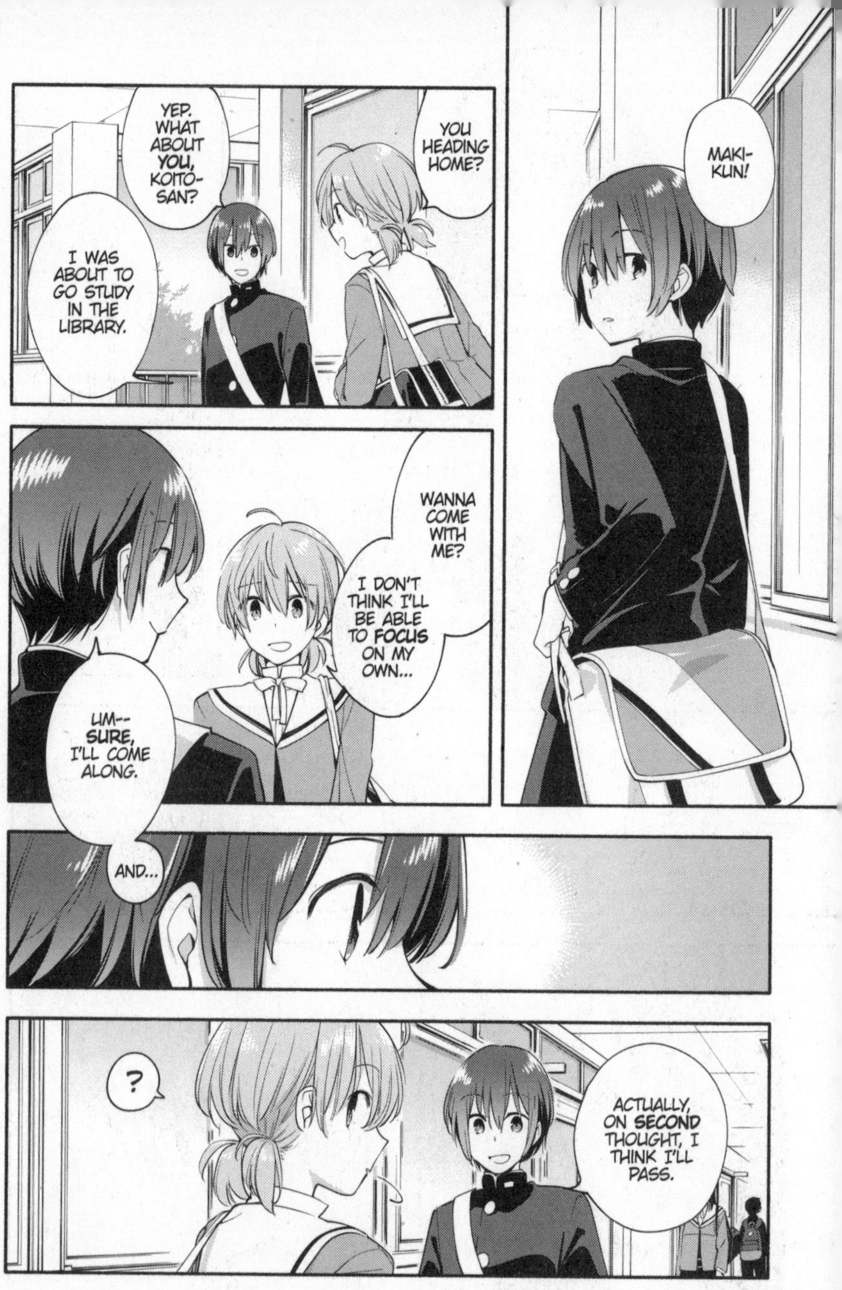
MAKI-KUN!
YOU HEADING HOME?
YEP. WHAT ABOUT YOU, KOITO-SAN?
I WAS ABOUT TO GO STUDY IN THE LIBRARY.
WANNA COME WITH ME?
I DON'T THINK I'LL BE ABLE TO FOCUS ON MY OWN...
UM-- SURE, I'LL COME ALONG.
AND...
ACTUALLY, ON SECOND THOUGHT, I THINK I'LL PASS.
?

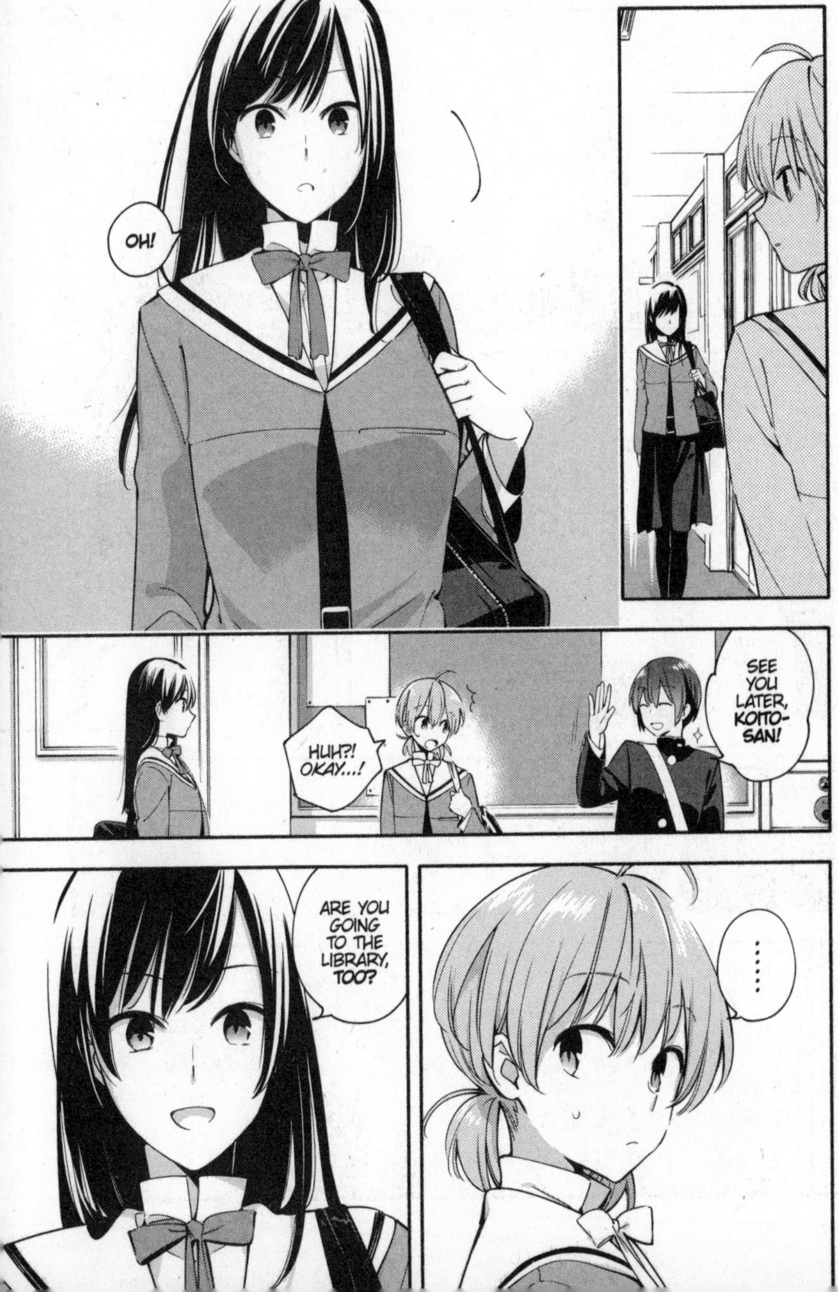
OH!
SEE YOU LATER, KOITO-SAN!
HUH?! OKAY...!
......
ARE YOU GOING TO THE LIBRARY, TOO?

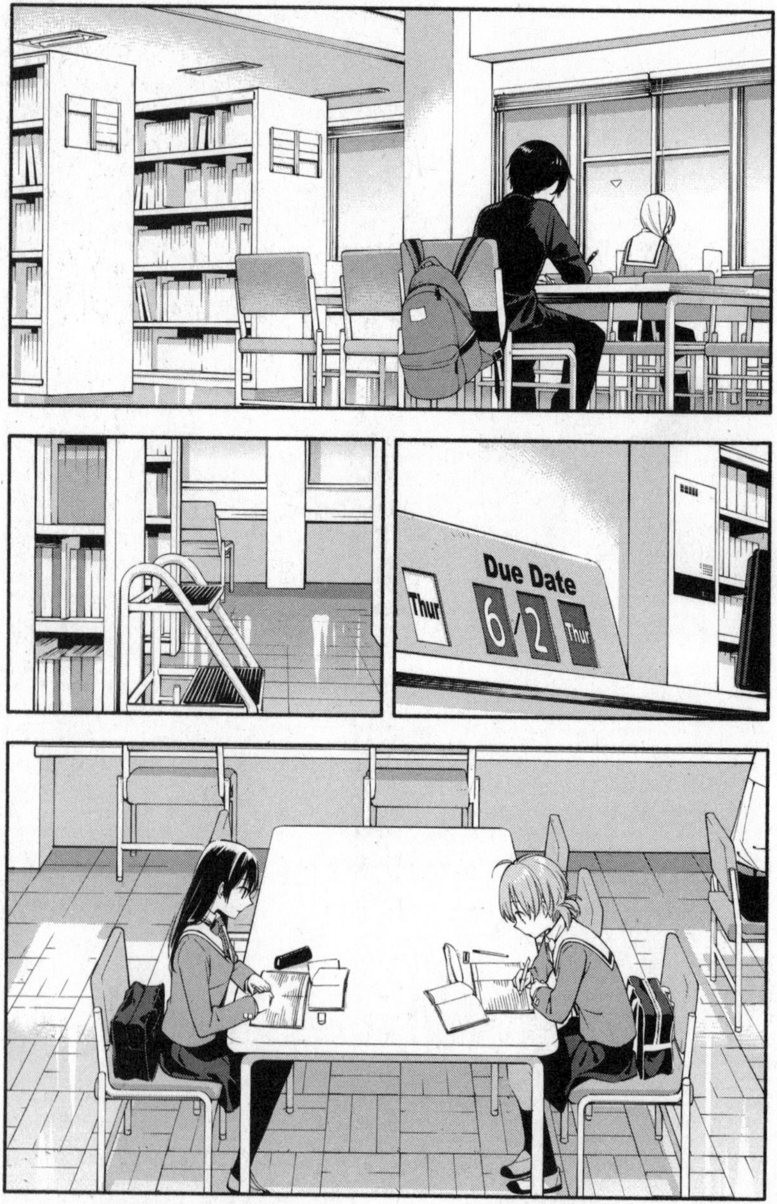
Thur
Due Date
6/2
Thur

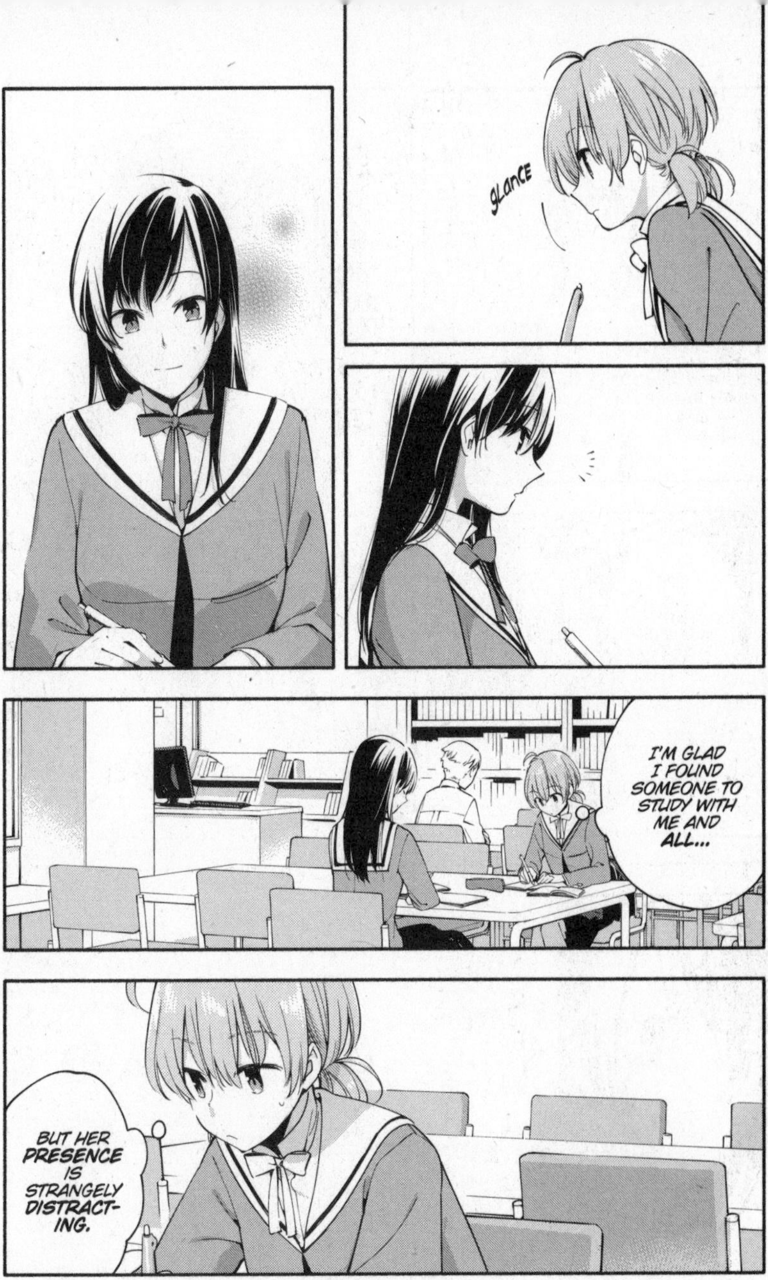
GLANCE
I'M GLAD I FOUND SOMEONE TO STUDY WITH ME AND ALL...
BUT HER PRESENCE IS STRANGELY DISTRACT-ING.

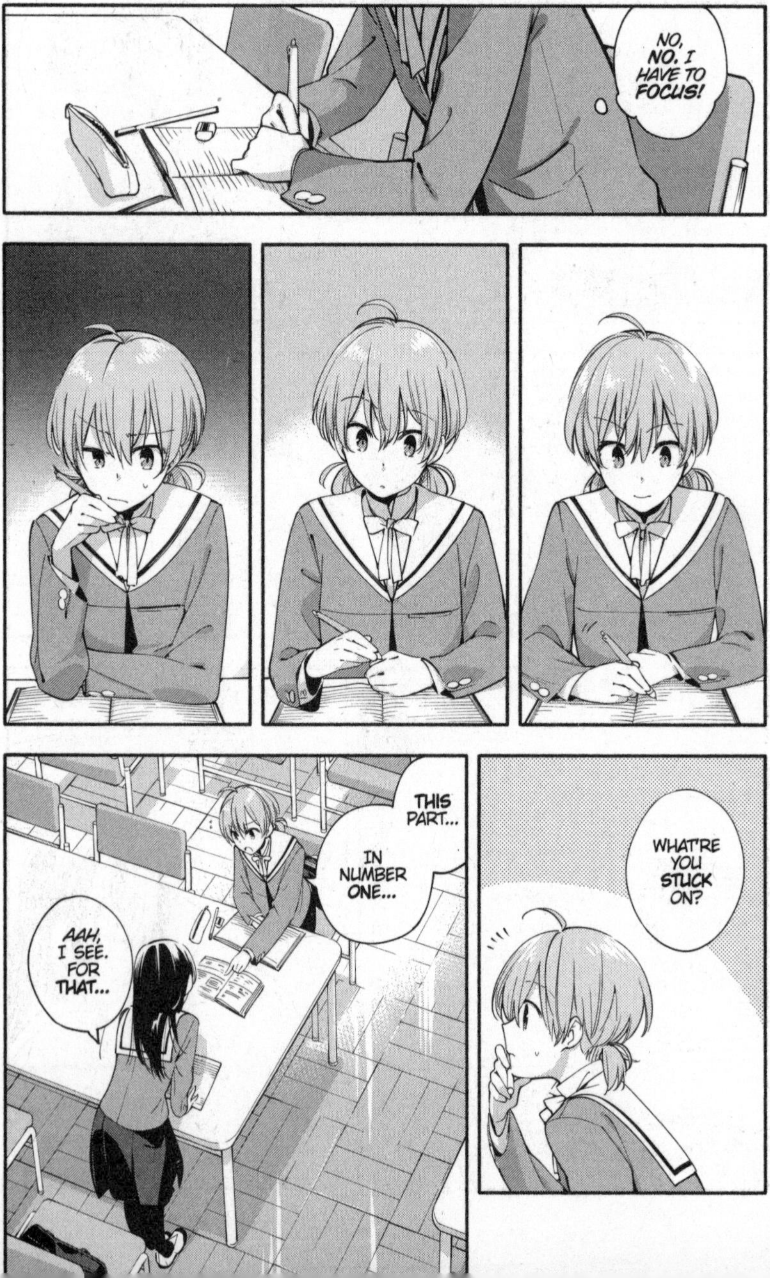
NO, NO. I HAVE TO FOCUS!
WHAT'RE YOU STUCK ON?
THIS PART...
IN NUMBER ONE...
AAH, I SEE. FOR THAT...

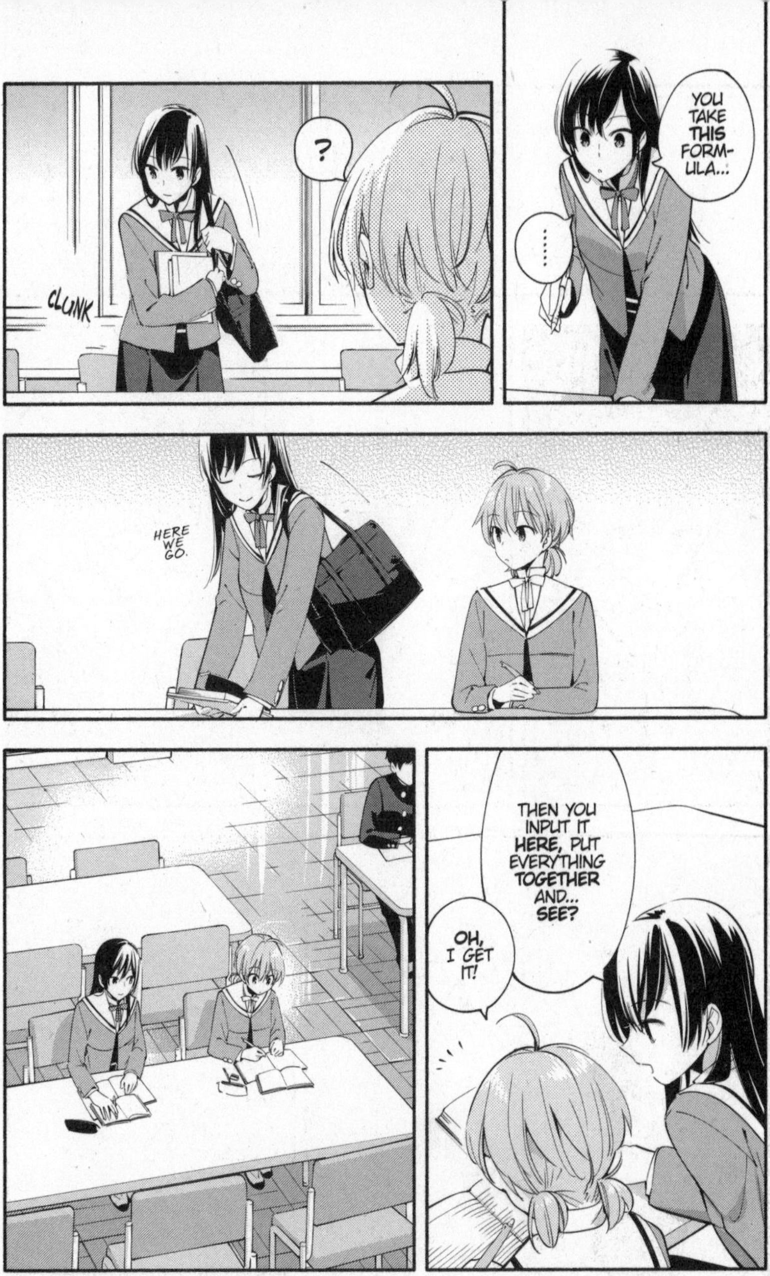
YOU TAKE THIS FORM-ULA...
......
?
CLUNK
HERE WE GO.
THEN YOU INPUT IT HERE, PUT EVERYTHING TOGETHER AND... SEE?
OH, I GET IT!

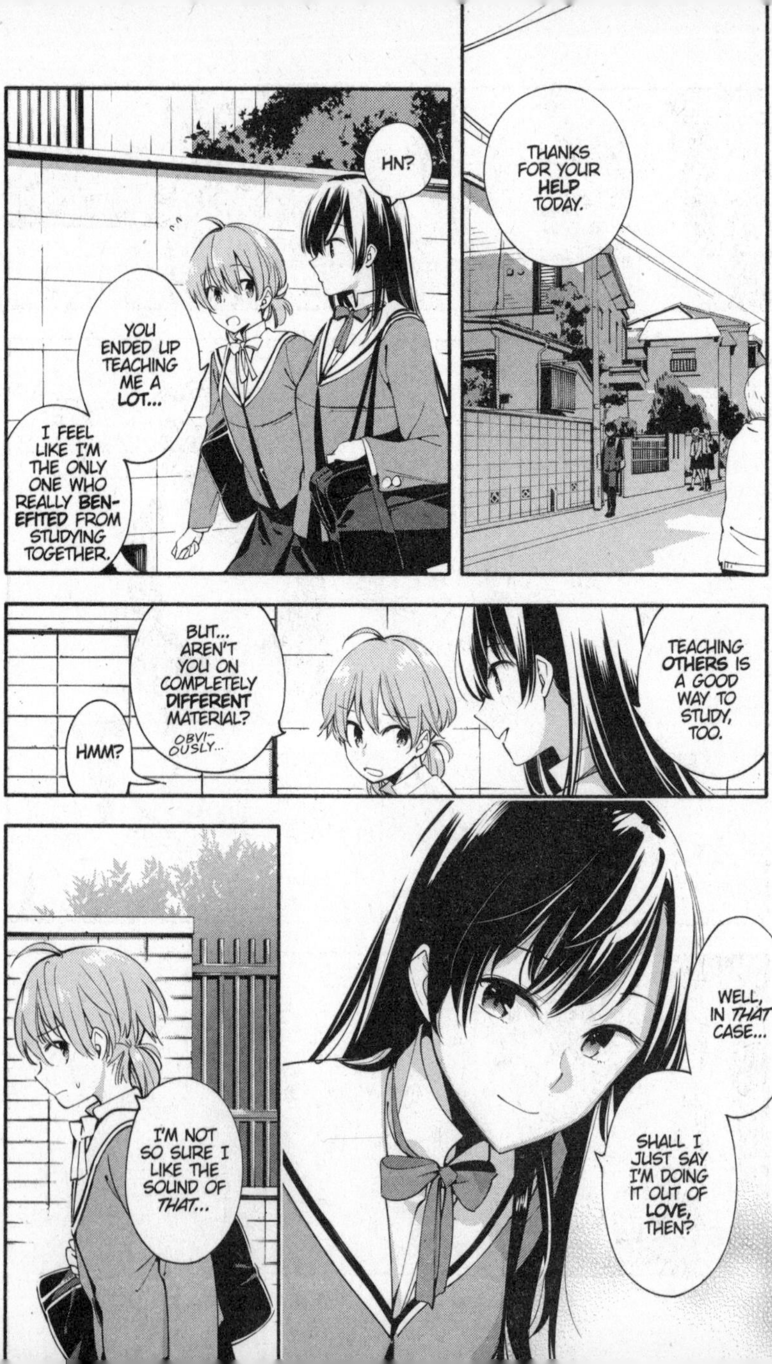
THANKS FOR YOUR HELP TODAY.
HN?
YOU ENDED UP TEACHING ME A LOT...
I FEEL LIKE I'M THE ONLY ONE WHO REALLY BEN-EFITED FROM STUDYING TOGETHER.
TEACHING OTHERS IS A GOOD WAY TO STUDY, TOO.
BUT... AREN'T YOU ON COMPLETELY DIFFERENT MATERIAL?
OBVI-OUSLY...
HMM?
WELL, IN *THAT* CASE...
SHALL I JUST SAY I'M DOING IT OUT OF LOVE, THEN?
I'M NOT SO SURE I LIKE THE SOUND OF *THAT*...

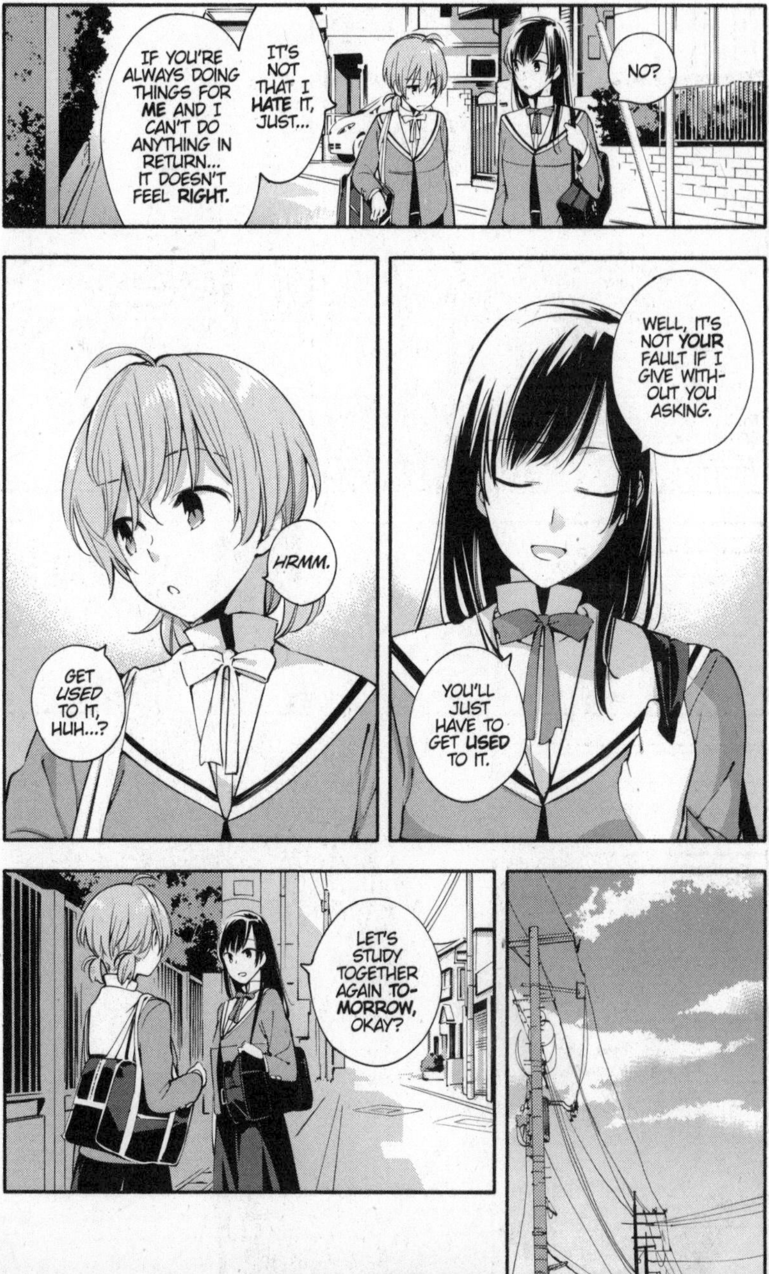
NO?
IT'S NOT THAT I HATE IT, JUST...
IF YOU'RE ALWAYS DOING THINGS FOR ME AND I CAN'T DO ANYTHING IN RETURN... IT DOESN'T FEEL RIGHT.
WELL, IT'S NOT YOUR FAULT IF I GIVE WITH-OUT YOU ASKING.
YOU'LL JUST HAVE TO GET USED TO IT.
HRMM.
GET USED TO IT, HUH...?
LET'S STUDY TOGETHER AGAIN TO-MORROW, OKAY?

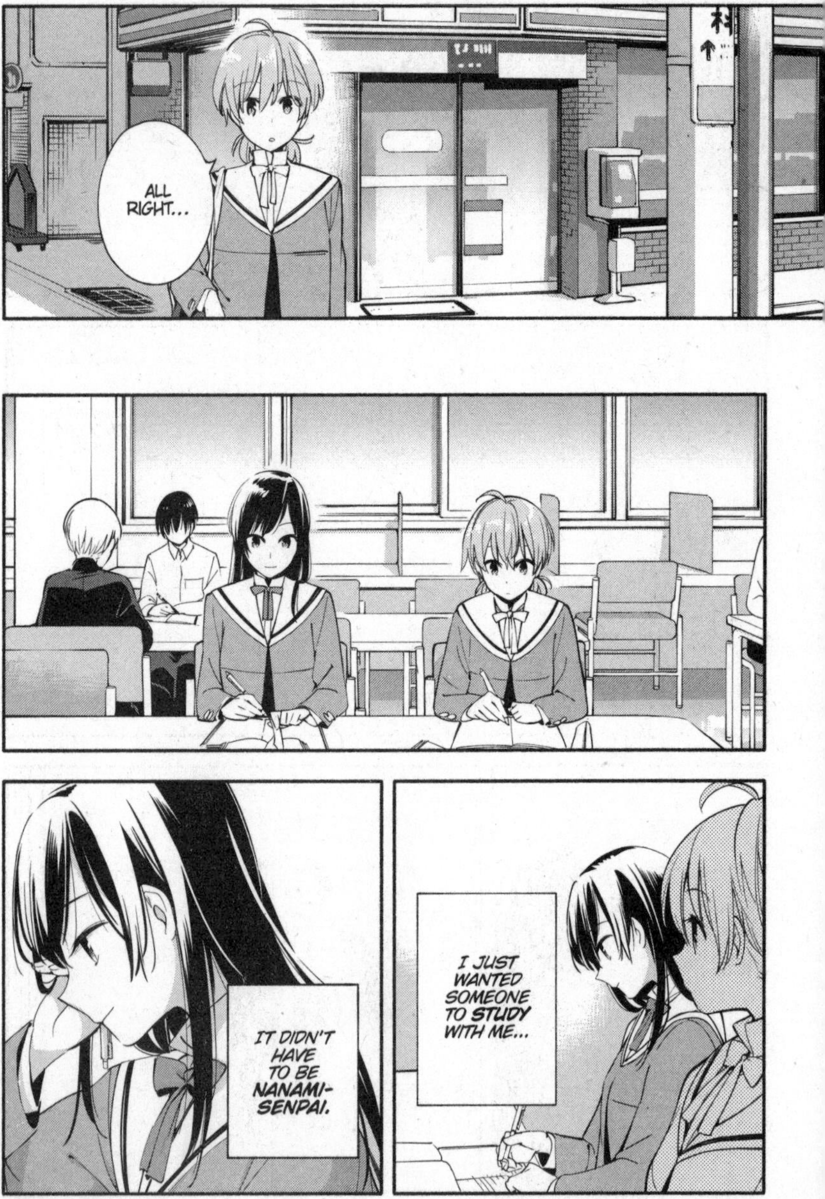
ALL RIGHT...
I JUST WANTED SOMEONE TO STUDY WITH ME...
IT DIDN'T HAVE TO BE NANAMI-SENPAI.

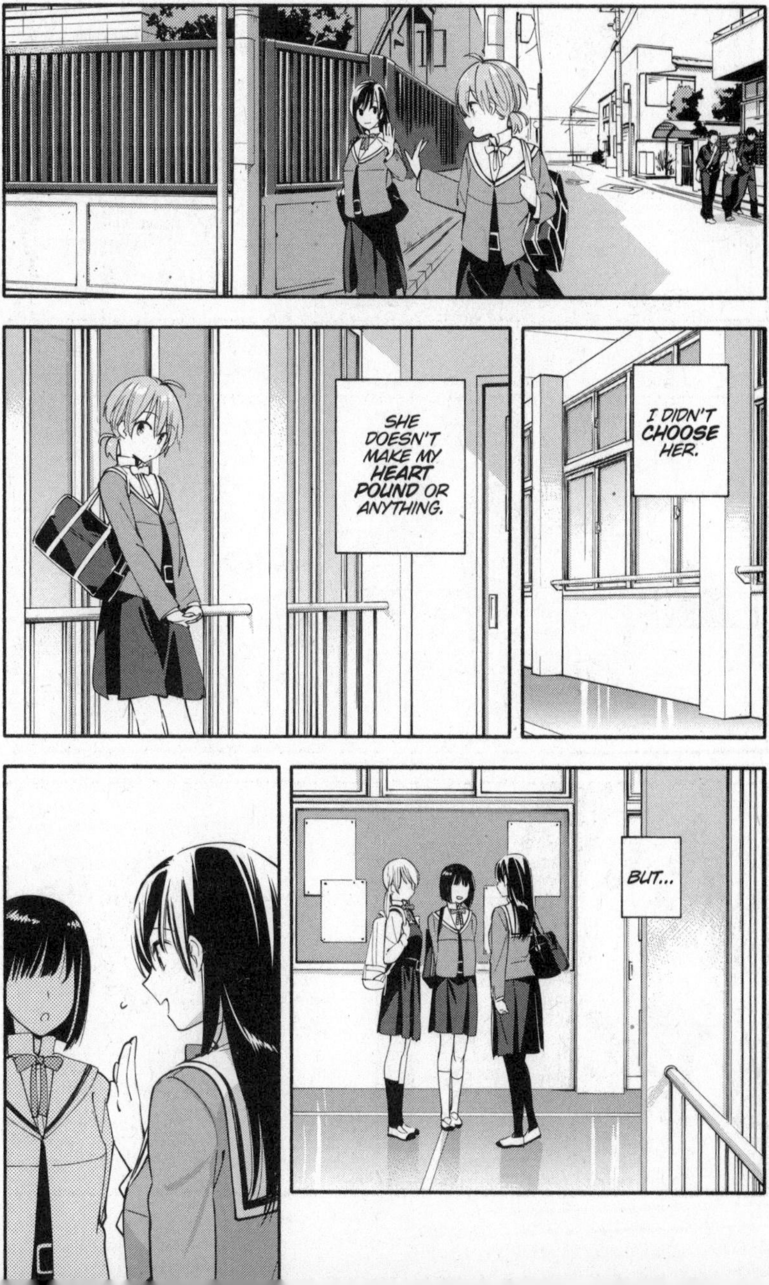
I DIDN'T CHOOSE HER.
SHE DOESN'T MAKE MY HEART POUND OR ANYTHING.
BUT...

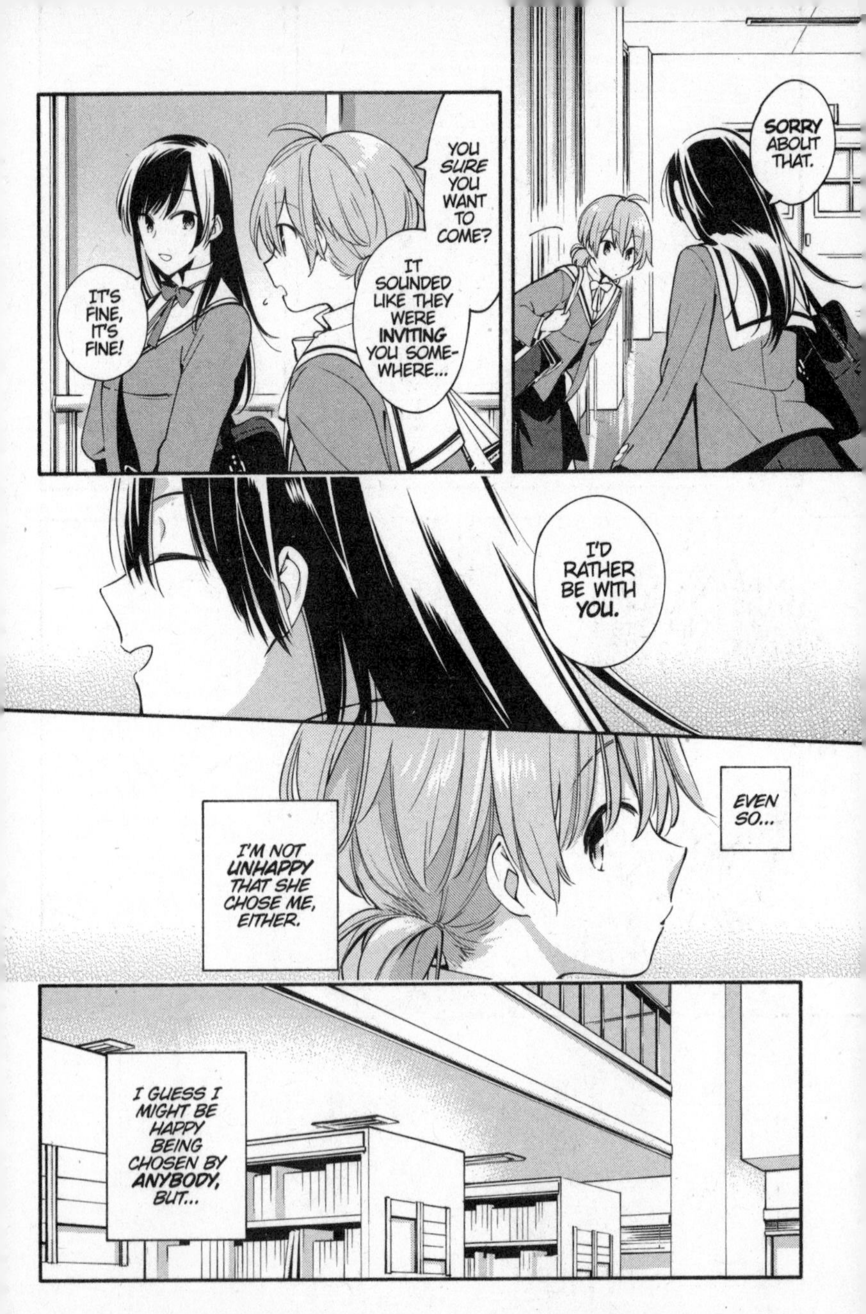
SORRY ABOUT THAT.
YOU SURE YOU WANT TO COME?
IT SOUNDED LIKE THEY WERE INVITING YOU SOME-WHERE...
IT'S FINE, IT'S FINE!
I'D RATHER BE WITH YOU.
EVEN SO...
I'M NOT UNHAPPY THAT SHE CHOSE ME, EITHER.
I GUESS I MIGHT BE HAPPY BEING CHOSEN BY ANYBODY, BUT...

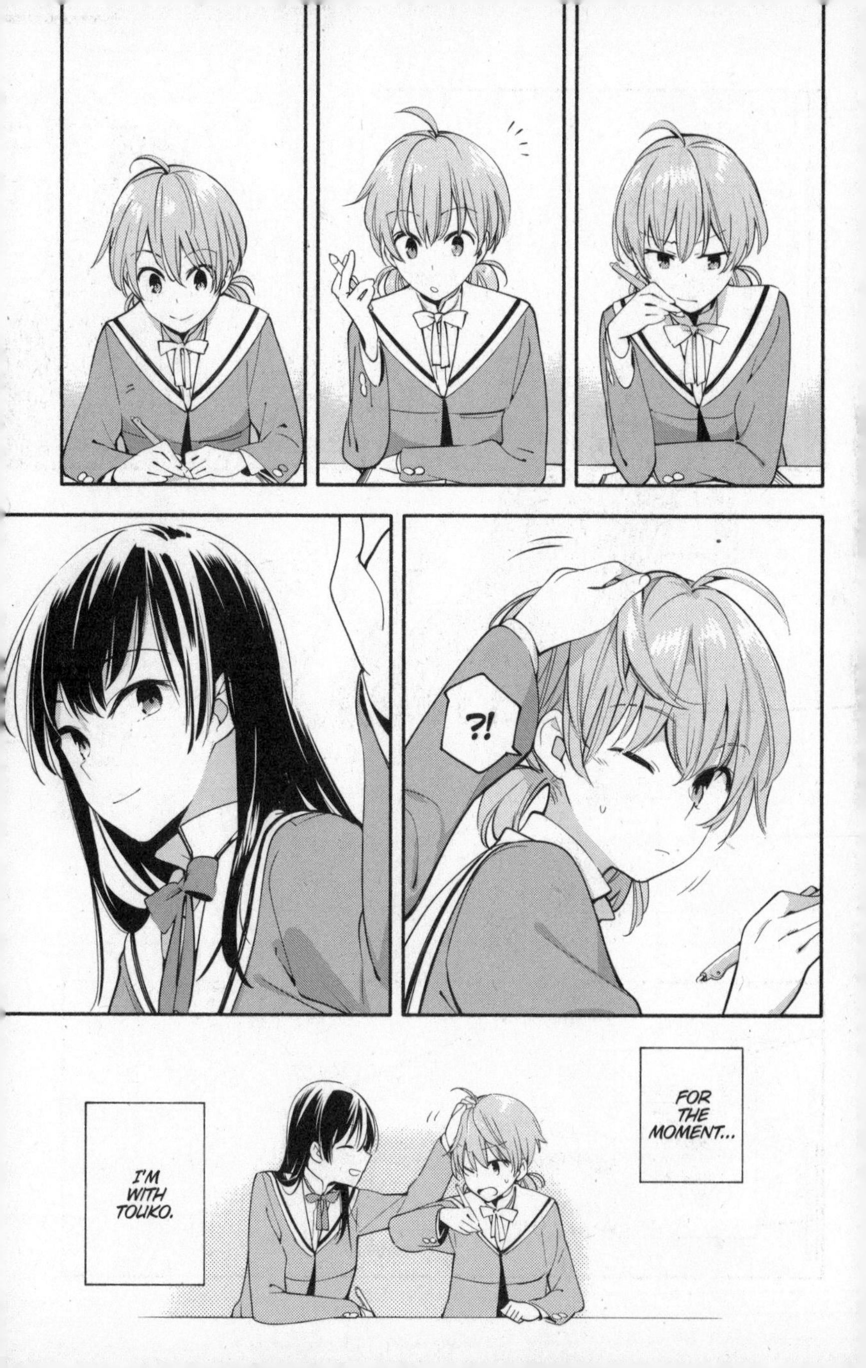
?!
FOR THE MOMENT...
I'M WITH TOUKO.

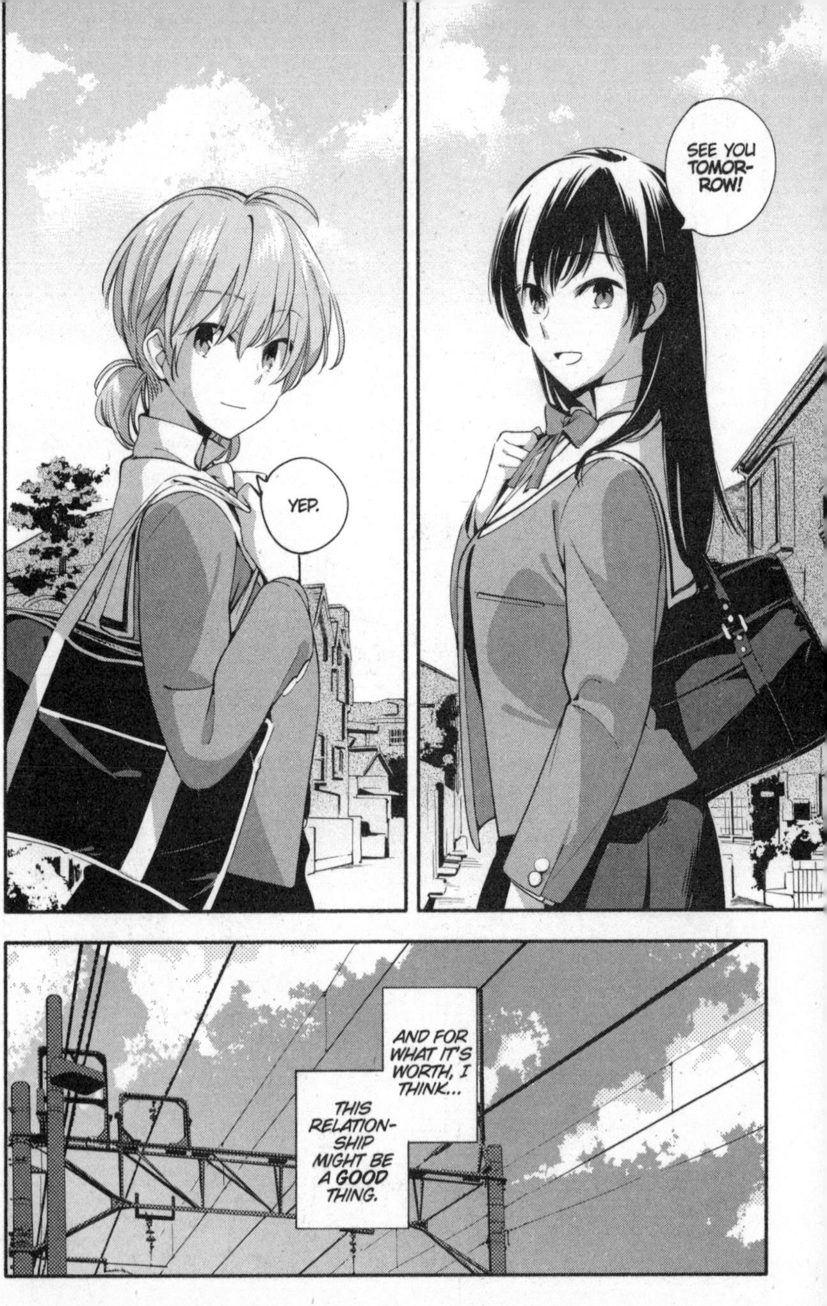
SEE YOU TOMORROW!
YEP.
AND FOR WHAT IT'S WORTH, I THINK...
THIS RELATIONSHIP MIGHT BE A GOOD THING.

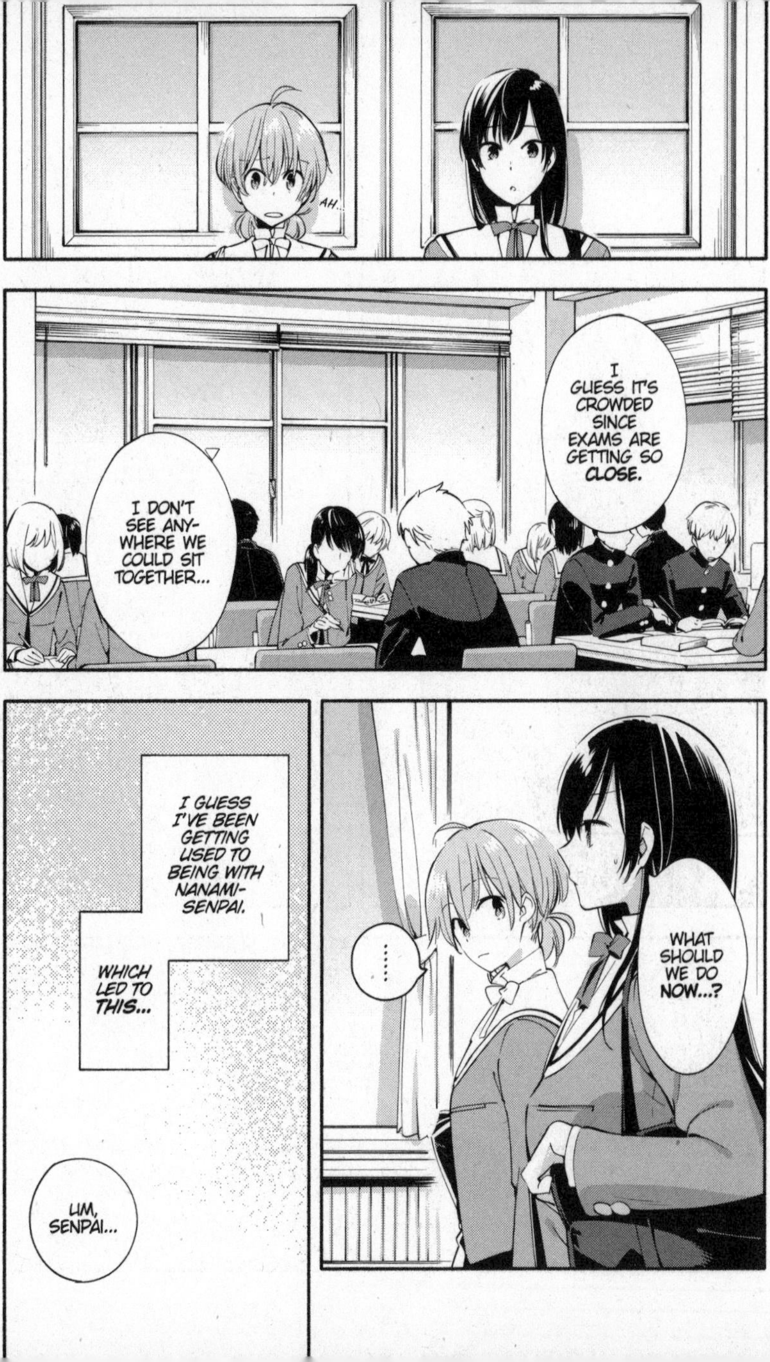
AH...
I GUESS IT'S CROWDED SINCE EXAMS ARE GETTING SO CLOSE.
I DON'T SEE ANYWHERE WE COULD SIT TOGETHER...
WHAT SHOULD WE DO NOW...?
......
I GUESS I'VE BEEN GETTING USED TO BEING WITH NANAMI-SENPAI.
WHICH LED TO THIS...
UM, SENPAI...

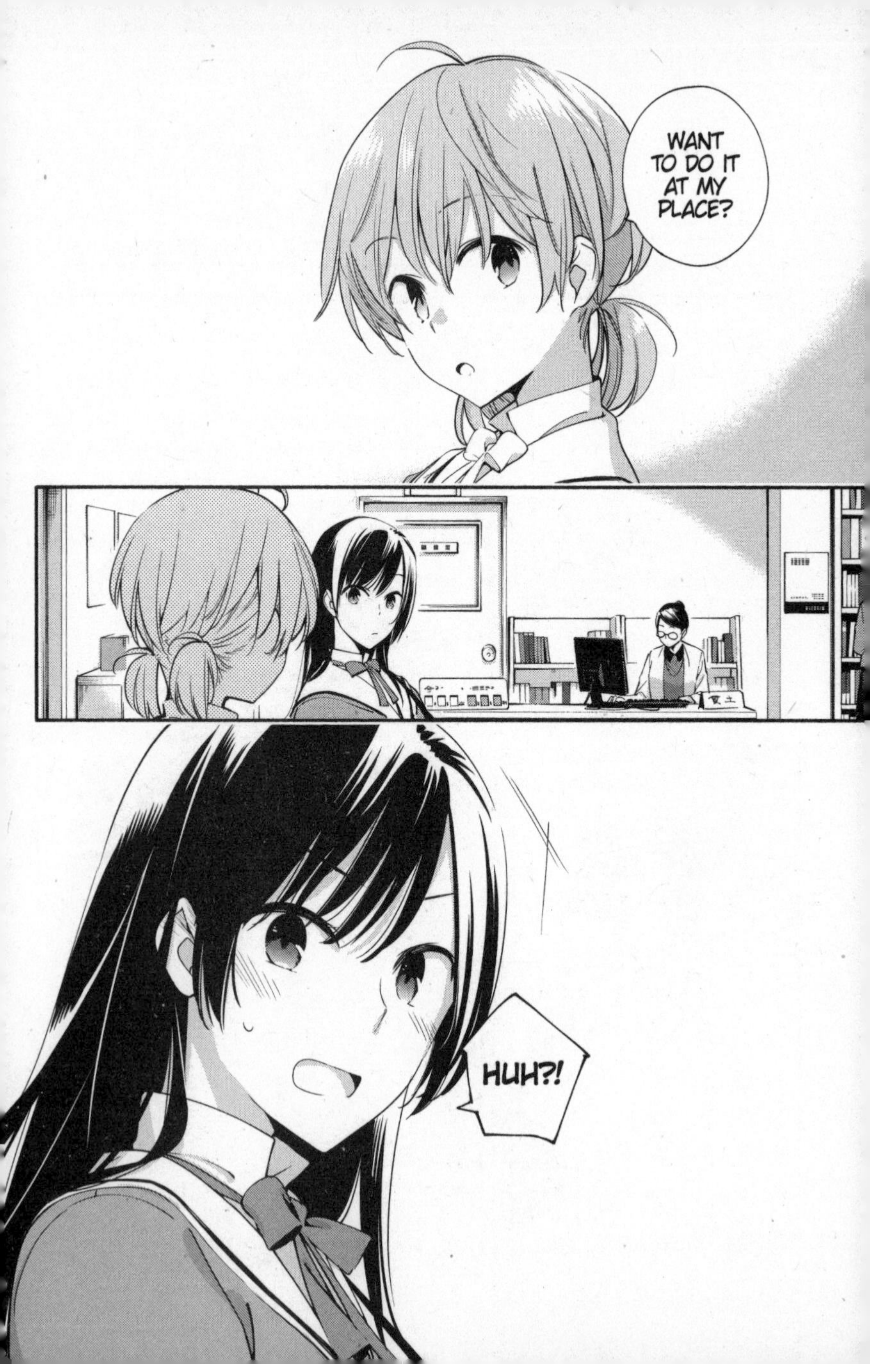
WANT TO DO IT AT MY PLACE?
HUH?!

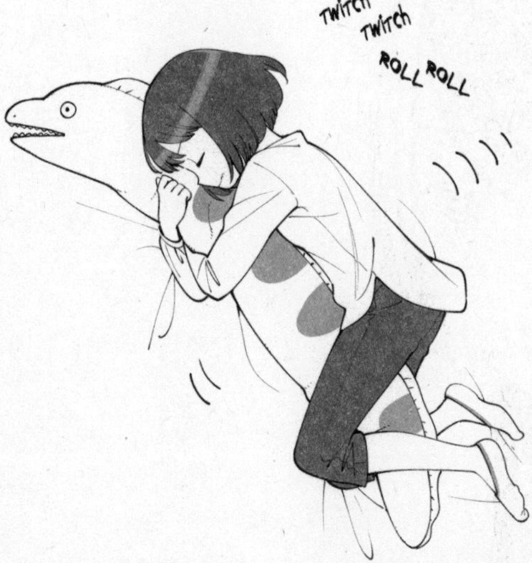
TWITCH
TWITCH
ROLL
ROLL

( **Bloom Into You** )

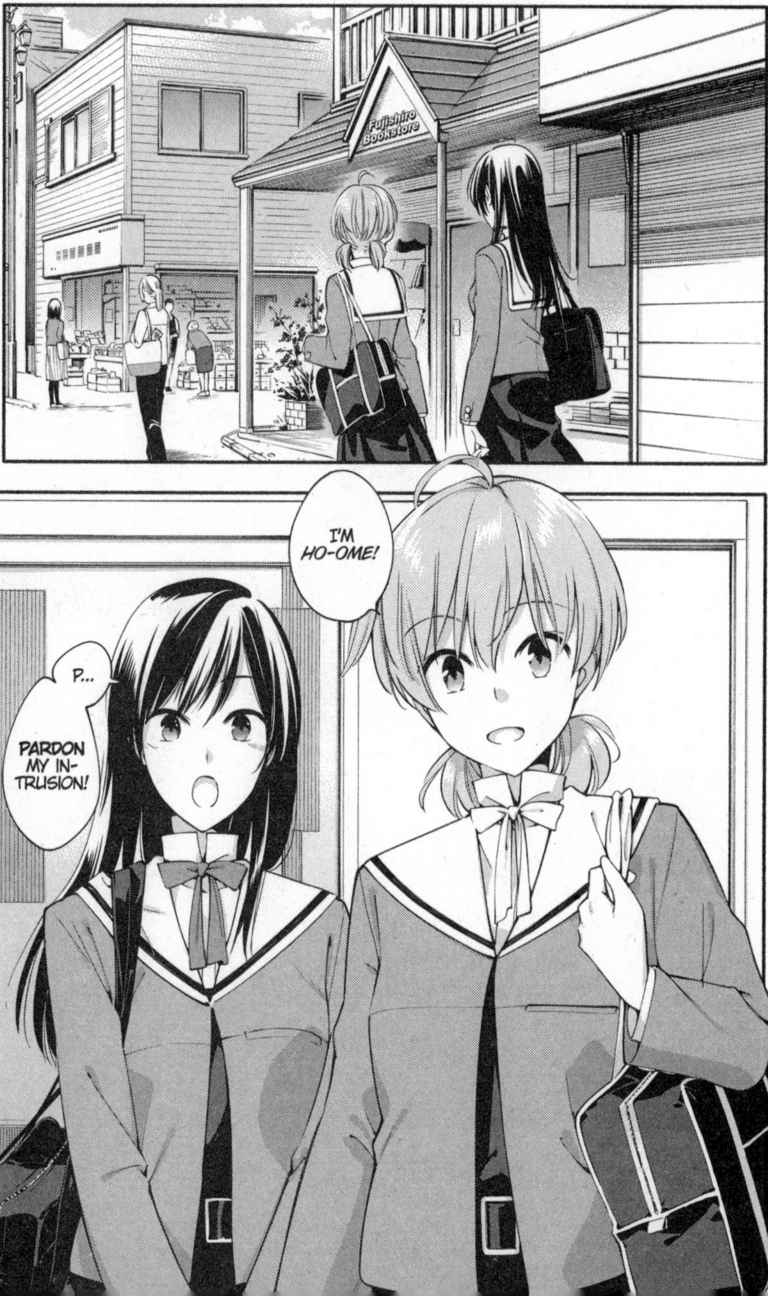
Fujishiro Bookstore
I'M HO-OME!
P...
PARDON MY IN-TRUSION!

# 9

## Multiple Choice ( Continued )

EPISODE NINE

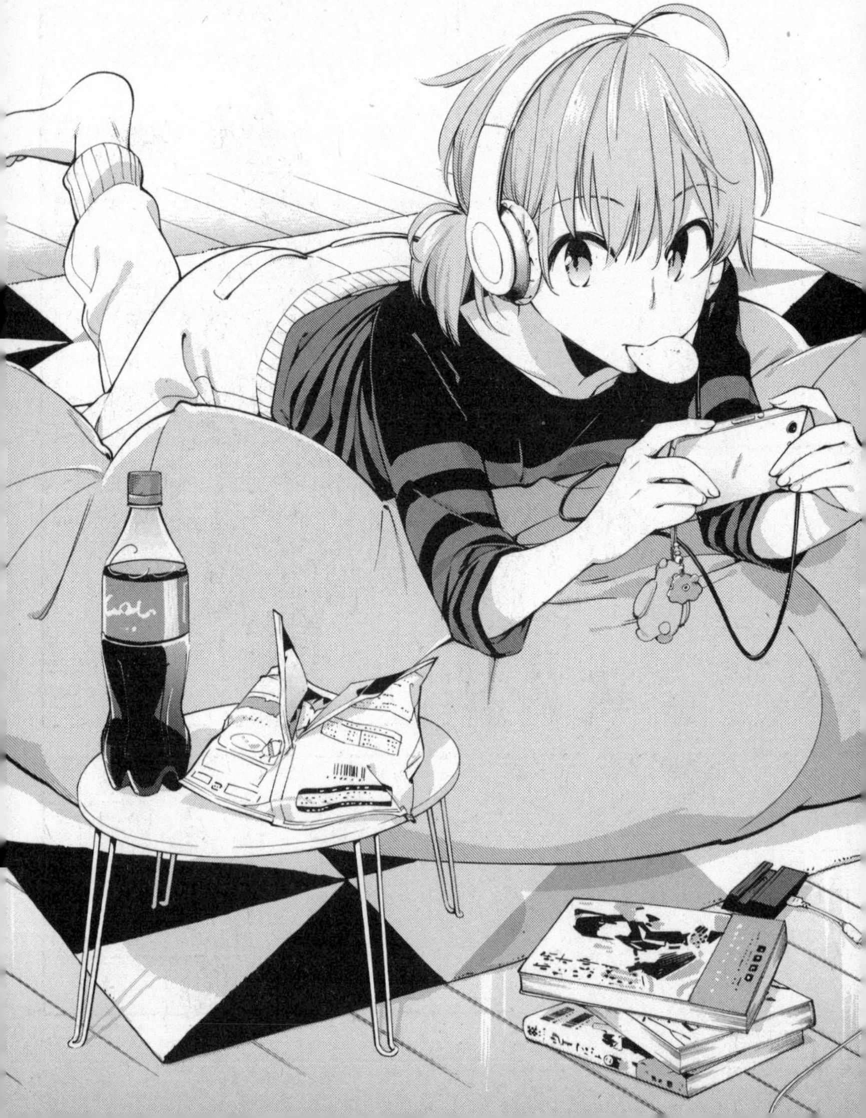

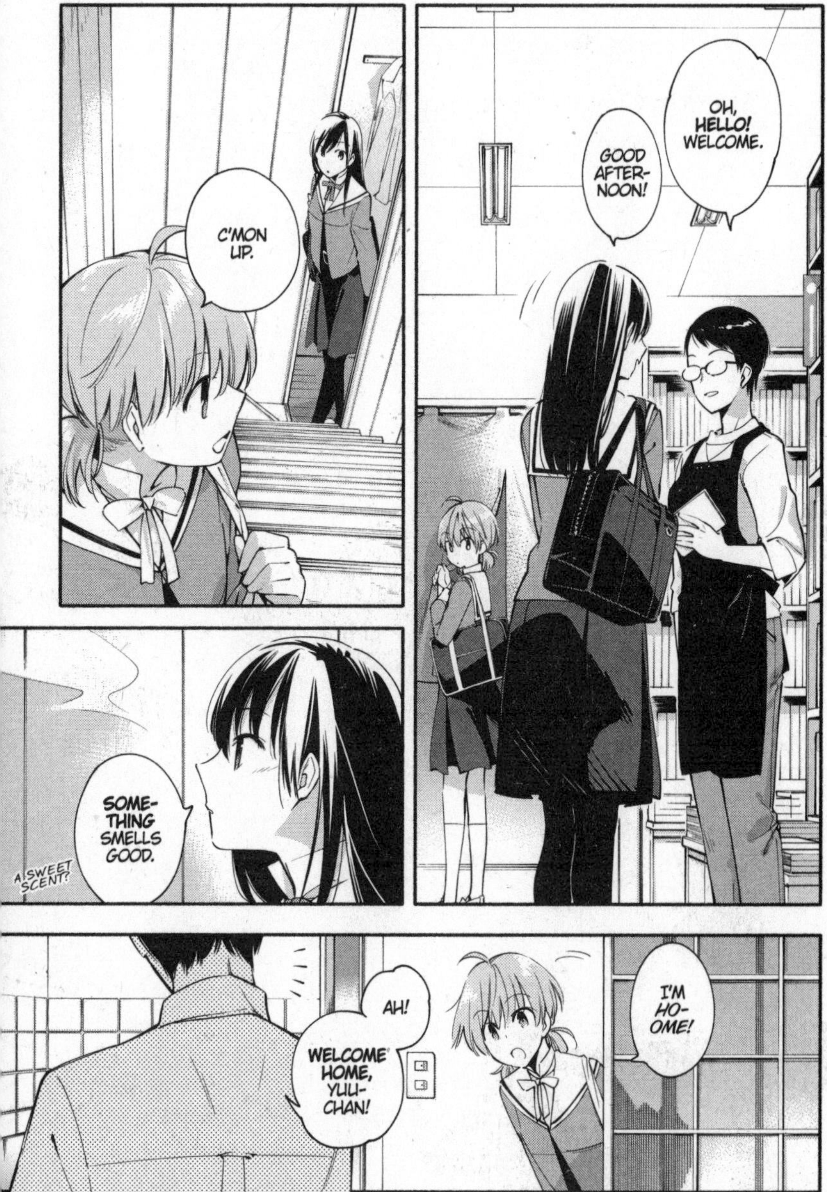
OH, HELLO! WELCOME.
GOOD AFTER-NOON!
C'MON UP.
SOME-THING SMELLS GOOD.
A SWEET SCENT?
I'M HO-OME!
AH!
WELCOME HOME, YUU-CHAN!

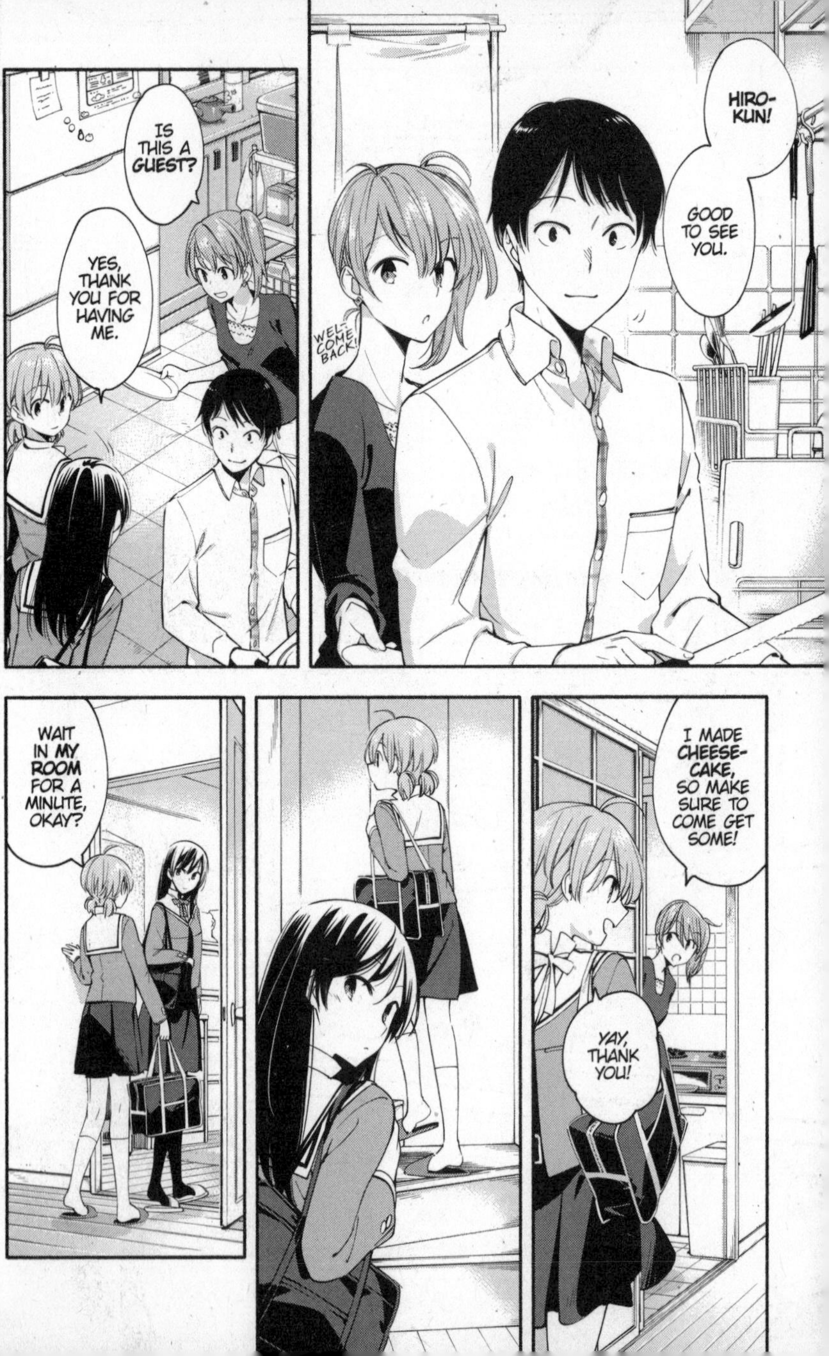
HIRO-KUN!
GOOD TO SEE YOU.
WEL-COME BACK!
IS THIS A GUEST?
YES, THANK YOU FOR HAVING ME.
I MADE CHEESE-CAKE, SO MAKE SURE TO COME GET SOME!
YAY, THANK YOU!
WAIT IN MY ROOM FOR A MINUTE, OKAY?

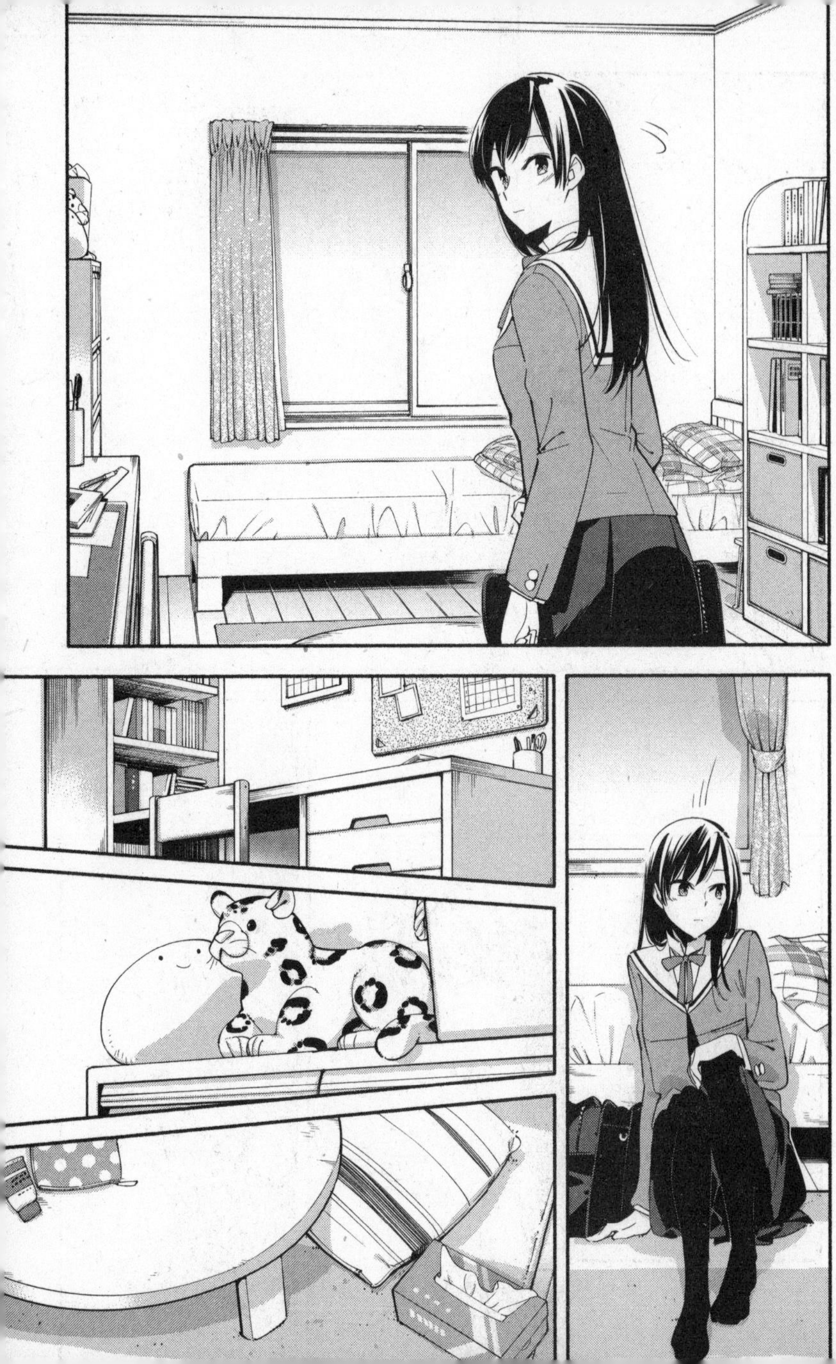

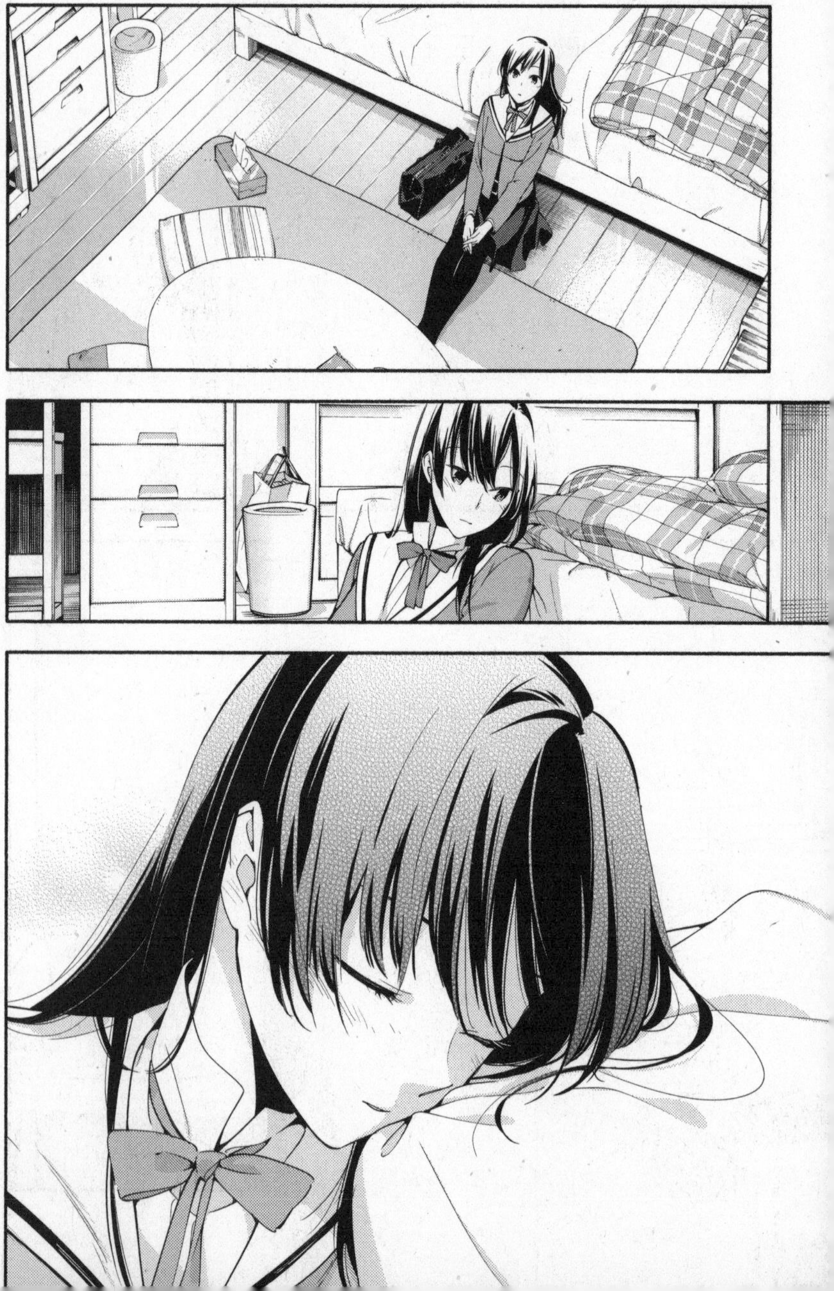

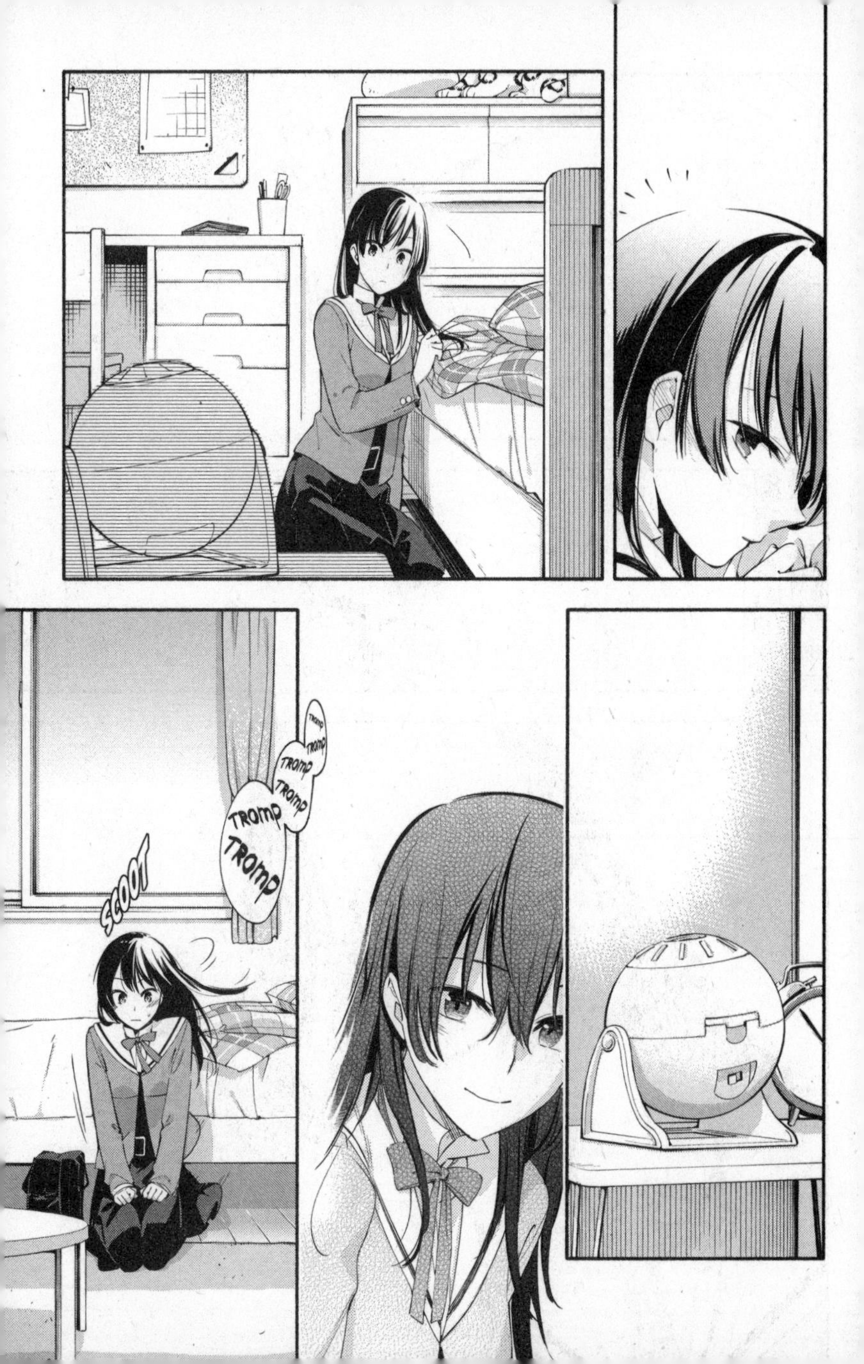
TROMP TROMP
TROMP TROMP
TROMP TROMP
SCOOT

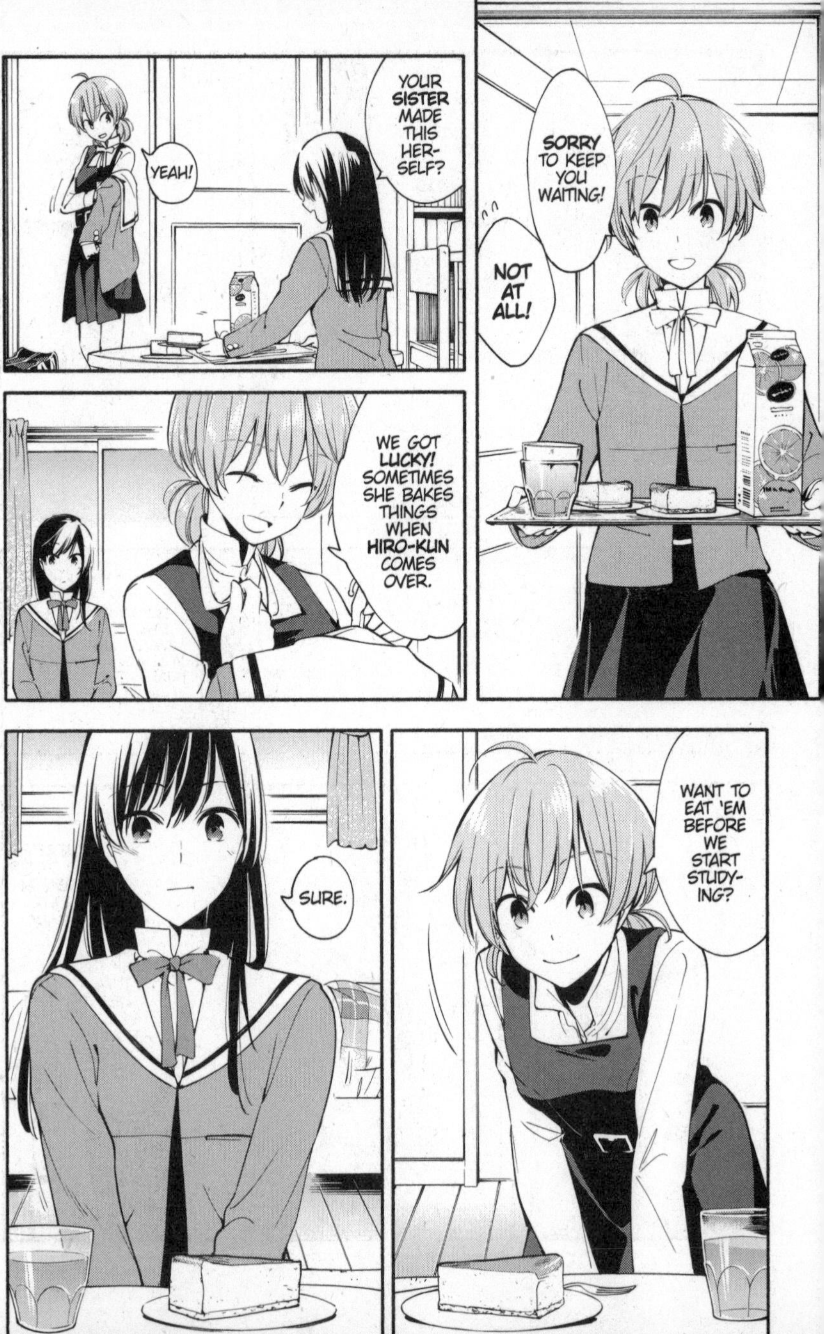
SORRY TO KEEP YOU WAITING!
NOT AT ALL!
YOUR SISTER MADE THIS HER-SELF?
YEAH!
WE GOT LUCKY! SOMETIMES SHE BAKES THINGS WHEN HIRO-KUN COMES OVER.
WANT TO EAT 'EM BEFORE WE START STUDY-ING?
SURE.

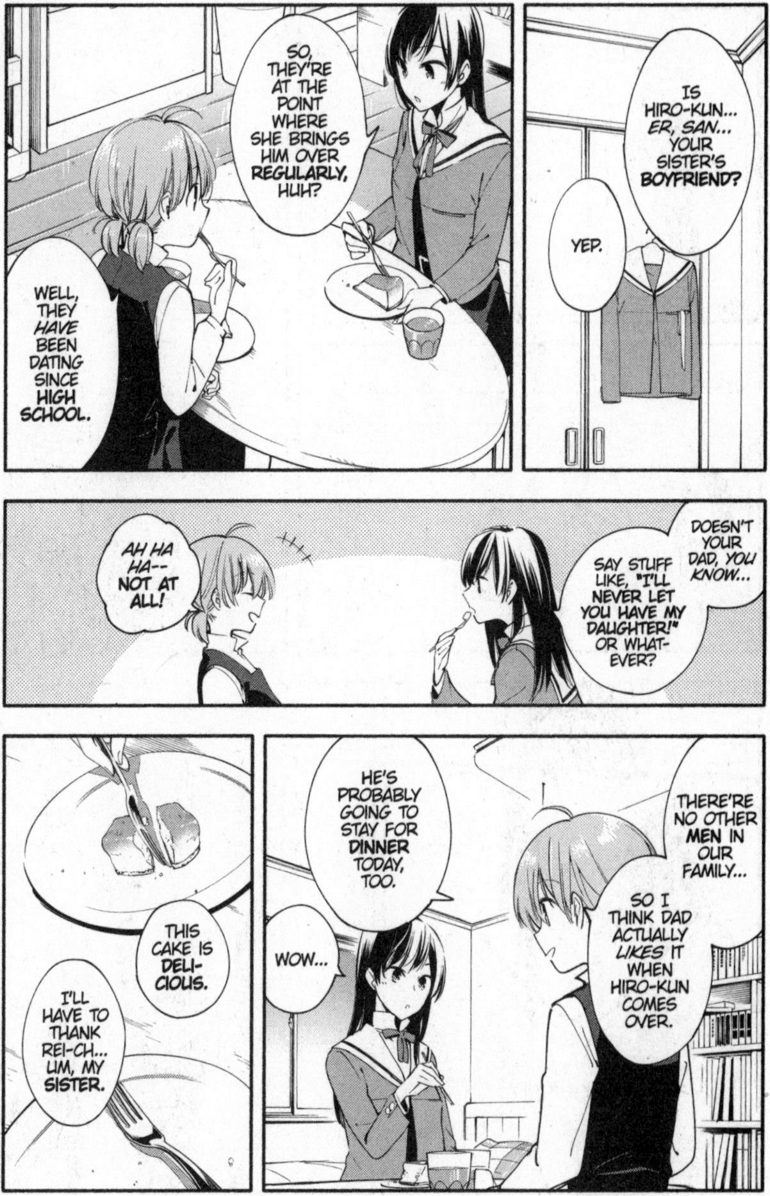
IS HIRO-KUN... ER, SAN... YOUR SISTER'S BOYFRIEND?
YEP.
SO, THEY'RE AT THE POINT WHERE SHE BRINGS HIM OVER REGULARLY, HUH?
WELL, THEY HAVE BEEN DATING SINCE HIGH SCHOOL.
DOESN'T YOUR DAD, YOU KNOW...
SAY STUFF LIKE, "I'LL NEVER LET YOU HAVE MY DAUGHTER!" OR WHATEVER?
AH HA HA-- NOT AT ALL!
THERE'RE NO OTHER MEN IN OUR FAMILY...
SO I THINK DAD ACTUALLY LIKES IT WHEN HIRO-KUN COMES OVER.
HE'S PROBABLY GOING TO STAY FOR DINNER TODAY, TOO.
WOW...
THIS CAKE IS DELICIOUS.
I'LL HAVE TO THANK REI-CH... UM, MY SISTER.

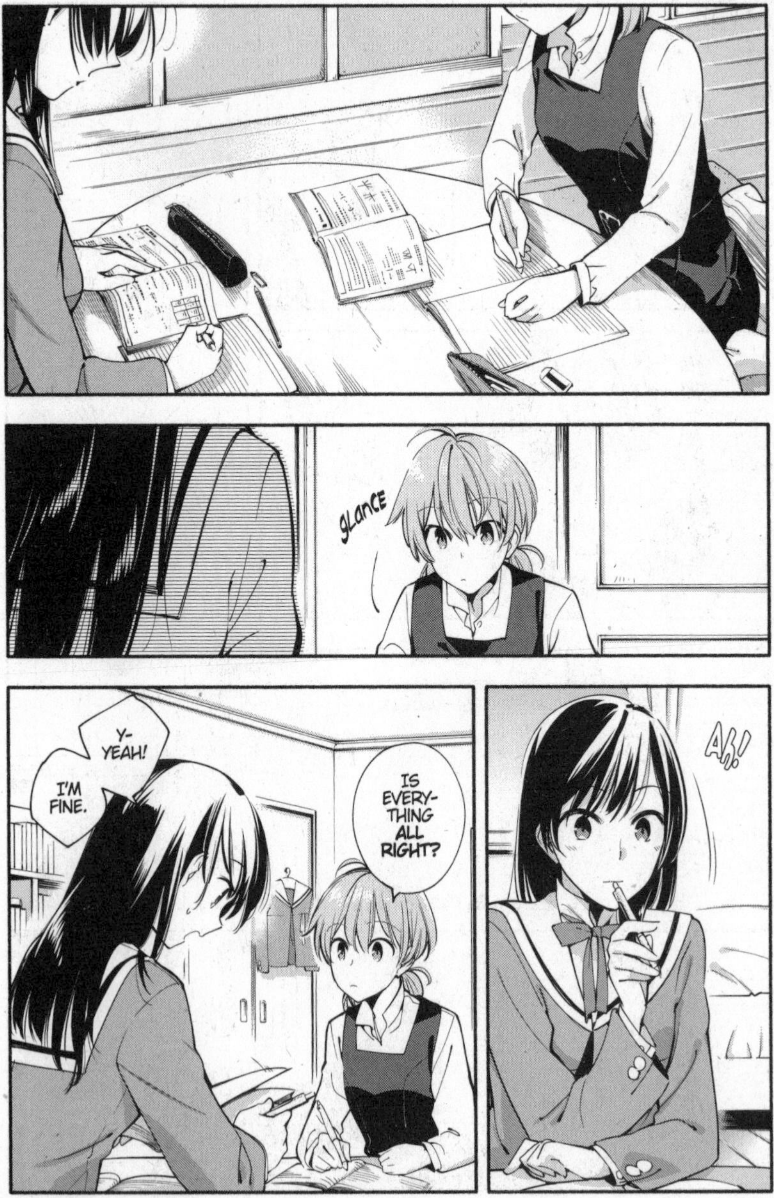
GLANCE
AH!
IS EVERY-THING ALL RIGHT?
Y-YEAH! I'M FINE.

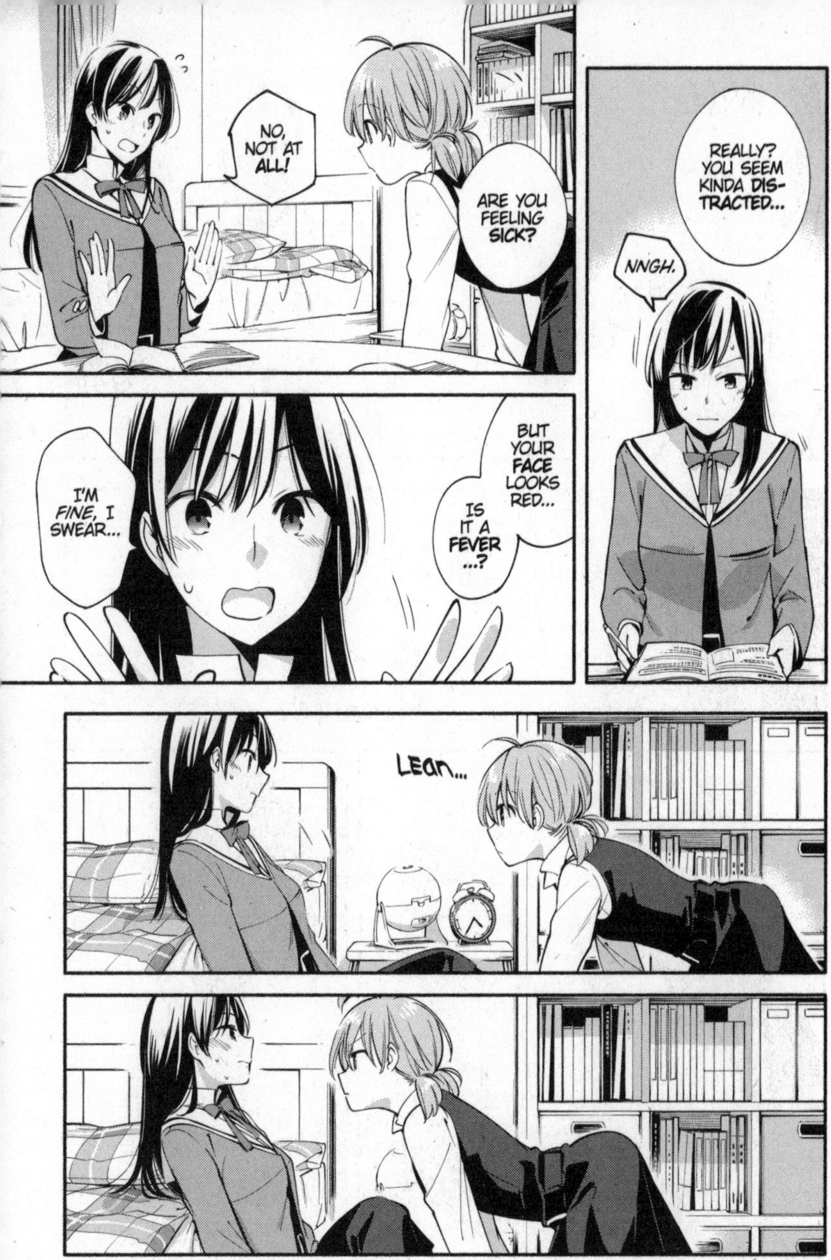
REALLY? YOU SEEM KINDA DISTRACTED...
NNGH.
ARE YOU FEELING SICK?
NO, NOT AT ALL!
BUT YOUR FACE LOOKS RED...
IS IT A FEVER ...?
I'M FINE, I SWEAR...
Lean...

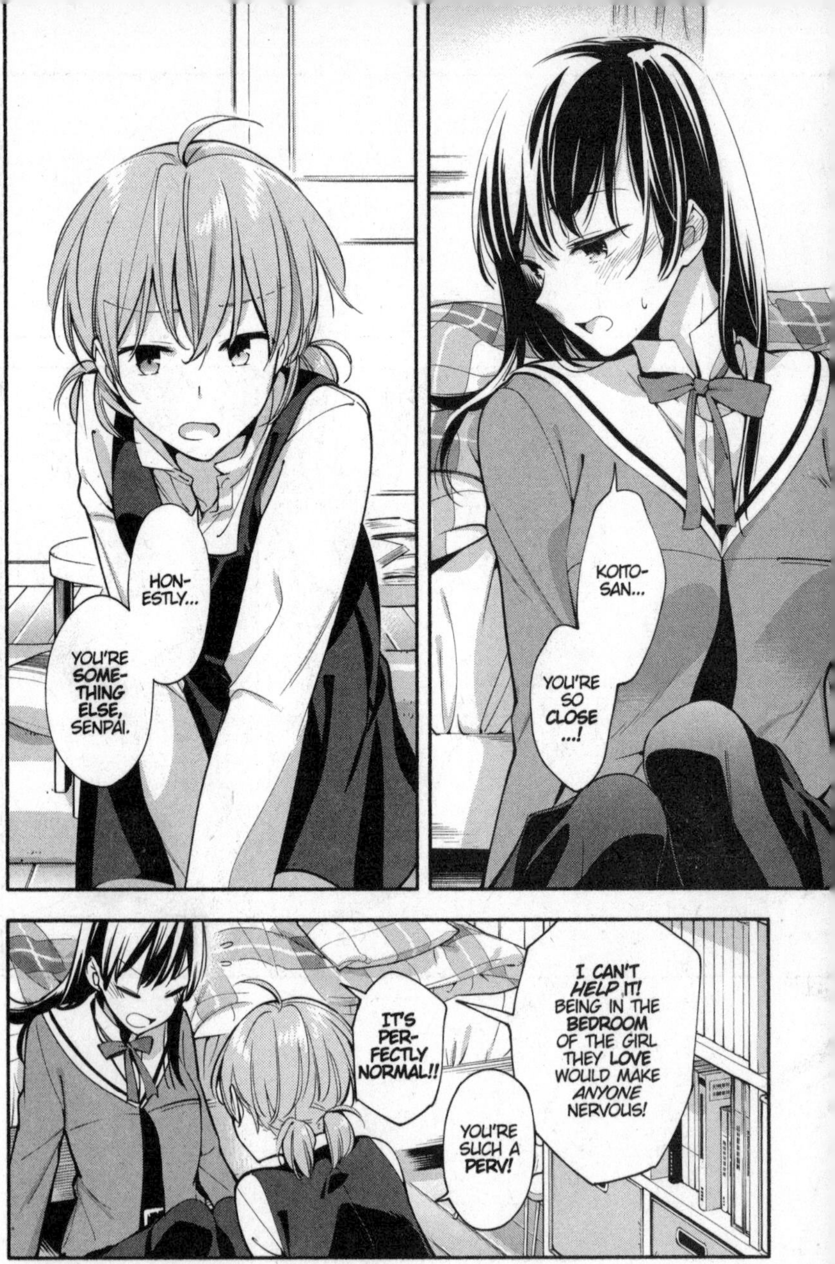
KOITO-SAN...
YOU'RE SO CLOSE ...!
HON-ESTLY...
YOU'RE SOME-THING ELSE, SENPAI.
I CAN'T *HELP* IT! BEING IN THE **BEDROOM** OF THE GIRL THEY **LOVE** WOULD MAKE *ANYONE* NERVOUS!
IT'S PER-FECTLY NORMAL!!
YOU'RE SUCH A **PERV**!

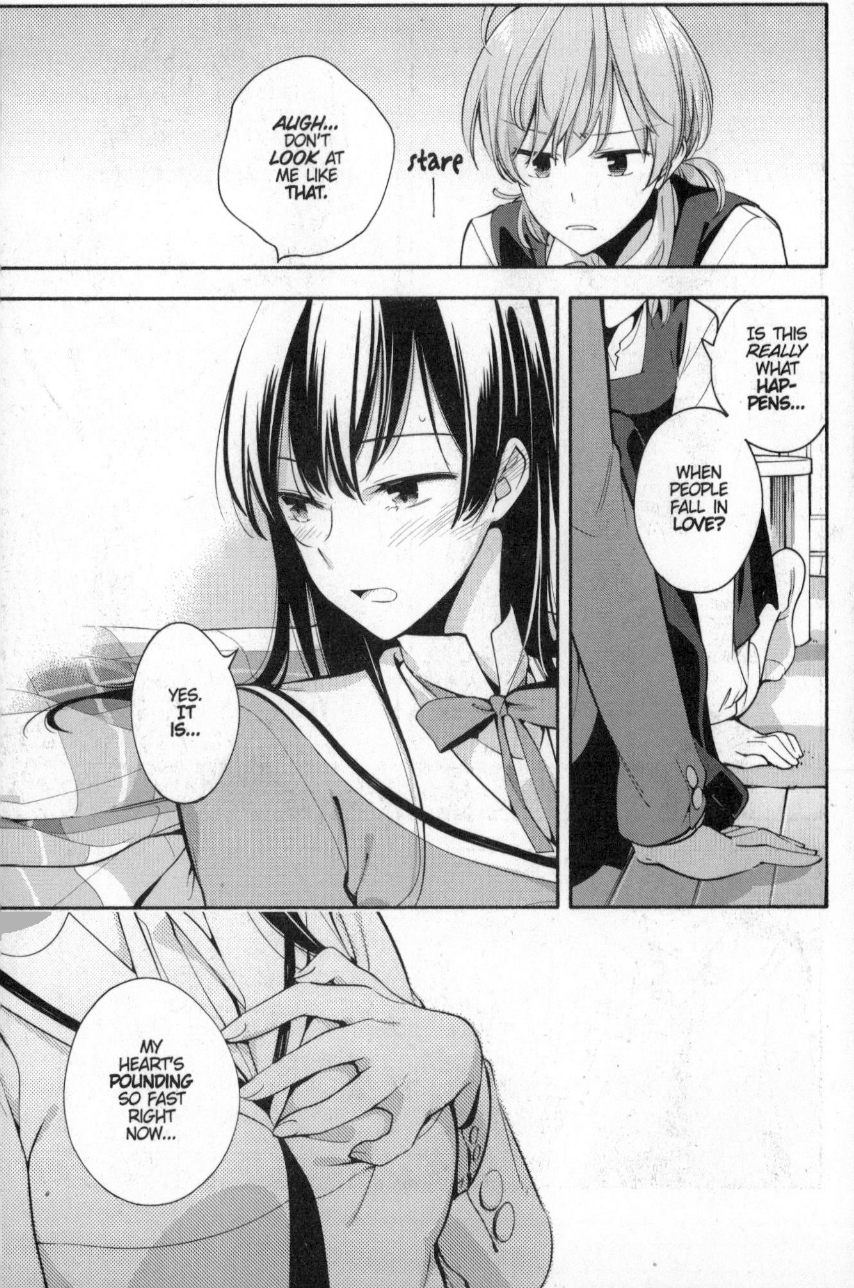
stare
AUGH... DON'T LOOK AT ME LIKE THAT.
IS THIS REALLY WHAT HAP-PENS...
WHEN PEOPLE FALL IN LOVE?
YES. IT IS...
MY HEART'S POUNDING SO FAST RIGHT NOW...

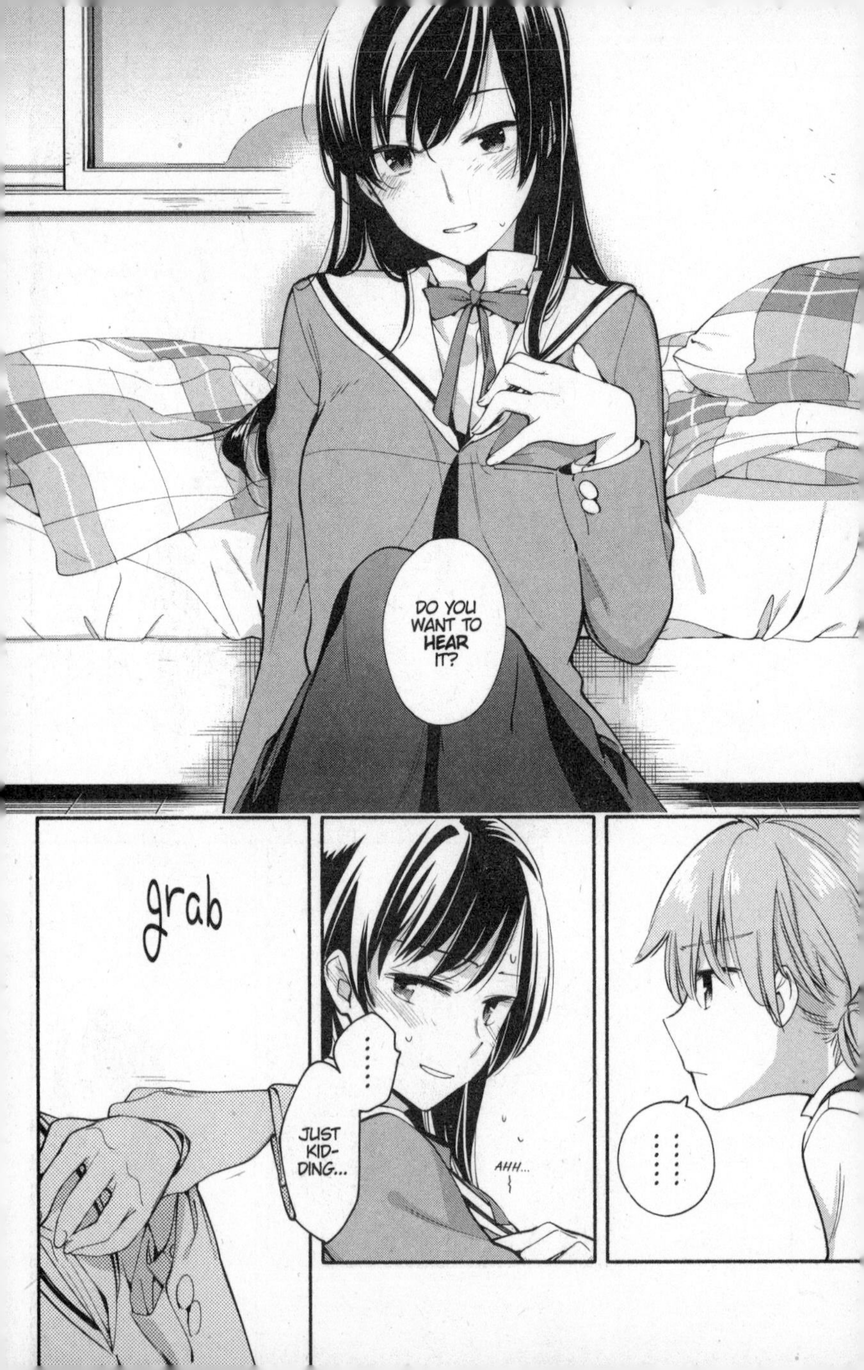
DO YOU WANT TO HEAR IT?
......
......
JUST KID-DING...
AHH...
grab

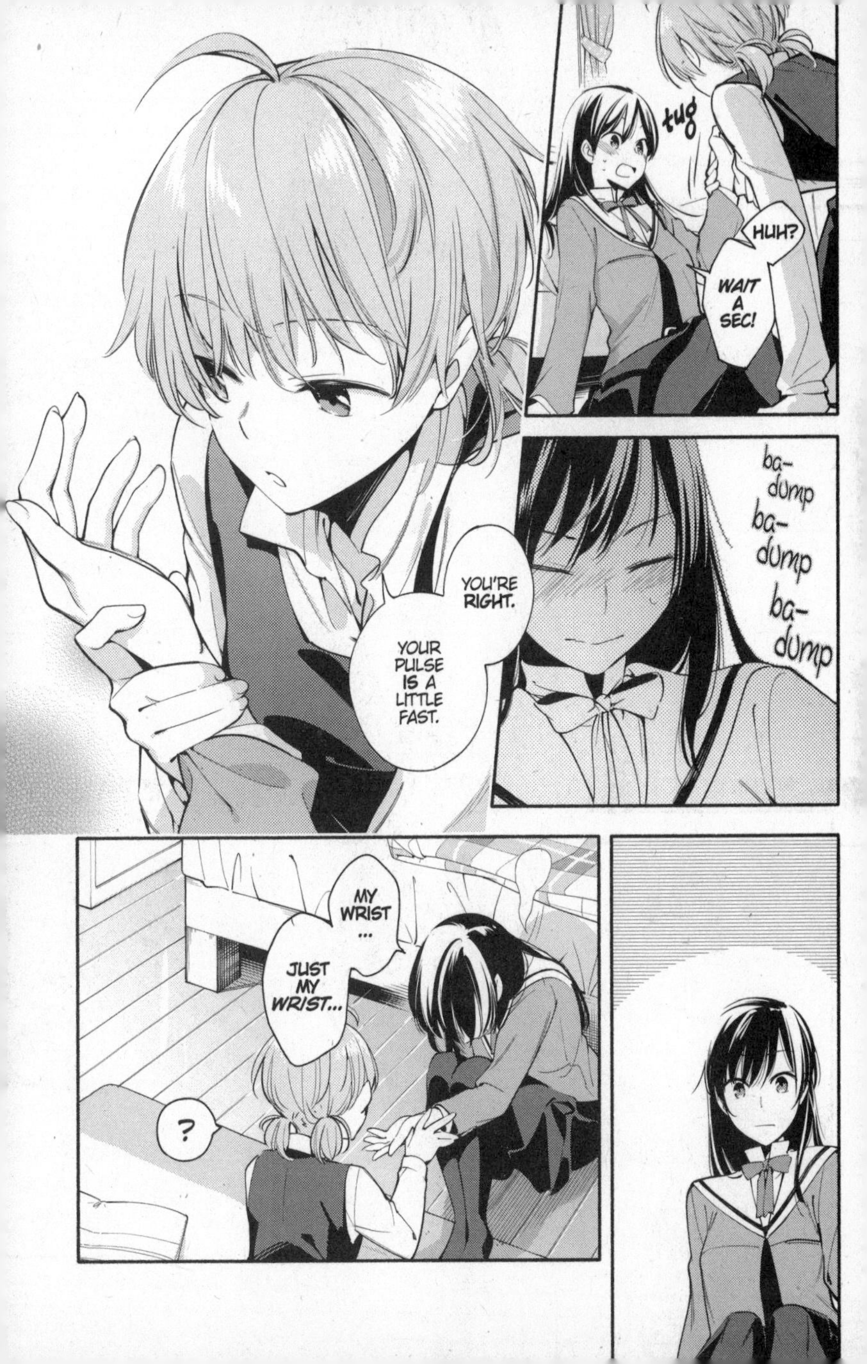
tug
HUH?
WAIT A SEC!
ba-dump ba-dump ba-dump
YOU'RE RIGHT.
YOUR PULSE IS A LITTLE FAST.
MY WRIST...
JUST MY WRIST...
?

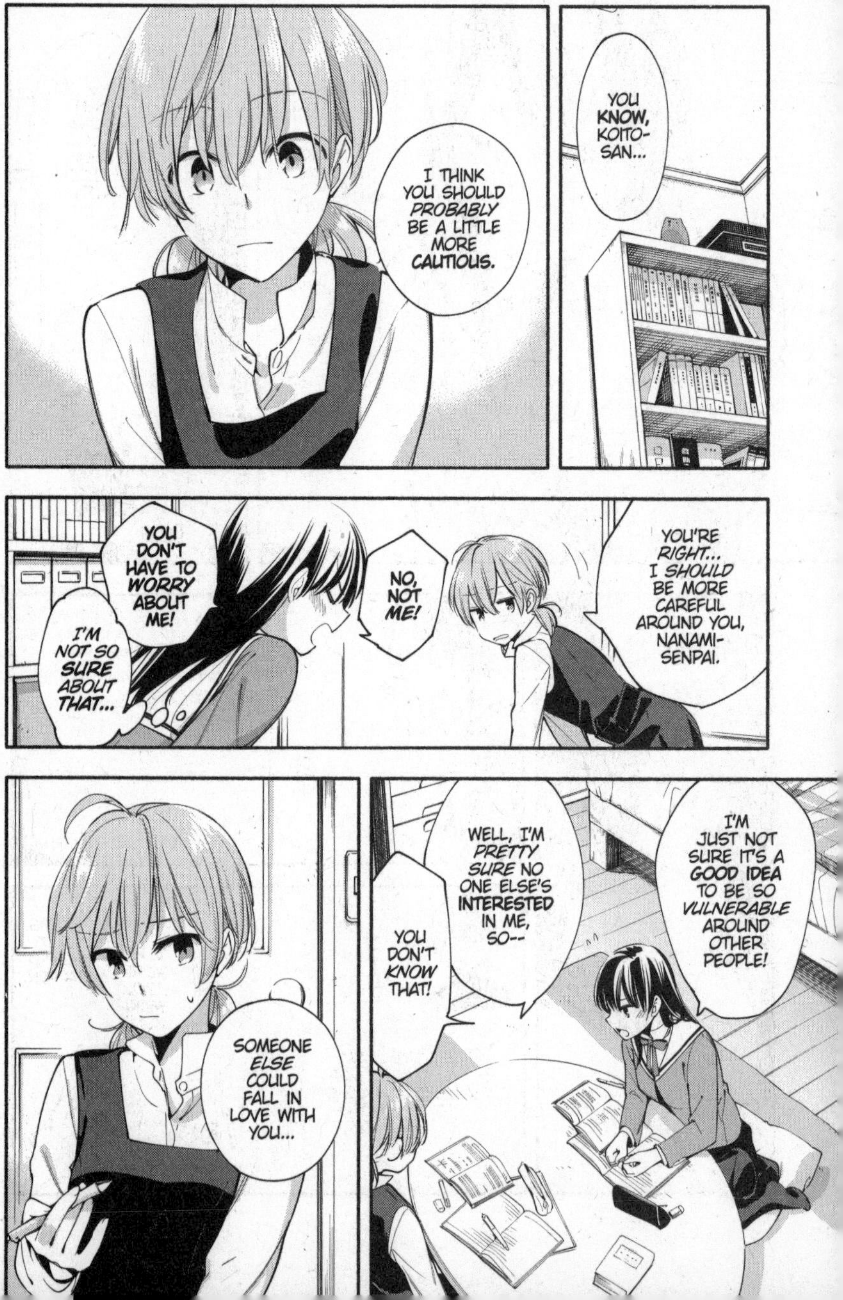
YOU KNOW, KOITO-SAN...
I THINK YOU SHOULD PROBABLY BE A LITTLE MORE CAUTIOUS.
YOU'RE RIGHT... I SHOULD BE MORE CAREFUL AROUND YOU, NANAMI-SENPAI.
NO, NOT ME!
YOU DON'T HAVE TO WORRY ABOUT ME!
I'M NOT SO SURE ABOUT THAT...
I'M JUST NOT SURE IT'S A GOOD IDEA TO BE SO VULNERABLE AROUND OTHER PEOPLE!
WELL, I'M PRETTY SURE NO ONE ELSE'S INTERESTED IN ME, SO--
YOU DON'T KNOW THAT!
SOMEONE ELSE COULD FALL IN LOVE WITH YOU...

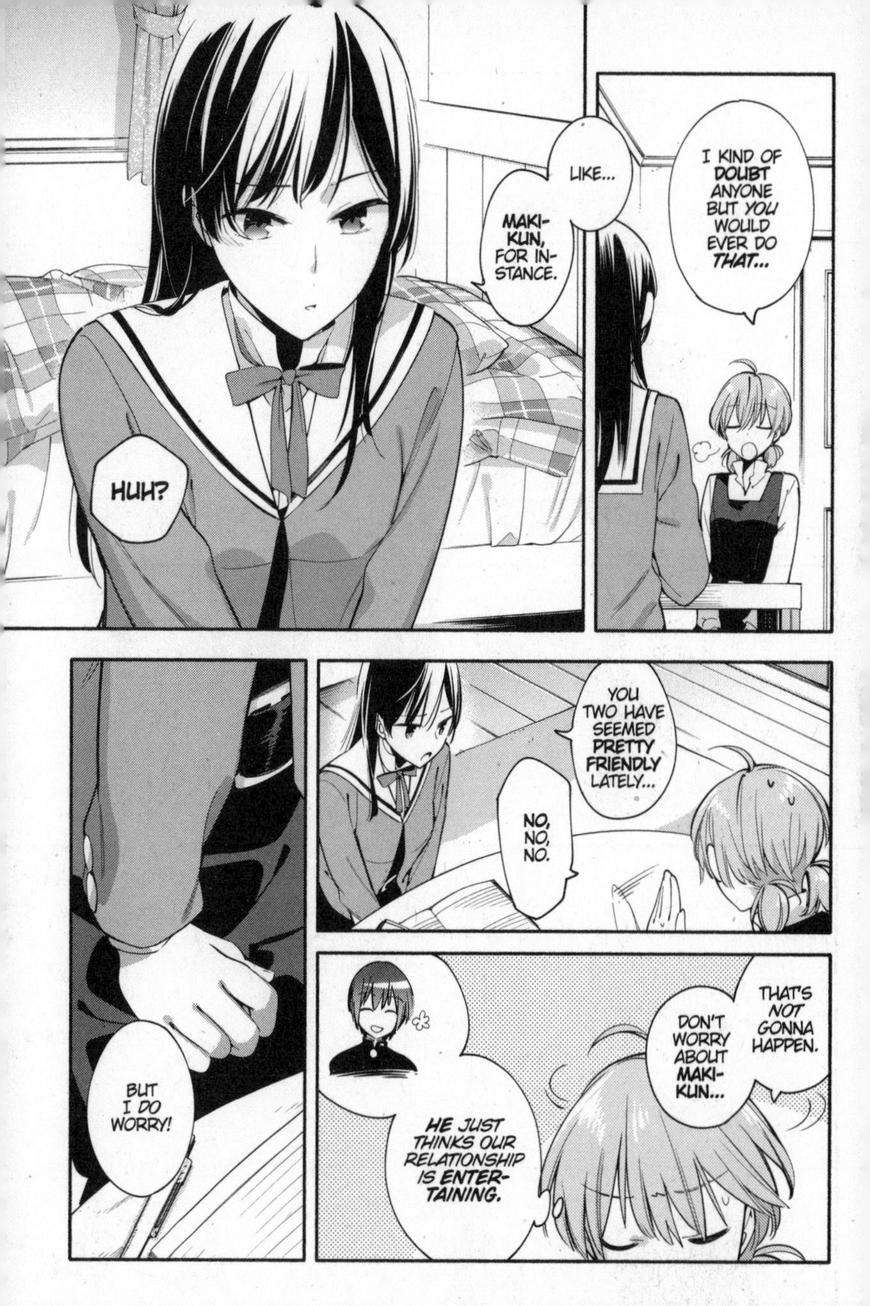
I KIND OF DOUBT ANYONE BUT YOU WOULD EVER DO THAT...
LIKE...
MAKI-KUN, FOR INSTANCE.
HUH?
YOU TWO HAVE SEEMED PRETTY FRIENDLY LATELY...
NO, NO, NO.
THAT'S NOT GONNA HAPPEN.
DON'T WORRY ABOUT MAKI-KUN...
HE JUST THINKS OUR RELATIONSHIP IS ENTERTAINING.
BUT I DO WORRY!

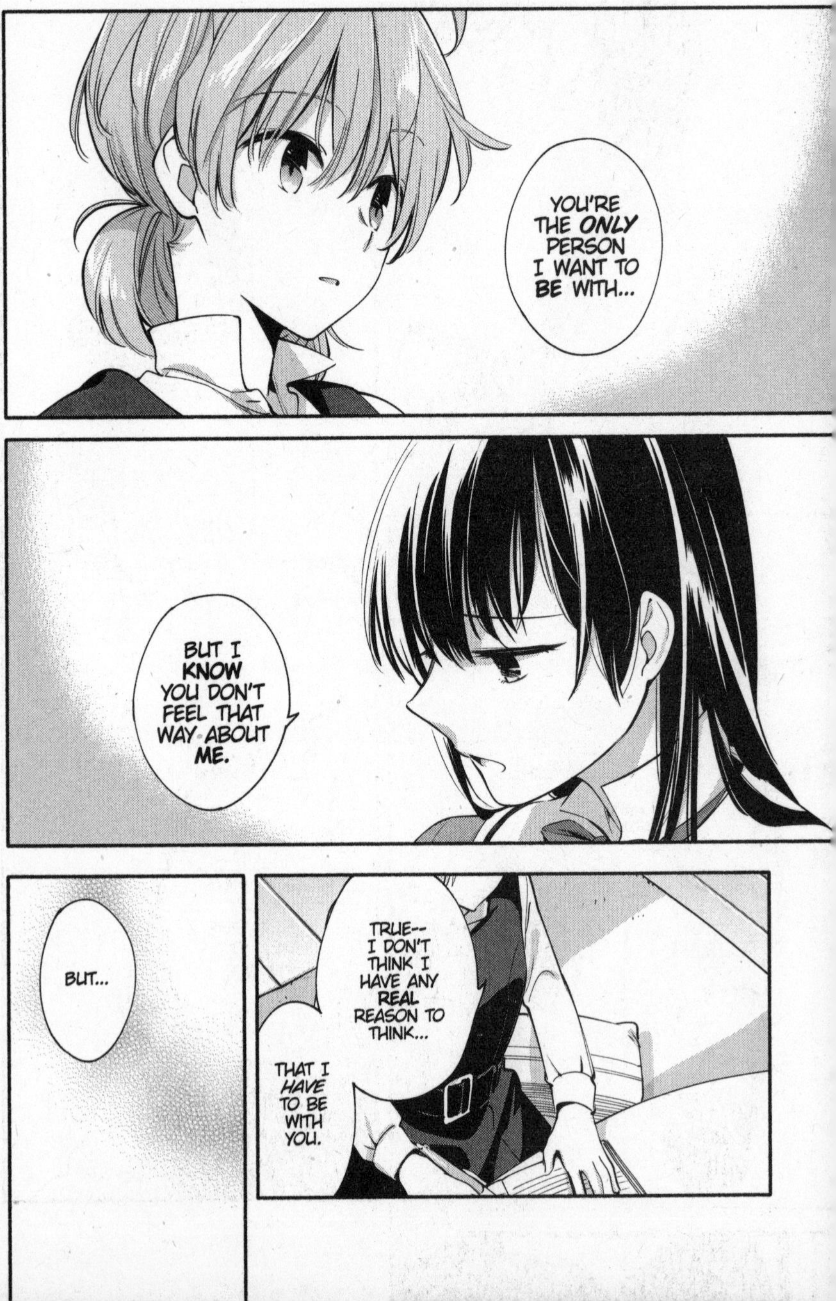
YOU'RE THE *ONLY* PERSON I WANT TO BE WITH...
BUT I KNOW YOU DON'T FEEL THAT WAY ABOUT ME.
TRUE-- I DON'T THINK I HAVE ANY REAL REASON TO THINK...
THAT I *HAVE* TO BE WITH YOU.
BUT...

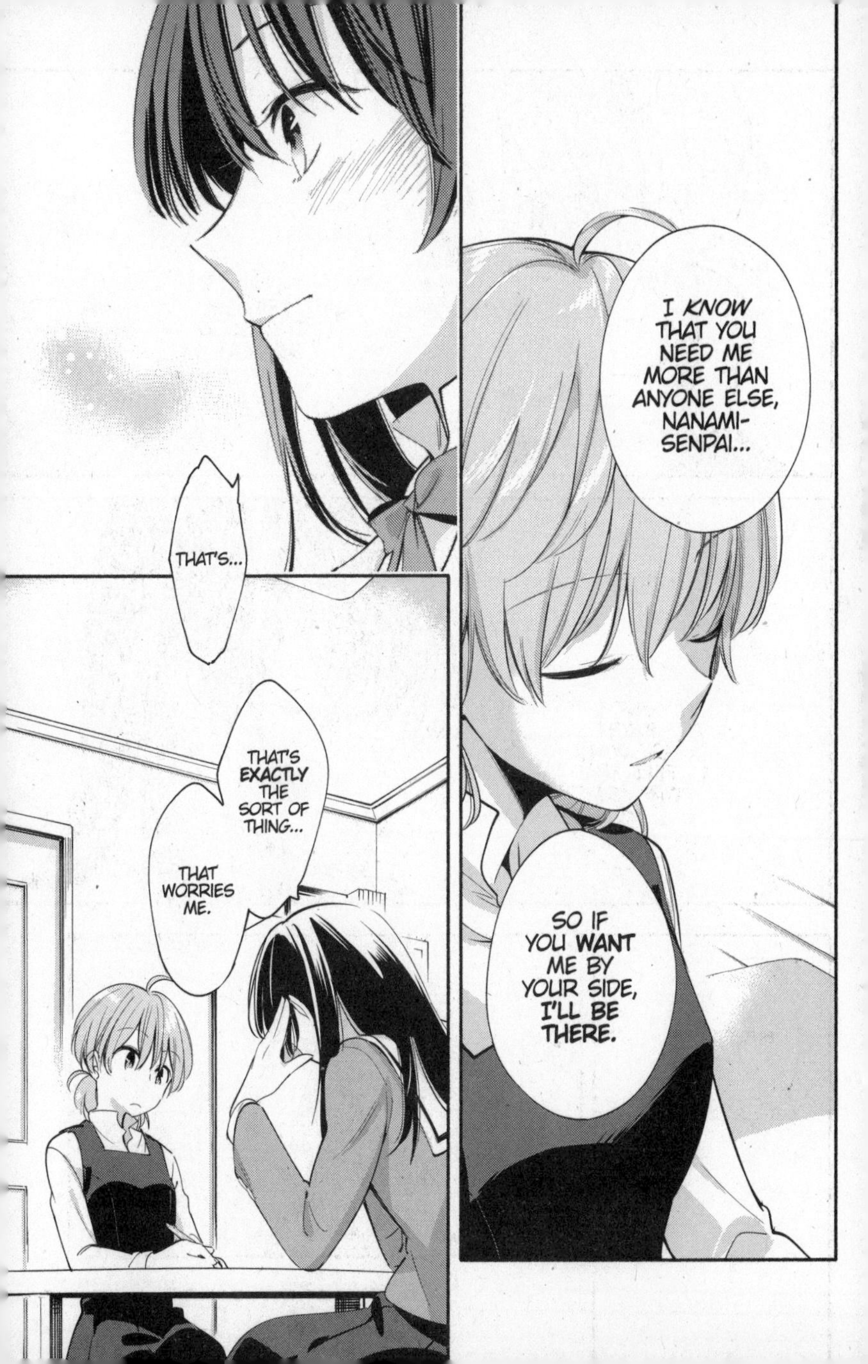
I KNOW THAT YOU NEED ME MORE THAN ANYONE ELSE, NANAMI-SENPAI...
SO IF YOU WANT ME BY YOUR SIDE, I'LL BE THERE.
THAT'S...
THAT'S EXACTLY THE SORT OF THING...
THAT WORRIES ME.

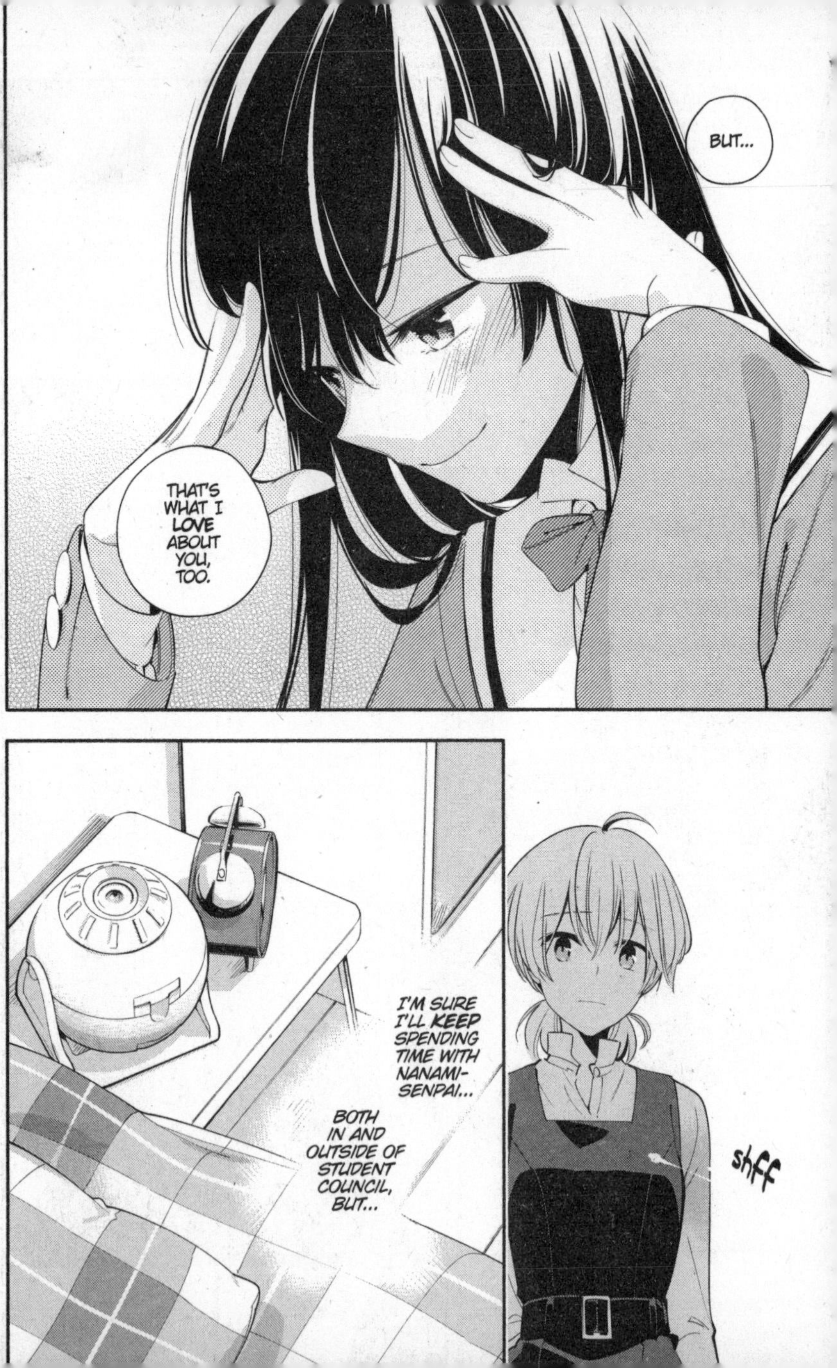
BUT...
THAT'S WHAT I LOVE ABOUT YOU, TOO.
shff
I'M SURE I'LL KEEP SPENDING TIME WITH NANAMI-SENPAI...
BOTH IN AND OUTSIDE OF STUDENT COUNCIL, BUT...

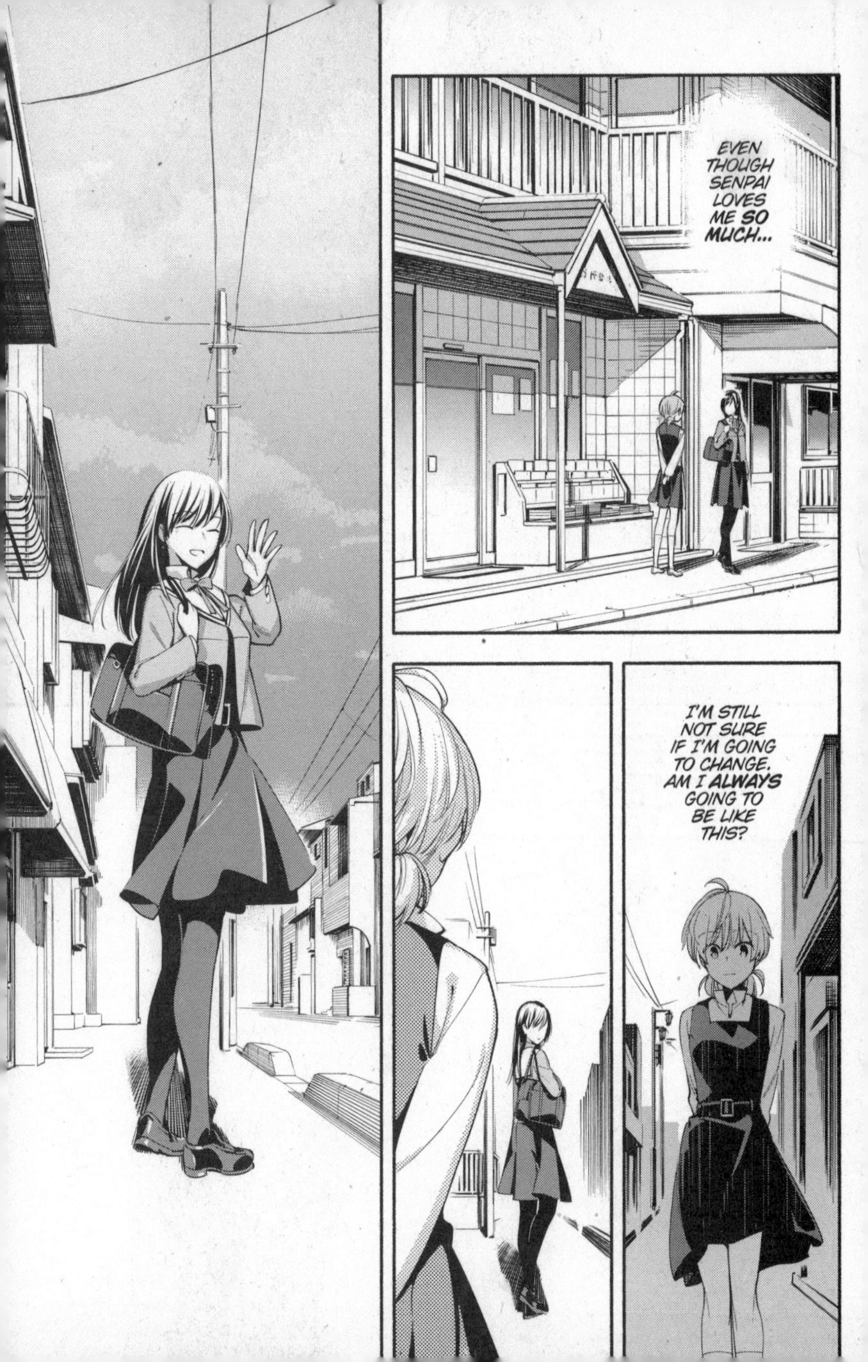
EVEN THOUGH SENPAI LOVES ME **SO MUCH...**
I'M STILL NOT SURE IF I'M GOING TO CHANGE. AM I **ALWAYS** GOING TO BE LIKE THIS?

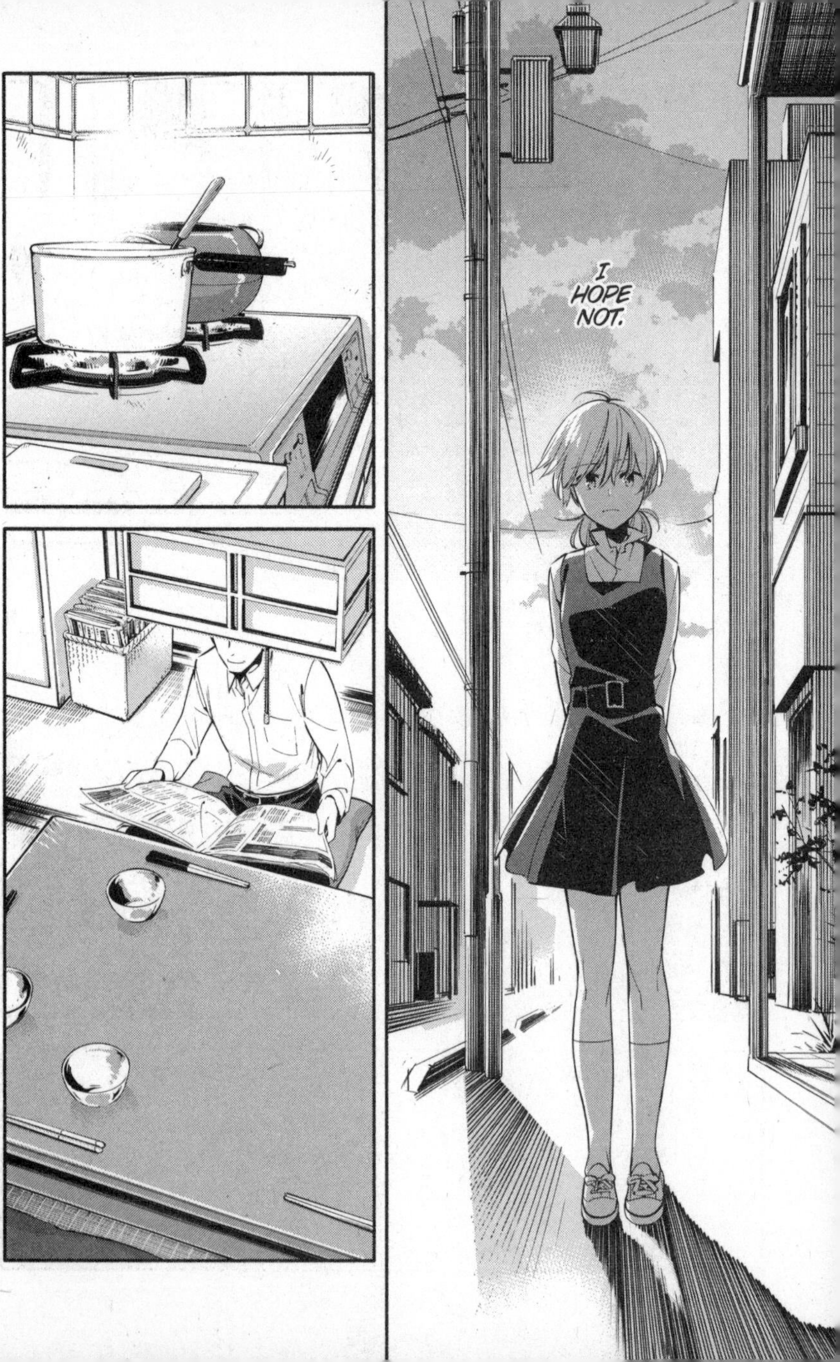
I HOPE NOT.

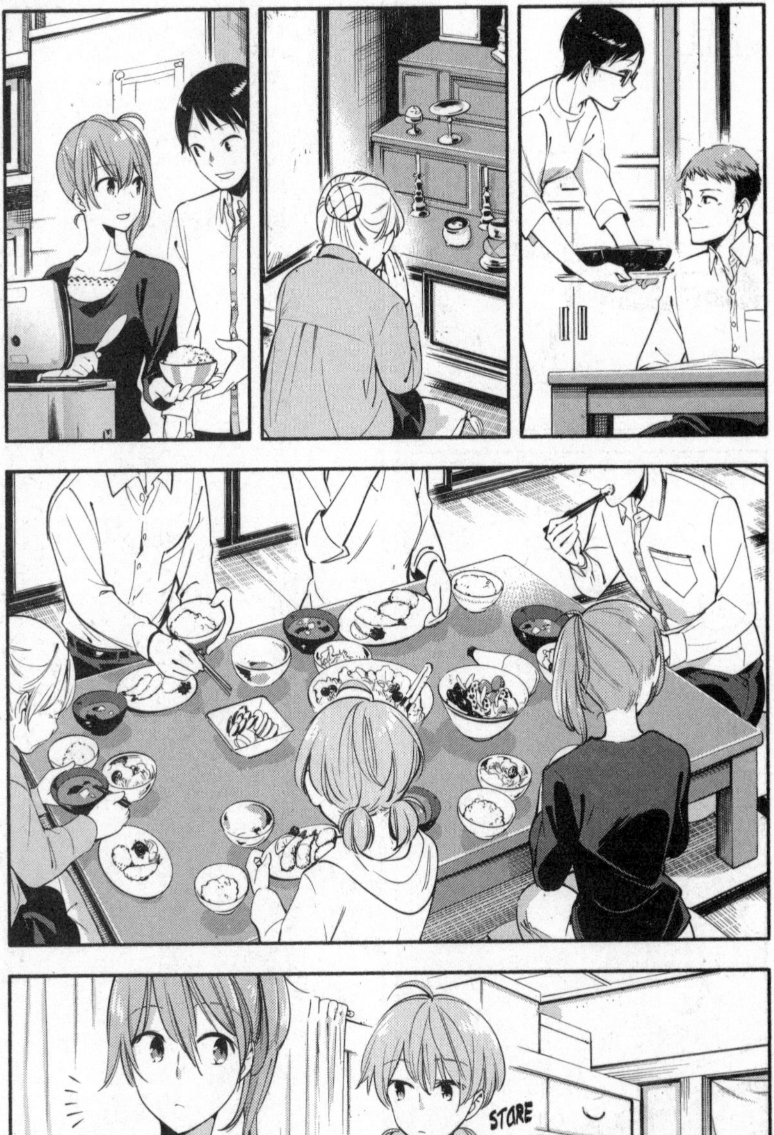
STARE

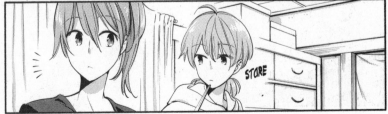

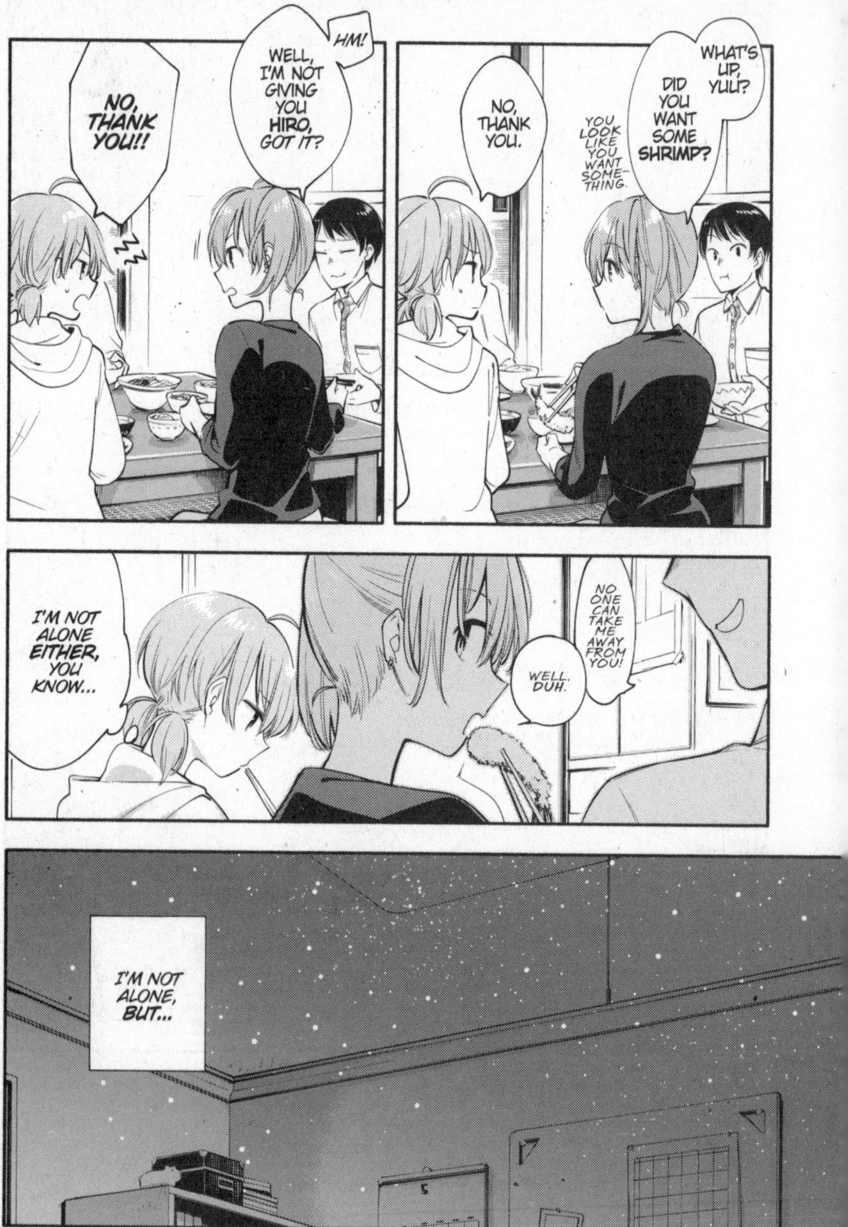
WHAT'S UP, YUU?
DID YOU WANT SOME SHRIMP?
YOU LOOK LIKE YOU WANT SOME-THING.
NO, THANK YOU.
HM!
WELL, I'M NOT GIVING YOU HIRO, GOT IT?
NO, THANK YOU!!
NO ONE CAN TAKE ME AWAY FROM YOU!
WELL, DUH.
I'M NOT ALONE EITHER, YOU KNOW...
I'M NOT ALONE, BUT...

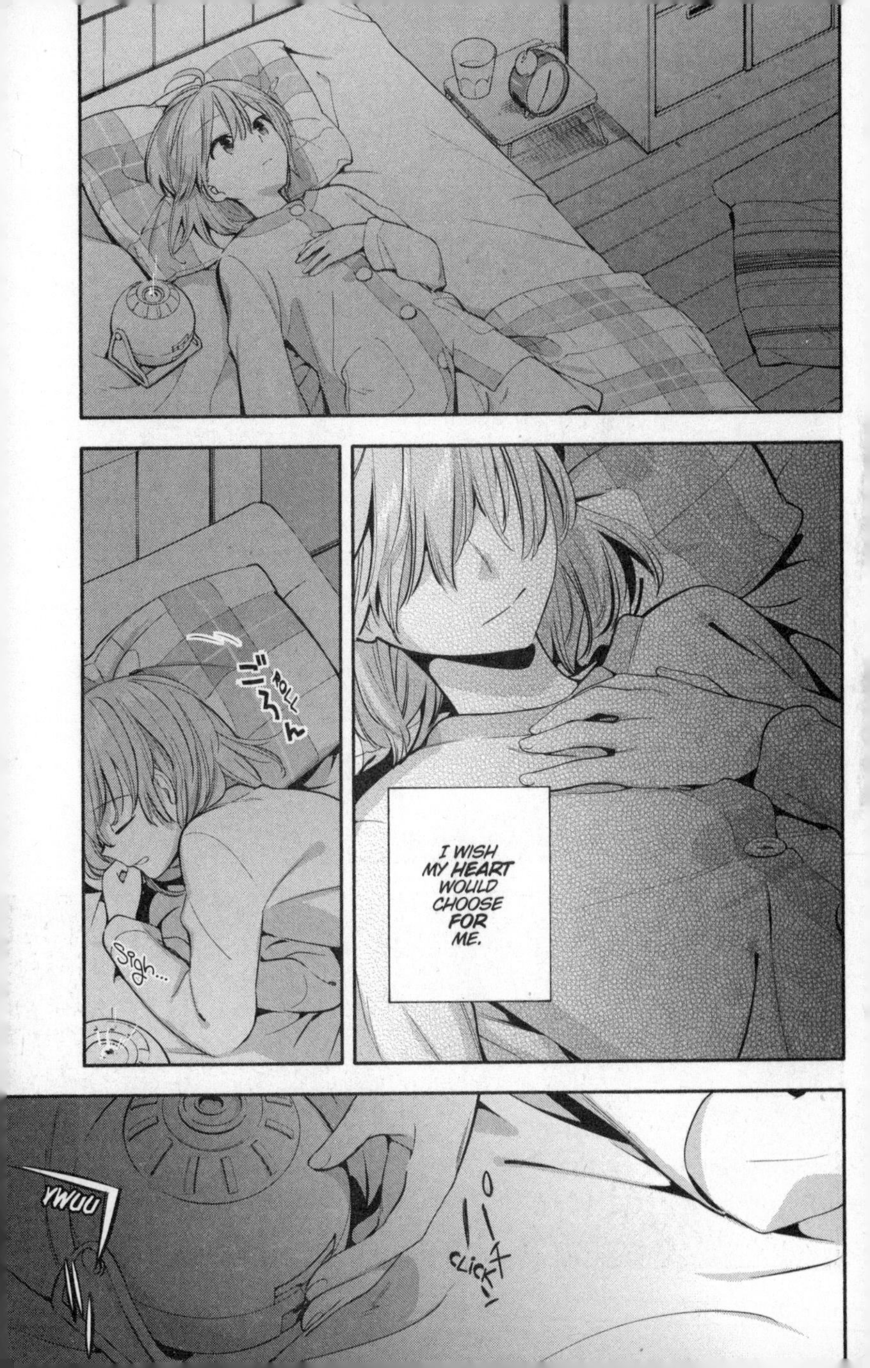
I WISH MY HEART WOULD CHOOSE FOR ME.
ROLL
Sigh...
CLICK
YWUU

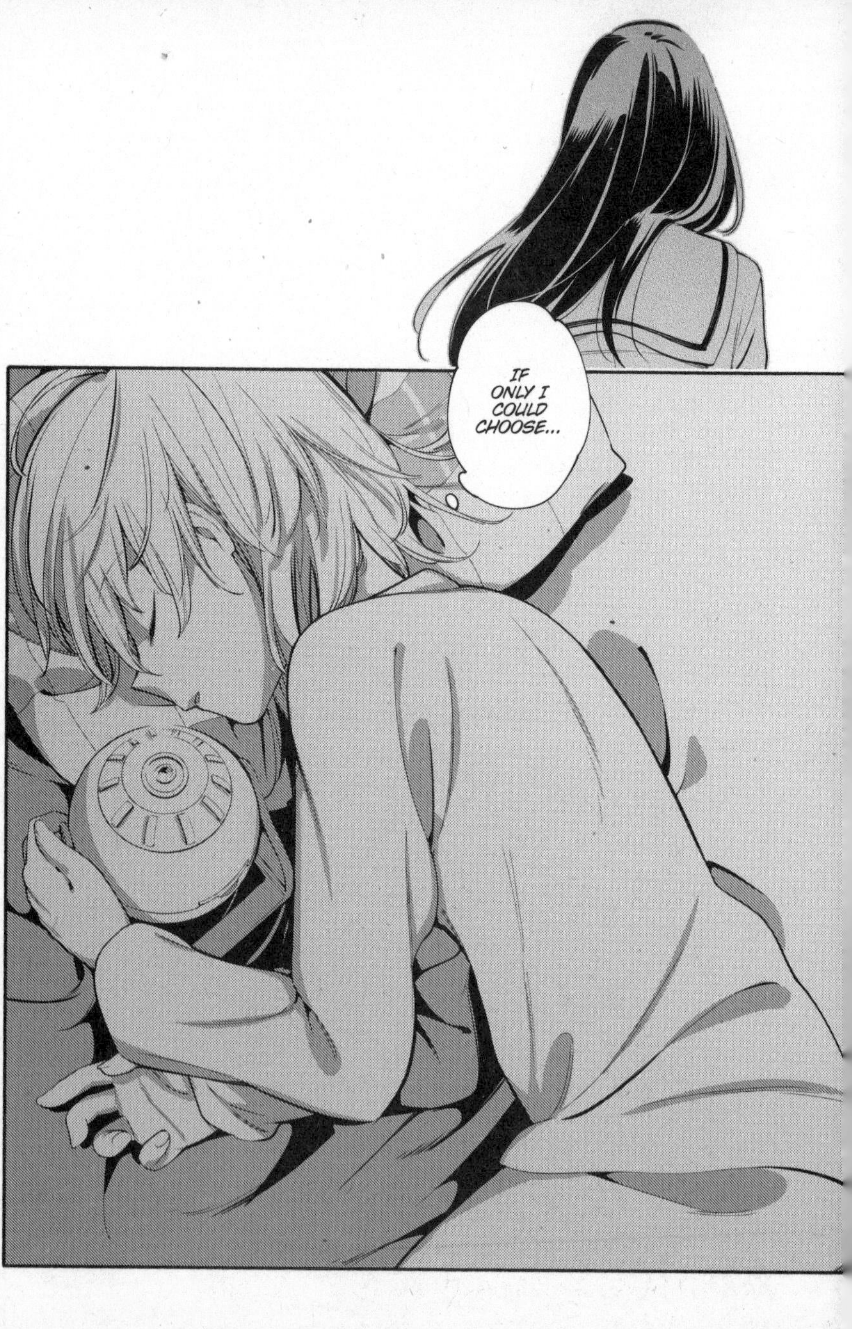
IF ONLY I COULD CHOOSE...

WE SEE EVERYTHING.

$\left( \text{several months ago} \right)$

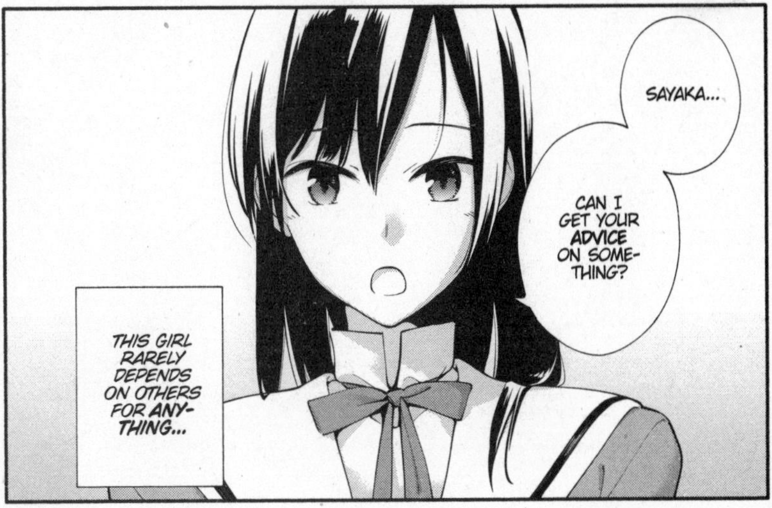
SAYAKA...
CAN I GET YOUR ADVICE ON SOME-THING?
THIS GIRL RARELY DEPENDS ON OTHERS FOR ANY-THING...

## Interlude: Before Dawn

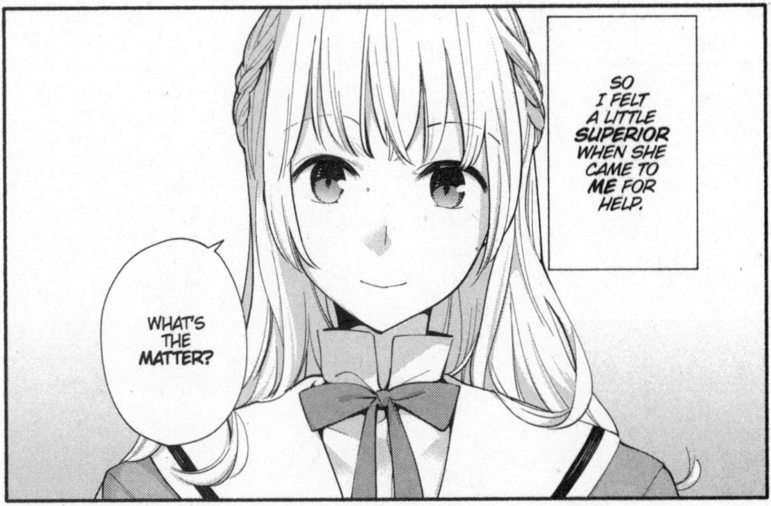
SO I FELT A LITTLE SUPERIOR WHEN SHE CAME TO ME FOR HELP.
WHAT'S THE MATTER?

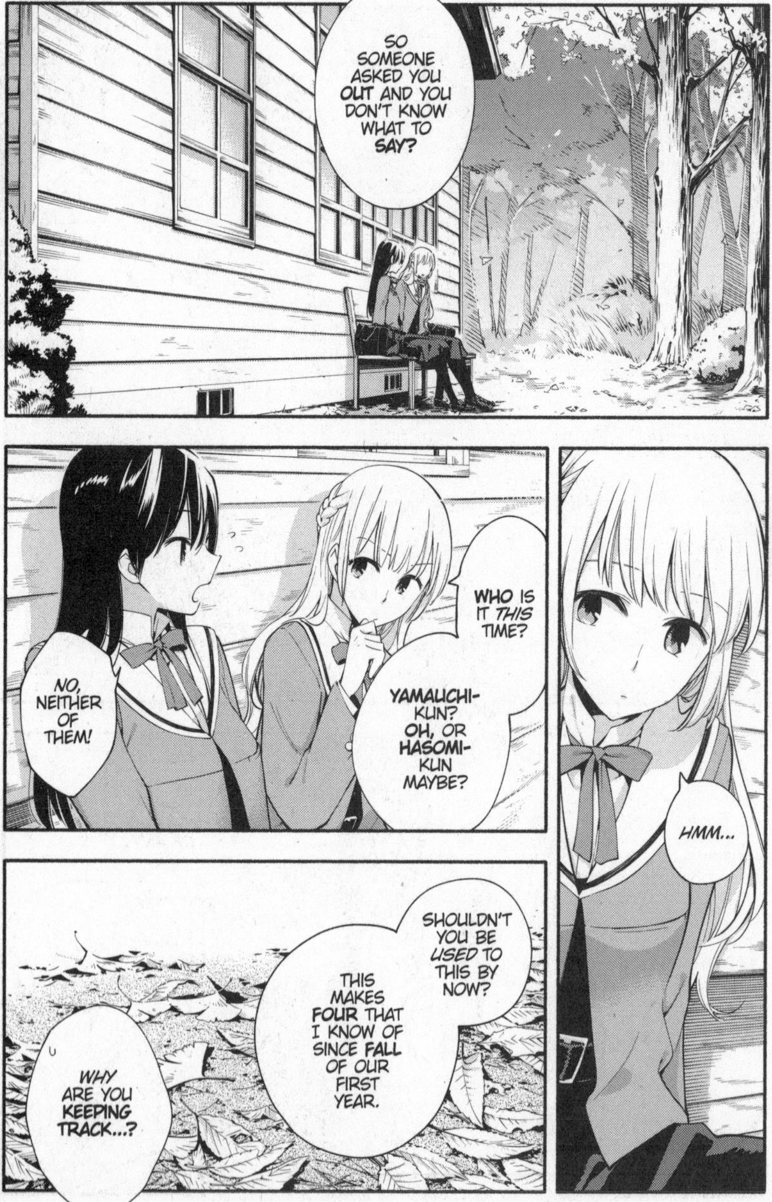
SO SOMEONE ASKED YOU OUT AND YOU DON'T KNOW WHAT TO SAY?
HMM...
WHO IS IT THIS TIME?
YAMAUCHI-KUN? OH, OR HASOMI-KUN MAYBE?
NO, NEITHER OF THEM!
SHOULDN'T YOU BE USED TO THIS BY NOW?
THIS MAKES FOUR THAT I KNOW OF SINCE FALL OF OUR FIRST YEAR.
WHY ARE YOU KEEPING TRACK...?

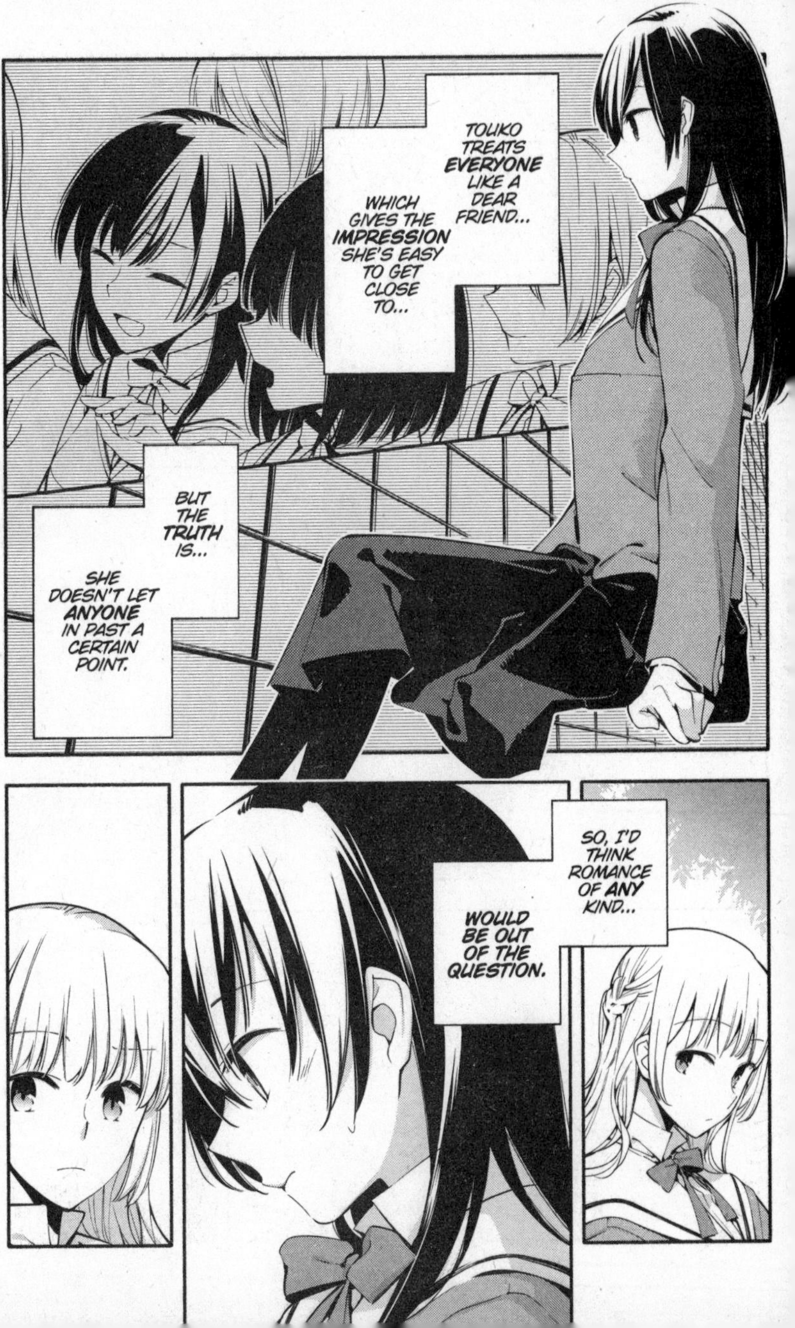
TOUKO TREATS EVERYONE LIKE A DEAR FRIEND...
WHICH GIVES THE IMPRESSION SHE'S EASY TO GET CLOSE TO...
BUT THE TRUTH IS...
SHE DOESN'T LET ANYONE IN PAST A CERTAIN POINT.
SO, I'D THINK ROMANCE OF ANY KIND...
WOULD BE OUT OF THE QUESTION.

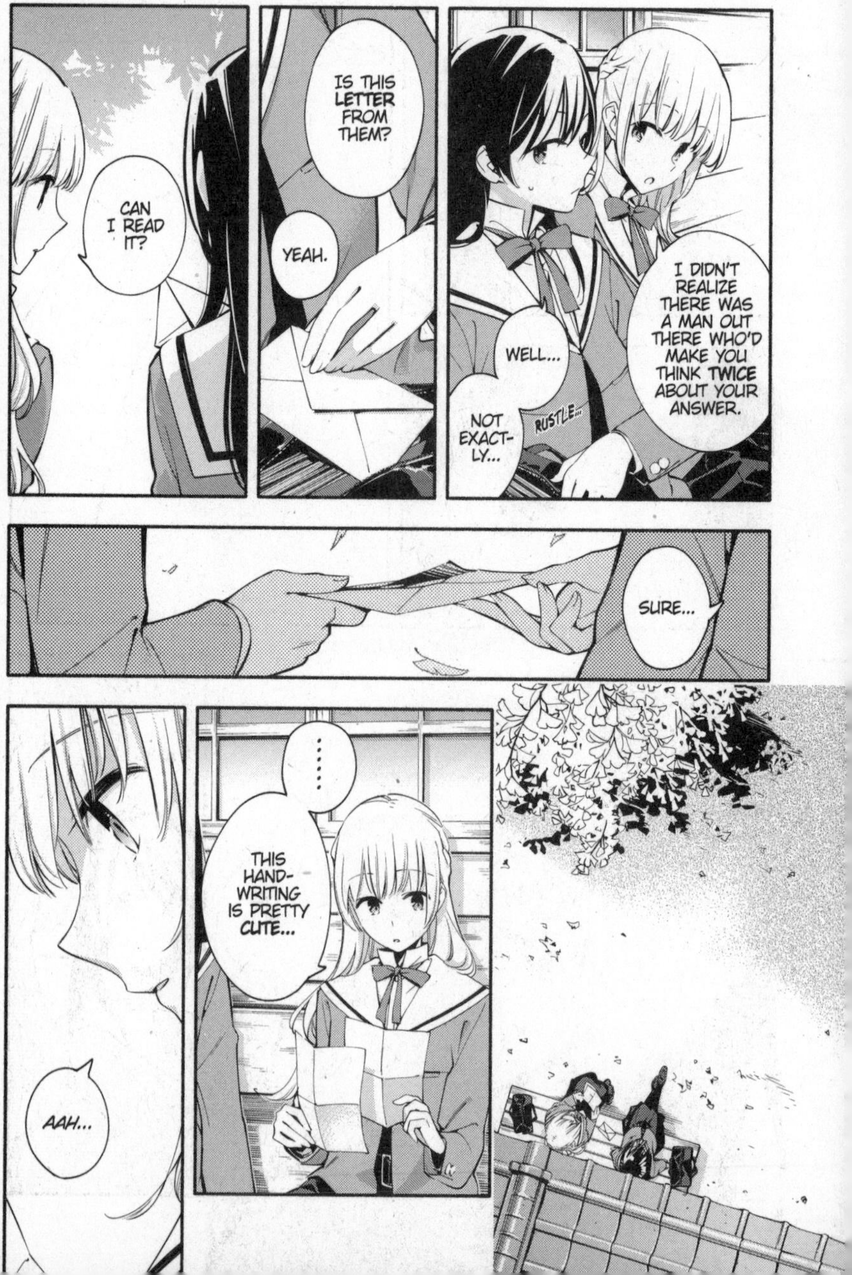
I DIDN'T REALIZE THERE WAS A MAN OUT THERE WHO'D MAKE YOU THINK TWICE ABOUT YOUR ANSWER.
WELL...
RUSTLE...
NOT EXACT-LY...
IS THIS LETTER FROM THEM?
YEAH.
CAN I READ IT?
SURE...
......
THIS HAND-WRITING IS PRETTY CUTE...
AAH...

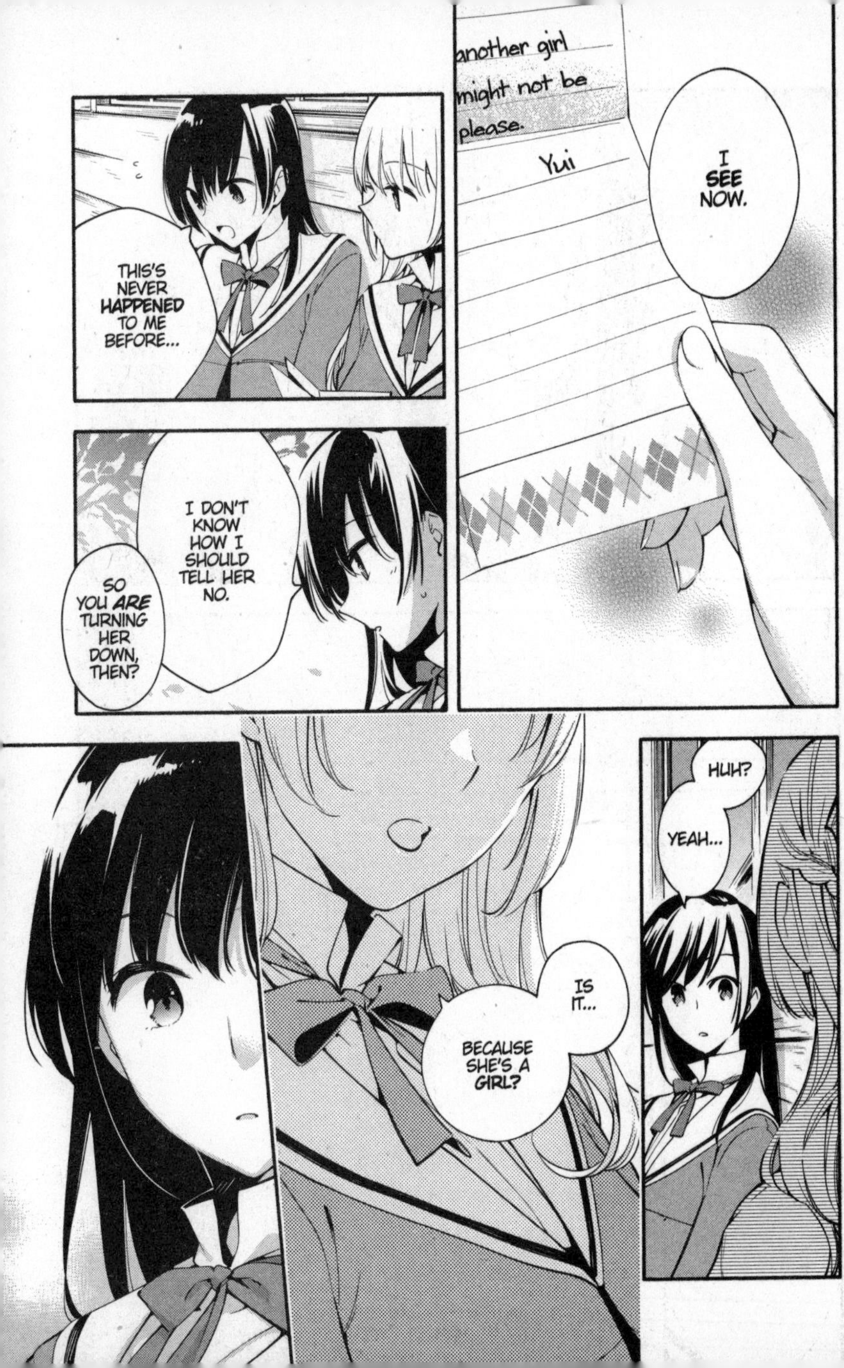
another girl
might not be
please.
Yui
I SEE NOW.
THIS'S NEVER HAPPENED TO ME BEFORE...
I DON'T KNOW HOW I SHOULD TELL HER NO.
SO YOU ARE TURNING HER DOWN, THEN?
HUH?
YEAH...
IS IT...
BECAUSE SHE'S A GIRL?

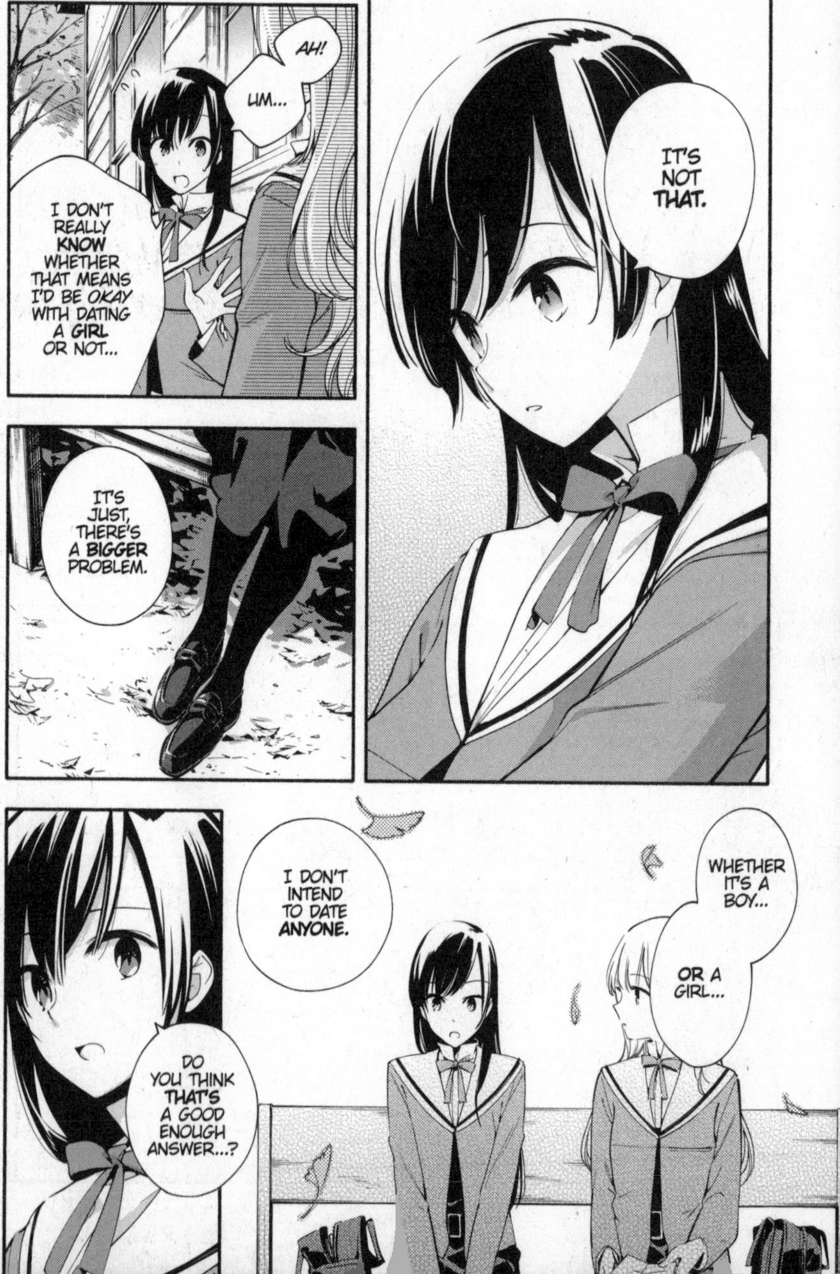
IT'S NOT THAT.
AH!
UM...
I DON'T REALLY KNOW WHETHER THAT MEANS I'D BE OKAY WITH DATING A GIRL OR NOT...
IT'S JUST, THERE'S A BIGGER PROBLEM.
WHETHER IT'S A BOY...
OR A GIRL...
I DON'T INTEND TO DATE ANYONE.
DO YOU THINK THAT'S A GOOD ENOUGH ANSWER...?

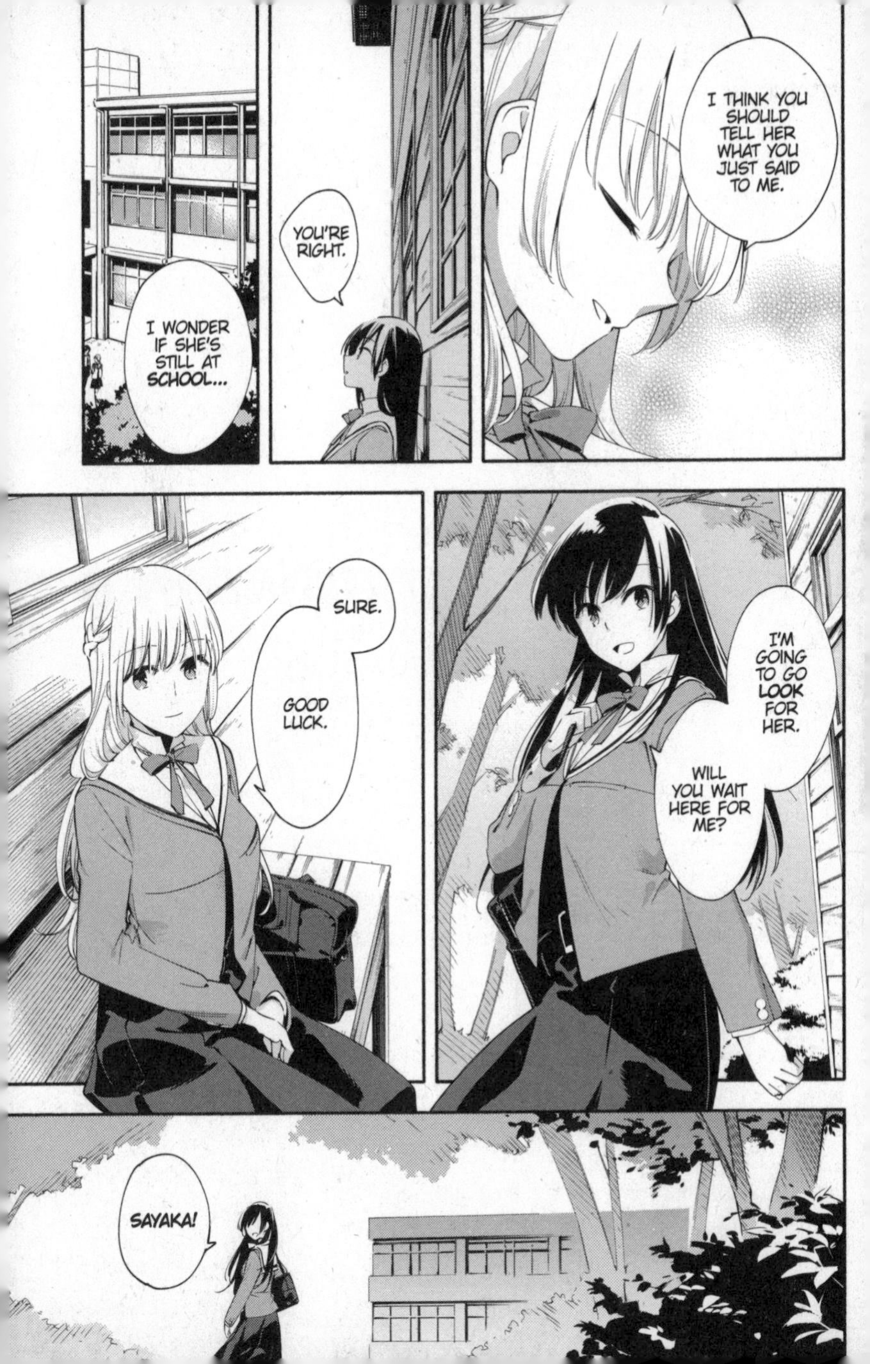
I THINK YOU SHOULD TELL HER WHAT YOU JUST SAID TO ME.
YOU'RE RIGHT.
I WONDER IF SHE'S STILL AT SCHOOL...
I'M GOING TO GO LOOK FOR HER.
WILL YOU WAIT HERE FOR ME?
SURE.
GOOD LUCK.
SAYAKA!

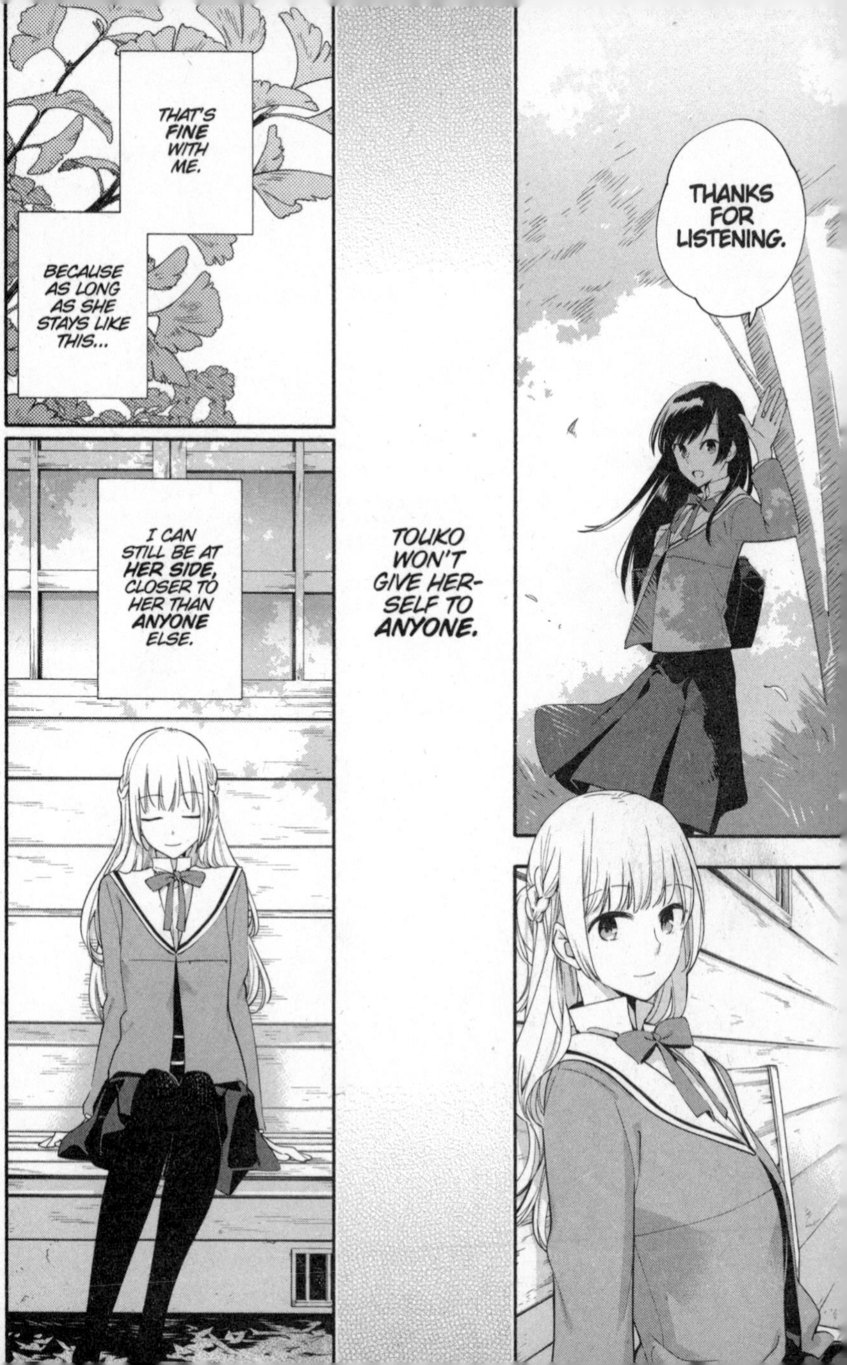
THANKS FOR LISTENING.
TOUKO WON'T GIVE HER-SELF TO ANYONE.
THAT'S FINE WITH ME.
BECAUSE AS LONG AS SHE STAYS LIKE THIS...
I CAN STILL BE AT HER SIDE, CLOSER TO HER THAN ANYONE ELSE.

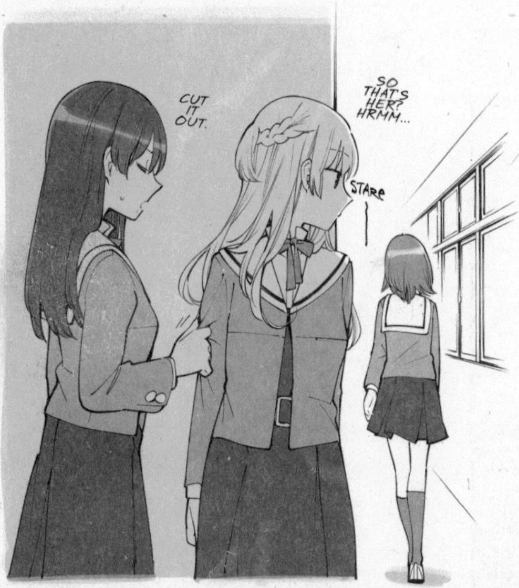
SO THAT'S HER? HRMM...
CUT IT OUT.
STARE

( **Bloom Into You** )

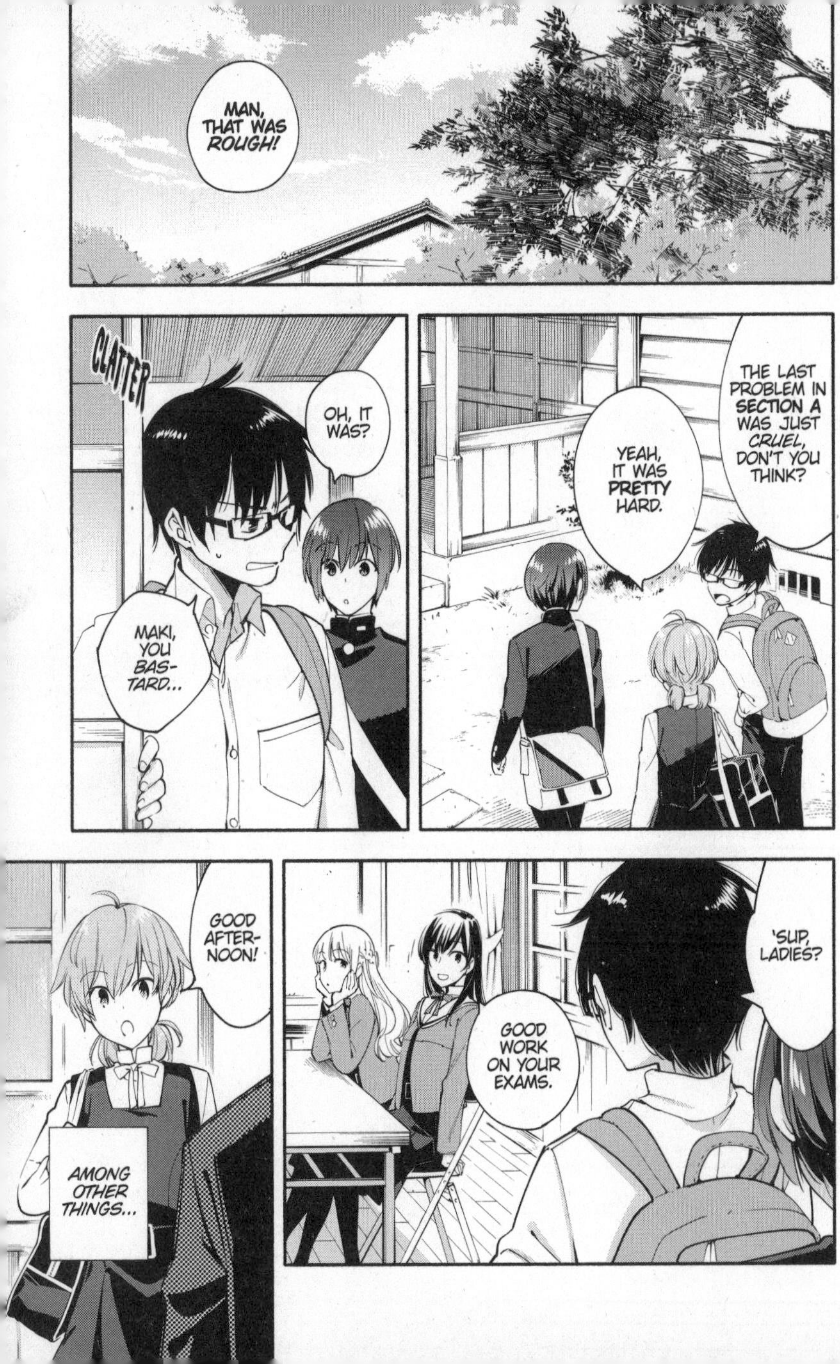
MAN, THAT WAS ROUGH!
THE LAST PROBLEM IN SECTION A WAS JUST CRUEL, DON'T YOU THINK?
YEAH, IT WAS PRETTY HARD.
OH, IT WAS?
CLATTER
MAKI, YOU BAS-TARD...
'SUP, LADIES?
GOOD WORK ON YOUR EXAMS.
GOOD AFTER-NOON!
AMONG OTHER THINGS...

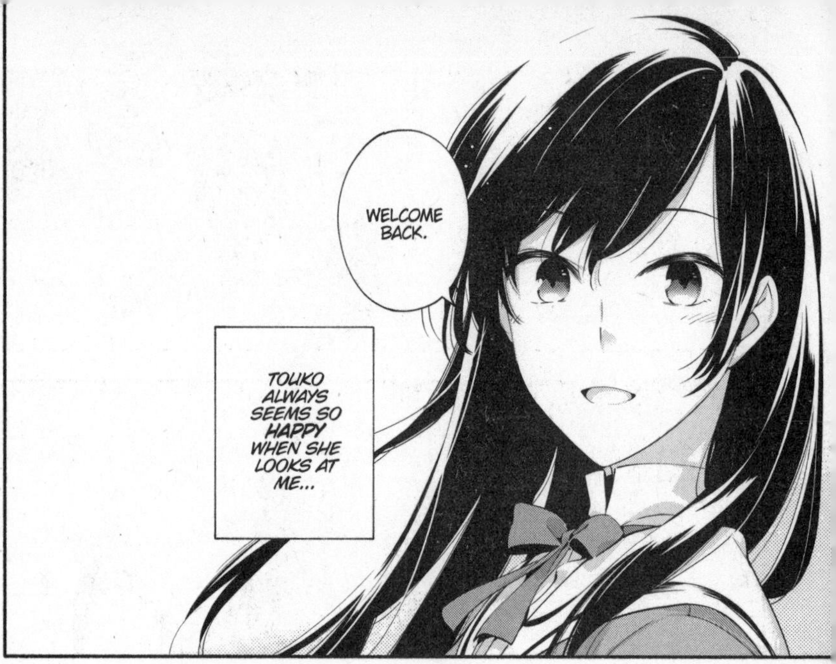
WELCOME BACK.
TOUKO ALWAYS SEEMS SO HAPPY WHEN SHE LOOKS AT ME...

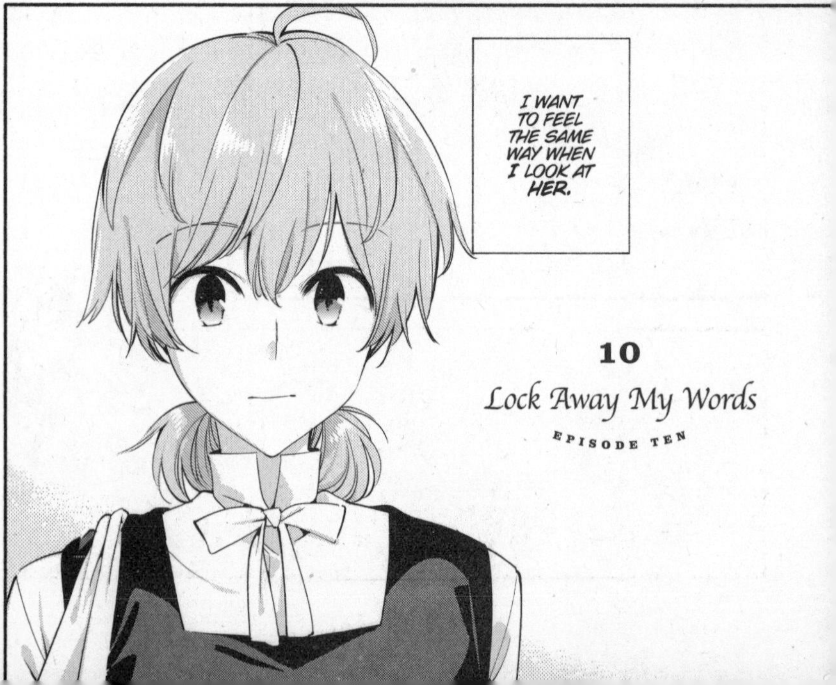
I WANT TO FEEL THE SAME WAY WHEN I LOOK AT HER.

# 10
# Lock Away My Words
EPISODE TEN

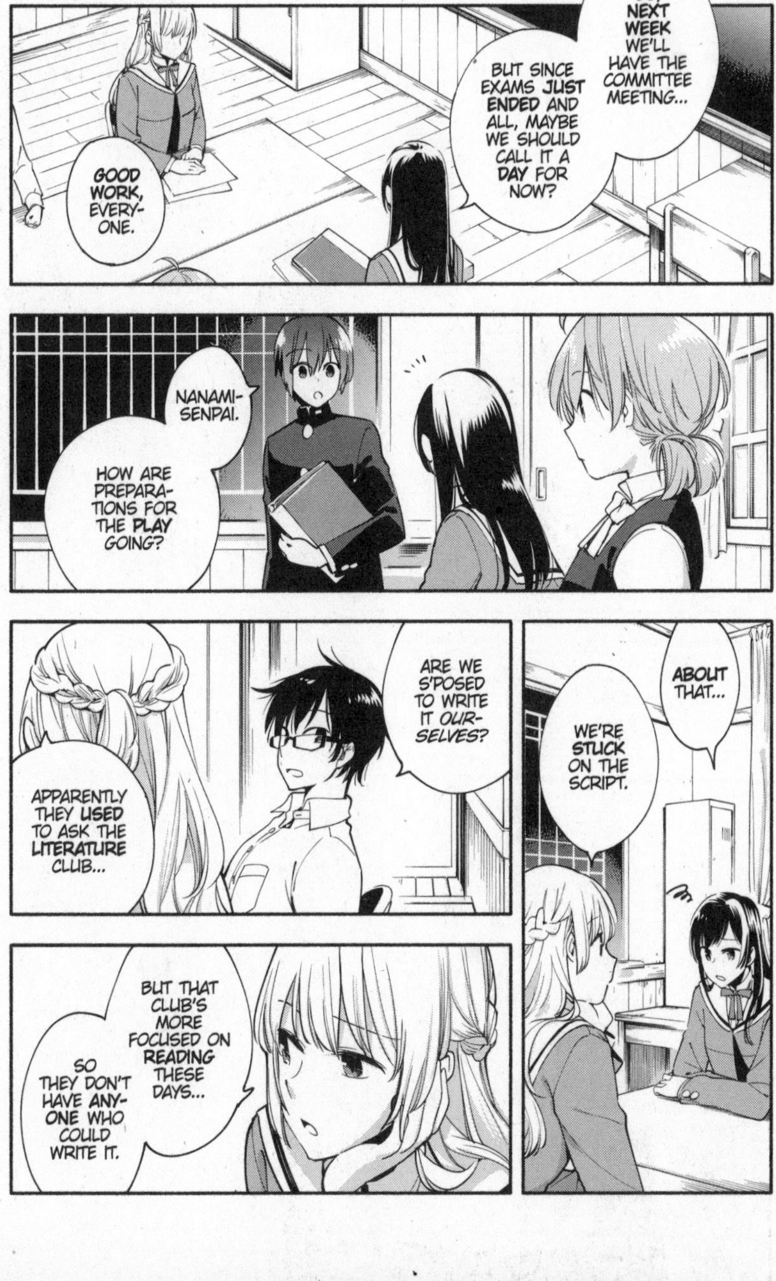
SO, NEXT WEEK WE'LL HAVE THE COMMITTEE MEETING...
BUT SINCE EXAMS JUST ENDED AND ALL, MAYBE WE SHOULD CALL IT A DAY FOR NOW?
GOOD WORK, EVERY-ONE.
NANAMI-SENPAI.
HOW ARE PREPARA-TIONS FOR THE PLAY GOING?
ABOUT THAT...
WE'RE STUCK ON THE SCRIPT.
ARE WE S'POSED TO WRITE IT OUR-SELVES?
APPARENTLY THEY USED TO ASK THE LITERATURE CLUB...
BUT THAT CLUB'S MORE FOCUSED ON READING THESE DAYS...
SO THEY DON'T HAVE ANY-ONE WHO COULD WRITE IT.

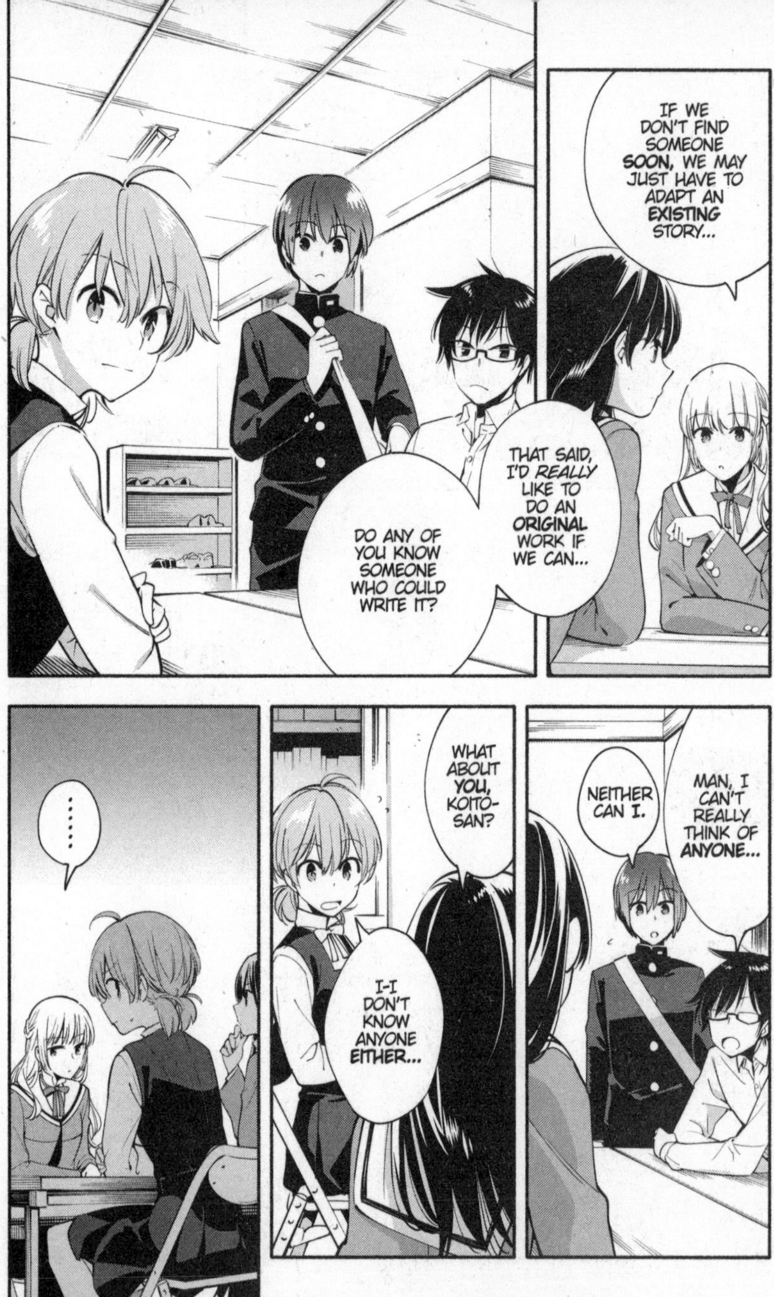
IF WE DON'T FIND SOMEONE SOON, WE MAY JUST HAVE TO ADAPT AN EXISTING STORY...
THAT SAID, I'D REALLY LIKE TO DO AN ORIGINAL WORK IF WE CAN...
DO ANY OF YOU KNOW SOMEONE WHO COULD WRITE IT?
MAN, I CAN'T REALLY THINK OF ANYONE...
NEITHER CAN I.
WHAT ABOUT YOU, KOITO-SAN?
I-I DON'T KNOW ANYONE EITHER...
......

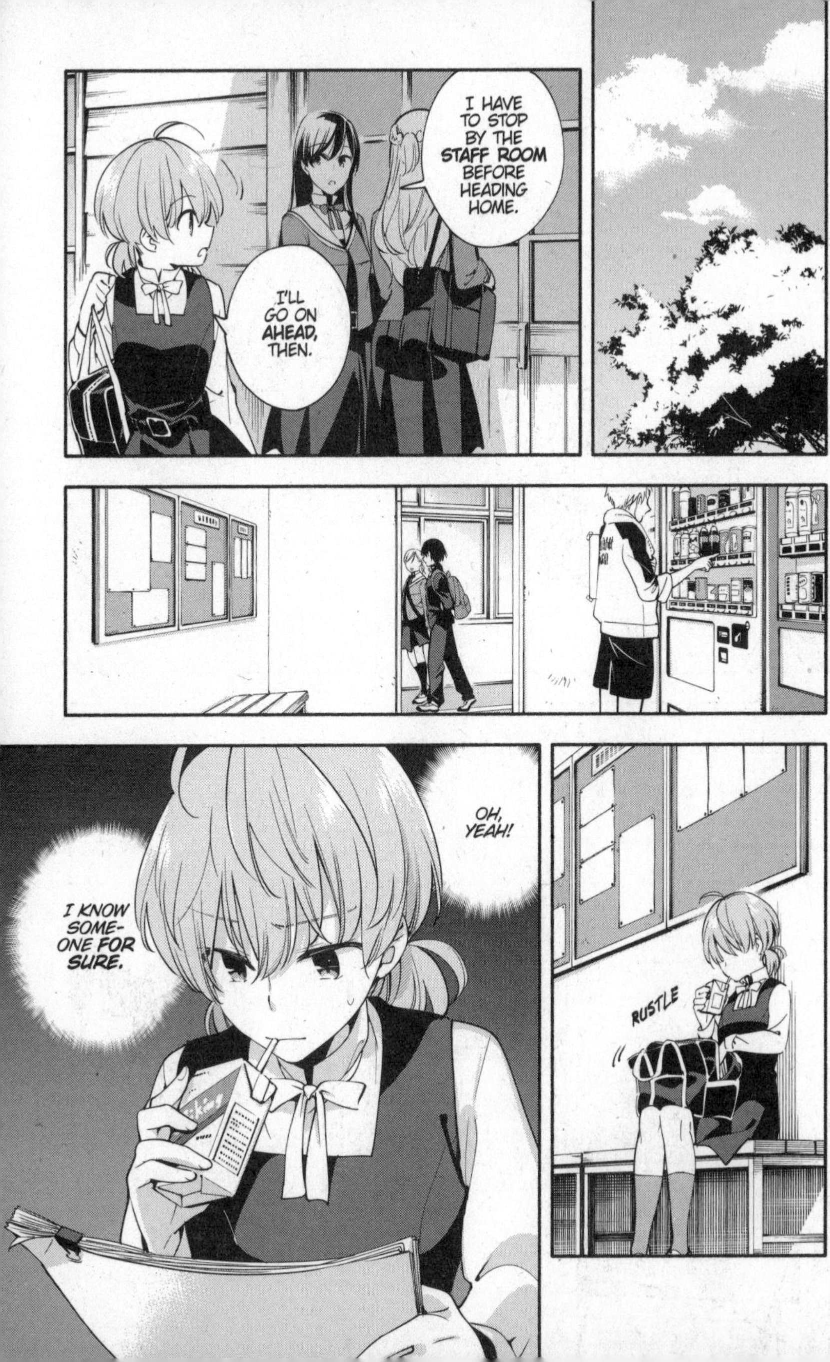
I HAVE TO STOP BY THE STAFF ROOM BEFORE HEADING HOME.
I'LL GO ON AHEAD, THEN.
RUSTLE
OH, YEAH!
I KNOW SOME-ONE FOR SURE.

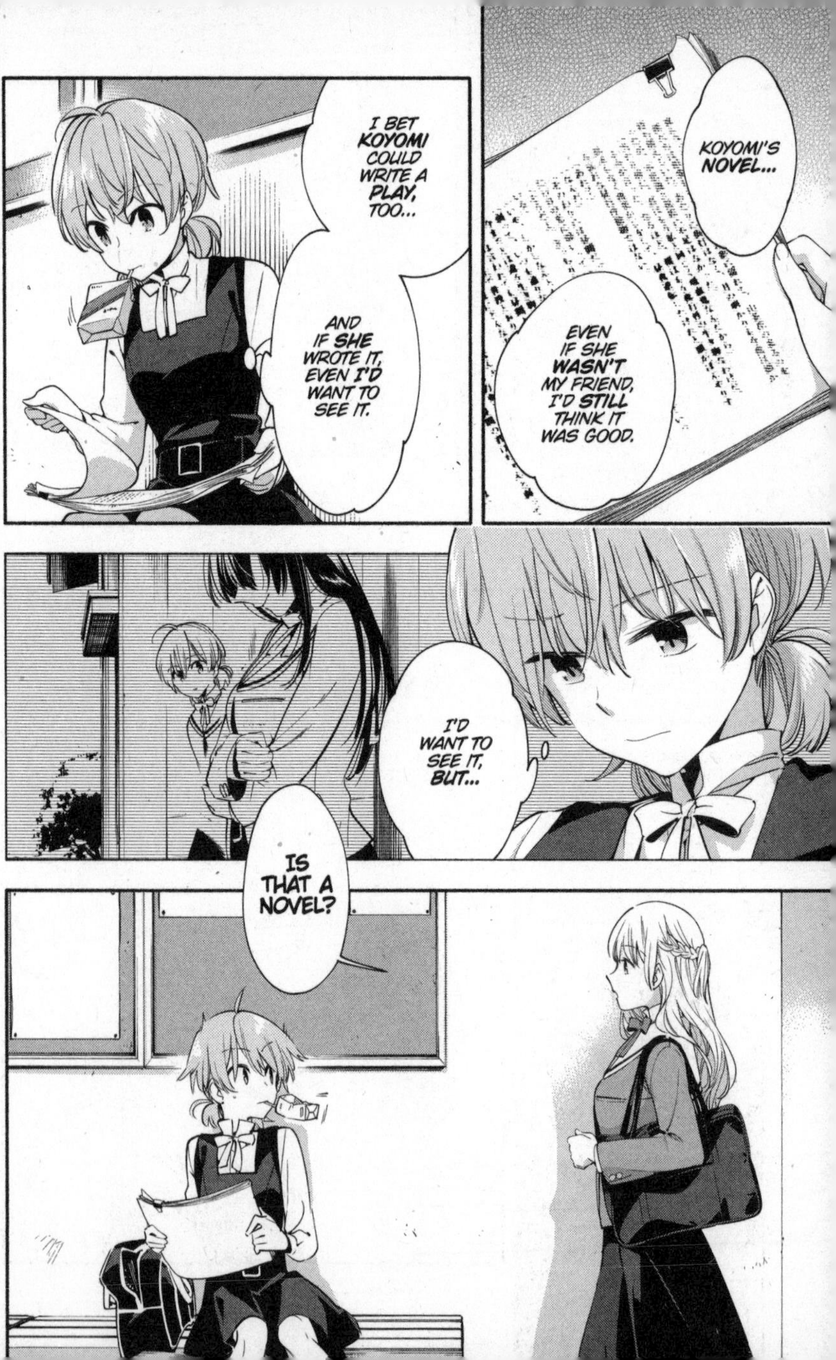
KOYOMI'S NOVEL...
EVEN IF SHE WASN'T MY FRIEND, I'D STILL THINK IT WAS GOOD.
I BET KOYOMI COULD WRITE A PLAY, TOO...
AND IF SHE WROTE IT, EVEN I'D WANT TO SEE IT.
I'D WANT TO SEE IT, BUT...
IS THAT A NOVEL?

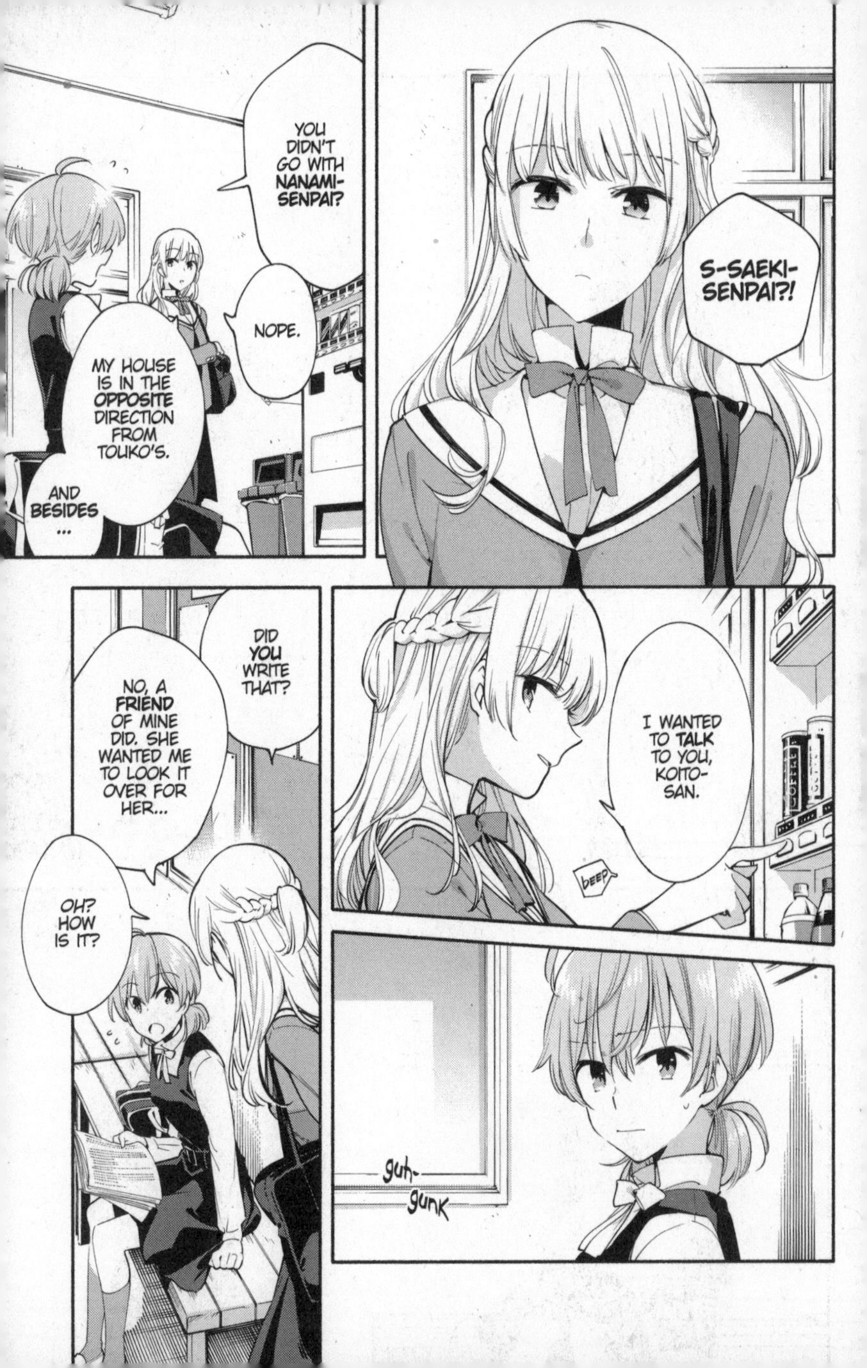
S-SAEKI-SENPAI?!
YOU DIDN'T GO WITH NANAMI-SENPAI?
NOPE.
MY HOUSE IS IN THE OPPOSITE DIRECTION FROM TOUKO'S.
AND BESIDES...
I WANTED TO TALK TO YOU, KOITO-SAN.
beep
guh-gunk
DID YOU WRITE THAT?
NO, A FRIEND OF MINE DID. SHE WANTED ME TO LOOK IT OVER FOR HER...
OH? HOW IS IT?

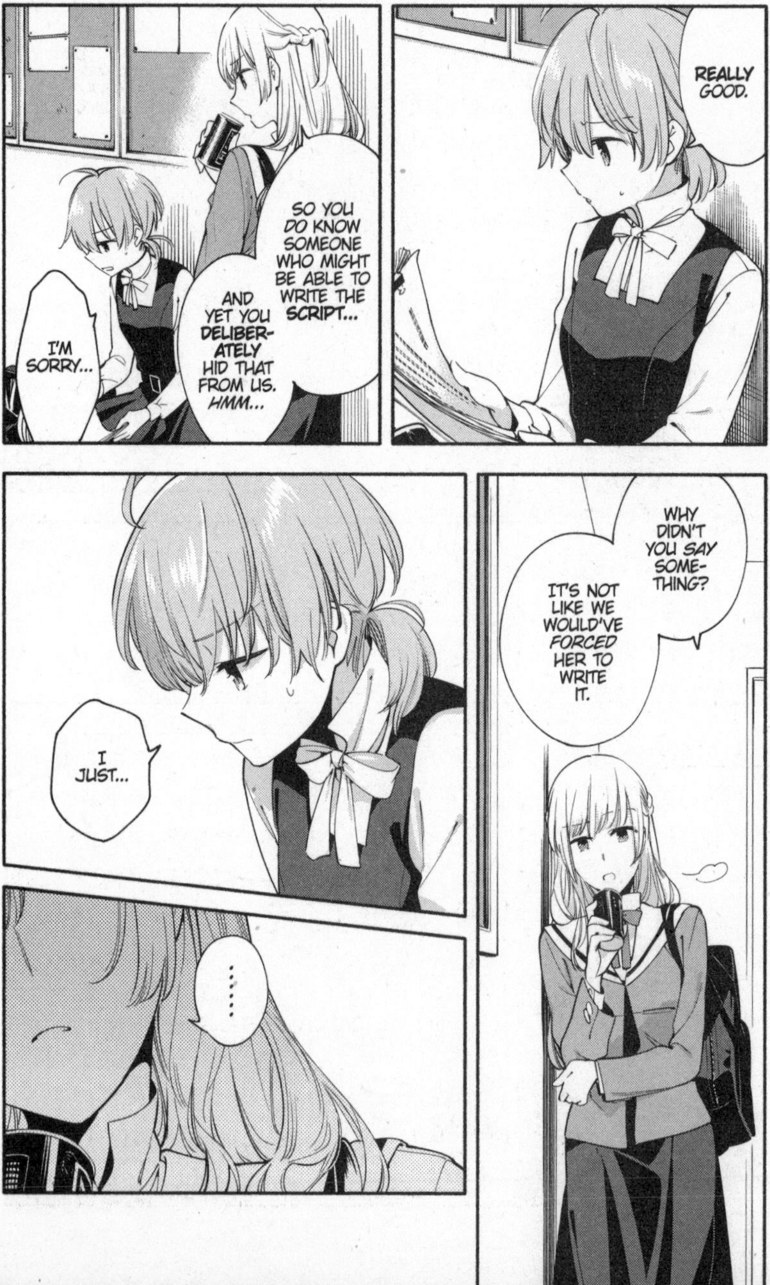
REALLY GOOD.
SO YOU *DO* KNOW SOMEONE WHO MIGHT BE ABLE TO WRITE THE **SCRIPT...**
AND YET YOU **DELIBERATELY** HID THAT FROM US. *HMM...*
I'M SORRY...
WHY DIDN'T YOU *SAY* SOMETHING?
IT'S NOT LIKE WE WOULD'VE *FORCED* HER TO WRITE IT.
I JUST...
......

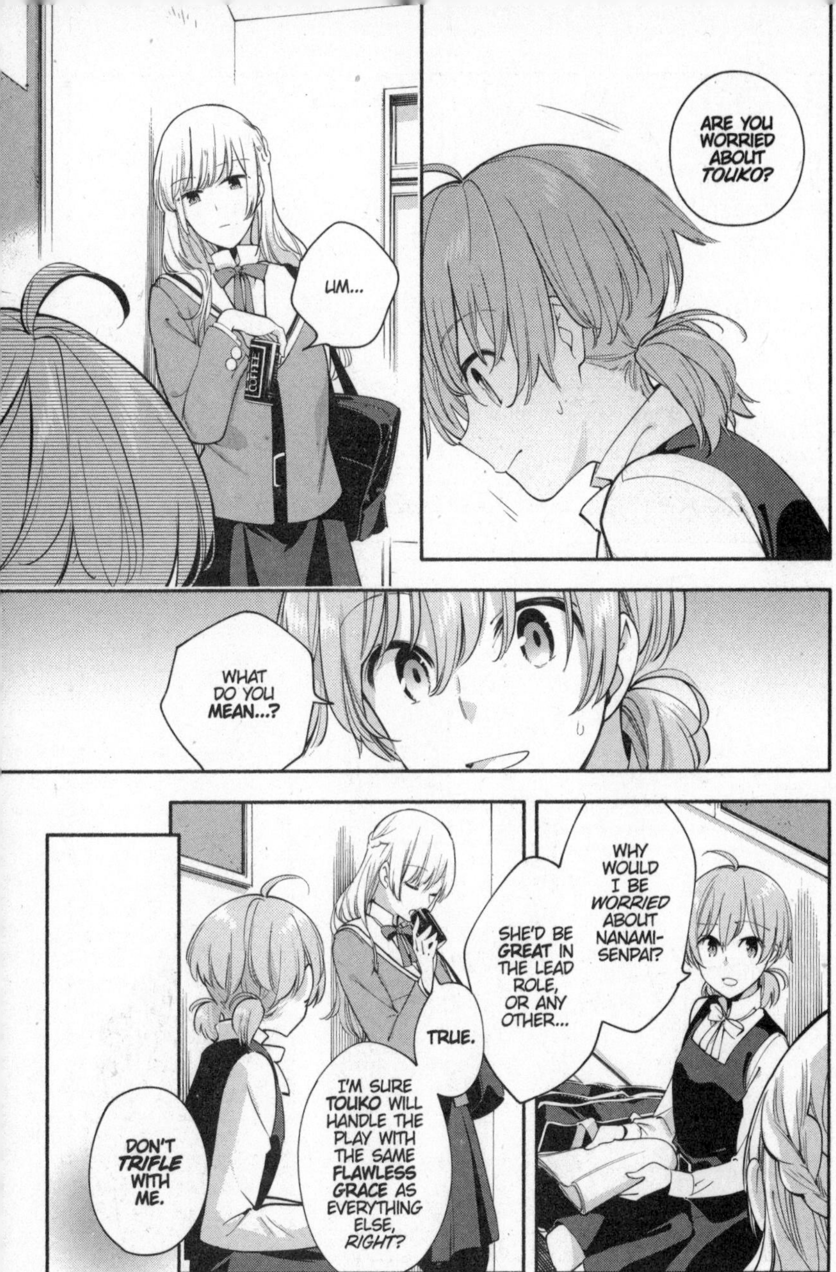

ARE YOU WORRIED ABOUT TOUKO?
UM...
COFFEE
WHAT DO YOU MEAN...?
WHY WOULD I BE WORRIED ABOUT NANAMI-SENPAI?
SHE'D BE GREAT IN THE LEAD ROLE, OR ANY OTHER...
TRUE.
I'M SURE TOUKO WILL HANDLE THE PLAY WITH THE SAME FLAWLESS GRACE AS EVERYTHING ELSE, RIGHT?
DON'T TRIFLE WITH ME.

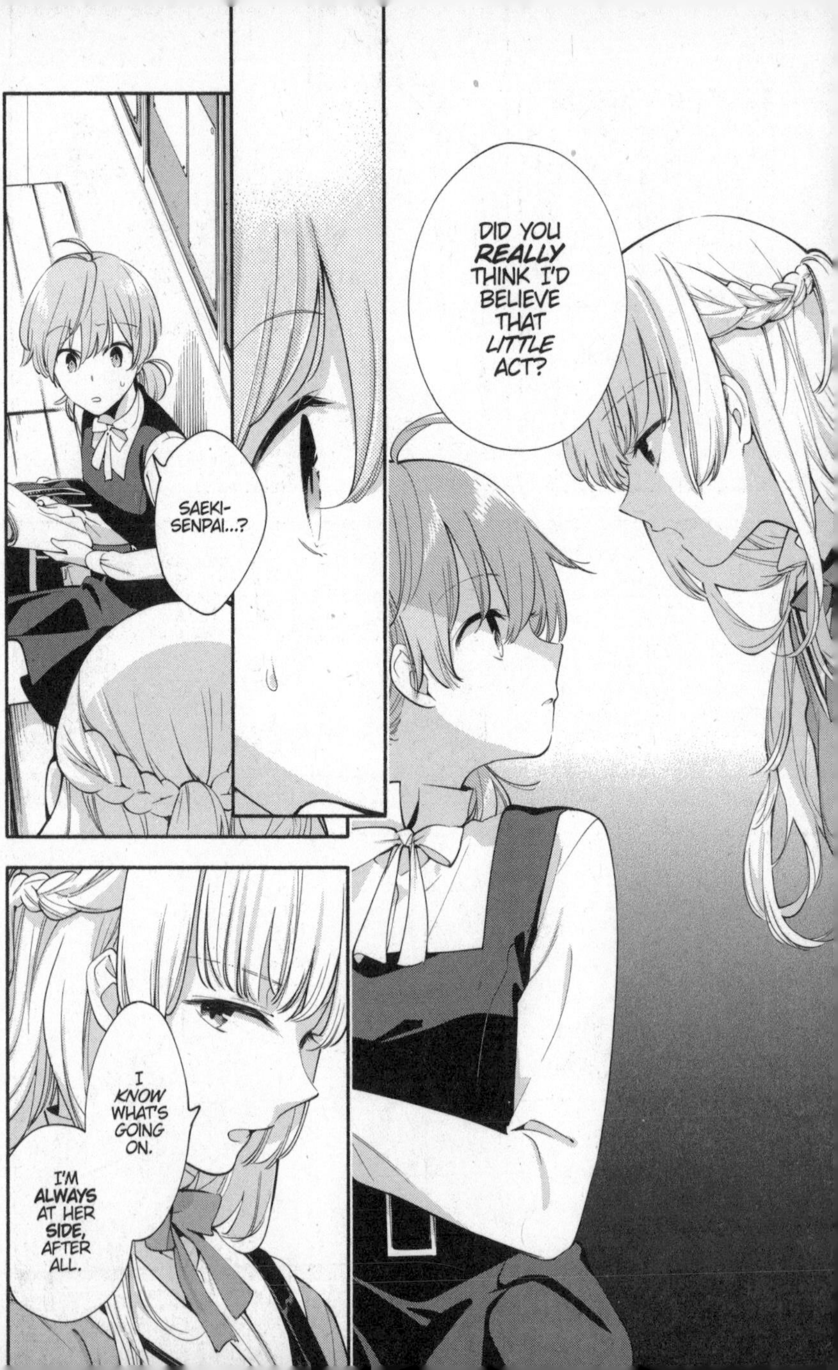
DID YOU *REALLY* THINK I'D BELIEVE THAT *LITTLE* ACT?
SAEKI-SENPAI...?
I *KNOW* WHAT'S GOING ON.
I'M **ALWAYS** AT HER **SIDE**, AFTER ALL.

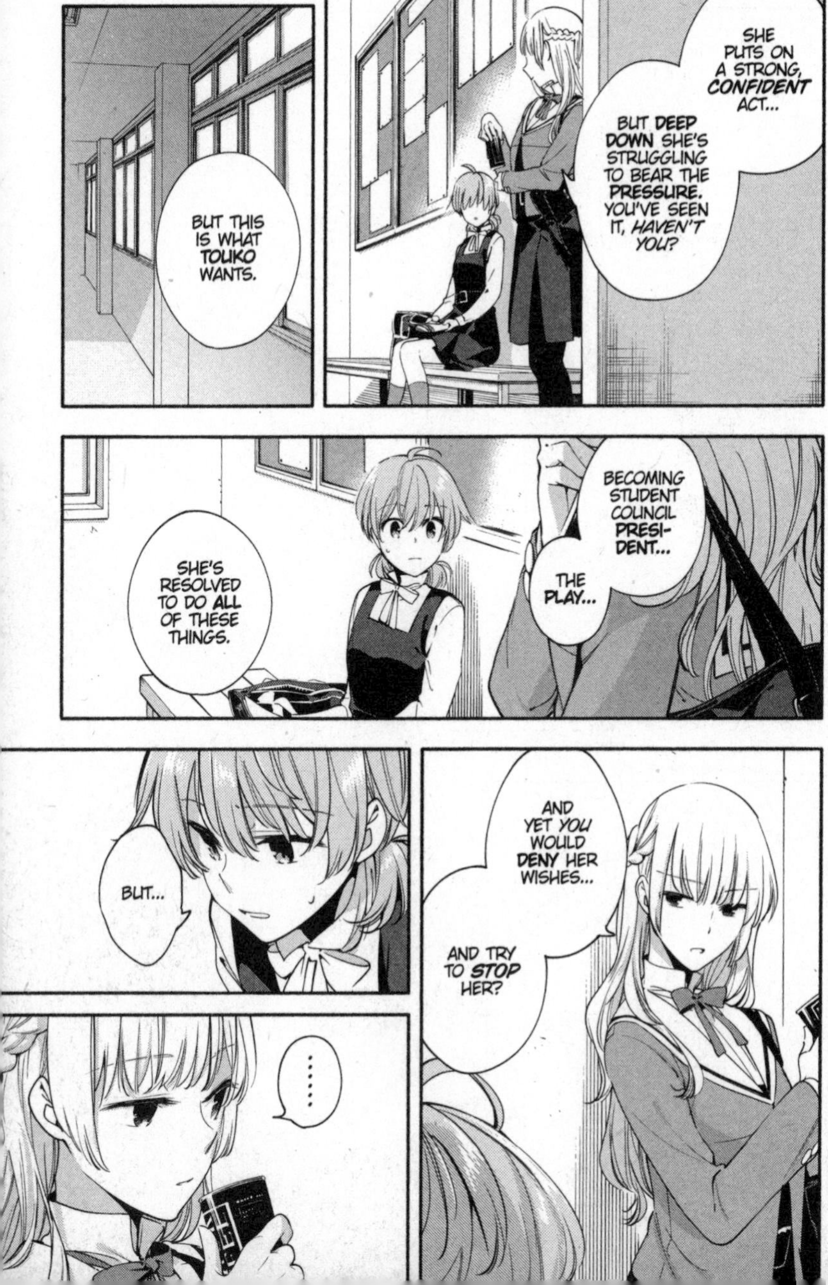
SHE PUTS ON A STRONG, CONFIDENT ACT...
BUT DEEP DOWN SHE'S STRUGGLING TO BEAR THE PRESSURE. YOU'VE SEEN IT, HAVEN'T YOU?
BUT THIS IS WHAT TOUKO WANTS.
BECOMING STUDENT COUNCIL PRESI-DENT...
THE PLAY...
SHE'S RESOLVED TO DO ALL OF THESE THINGS.
AND YET YOU WOULD DENY HER WISHES...
AND TRY TO STOP HER?
BUT...
......

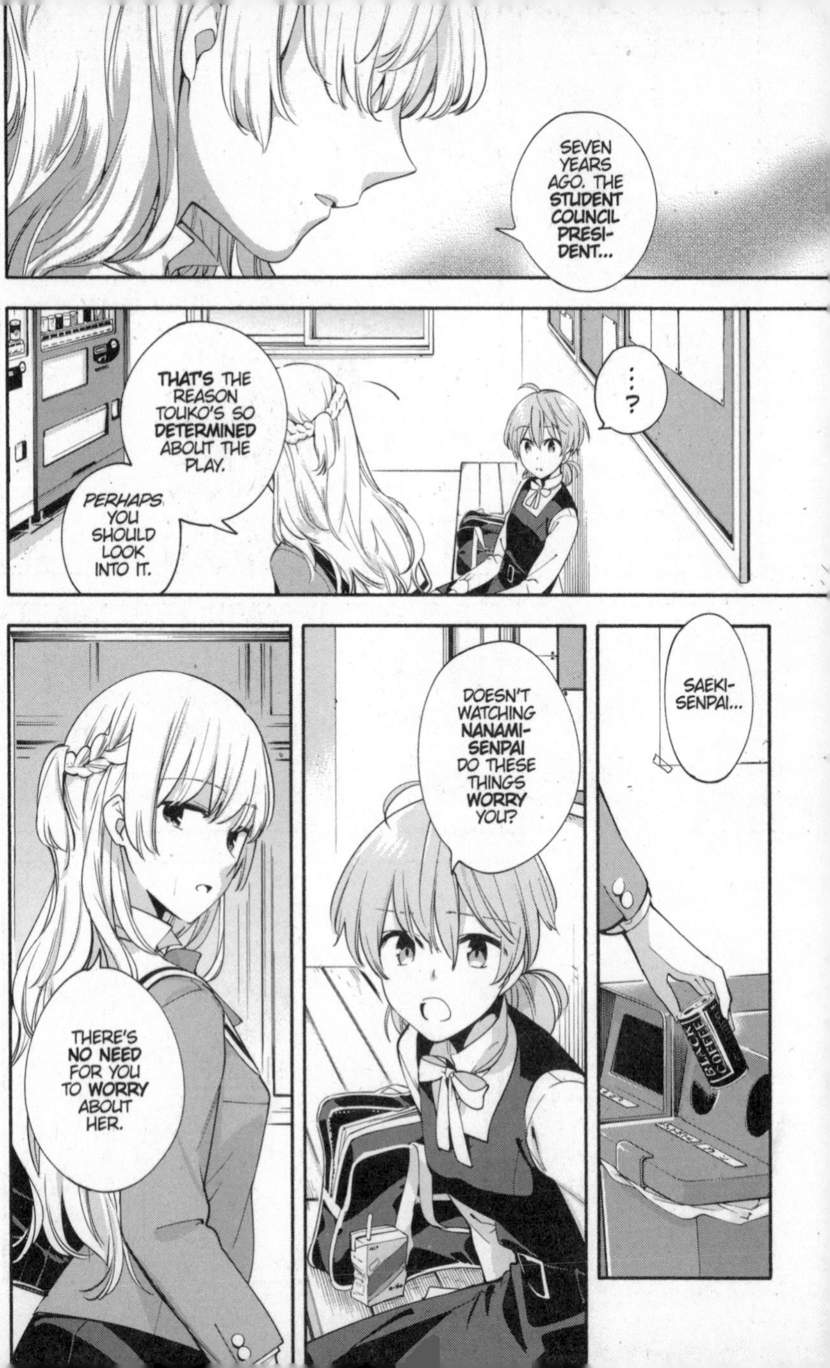
SEVEN YEARS AGO. THE STUDENT COUNCIL PRESI- DENT...
...?
THAT'S THE REASON TOUKO'S SO DETERMINED ABOUT THE PLAY.
PERHAPS YOU SHOULD LOOK INTO IT.
SAEKI-SENPAI...
BLACK COFFEE
DOESN'T WATCHING NANAMI-SENPAI DO THESE THINGS WORRY YOU?
THERE'S NO NEED FOR YOU TO WORRY ABOUT HER.

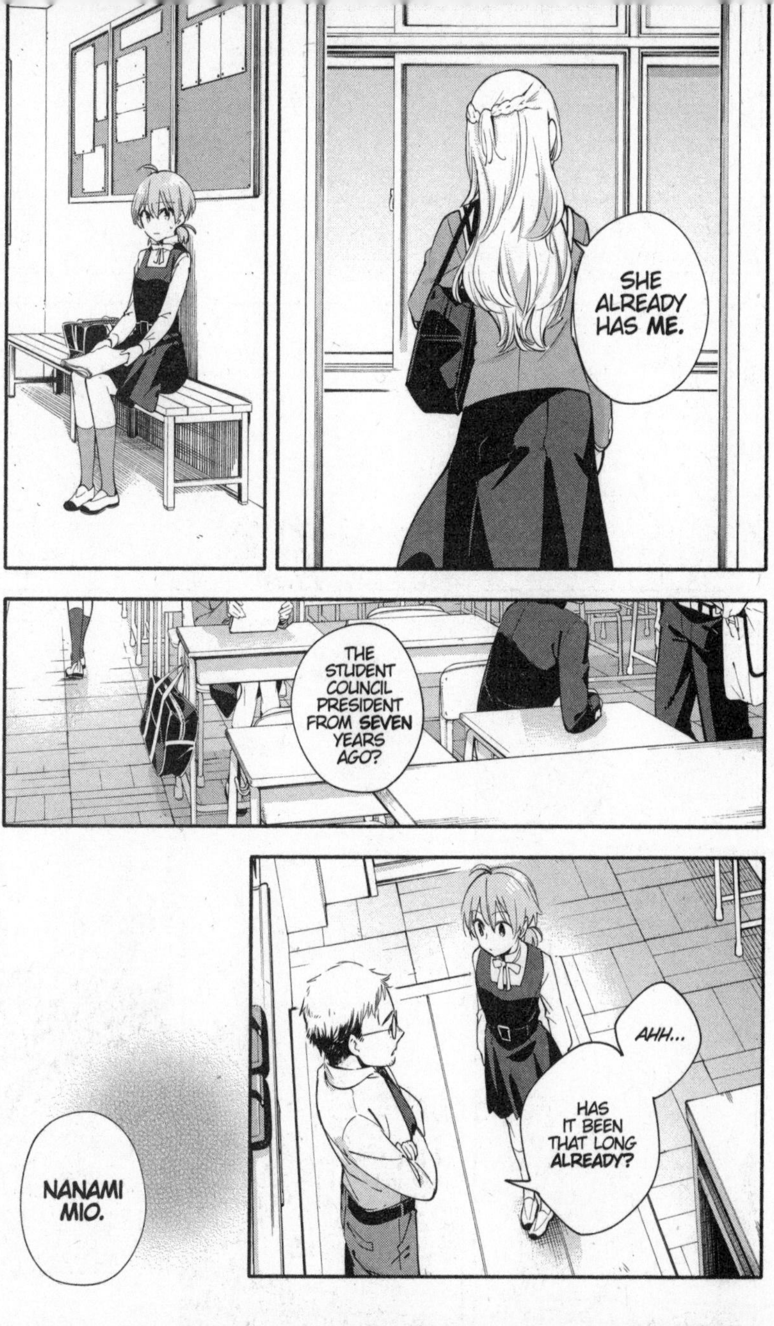
SHE ALREADY HAS ME.
THE STUDENT COUNCIL PRESIDENT FROM SEVEN YEARS AGO?
AHH...
HAS IT BEEN THAT LONG ALREADY?
NANAMI MIO.

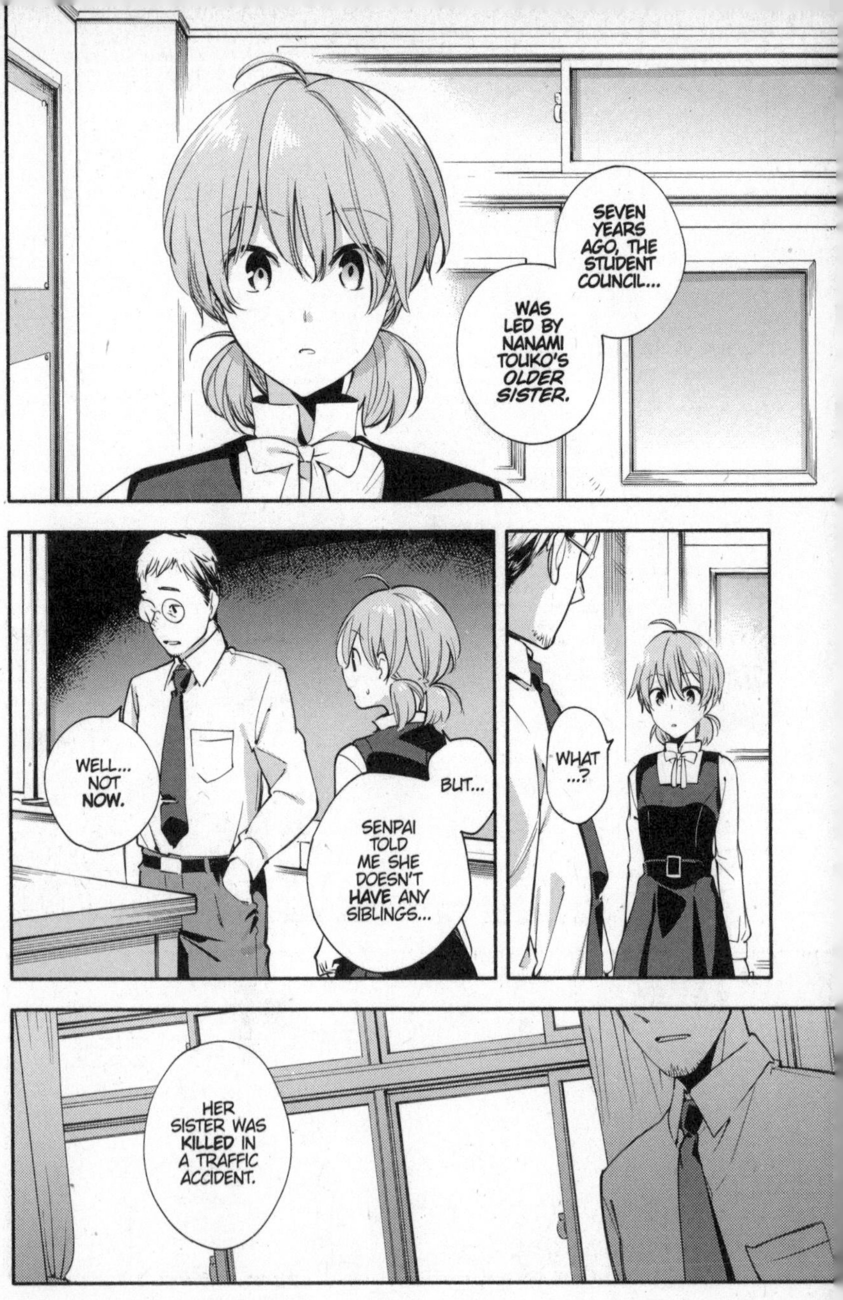
SEVEN YEARS AGO, THE STUDENT COUNCIL...
WAS LED BY NANAMI TOUKO'S OLDER SISTER.
WHAT ...?
BUT...
SENPAI TOLD ME SHE DOESN'T HAVE ANY SIBLINGS...
WELL... NOT NOW.
HER SISTER WAS KILLED IN A TRAFFIC ACCIDENT.

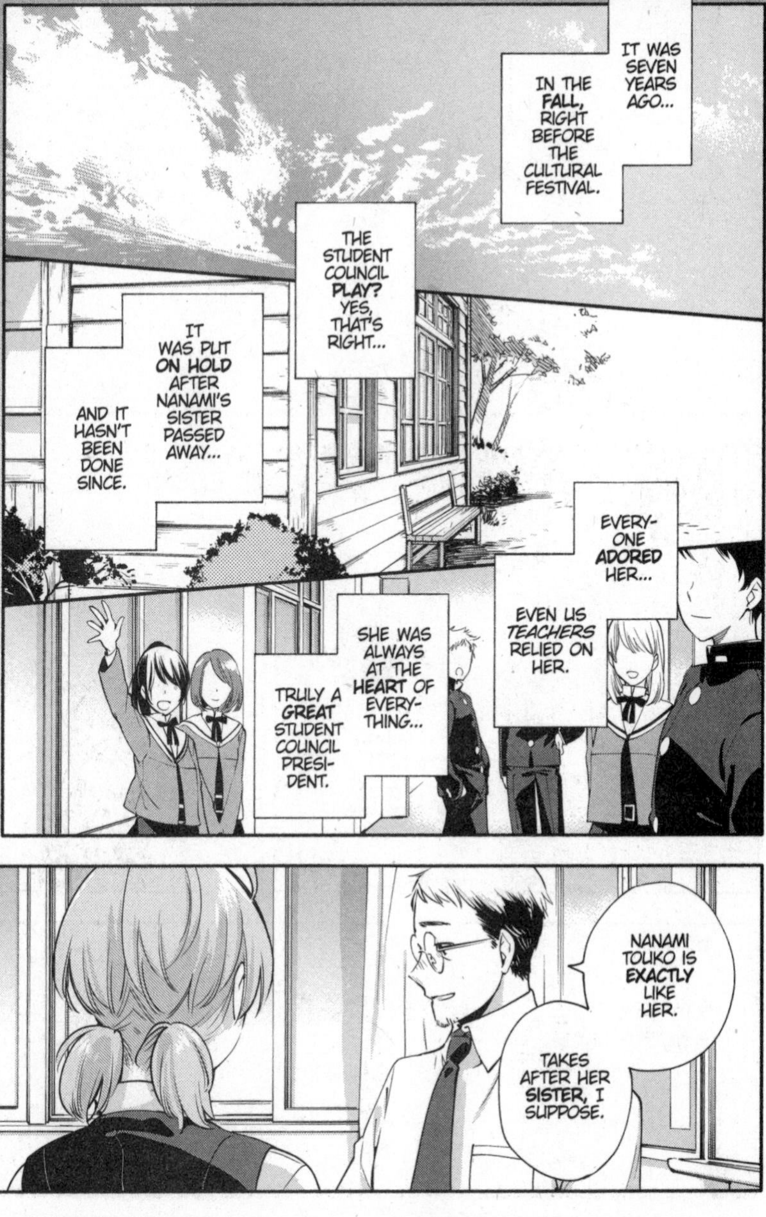
IT WAS SEVEN YEARS AGO...
IN THE FALL, RIGHT BEFORE THE CULTURAL FESTIVAL.
THE STUDENT COUNCIL PLAY? YES, THAT'S RIGHT...
IT WAS PUT ON HOLD AFTER NANAMI'S SISTER PASSED AWAY...
AND IT HASN'T BEEN DONE SINCE.
EVERY-ONE ADORED HER...
EVEN US TEACHERS RELIED ON HER.
SHE WAS ALWAYS AT THE HEART OF EVERY-THING...
TRULY A GREAT STUDENT COUNCIL PRESI-DENT.
NANAMI TOUKO IS EXACTLY LIKE HER.
TAKES AFTER HER SISTER, I SUPPOSE.

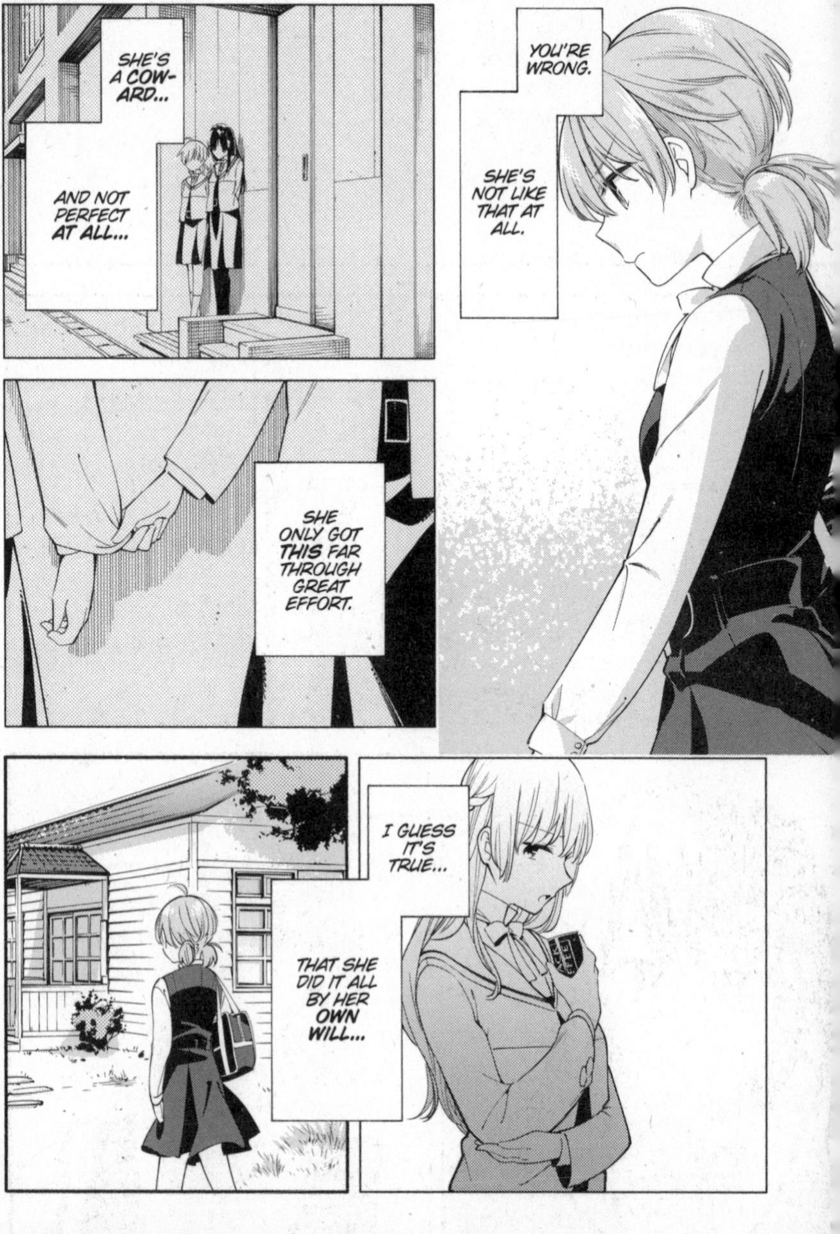
YOU'RE WRONG.
SHE'S NOT LIKE THAT AT ALL.
SHE'S A COWARD...
AND NOT PERFECT AT ALL...
SHE ONLY GOT THIS FAR THROUGH GREAT EFFORT.
I GUESS IT'S TRUE...
THAT SHE DID IT ALL BY HER OWN WILL...

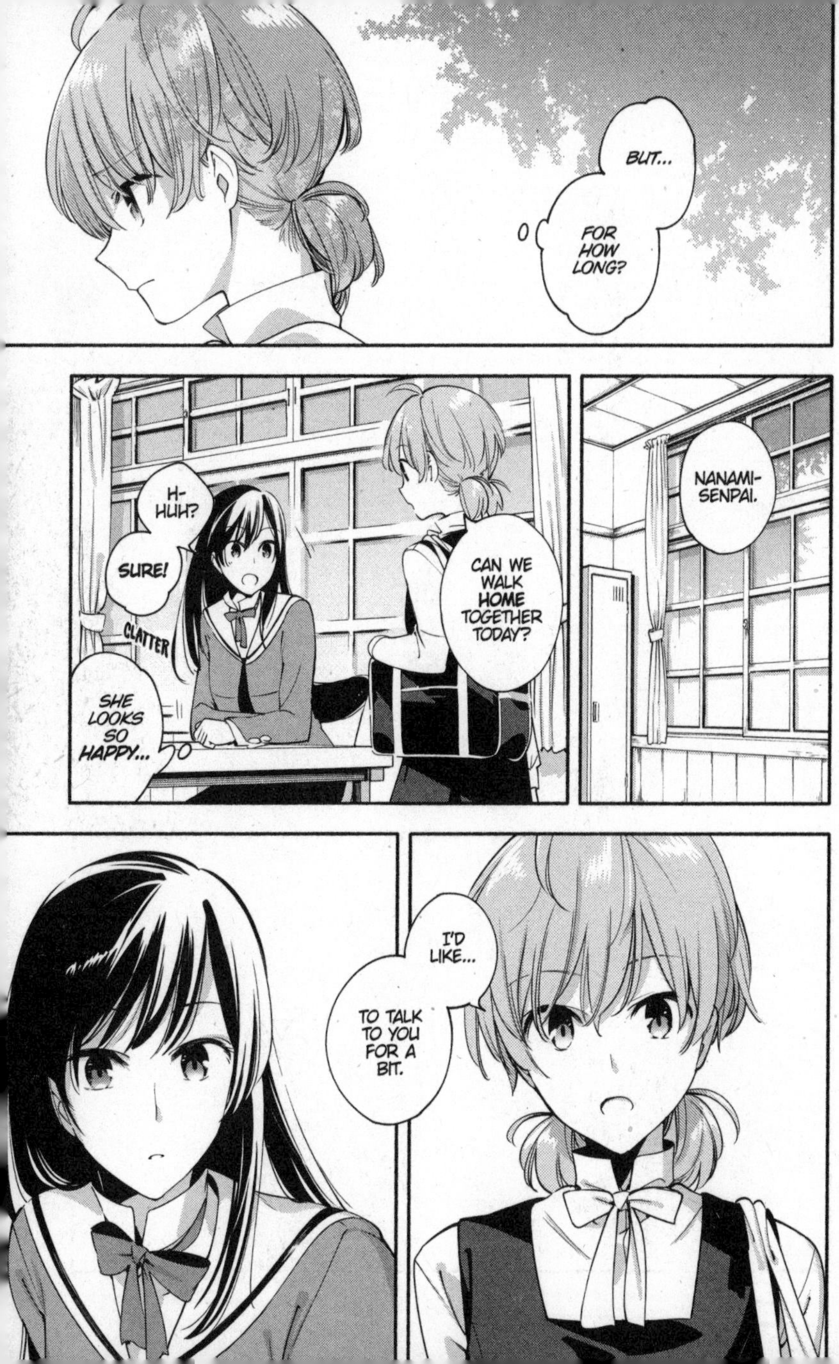
BUT...
FOR HOW LONG?
NANAMI-SENPAI.
CAN WE WALK HOME TOGETHER TODAY?
H-HUH?
SURE!
CLATTER
SHE LOOKS SO HAPPY...
I'D LIKE...
TO TALK TO YOU FOR A BIT.

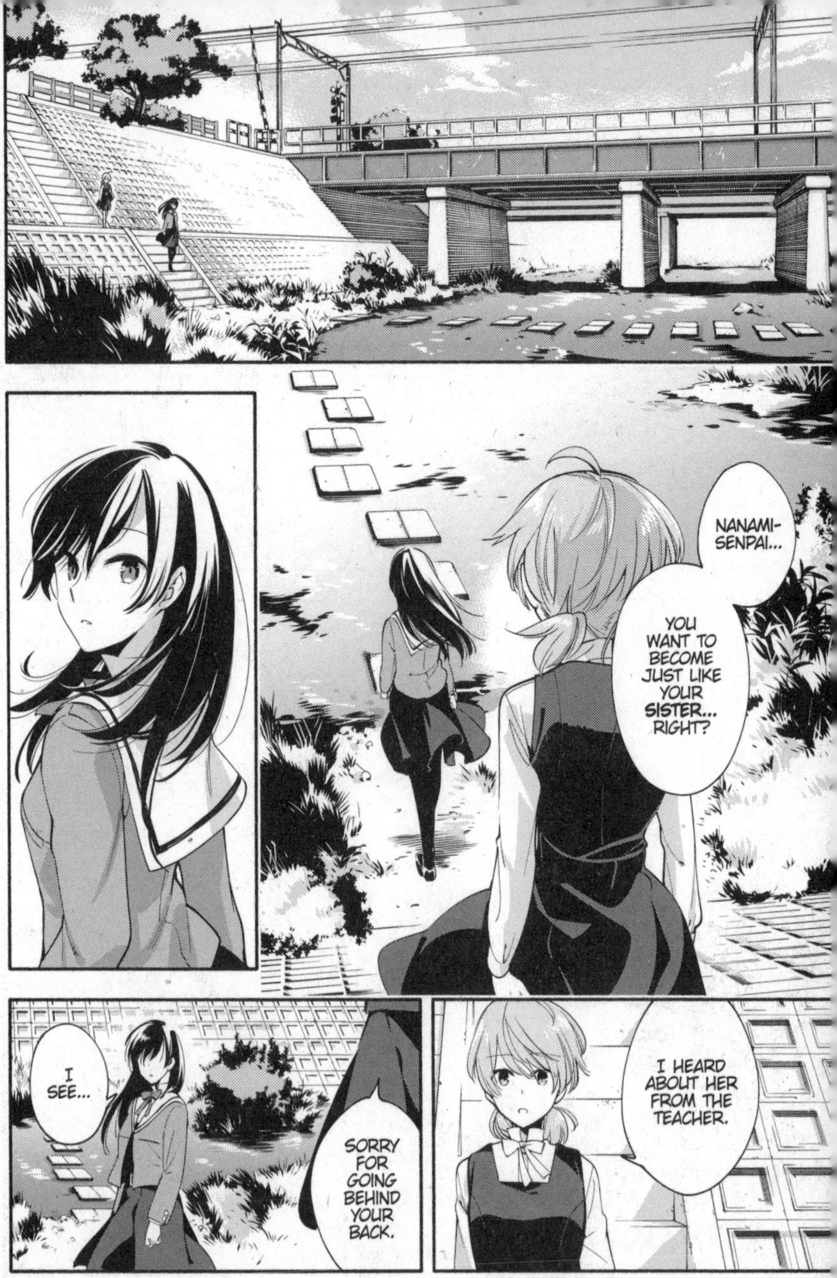
NANAMI-SENPAI...
YOU WANT TO BECOME JUST LIKE YOUR SISTER... RIGHT?
I HEARD ABOUT HER FROM THE TEACHER.
SORRY FOR GOING BEHIND YOUR BACK.
I SEE...

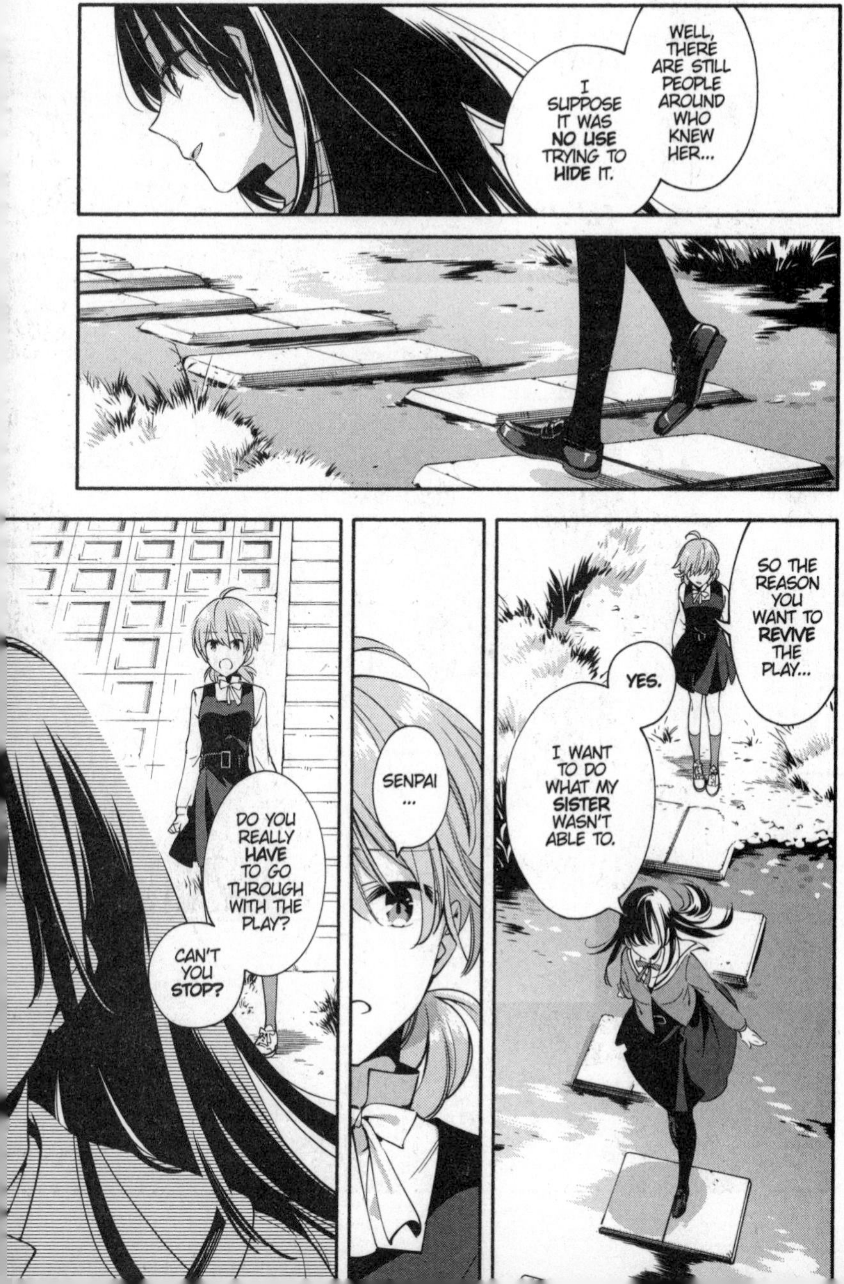
WELL, THERE ARE STILL PEOPLE AROUND WHO KNEW HER...
I SUPPOSE IT WAS NO USE TRYING TO HIDE IT.
SO THE REASON YOU WANT TO REVIVE THE PLAY...
YES.
I WANT TO DO WHAT MY SISTER WASN'T ABLE TO.
SENPAI...
DO YOU REALLY HAVE TO GO THROUGH WITH THE PLAY?
CAN'T YOU STOP?

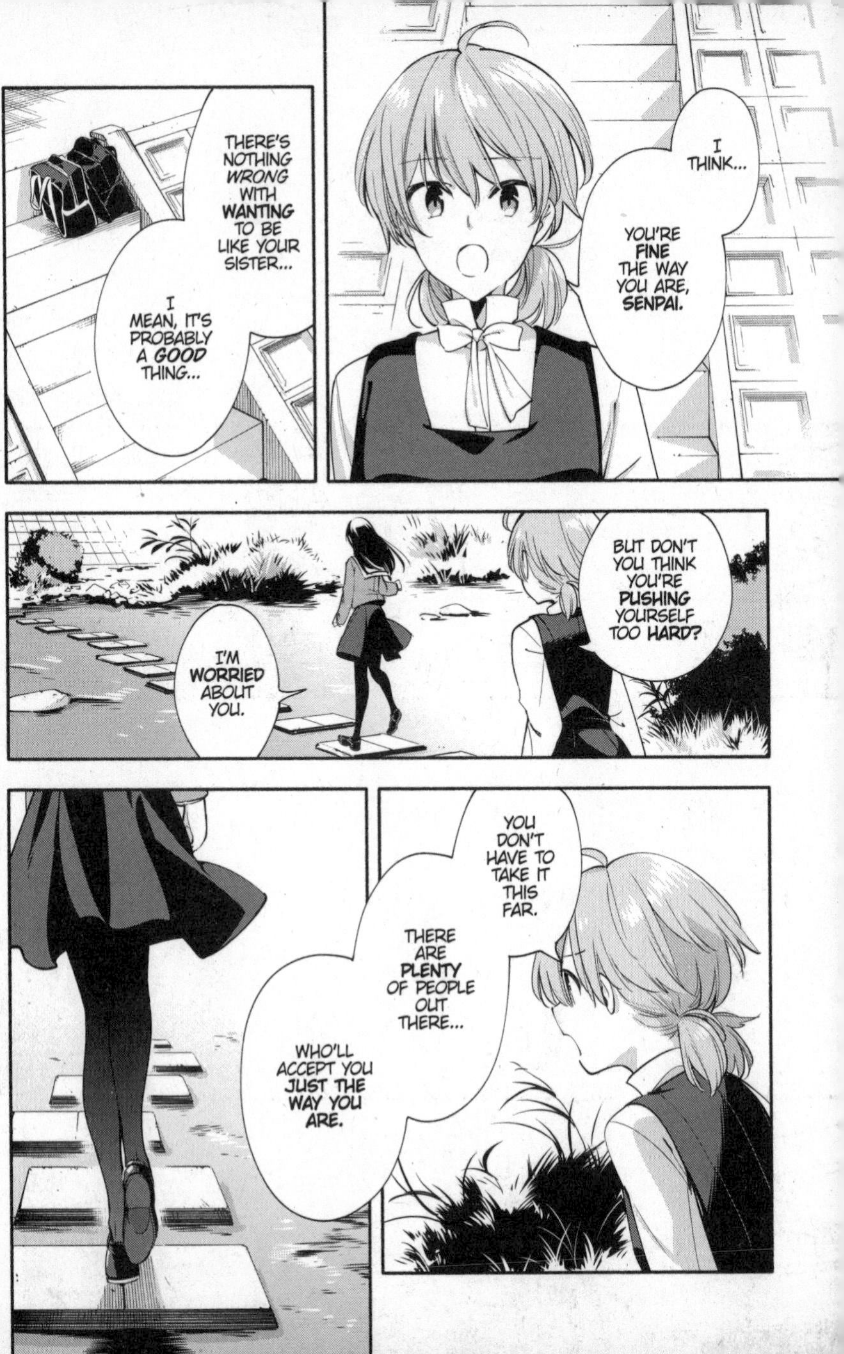
I THINK...
YOU'RE **FINE** THE WAY YOU ARE, **SENPAI.**
THERE'S NOTHING *WRONG* WITH **WANTING** TO BE LIKE YOUR SISTER...
I MEAN, IT'S PROBABLY A **GOOD** THING...
BUT DON'T YOU THINK YOU'RE **PUSHING** YOURSELF TOO **HARD?**
I'M **WORRIED** ABOUT YOU.
YOU DON'T HAVE TO TAKE IT THIS FAR.
THERE ARE **PLENTY** OF PEOPLE OUT THERE...
WHO'LL ACCEPT YOU **JUST THE WAY YOU ARE.**

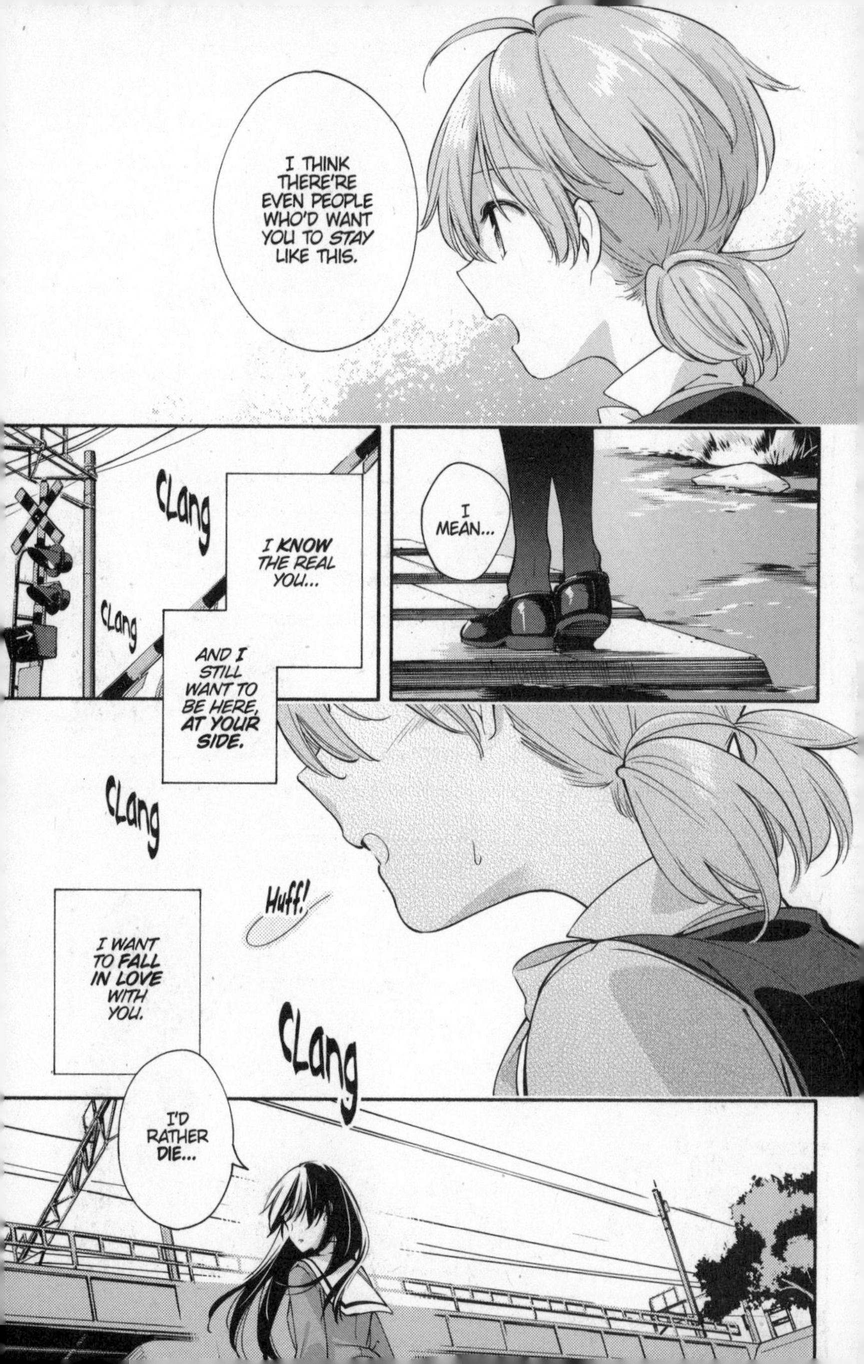
I THINK THERE'RE EVEN PEOPLE WHO'D WANT YOU TO *STAY* LIKE THIS.
I MEAN...
CLang
I KNOW THE REAL YOU...
CLang
AND I STILL WANT TO BE HERE, AT YOUR SIDE.
CLang
Huff!
I WANT TO FALL IN LOVE WITH YOU.
CLang
I'D RATHER DIE...

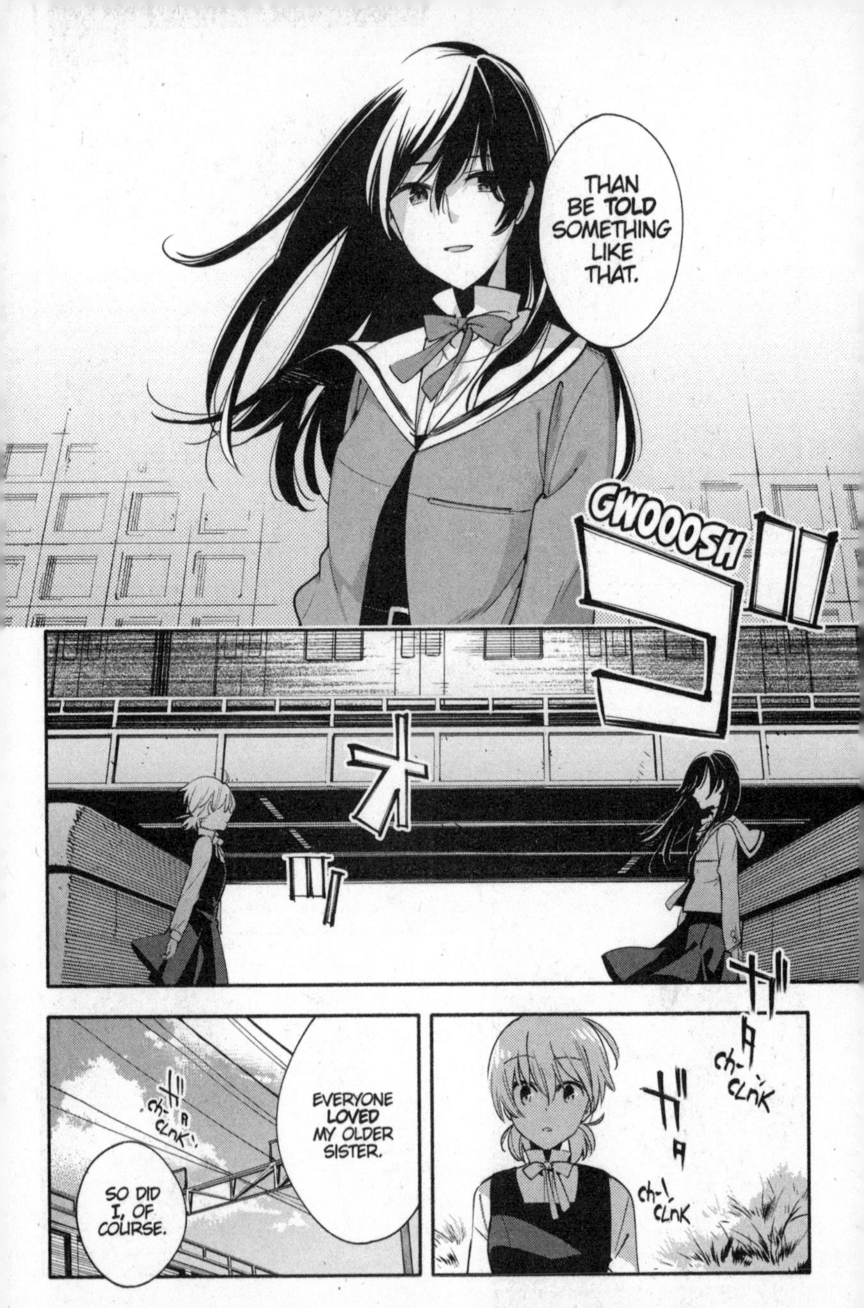
THAN BE TOLD SOMETHING LIKE THAT.
GWOOOSH
CH- CLNK
CH-! CLNK
EVERYONE LOVED MY OLDER SISTER.
CH- CLNK!
SO DID I, OF COURSE.

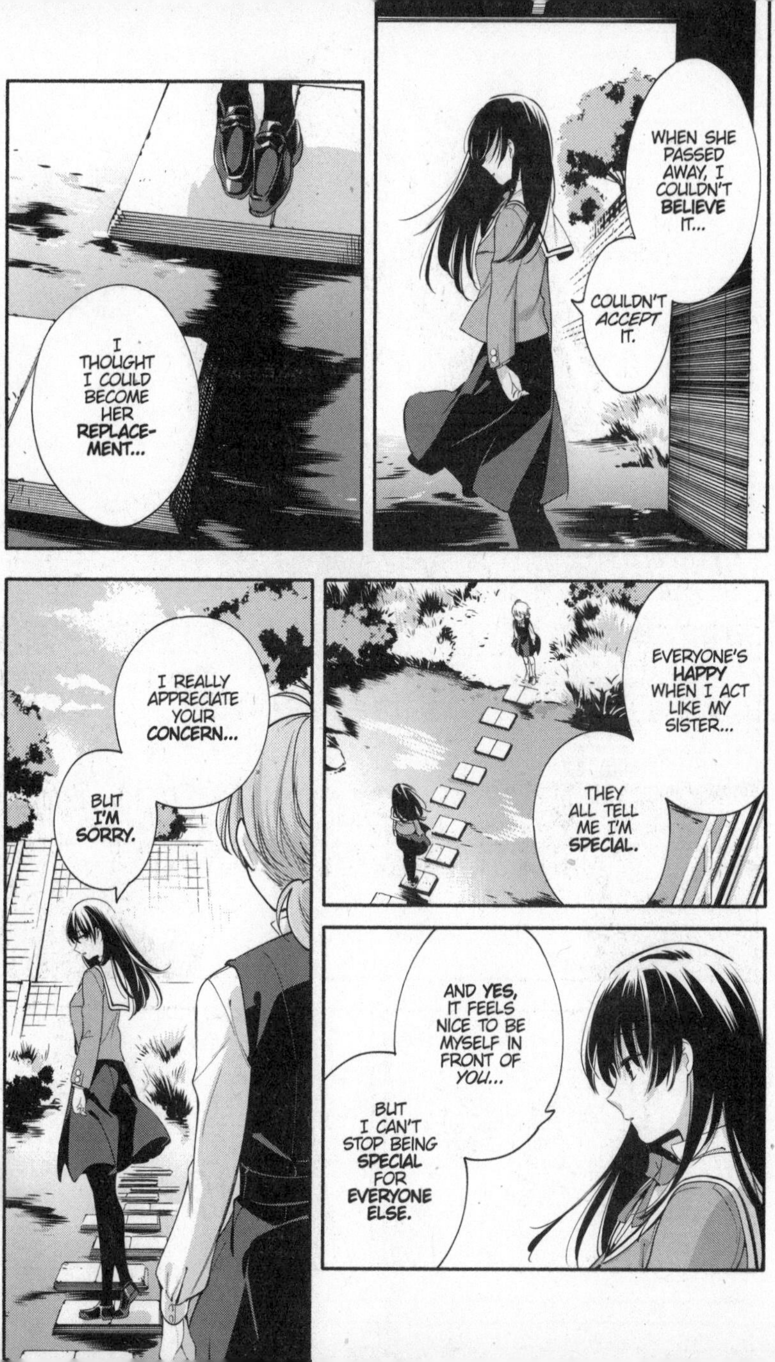
WHEN SHE PASSED AWAY, I COULDN'T BELIEVE IT...
COULDN'T ACCEPT IT.
I THOUGHT I COULD BECOME HER REPLACE-MENT...
EVERYONE'S HAPPY WHEN I ACT LIKE MY SISTER...
THEY ALL TELL ME I'M SPECIAL.
AND YES, IT FEELS NICE TO BE MYSELF IN FRONT OF YOU...
BUT I CAN'T STOP BEING SPECIAL FOR EVERYONE ELSE.
I REALLY APPRECIATE YOUR CONCERN...
BUT I'M SORRY.

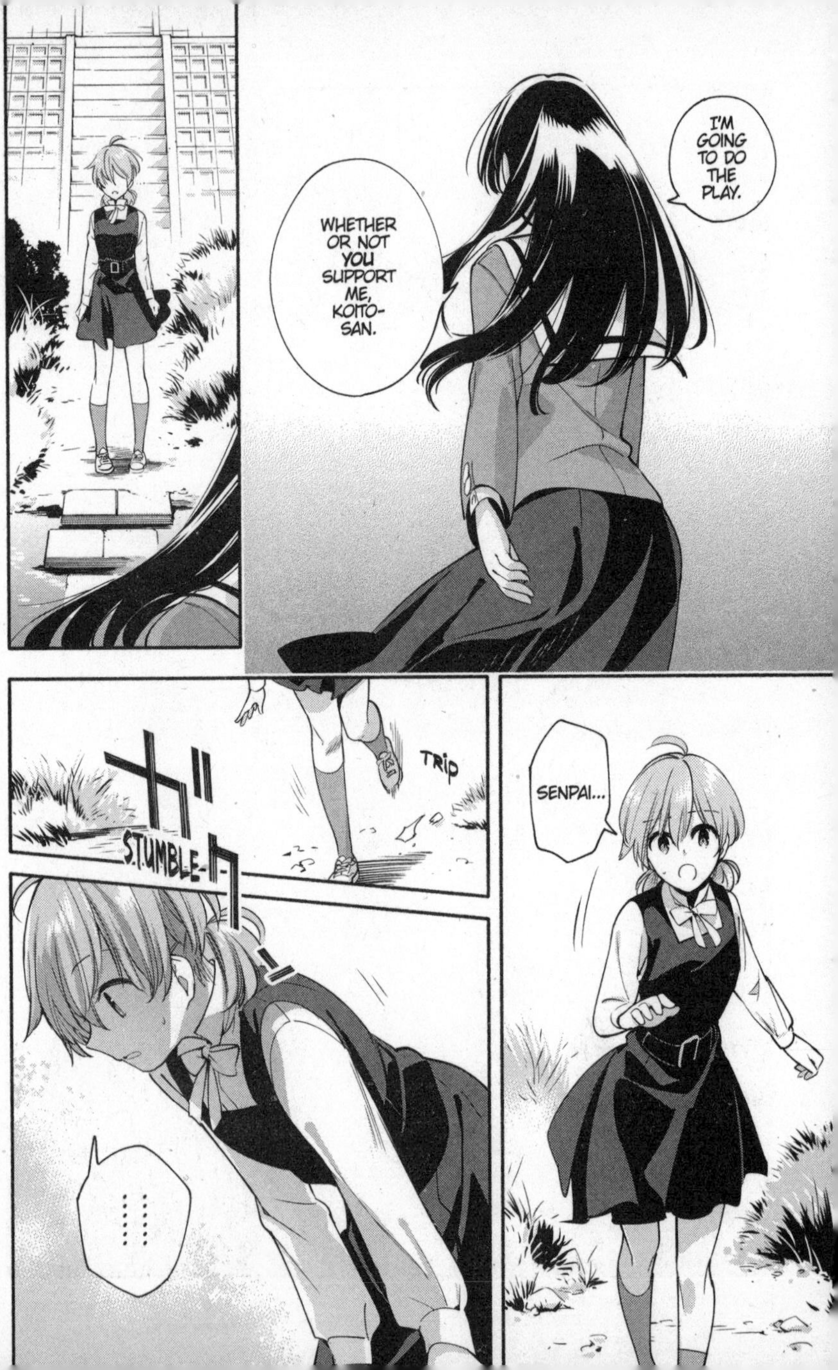
I'M GOING TO DO THE PLAY.
WHETHER OR NOT YOU SUPPORT ME, KOITO-SAN.
SENPAI...
TRIP
STUMBLE
......

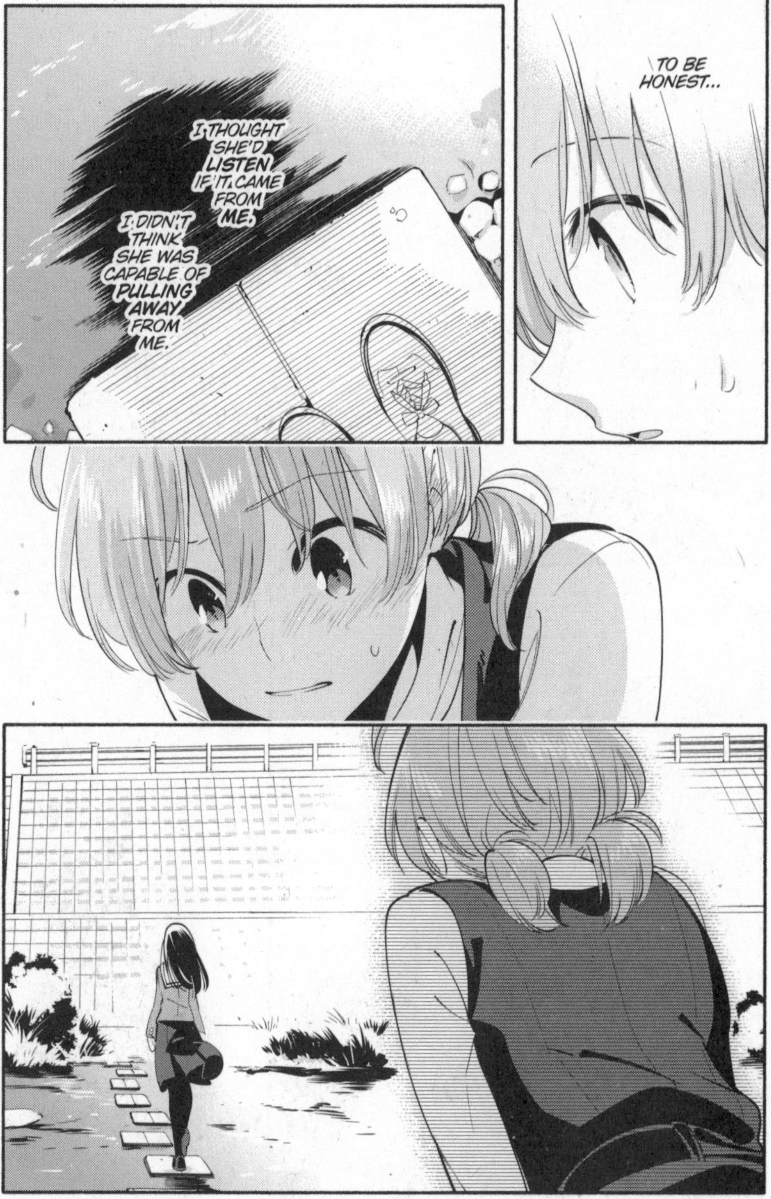
TO BE HONEST...
I THOUGHT SHE'D LISTEN IF IT CAME FROM ME.
I DIDN'T THINK SHE WAS CAPABLE OF PULLING AWAY FROM ME.

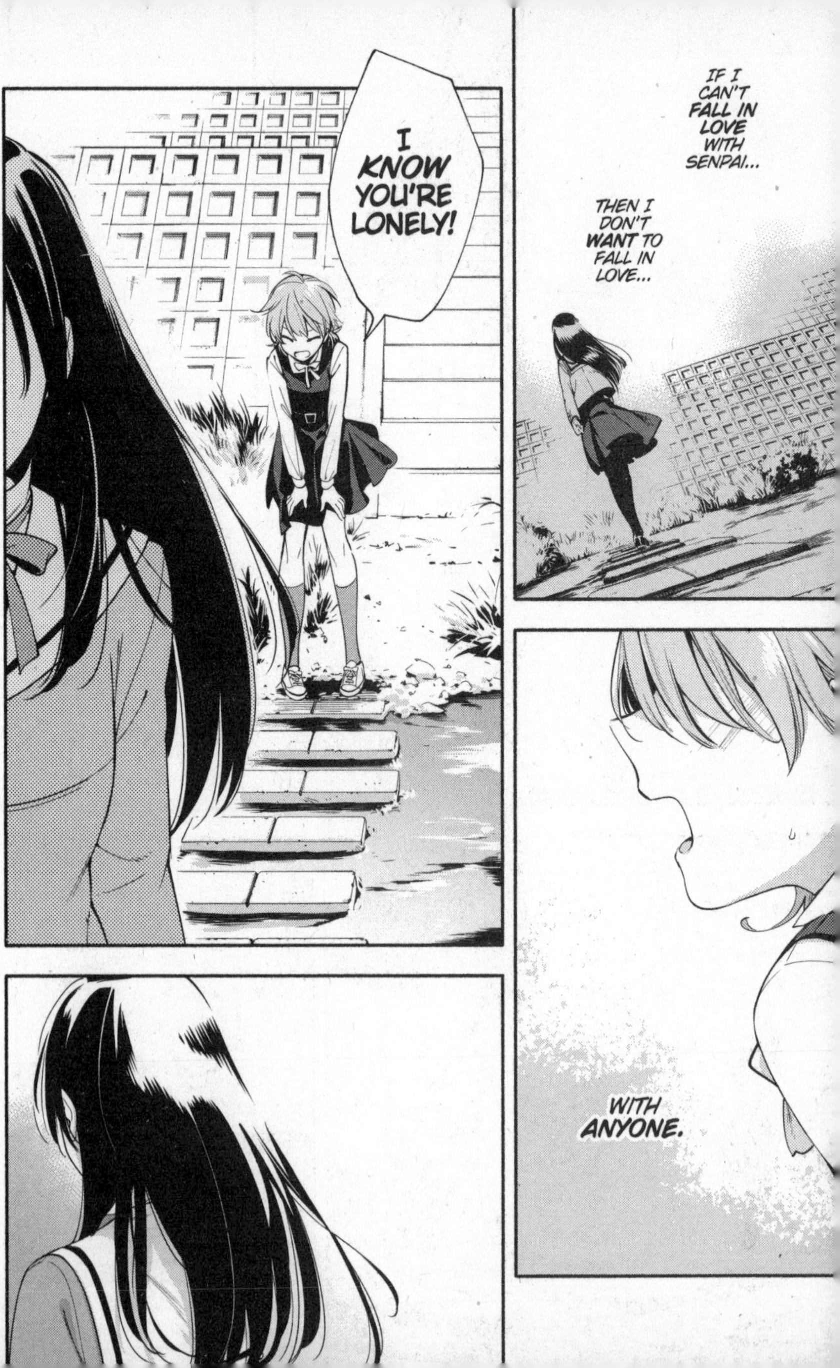
IF I CAN'T FALL IN LOVE WITH SENPAI...
THEN I DON'T WANT TO FALL IN LOVE...
WITH ANYONE.
I KNOW YOU'RE LONELY!

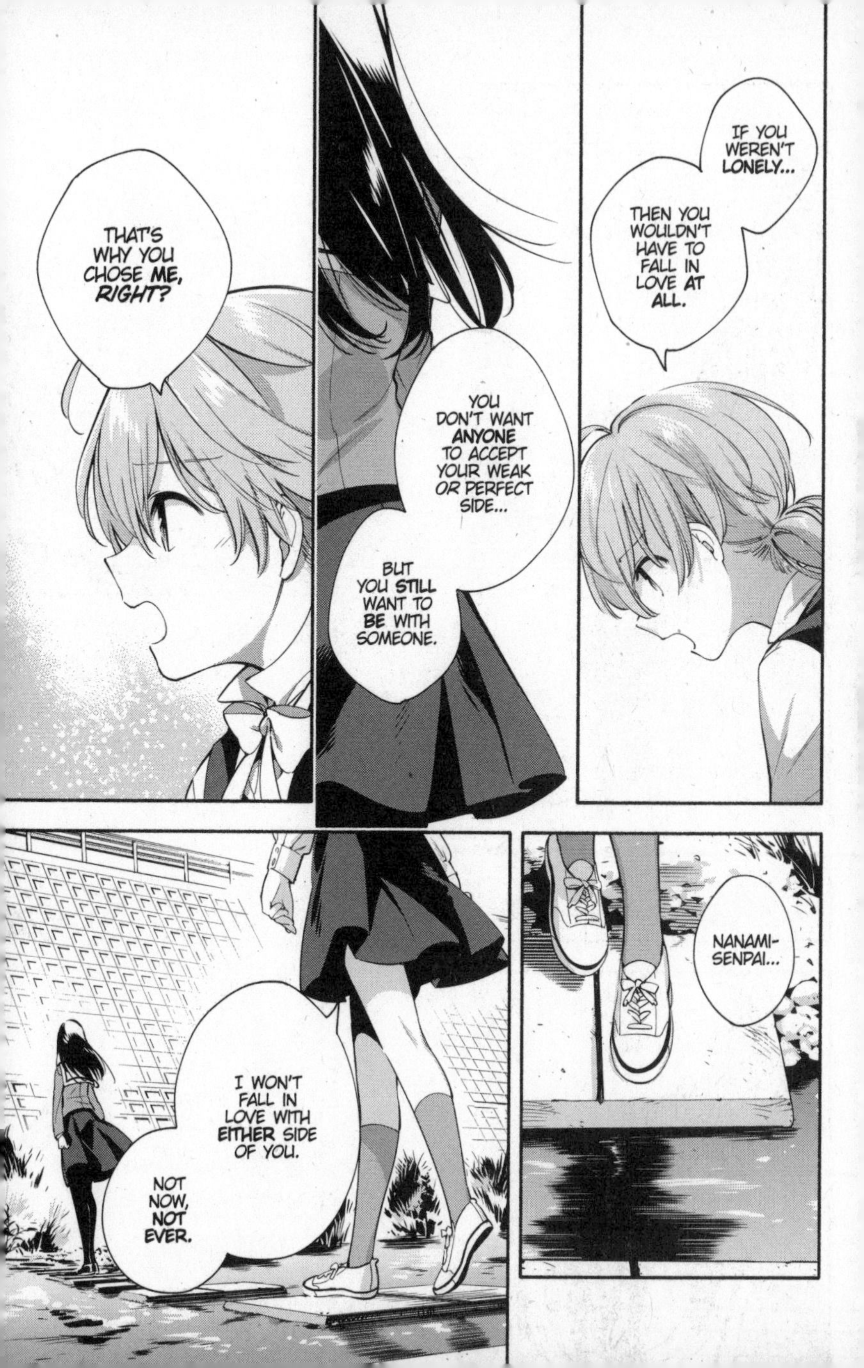
IF YOU WEREN'T LONELY...
THEN YOU WOULDN'T HAVE TO FALL IN LOVE AT ALL.
YOU DON'T WANT ANYONE TO ACCEPT YOUR WEAK OR PERFECT SIDE...
BUT YOU STILL WANT TO BE WITH SOMEONE.
THAT'S WHY YOU CHOSE ME, RIGHT?
NANAMI-SENPAI...
I WON'T FALL IN LOVE WITH EITHER SIDE OF YOU.
NOT NOW, NOT EVER.

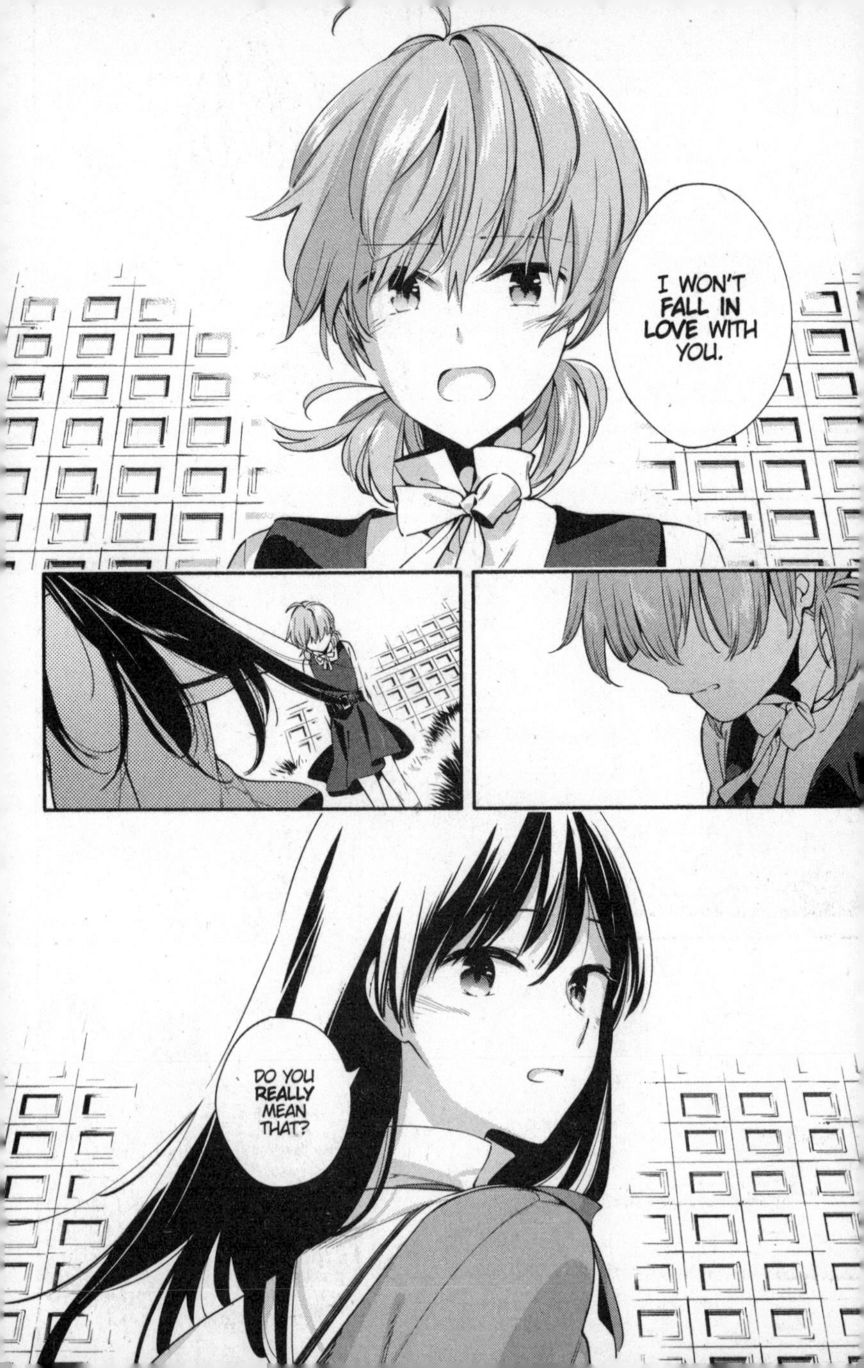
I WON'T FALL IN LOVE WITH YOU.
DO YOU REALLY MEAN THAT?

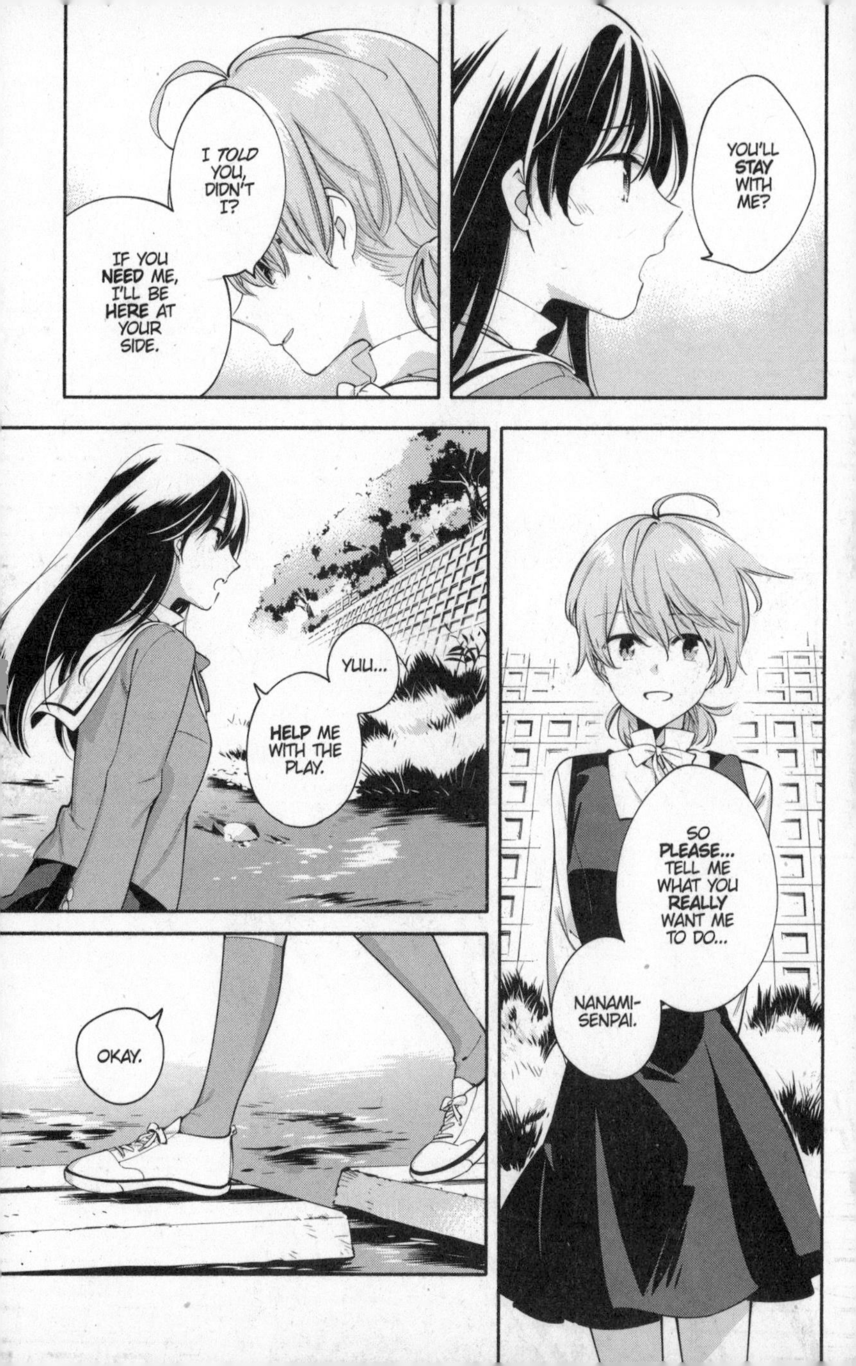
YOU'LL STAY WITH ME?
I *TOLD* YOU, DIDN'T I?
IF YOU NEED ME, I'LL BE HERE AT YOUR SIDE.
SO PLEASE... TELL ME WHAT YOU REALLY WANT ME TO DO...
NANAMI-SENPAI.
YUU...
HELP ME WITH THE PLAY.
OKAY.

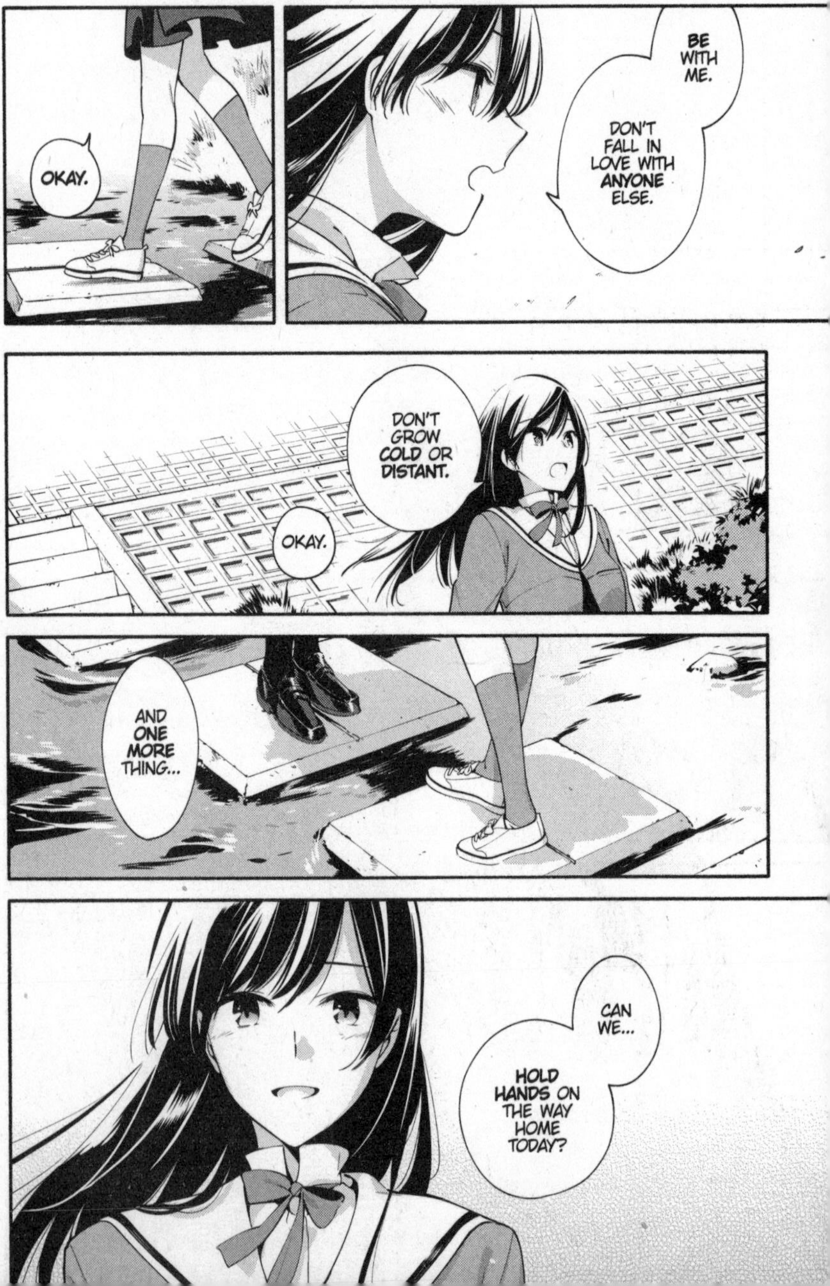
BE WITH ME.
DON'T FALL IN LOVE WITH ANYONE ELSE.
OKAY.
DON'T GROW COLD OR DISTANT.
OKAY.
AND ONE MORE THING...
CAN WE...
HOLD HANDS ON THE WAY HOME TODAY?

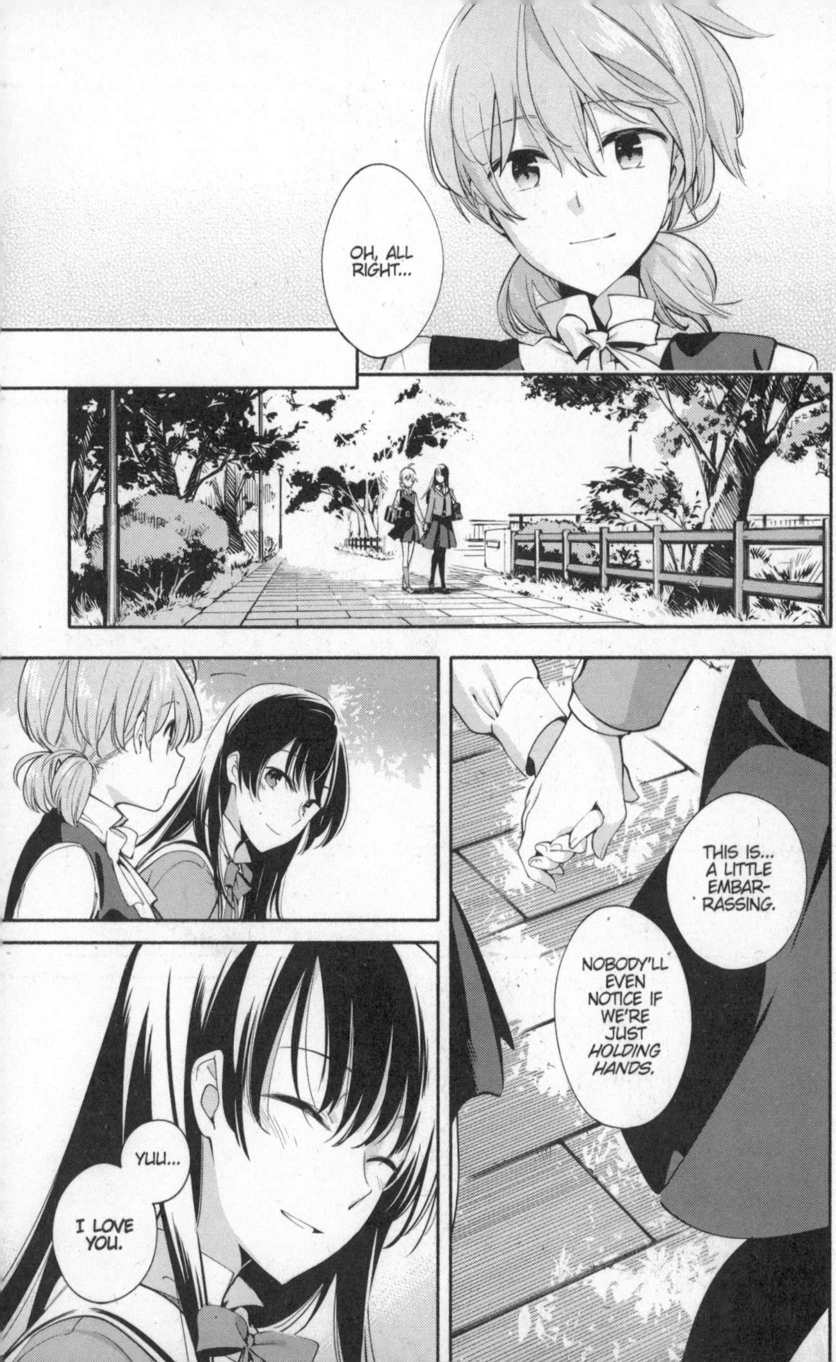
OH, ALL RIGHT...
THIS IS... A LITTLE EMBARRASSING.
NOBODY'LL EVEN NOTICE IF WE'RE JUST *HOLDING HANDS.*
YUU...
I LOVE YOU.

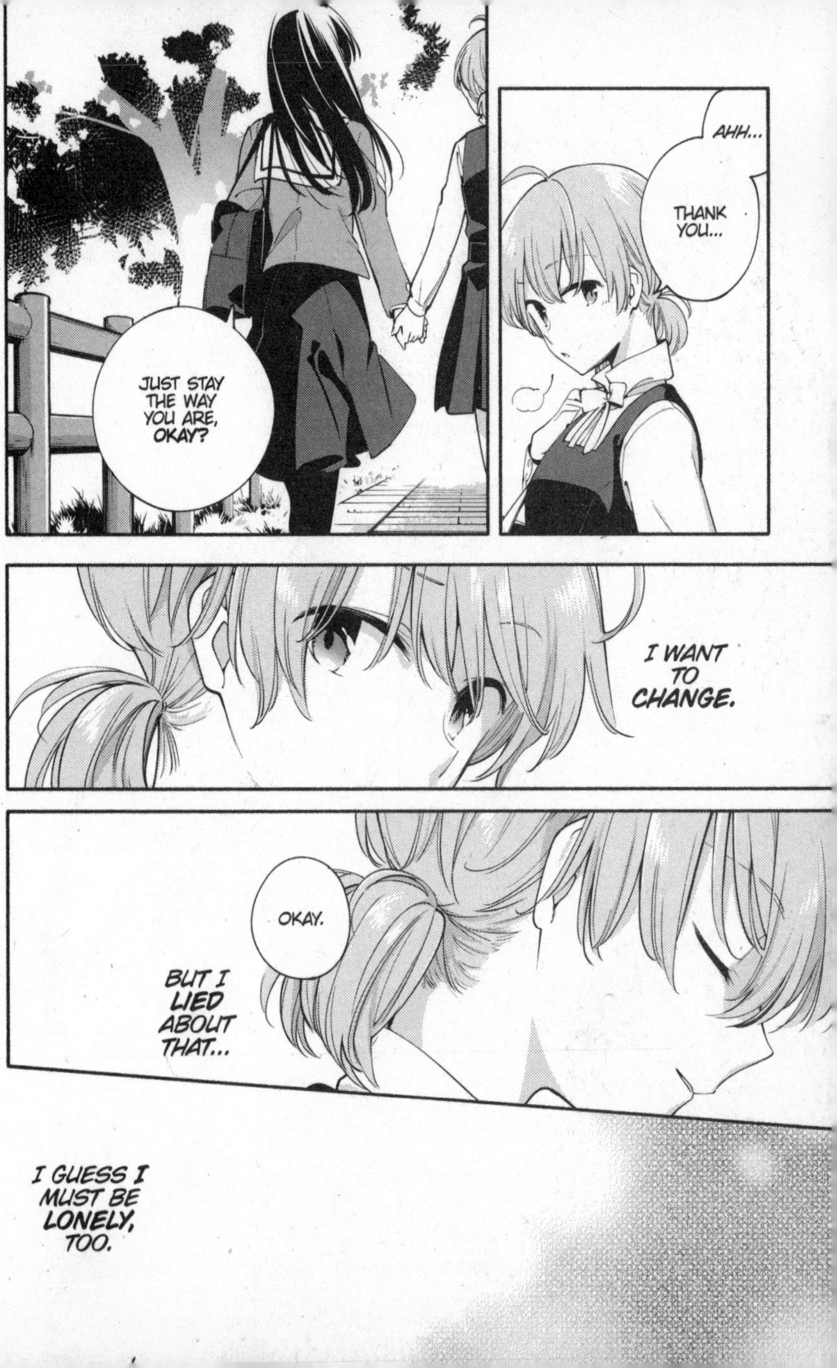
AHH...
THANK YOU...
JUST STAY THE WAY YOU ARE, OKAY?
I WANT TO CHANGE.
OKAY.
BUT I LIED ABOUT THAT...
I GUESS I MUST BE LONELY, TOO.

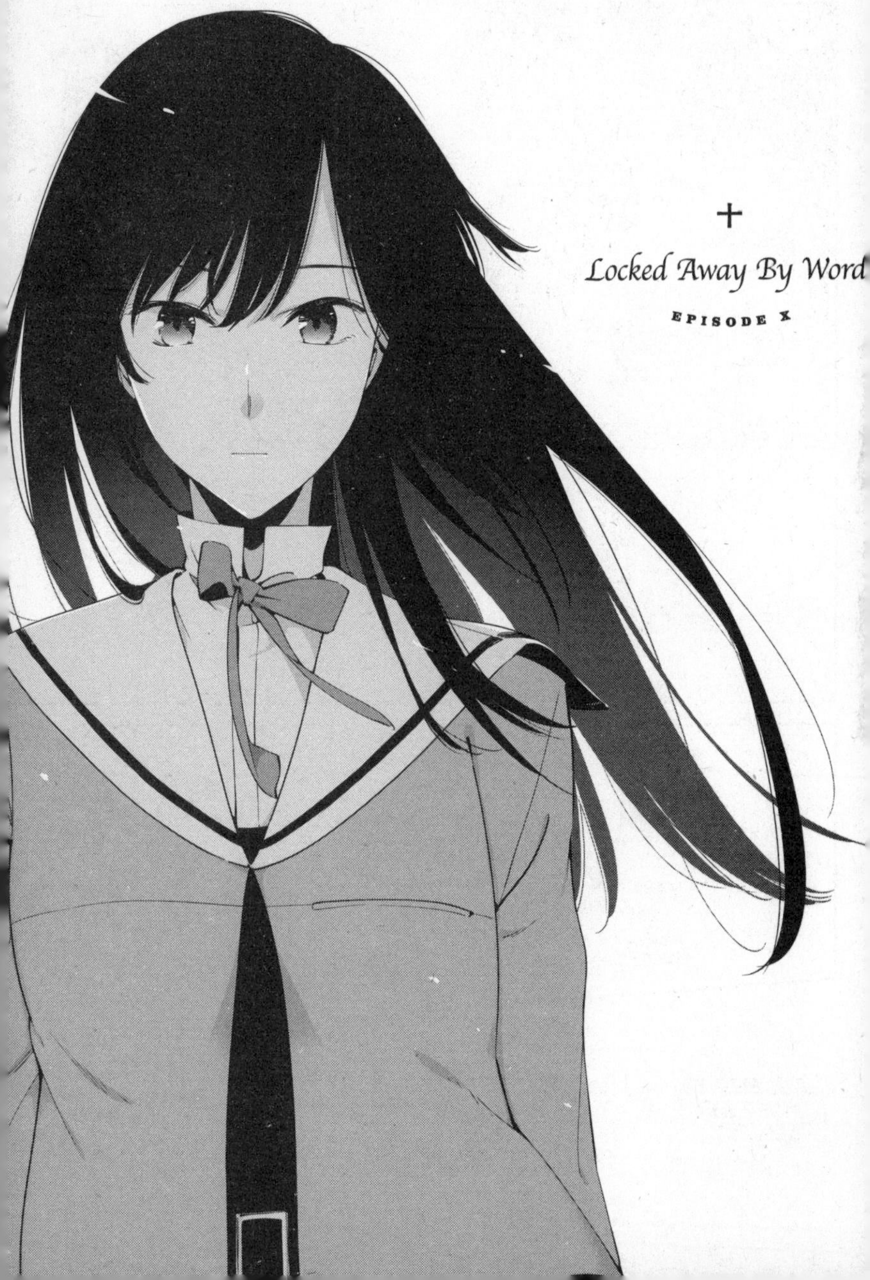

# Locked Away By Word

EPISODE X

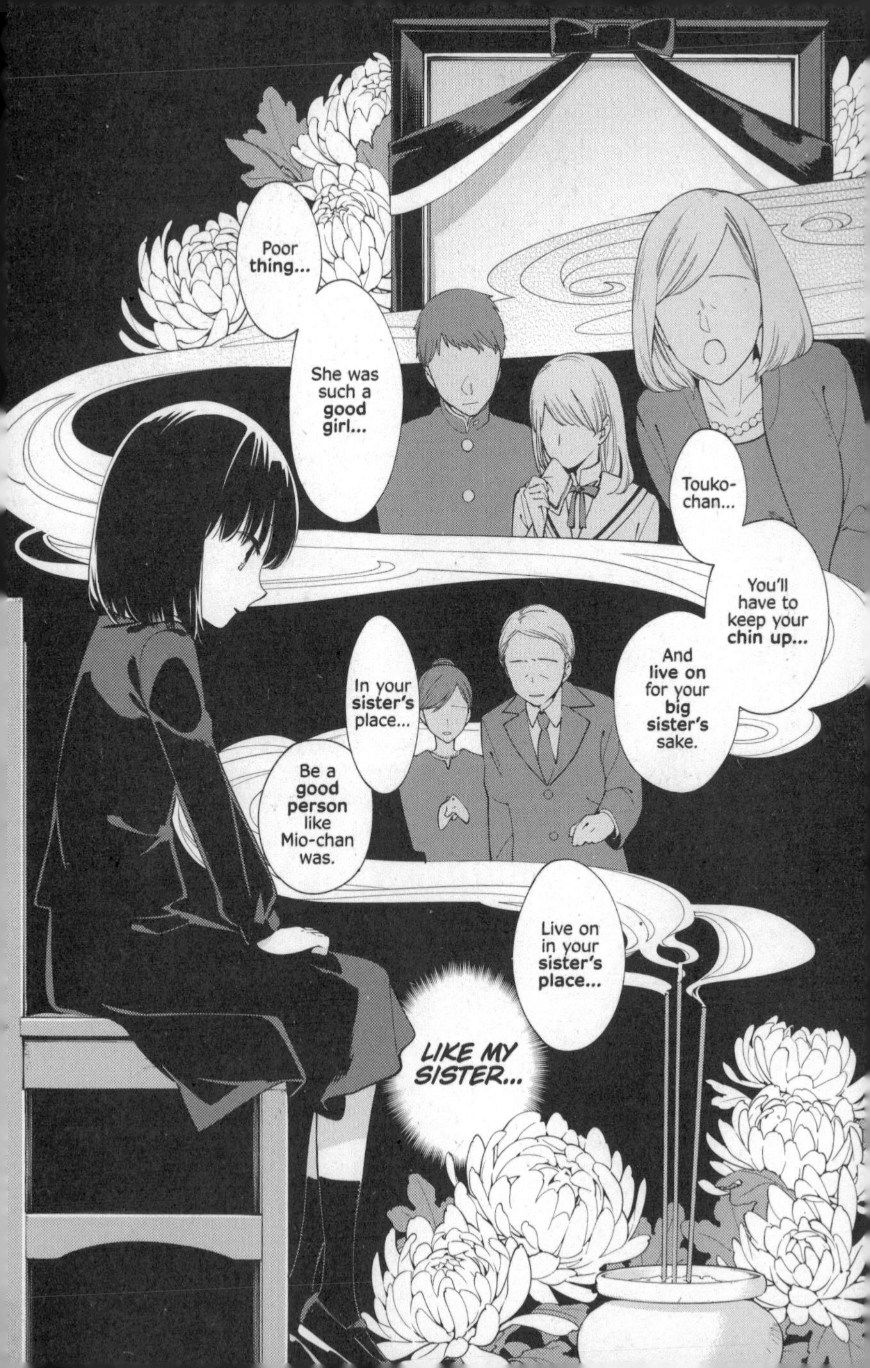
Poor thing...
She was such a good girl...
Touko-chan...
You'll have to keep your chin up...
And live on for your big sister's sake.
In your sister's place...
Be a good person like Mio-chan was.
Live on in your sister's place...
LIKE MY SISTER...

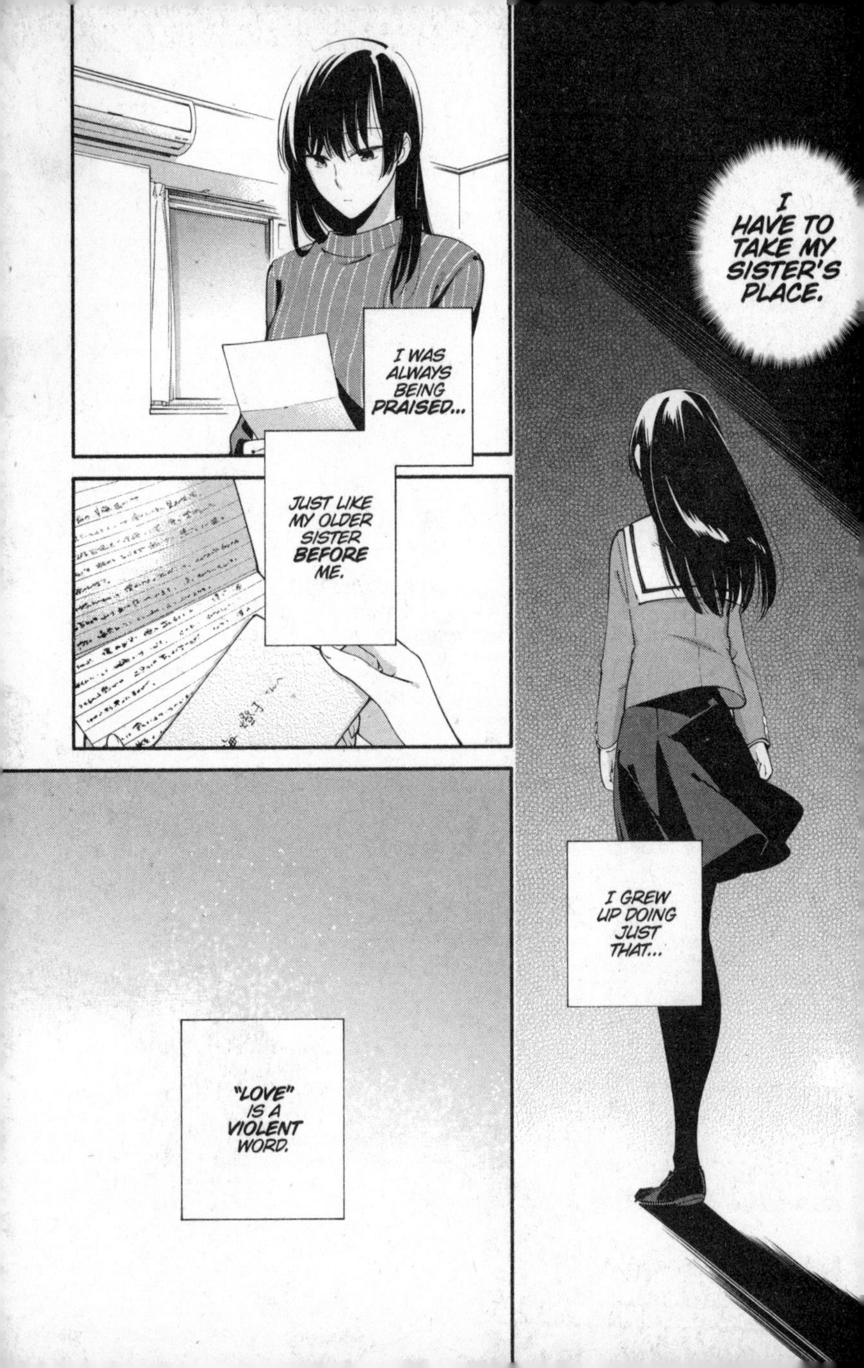
I HAVE TO TAKE MY SISTER'S PLACE.
I GREW UP DOING JUST THAT...
I WAS ALWAYS BEING PRAISED...
JUST LIKE MY OLDER SISTER BEFORE ME.
"LOVE" IS A VIOLENT WORD.

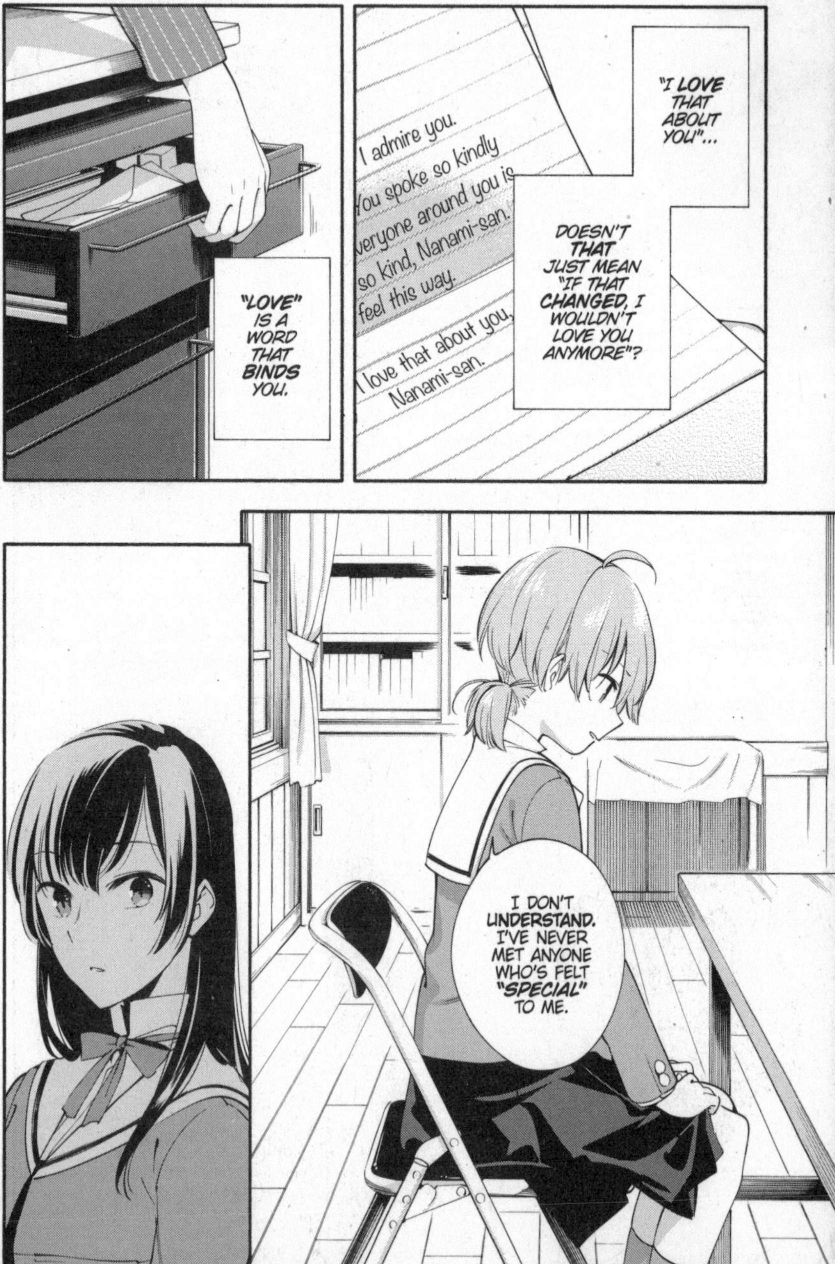
I admire you.
You spoke so kindly
veryone around you is
so kind, Nanami-san.
feel this way.
I love that about you,
Nanami-san.
"I LOVE THAT ABOUT YOU"...
DOESN'T THAT JUST MEAN "IF THAT CHANGED, I WOULDN'T LOVE YOU ANYMORE"?
"LOVE" IS A WORD THAT BINDS YOU.
I DON'T UNDERSTAND. I'VE NEVER MET ANYONE WHO'S FELT "SPECIAL" TO ME.

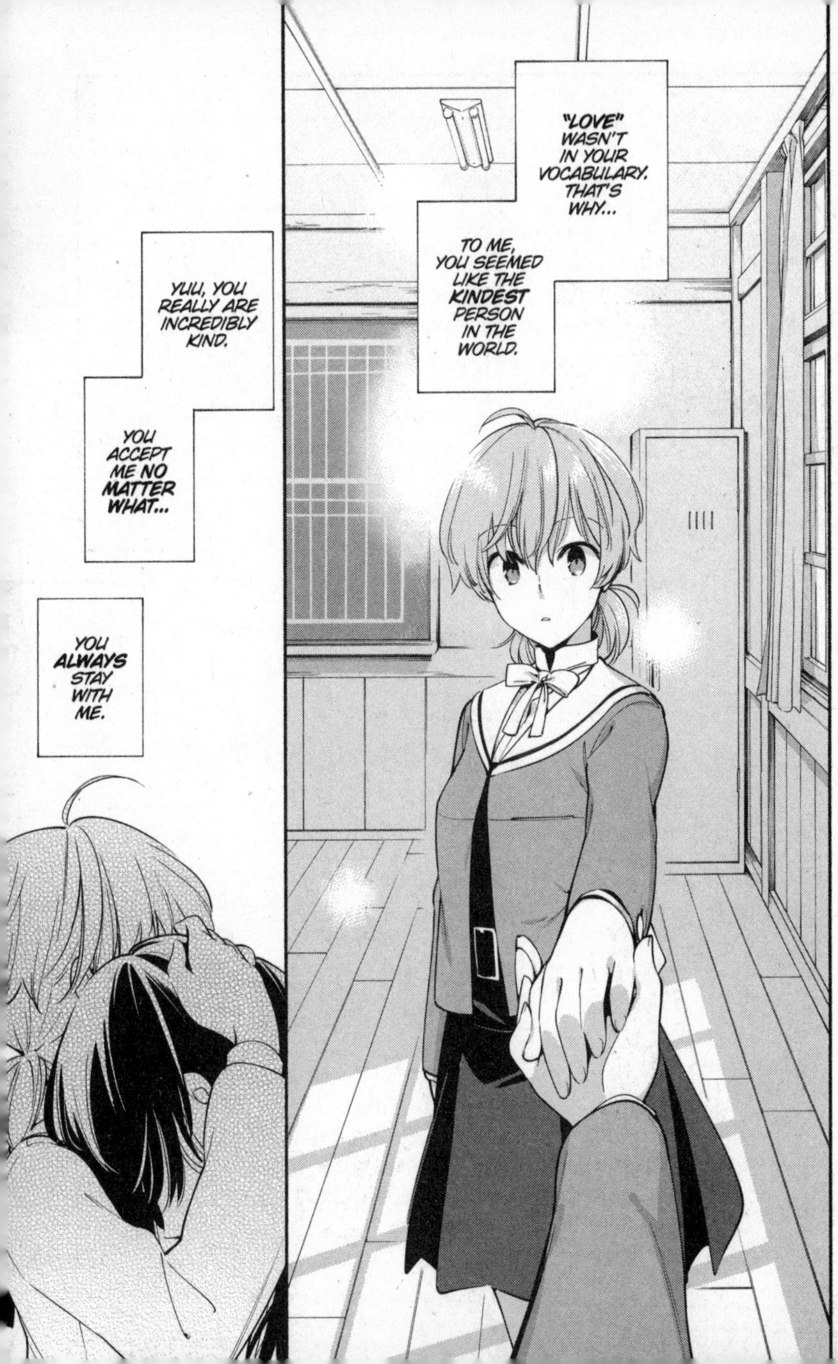
"LOVE" WASN'T IN YOUR VOCABULARY. THAT'S WHY...
TO ME, YOU SEEMED LIKE THE KINDEST PERSON IN THE WORLD.
YUU, YOU REALLY ARE INCREDIBLY KIND.
YOU ACCEPT ME NO MATTER WHAT...
YOU ALWAYS STAY WITH ME.

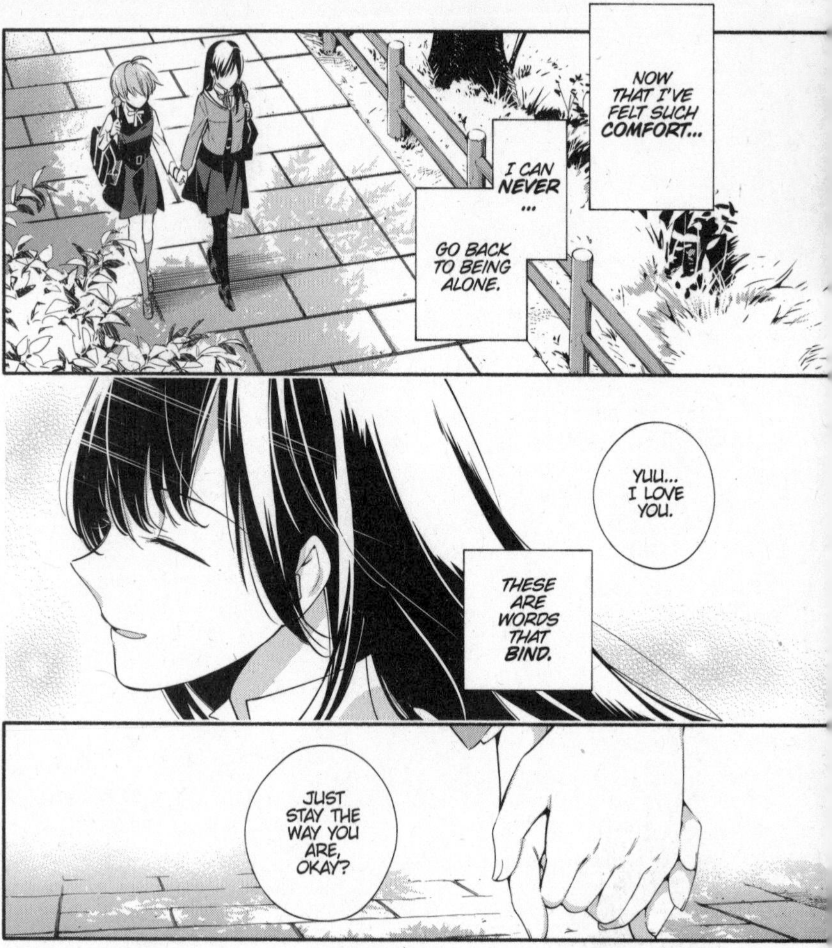
NOW THAT I'VE FELT SUCH COMFORT...
I CAN NEVER ...
GO BACK TO BEING ALONE.
YUU... I LOVE YOU.
THESE ARE WORDS THAT BIND.
JUST STAY THE WAY YOU ARE, OKAY?

PLEASE, YUU...

DON'T FALL IN LOVE WITH ME.

These two girls...

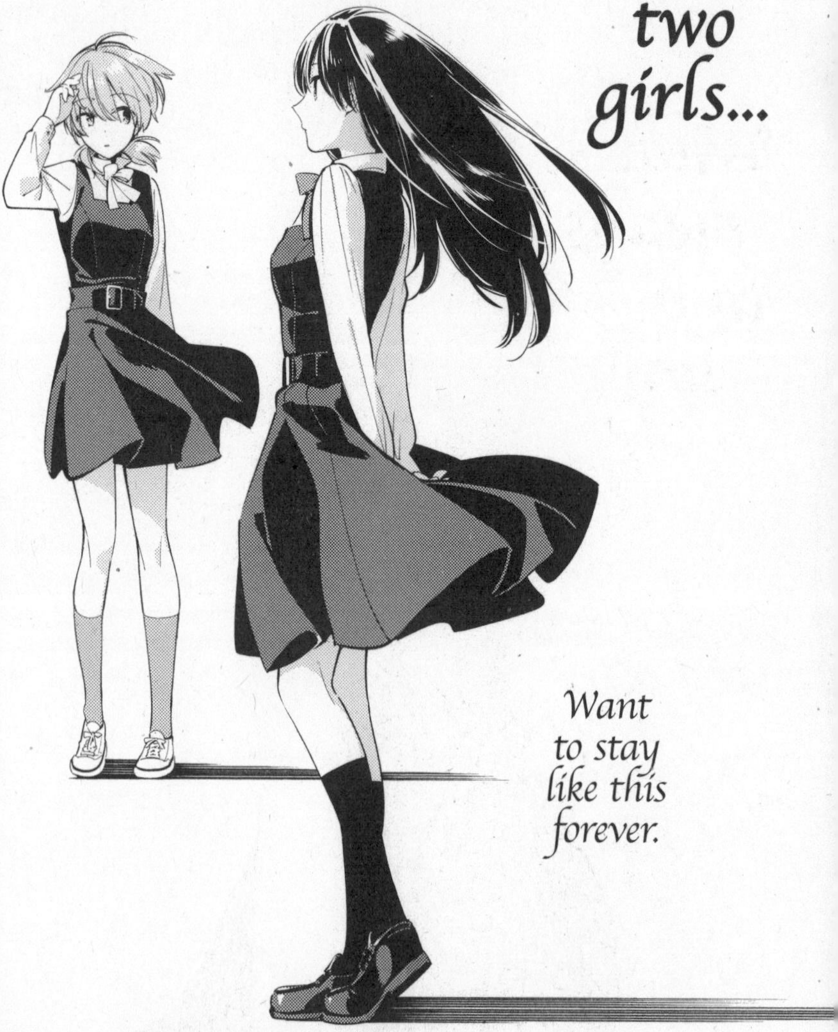

Want to stay like this forever.

**Bloom Into You** Vol. 3

Coming Soon

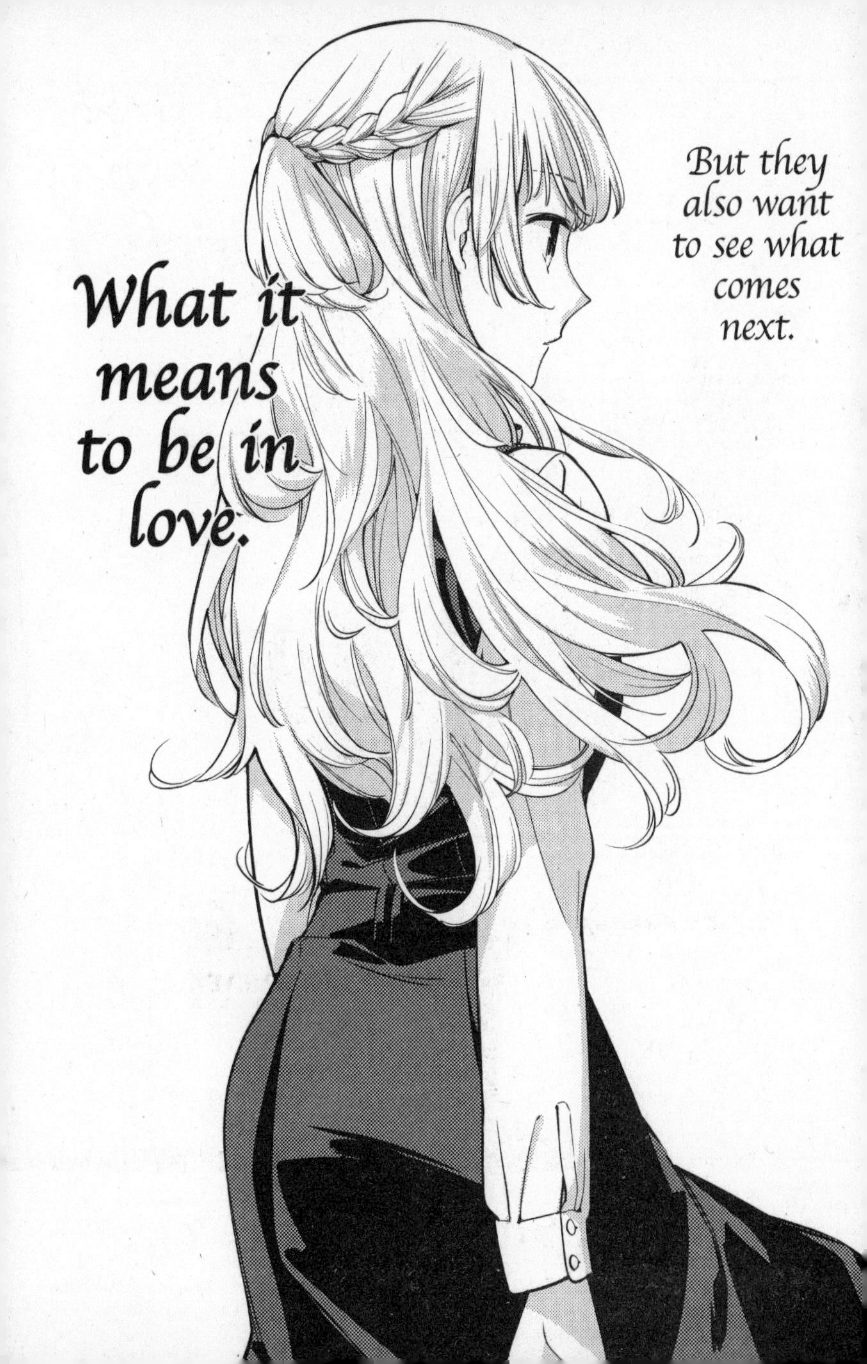
But they also want to see what comes next.
What it means to be in love.

# AFTERWORD

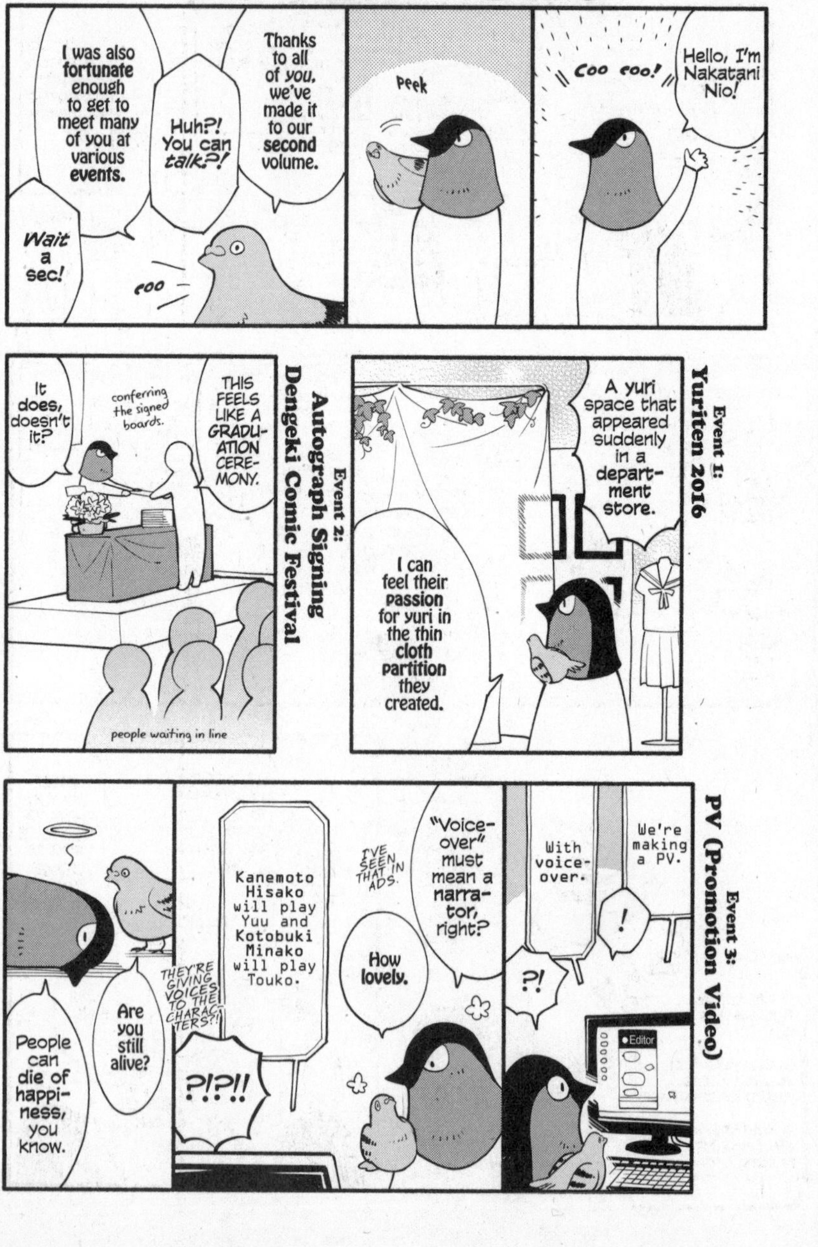

Coo coo!
Hello, I'm Nakatani Nio!
Peek
Thanks to all of you, we've made it to our second volume.
Huh?! You can talk?!
I was also fortunate enough to get to meet many of you at various events.
Wait a sec!
coo
Event 1: Yuriten 2016
A yuri space that appeared suddenly in a department store.
I can feel their passion for yuri in the thin cloth partition they created.
Event 2: Autograph Signing Dengeki Comic Festival
THIS FEELS LIKE A GRADUATION CEREMONY.
conferring the signed boards.
It does, doesn't it?
people waiting in line
Event 3: PV (Promotion Video)
We're making a PV.
With voice-over.
!
?!
"Voice-over" must mean a narrator, right?
I'VE SEEN THAT IN ADS.
How lovely.
Kanemoto Hisako will play Yuu and Kotobuki Minako will play Touko.
THEY'RE GIVING VOICES TO THE CHARACTERS?!
?!?!!
Are you still alive?
People can die of happiness, you know.

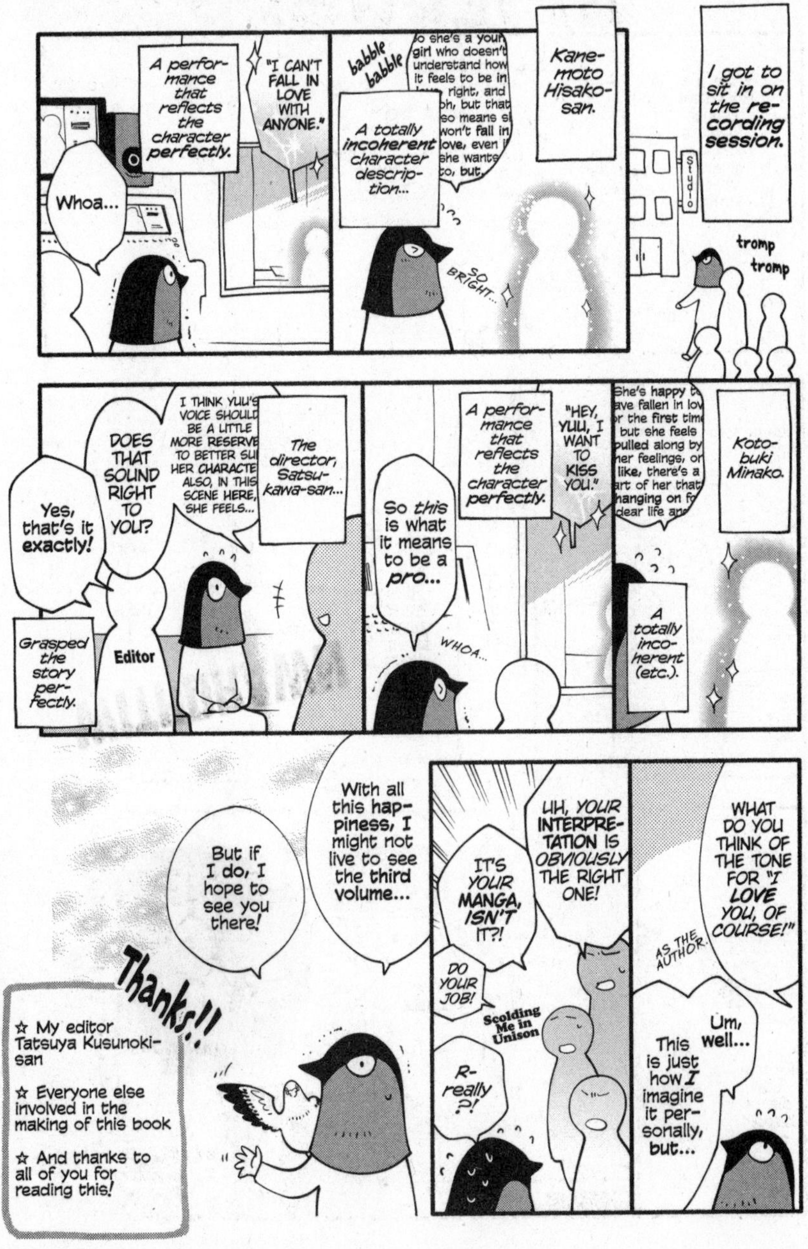
I got to sit in on the recording session.
Studio
tromp tromp
Kane-moto Hisako-san.
o she's a youn girl who doesn't understand how it feels to be in lo right, and oh, but that so means s won't fall in love, even i she wants to, but,
babble babble
A totally incoherent character description...
SO BRIGHT...
"I CAN'T FALL IN LOVE WITH ANYONE."
A performance that reflects the character perfectly.
Whoa...
Koto-buki Minako.
She's happy t ave fallen in lov or the first tim but she feels pulled along by her feelings, or like, there's a art of her that hanging on f dear life an
A totally inco-herent (etc.).
"HEY, YUU, I WANT TO KISS YOU."
A performance that reflects the character perfectly.
So this is what it means to be a pro...
WHOA...
The director, Satsu-kawa-san...
I THINK YUU'S VOICE SHOULD BE A LITTLE MORE RESERVE TO BETTER SU HER CHARACTE ALSO, IN THIS SCENE HERE, SHE FEELS...
DOES THAT SOUND RIGHT TO YOU?
Yes, that's it exactly!
Grasped the story perfectly.
Editor
WHAT DO YOU THINK OF THE TONE FOR "I LOVE YOU, OF COURSE!"
AS THE AUTHOR.
Um, well...
This is just how I imagine it personally, but...
UH, YOUR INTERPRETATION IS OBVIOUSLY THE RIGHT ONE!
IT'S YOUR MANGA, ISN'T IT?!
DO YOUR JOB!
Scolding Me in Unison
R-really?!
With all this happiness, I might not live to see the third volume...
But if I do, I hope to see you there!
Thanks!!
☆ My editor Tatsuya Kusunoki-san
☆ Everyone else involved in the making of this book
☆ And thanks to all of you for reading this!

SEVEN SEAS ENTERTAINMENT PRESENTS

# Bloom into You

story and art by NAKATANI NIO

VOLUME 2

TRANSLATION
Jenny McKeon

ADAPTATION
Jenn Grunigen

LETTERING AND LAYOUT
CK Russell

LOGO DESIGN
KC Fabellon

COVER DESIGN
Nicky Lim

PROOFREADER
Tom Speelman
Danielle King

PRODUCTION MANAGER
Lissa Pattillo

EDITOR-IN-CHIEF
Adam Arnold

PUBLISHER
Jason DeAngelis

BLOOM INTO YOU VOL. 2

Edited by ASCII MEDIA WORKS.
First published in Japan in 2016 by KADOKAWA CORPORATION, Tokyo.
English translation rights arranged with KADOKAWA CORPORATION, Tokyo.



Seven Seas books may be purchased in bulk for promotional, educational, or business use. Please contact your local bookseller or the Macmillan Corporate and Premium Sales Department at 1-800-221-7945, extension 5442, or by e-mail at MacmillanSpecialMarkets@macmillan.com.





ISBN: 978-1-626924-79-6

Printed in Canada

First Printing: May 2017

10 9 8 7 6 5 4 3 2 1

FOLLOW US ONLINE: ***www.gomanga.com***

## READING DIRECTIONS

This book reads from ***right to left***, Japanese style. If this is your first time reading manga, you start reading from the top right panel on each page and take it from there. If you get lost, just follow the numbered diagram here. It may seem backwards at first, but you'll get the hang of it! Have fun!!

1
2
3
4
5
6
7
8
9

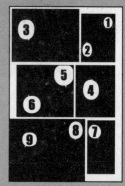